She didn't believe in

love—until the right

man came along....

Praise for the romances of
***New York Times* bestselling author**
Catherine Anderson

"Anderson comes up with another winner by deftly blending sweetness and sensuality in a poignantly written story."

—*Booklist*

"Count on Catherine Anderson for intense emotion."

—Jayne Ann Krentz

"Catherine Anderson is an amazing talent."

—Elizabeth Lowell

"Catherine Anderson has a gift for imbuing her characters with dignity, compassion, courage, and strength that inspire readers."

—*Romantic Times*

"A major voice in the romance genre." —*Publisher Weekly*

"Not only does author Catherine Anderson push the envelope, she seals, stamps, and sends it to the reader with love."

—*Affaire de Coeur*

continued . . .

Praise for the contemporary romances of Catherine Anderson

Blue Skies

"Readers may need to wipe away tears . . . since few will be able to resist the power of this beautifully emotional, wonderfully romantic love story." —*Booklist*

"A keeper and a very strong contender for Best Contemporary Romance of the Year." —Romance Reviews Today

Only by Your Touch

"Ben Longtree is a marvelous hero whose extraordinary gifts bring a unique and special magic to this warmhearted novel. No one can tug your heartstrings better than Catherine Anderson." —*Romantic Times* (4½ Stars, Top Pick)

"This delightful story by Catherine Anderson will warm your heart. Her portrayal of her characters (two- and four-legged alike) will make you feel every emotion. Don't miss this well-done book." —*Rendezvous*

"Ms. Anderson has woven a tale that touched my soul and will live forever as a cherished keeper to read again and again. . . . I am pleased to award it Romance Reviews Today's Perfect Ten." —Romance Reviews Today

Always in My Heart

"Emotionally involving, family-centered, and relationship oriented, this story is a rewarding read." —*Library Journal*

"[A] superbly written contemporary romance, which features just the kind of emotionally nourishing, comfortably compassionate type of love story this author is known for creating." —*Booklist*

Sweet Nothings

"Pure reading magic." —*Booklist*

Phantom Waltz

"Anderson departs from traditional romantic stereotypes in this poignant, contemporary tale of a love that transcends all boundaries . . . romantic through and through."
—*Publishers Weekly*

"Coulter Family" books by Catherine Anderson

Phantom Waltz
Sweet Nothings
Blue Skies

Other Signet Books by Catherine Anderson

Always in My Heart
Only by Your Touch

Bright Eyes

❀

Catherine Anderson

SIGNET
Published by New American Library, a division of
Penguin Group (USA) Inc., 375 Hudson Street,
New York, New York 10014, U.S.A.
Penguin Books Ltd, 80 Strand,
London WC2R 0RL, England
Penguin Books Australia Ltd, 250 Camberwell Road,
Camberwell, Victoria 3124, Australia
Penguin Books Canada Ltd, 10 Alcorn Avenue,
Toronto, Ontario, Canada M4V 3B2
Penguin Books (NZ), cnr Rosedale and Airborne Roads,
Albany, Auckland 1310, New Zealand

Penguin Books Ltd, Registered Offices:
80 Strand, London WC2R 0RL, England

First published by Signet, an imprint of New American Library,
a division of Penguin Group (USA) Inc.

First Printing, June 2004
10 9 8 7 6 5 4 3 2 1

Printed in the United States of America

PUBLISHER'S NOTE
This is a work of fiction. Names, characters, places, and incidents either are the product of the author's imagination or are used fictitiously, and any resemblance to actual persons, living or dead, business establishments, events, or locales is entirely coincidental.

To Julie Seybert, a.k.a. Jules Maree, whose voice is almost as beautiful as she is. Don't give up on your dreams, my friend. Nashville is waiting, and the world will be a much poorer place without your music.

And also, as always, to my husband, Sid, who has been my anchor in every storm and never failed me.

Chapter One

As Zeke Coulter parked his red Dodge Ram in front of his new ranch-style home that August afternoon, he was eagerly anticipating the weekend. One of the drawbacks of owning a ranch-supply store was that he had to work most Saturdays, but he'd rearranged the employee shift schedule that morning to give himself a mini-vacation, two entire days to do exactly as he pleased. Although a half rack of cold longnecks sat beside him on the seat, there would be no beer on tap for him tonight. He planned to work outside in the garden until dark and then spend the remainder of the evening putting up vegetables for winter.

Just as he reached to turn off the truck ignition, his cell phone rang. He expected it to be someone at the store. Randall, the night manager, couldn't wipe his own ass without Zeke telling him how.

"Zeke here," he answered, his voice edged with frustration.

"You got a hot date tonight?"

Zeke grinned. He hadn't heard from his younger brother Hank in over a week. "Hey, little brother. I thought your dialing finger was broken." Hank was newly married, and

Zeke couldn't resist teasing him. "That pretty little bride must be keeping you mighty busy."

"We come up for air occasionally," Hank replied good-naturedly. "Carly and I were hoping you might come out for dinner. Southern-fried chicken with all the trimmings."

"I thought the smell of fried food made her sick."

"Not anymore. She's over that and having sudden cravings again. Tonight it's fried chicken and mashed potatoes with gravy."

"Which one of you is pregnant? Sounds highly suspicious to me. That's your favorite meal."

Hank chuckled. "We've got similar tastes. What can I say? You comin' out or not?"

With genuine regret, Zeke explained that he had other plans for the evening.

"Picking vegetables and canning?" Hank echoed with unveiled disgust. "You've got the Coulter reputation to uphold, remember. It comes as part of the genetic package, right along with the nose."

Zeke couldn't help but laugh. It was true; he and all his brothers had their father's looks—sable hair, dark skin, blue eyes, and sharply chiseled features, the most prominent of which was a large nose that their mother often likened to the blade of a bowie knife.

"If I don't get my tomatoes put up this weekend, they'll ruin. I worked too damned hard growing that garden to let the produce go to waste."

"What's the matter with you, bro? Thirty-three and single on a Friday night, and you're going to can tomatoes? You're supposed to be having fun."

"Almost thirty-four, and I enjoy canning."

"Don't tell anyone."

Zeke laughed again. "You had enough fun for both of us, and look how you ended up. Canning tomatoes is safer."

"I like the way I ended up," Hank retorted, his tone mellow with contentment.

Hank did seem to be truly happy, and Zeke was glad for him. But getting married and raising a family weren't for everyone. "I'm sorry I can't make it for dinner, bro. Tell Carly thanks for the invite."

Zeke had just ended the call when he saw a boy who looked to be about twelve racing from behind the house. Just the way the kid ran, shoulders hunched and body low to the ground, told Zeke that trouble was afoot. Cursing under his breath, he swung out of the vehicle.

"Hey!" he yelled.

His T-shirt flapping and sneakers flying, the kid never broke stride. Zeke watched him cut across the field that lay between his forty acres and the neighboring farm. *Fantastic.* He could well remember being that age. Summers in the country could be long and boring for a boy who wasn't kept busy, and boredom often led to mischief.

The late-afternoon sunlight burned through Zeke's blue shirt as he strode along the west end of the house to see what the kid had been up to. When he reached the side porch, he saw a splash of red on the cream-colored siding just below the kitchen window. He snapped to a halt and circled the flagstone steps to get a better look. The pulp of a ripe tomato had been splattered on the new paint.

"Damn it!" Swearing to turn the air blue, Zeke rounded the corner of the house to find countless more splotches of red on the siding. And that wasn't all. The family room slider and bathroom window were shattered, and the door of the storage shed hung from one hinge, the cross bucks broken clean in two.

When Zeke turned to survey his garden, a wave of regret washed over him. His tomato plants and corn looked as if a tornado had flattened them. Fury, sudden and searing, fired his blood. This wasn't mere mischief, but malicious vandalism. The tomato stains would never wash off his house. He'd have to repaint. And that wasn't to mention the cost of replacing the windows and the storage shed door.

Spurred by rage, Zeke set off across the field, following the boy's footprints. *What the hell is the world coming to?* he asked himself as he marked off the distance with angry strides. Just as he suspected, the kid's tracks led directly to the old farmhouse, a white, two-story monstrosity with a wraparound veranda, peeling paint, and a green shingle roof sorely in need of repair. As Zeke entered the patchy side yard, which was peppered with shady elms and oaks, he saw movement on the front lawn. His steps long and purposeful, he circled the house, hoping to collar the child before he escaped inside.

Instead of finding the boy, Zeke came upon a woman. No question about her gender. She was bent over a long plank table, struggling to cover an assortment of odds and ends with a blue plastic tarp that kept catching in the breeze. Her skimpy black dress rode high on her bare thighs, revealing long, shapely legs the color of coffee generously laced with cream. When she stretched farther forward to catch the tarp, her hemline inched higher. *Sweet Lord.* If he had known someone like this lived next door, he'd have come over to borrow a cup of sugar.

"Excuse me," he said to her attractive backside.

"Oh!" Startled by his voice, she jerked erect and spun around.

The front of her was just as delightful to look at as the back. Normally Zeke preferred fashionably slender women, but he quickly decided there was something to be said for females who were generously round in all the right places, especially when the roundness was showcased in clingy black stuff that revealed every dip and swell.

"I'm sorry. I didn't hear you drive up." She tugged her skirt down and fluttered a hand at the collection of stuff on the table. "I was just closing up shop until morning, but if you'd like to take a quick look, feel free. This is the third day, and I just marked everything down."

Zeke decided she was having a yard sale. Unfortunately, the only item of interest didn't sport a price tag. Despite the heavy layer of makeup, she was beautiful. A mane of curly black hair cascaded past her slender shoulders, which were bare except for thin black straps. Her mouth was lush, soft, and defined with deep burgundy gloss, the lower lip pouted and glistening in the sunlight, the upper shaped in a tempting bow. Above the bodice of the dress, full, creamy breasts plumped up, displaying a dusky cleavage that invited him to look. Raised to be a gentleman, Zeke resisted the urge, dropped his gaze, and found himself staring at her legs instead. *Not good.*

He caught the scent of vanilla, which rattled him even more. His most pleasurable moments were spent in the kitchen. "I, um—I'm not interested in buying anything," he finally found the presence of mind to say.

Smoothing her short skirt again, she gave him a questioning look, her sherry-brown eyes warming as she smiled. "Are you here to see my father then?"

For an awful moment, Zeke couldn't recall why the hell he was there. Then he glanced at his feet, saw a chunk of tomato clinging to the toe of his Western-style boot, and remembered in a rush. Before he could launch into an explanation, she dimpled a cheek at him and said, "Are you *sure* I can't sell you something? I have a set of Ping golf clubs that are like brand-new."

You could sell me almost anything. Zeke shook his head. "I'm not into golf."

"How about some perfectly good warm-up pants?" She gave him a measuring look. "Probably not. Robert is quite a bit shorter than you." Her eyes fairly danced with mischief. "I've got a great shotgun, though, that I'm willing to sell cheap, along with a reloading kit that has never been used. I've also got every issue of *Playboy,* dating back to March 1970. You can have the entire lot for a dollar."

"That's quite a collection."

"Yes, well, Robert is—" She broke off and shrugged. Something dark flashed in her eyes, momentarily veiling the shimmers of brightness. "He's an enthusiast, I guess you might say."

Zeke wondered how any man in his right mind could ogle other women when he had this one at home. With a soft sigh, she regained her composure, and the shadows left her eyes. Her mischievous smile was infectious, and Zeke found himself grinning.

"You aren't, by any chance, getting a divorce?" he asked.

"Done deal. Now I'm just trying to recoup some of my losses and exact a little revenge while I'm at it."

She could make any man cry with one swing of her hips. Zeke kept his gaze fixed on her face and did his damnedest to look like a choirboy.

"If you're interested in a tried-and-true lucky shirt or a prized letterman's sweater, you've come to the right place." She wore sexy black stilettos with snappy straps that showcased her slender ankles and shapely calves. As she circled the table to retrieve the tarp, she balanced her weight on her toes to prevent the thin heels from sinking into the grass. "I don't mean to be rude, but I'm running late for work. If you're here for eggs or milk, you'll find my dad in the house."

Zeke wondered what kind of work she did, to be dressed like that. *Don't even go there, son.* She looked to be in her late twenties or early thirties, which, if she had married young, put her at about the right age to be the tomato thrower's mother. Zeke looked into her pretty eyes and regretted his reason for being there. He doubted she'd be happy to hear that her son had just inflicted costly damages to her neighbor's house and garden.

"I'm Zeke Coulter. I live next door."

"Ah, Pop's new neighbor." She finished drawing the tarp over the table and stepped forward to offer him her hand. "It's good to finally meet you. Right after you moved in, I baked you a cake, but it met with disaster before I got it out of the oven. My daughter, Rosie, jumped rope in the kitchen."

"Uh-oh. Rope jumpers and rising cakes don't mix." Taking care not to squeeze too hard, Zeke shook hands with her. Her fingers felt slim and soft against his calloused palm. "That's a shame. I love a good cake."

"I didn't say it was a good cake." She wrinkled her nose. "I'm not much of a cook, I'm afraid. It probably would have fallen, regardless. Rosie just gave me a good excuse."

With those looks, who needed culinary skills? Zeke hated to let go of her hand. "And your name is?"

"Oh!" She laughed again and rolled her eyes. "I'm sorry. Natalie Patterson." She tugged her fingers free and glanced at her watch. "I'm sure you'd like to meet my father. If you'll step into the house, I'll introduce you before I grab my purse and run."

Again Zeke wondered what kind of work she did. A barmaid, possibly, only how could she survive an eight-hour shift in those impractical shoes?

"Actually, meeting your father isn't what brought me over." Zeke wished he knew a gentle way to say this, but straight and to the point was more his style. "When I got home from work a few minutes ago, I saw a boy running from my backyard. I followed him here."

Her smile slowly faded. "That would be my son, Chad. Is there some sort of problem?"

"You could say so, yes." Zeke told her about the vandalism to his property. "At a quick guess, if I do the repairs myself, I'd say about a thousand dollars' worth of damage has been done. That isn't to mention all my hard work on the garden down the drain. I've been babying those tomato plants since early June, and the fruit was just getting ripe enough to pick."

Her finely arched brows drew together in a frown. "Oh, Mr. Coulter, I'm so sorry."

Zeke had expected her to jump to the defense of her son, not immediately conclude that the boy was guilty. "No sorrier than I am."

She rubbed her bare arms as though to ward off a chill as she turned toward the house. "Chad!" she called. "Can I see you out here for a moment, please?"

Zeke saw that the old-fashioned, double-hung windows of the house had been raised to let in a breeze. Through a living-room screen discolored with age, an elderly man with unkempt white hair peered out at them. "What's happenin', Nattie? You need me out there?"

"Nothing's happening, Gramps. I just want to talk to Chad."

"Chad!" the old man yelled. "Yer mama's hollerin' fer ya!"

The wind picked up, bringing with it the refreshing evening coolness that made summers in Central Oregon so enjoyable. *Nattie*. Zeke liked the ring of that. It suited her, somehow—sweet yet sassy. The breeze trailed black strands of curly hair across her face. As she brushed at her cheek, he took the opportunity to study her features, which seemed only more perfect upon closer inspection. Sculpted cheekbones, a dainty little nose, a mouth that begged to be kissed, and a flawless, sun-kissed complexion.

The front screen door slapped open, and the boy emerged onto the veranda. He cast Zeke a look that burned with resentment. Then he hung his head and tromped down the rickety porch steps. When he reached his mother, he shoved his hands in his jeans pockets, slouched his shoulders, and toed a clump of overgrown grass.

"Chad," Natalie began, "this gentleman says that you ruined his garden, threw tomatoes at his house, broke two windows, and wrecked his shed door."

The boy finally raised his head. A shock of honey-brown hair fell into his eyes, which were a mirror image of his mom's. "So?"

It wasn't what Zeke expected. No denials? Not that lying would have been a smart move. The boy's Portland Trailblazer T-shirt and Nike running shoes were smeared with tomato pulp and seeds.

"So?" Natalie grasped the child's arm and gave him a light shake. "Is that all you have to say? Mr. Coulter claims you've inflicted at least a thousand dollars in damages. I don't have that kind of money right now. You know that."

The kid's eyes flashed with anger. "Call Dad. He's got plenty of money."

Natalie looked as if she meant to say something, but then she caught her lower lip between her teeth and remained silent. Finally she whispered, "Oh, Chad. Your father isn't even paying his child support. What makes you think he'll come through for you on this?"

The boy jerked his arm from her grasp. "It's your fault Dad doesn't send any checks. He hates your guts, that's why. If he finds out I'm in trouble, it'll be different. You'll see."

Before Natalie could respond, the screen door slapped open again. The elderly man Zeke had glimpsed through the window screen shuffled across the porch and down the steps. He wore faded denim overalls and a dingy undershirt. Old, leather-soled house shoes flopped on his bony feet as he hobbled across the grass.

"What seems to be the problem out here?" he demanded, his grizzled brows snapping together over rheumy blue eyes.

Natalie rested a staying hand on her son's shoulder as she turned to address her grandfather. "This gentleman is our new next-door neighbor, Gramps. It seems that Chad wreaked havoc over at his place, throwing tomatoes at his house, among other things. He estimates the damage at a thousand dollars or more."

"Ha!" the old man snorted. He nailed Zeke with an imperious stare. "You find any fingerprints on them there tomaters, mister?"

The absurdity of the question gave Zeke pause. Then he glanced at the boy. "Dusting for prints wasn't necessary. The kid is covered with tomato pulp."

Natalie's grandfather leaned around, narrowed his eyes, and peered at his great-grandson. When the old man straightened, he said, "Tomaters is a purdy common crop. We got a bunch ripe for pickin' ourselves."

"Gramps," Natalie inserted. "*Please*. You're only making matters worse."

"Hmph. Worse how?" Gramps hooked his thumbs under his overall straps, rocked back on his worn-down heels, and glared at Zeke. "You know who yer messin' with, boy? Westfields, that's who."

The name didn't ring any bells, but Zeke refrained from saying so.

"Been Westfields in this area for nigh on to a hundred years," the old man continued. "Don't come on this property makin' wild accusations without no proof. We don't take kindly to smears on the family name."

Zeke didn't take kindly to smears on his house, but again he held his tongue. The old man's face was an angry red. Zeke didn't want him to have a stroke.

Natalie released her son to curl an arm around her grandfather's frail shoulders. "Gramps, you're missing your game show."

"To hell and tarnation with game shows!" Gramps said with a snort. "Like I got nothin' better to do?" His withered mouth puckered like a drawstring pouch. "I'm politely invitin' you to get off this property, mister. Our Chad's a good boy. He wouldn't do nothin' like you say he done. You readin' me loud and clear?"

"Gramps, *please,*" Natalie said again, only her voice was firmer this time. "That's enough. Mr. Coulter hasn't been unpleasant, and Chad has confessed to doing the damage."

"Say what?" Gramps blinked. Then he leaned around Natalie to peer at the child again. "That true, Chad?"

Chad nodded sullenly. Just about then, the screen door whacked the exterior of the house again, and a dark-haired siren in a red miniskirt and cropped tank top appeared on the veranda. She looked a lot like Natalie, but her long, curly hair was stiff with styling gel and she was walking straight legged, balancing her weight on her heels. Zeke glanced at her bare feet and saw that she had cotton balls between her toes.

"Hey," she said, flashing him a sultry smile. "I'm Valerie, Nat's younger sister." Coming to a stop at the porch rail, she relaxed her stance, splayed a slender hand over one shapely hip, and winked. "Did I hear someone say 'new neighbor'?"

"I'm Zeke Coulter." Zeke would have known the girl was Natalie's younger sister without being told. The two women might have been poured from the same mold. He guessed the younger version to be in her early twenties, not exactly jailbait, but close. "I bought the place next door."

"Way cool," Valerie said, smoothing her fingertips provocatively over her hipbone. "Finally, something *interesting* happens out here in the back of beyond." She popped her chewing gum, a habit that drove Zeke crazy, and grinned, flashing a dimple similar to Natalie's. "I've been home for only two weeks, and already I'm dying of boredom."

The insinuation was that Zeke might provide her with

some much-needed diversion. The smell of her perfume drifted across the yard. *Obsession.* He recognized the scent because his sister Bethany often wore it. No question about it. Valerie was a hot little package, all curves and long legs, with big, dark, expressive eyes to suck a man under before he realized he was drowning. Zeke had long since learned not to wade in deep water. He just felt older than dirt when he looked at her.

He bit back a smile, *no offense intended,* and returned his attention to Natalie, who was still trying to soothe her grandfather. She wasn't his type, either. *Nice to look at, though.* He preferred naturally beautiful women who didn't need heavy makeup, stiletto heels, and slinky black dresses to catch a man's eye.

Natalie glanced at her watch again. Patting her grandfather's shoulder, she said, "I want you to go back in the house now, Gramps." She turned to her son. "You, too. And to your bedroom, young man. No television, no computer games, no music, no *Harry Potter.* I want you to stare at the ceiling and think about what you've done. In the morning, we'll discuss this further and decide on a punishment."

In Zeke's day, the punishment would have been meted out with a wide leather belt. As a kid, he'd detested those trips to the barn with his dad, but the sting had stayed with him for hours and made him think twice before he messed up again. Watching Chad slouch away, struggling to preserve his tough-guy image, Zeke couldn't help but think that an old-fashioned march to the barn might be just what he needed.

Zeke heard the screen door slap open again. *Why am I not surprised?* He was one of six kids and had family members oozing out from under the baseboards. As he focused on the newest character in the Westfield clan, a younger version of Gramps with salt-and-pepper hair, a few less wrinkles, and patched overalls with holes at the knees, Zeke decided that his relatives were downright normal by comparison.

"Dad, what're you doing out here?" the younger gramps asked as he gimped across the patchy lawn, one hand pressed to his lower back. "Sounds to me like Natalie is telling you to shut up, and you aren't listening."

Natalie sent the new arrival an imploring look. "Pop, would you make Gramps go back inside? He isn't helping this situation any."

Pop scratched his head, which, to his credit, didn't look as if it needed shampooing. "Dad, you need to come back in the house. Nattie can handle this."

"She can't, either. She needs a man to stand up for her and the boy. That no-account husband of hers is too durned busy with that blond harlot to take care of his family. That leaves you and me."

Pop, whom Zeke guessed to be Natalie's father, hooked an arm around the older man's shoulders. "Come on, Dad. You ever heard that joke about the Chihuahua pissin' on a fire hydrant? Positive thinking can only take you so far."

"A *what* pissin' on a *what?*" Gramps clearly didn't appreciate the comparison. "The bastard's big, I'll grant you that, but I'm not afraid of him. If I hit a man and he don't fall, I'll walk around behind to see what's holdin' him up!"

Natalie closed her eyes as her father and grandfather shuffled away. With every step, Gramps muttered under his breath about Court TV and Natalie selling Chad down the river. Natalie's father just shook his head and continued herding the old man toward the porch.

Natalie sighed, fixed Zeke with an imploring gaze, and said, "I wish I could say he has Alzheimer's."

Zeke could sympathize. His relatives weren't quite so colorful, but on occasion, his boisterous brothers had given him cause for embarrassment. He glanced past Natalie to spare a long look at Valerie's shapely legs as she helped her father and grandfather up the steps, no easy feat with cotton balls between her toes.

"Valerie just broke up with her boyfriend and lost her job." Natalie shrugged. "A family trait, I guess. When everything goes wrong, we run home to the farm." Her smile was tremulous. She drew in a bracing breath. "I'll happily pay for the repairs to your house and garden," she assured him. "Chad is having a rough time right now, accepting the divorce—and other things. He's been acting out and being difficult. I think he's hoping that he'll finally do something bad enough to get his father's attention."

"Does his dad live out of town?"

She shook her head. "No. Right here in Crystal Falls. He's just—busy."

With the blond harlot? Zeke couldn't imagine any father worth his salt letting a woman take precedence over his child.

Natalie's slender throat convulsed as she swallowed. "Look, Mr. Coulter." Her gaze chased off to the fields. "I'm sure you're not interested in our family dynamics. Suffice it to say that I know Chad did the damage to your house and garden. No contest." She looked him straight in the eye again. "It's just—well, I'm not in the best position right now to make restitution. Things have been tight." She swung her hand at the table behind her, which told him the yard sale had been prompted more by sheer necessity than a need for revenge. "I'd like to say I could pay you next month—or the month after that." She straightened her shoulders. "But the truth is, I honestly don't know when I'll be a thousand dollars ahead. Would you let me make installments?"

Zeke understood that this must be a difficult time for her. He'd overheard enough to know that her ex-husband wasn't fulfilling his responsibilities, and supporting two kids without help couldn't be easy. On the other hand, though, her son had damaged Zeke's property. Zeke didn't want to be a hard ass and call the cops, but there was no way he could let it slide, either. When a boy inflicted costly damages, he had to be held accountable.

Zeke rubbed his jaw. He didn't want this prank, if it could be called that, to go on Chad's record. "How about if we strike a deal?"

Her eyes filled with suspicion. "What kind of deal?"

Zeke almost grinned. She was a tempting package, but he wasn't into bargaining for a piece of ass, as appealing as the prospect might be.

"I was thinking that Chad could work off the debt. It'll be cheaper if I do the repairs myself. Why can't he come over and help me?"

"I'm not sure that's a good idea."

The more Zeke considered the solution, the more he thought it was a great idea. Inspired, even. The kid had a problem. A little hard work might be good for him. "The way I figure, paying minimum wage, he owes me"—he broke off to do some quick calculations—"about a hundred and forty hours. Calculating on a forty-hour week, that works out to be"—he paused again—"three and a half weeks."

She looked distressed. "But he has *camp*."

"Camp?"

"At the Lake of the Woods the last week of August. He goes every year."

Zeke arched an eyebrow. "Isn't camp expensive?"

"It's church camp. The kids raise the money themselves with bake sales and car washes. So much else has been turned upside down in his life. I can't take that away, too." Her expression grew pensive. "Could he work for three weeks? I'll come over and finish up for him, no problem."

Zeke couldn't believe she was offering. He'd seen her check her watch more than once. She worked swing shift somewhere. What did she mean to do, get up after a few hours of sleep and work all day for half a week, paying off her son's debt? No way.

"This is the boy's mess to clean up." It seemed simple enough to Zeke. If you screwed up, you had to pay. "He'll work off the debt himself, or I'll call the law, your choice."

"But—"

Zeke had been raised by his father's iron hand. Right was right. If he'd been in Chad's shoes, he'd have gotten a whipping and still been made to work off the debt. "Let me make myself clear, Mrs. Patterson. I'm bending as far as I intend to bend."

"Chad is very—" She broke off to fix him with an imploring look. "He's been through so much, Mr. Coulter, things you don't understand. He's very delicate right now."

Delicate? The kid was a bank robbery waiting to happen. "That's my offer. Take it or leave it."

"I understand that you're angry. That's one of my concerns. I don't want my son indentured to an unreasonable taskmaster for three and a half weeks. He needs to go to camp. He needs the interaction with other kids and some time with the counselors."

He needed a swift kick in the ass. But Zeke was through arguing. "I'll expect to see your son at my door at eight tomorrow morning," he said in his "boss" voice, which came fairly easy after dealing with the incompetent Randall for six months. "If he doesn't show, I'll turn this matter over to the police."

Zeke didn't trust himself to stand there, looking into those pleading brown eyes, so he pivoted and took off. He'd gone about three paces when he heard a malevolent hissing sound. Before he could whip around, something bit him on the ass. He whirled to confront a flapping, maniacal gander, bent on doing him physical injury.

"Chester! Stop it!" Natalie cried. "Oh, God, Mr. Coulter, I'm sorry! Rosie must have let him out. I've had him in the pen all day because of the yard sale. He hates strangers."

Trying to maintain his dignity, Zeke swatted at the gander as it flapped its way airborne to nip at his chest. *Problem.* There was nothing meaner or more viciously effective than a gander protecting its territory. Not even a Rottweiler was as ominous.

Zeke did the only thing any self-respecting cowboy could do.

He ran.

Chapter Two

Wavering between laughter and tears, Natalie watched Zeke Coulter race for home. His lean body roped with muscle from years of hard work, he carried himself with a relaxed confidence that told her the cowboy attire wasn't only for looks. Yet with every few steps, he shot a glance over his shoulder to be sure he wasn't in danger of being attacked from behind by the Westfield family goose.

Normally Natalie would have felt terrible about Chester pinching their neighbor, but Coulter's uncaring attitude about an eleven-year-old boy missing summer camp went a long way toward tempering her regret. Chad had committed a grave wrong, and he deserved to suffer the consequences, but making him miss camp after he'd looked forward to it all summer seemed too severe a punishment.

When the gander finally gave up the chase and waddled back to the yard, Natalie leaned down to stroke his neck. "Good *boy,* Chester!" She knew it was an uncharitable thing to say, but she couldn't quite help herself. Chad had taken so many hard hits over the last few months. It wasn't fair that he should take another one. With a snicker, she added, "Just deserts. You put him on the run in short order."

Chester quacked and nudged her hand for a treat.

"Sorry," she murmured. "I didn't know in advance that you were going to be my knight in feathered armor."

Clearly proud of himself, Chester lifted his wings and quacked softly. Sometimes Natalie could have sworn the silly old gander could talk.

She tapped his beak with a fingernail. "Yes, you did a good job," she agreed. "Maybe that'll teach the big old meanie not to be so obnoxious and dictatorial the next time."

Next time? Natalie shuddered at the thought. If Chad stepped out of line again, Zeke Coulter might call the police.

From the corner of her eye, she saw her daughter Rosie approaching. Chester waddled away as Natalie straightened and turned toward the child.

"Hi, sweetie. How was your snooze?" It was the third time this week that Rosie had fallen asleep while watching television in the late afternoon. Normally the little girl took naps only under duress. The sudden change in her sleep patterns concerned Natalie. Was Rosie more upset by the upheaval in her life than she was letting on? "You were zonked for three whole hours."

"I missed *Scooby-Doo,*" Rosie complained.

"Uh-oh." Natalie crouched down to look her daughter in the eye. "Maybe it'll come on again later and Gramps will let you watch it."

"Maybe." Rosie rubbed her brown eyes and then squinted to see across the field. "Who's that man, Mommy?"

Natalie glanced over her shoulder. Pop's new neighbor was now only a denim-blue blotch in the distance. "That's Mr. Coulter. He moved in next door."

"Did he come to look at our yard-sale stuff?"

Natalie chose to ignore the question. The less Rosie knew

about her brother's shenanigans the better. "Where are your shoes, sweetie? If you walk barefoot on the grass, you're liable to get stung by a bee."

"I forgot them in the house." Rosie wiggled her bare toes and then lifted her arms. "I need a hug before you go to work."

Natalie drew her daughter close. "A big hug or a little one?"

"Gigantic."

Natalie pretended to squeeze as hard as she could, which made Rosie giggle. "Miss me while I'm gone?"

"Yes. I don't like it when you leave."

Natalie wished she didn't have to go. Before the divorce, her mom had stayed with the kids at night, but that was no longer possible now that the marital residence had sold and Natalie lived with her dad. Naomi Westfield refused to be in the same house with her ex-husband, Pete, on a regular basis.

Right after the house sold, Natalie had dropped the children off at her mother's on the way to work and picked them up when her shift ended, but that hadn't lasted long. Naomi's rented condo was in an all-adult community, and after only a week, the neighbors had started to complain about the kids being there so much.

"I have to go to work, sweetie. We can't buy your Barbie a dune buggy without money, and I can't make money unless I work. Bummer, huh?"

Rosie nodded.

Natalie sat back on her heels to smooth her daughter's sleep-tousled curls. Rosie was so darling, a dark-haired, sloe-eyed little angel. Whenever Natalie started thinking of her marriage as a horrible mistake, she had only to look at her kids to know that all the heartbreak and disillusionment had been worth it. "You have fun at night with Aunt Valerie, don't you?"

"Uh-huh. I just miss you and Grammy."

Natalie could understand that. Valerie loved her niece and nephew, and she was making a gallant effort to fill in for Natalie at night, but her zany personality and fun-and-games approach to babysitting were a far cry from what the kids were used to. Grammy and Mommy had rules and enforced them. Valerie felt that rules stifled a child's personality. Instead of making Chad and Rosie eat their vegetables, she fashioned baked-potato dolls with spinach hair or created landscapes on their plates, using smashed peas for grass, broccoli spears for trees, and carrots julienne to build split-rail fencing around cauliflower sheep.

In a more perfect world, Robert would be playing a larger role in the children's lives to make this transition easier for them. Unfortunately, he had never been very family oriented and was even less so now, far too busy cruising through town in his red Corvette with a sexy blonde tucked under one arm to spend time with his son and daughter.

"What're you going to do with Aunt Valerie tonight?" Natalie asked.

"She's going to paint my fingernails, and then we're going to put on makeup and play dress up."

"That sounds fun."

"I just wish you could play dress up with us."

"Oh, sweetheart, I'd like nothing better." Natalie kissed the tip of Rosie's nose. "But mommies don't always get their druthers. I have to earn a living."

"I know," Rosie said dismally. "Maybe Poppy will win the lottery tomorrow night."

Natalie smiled in spite of herself. Without fail, her father and grandfather wagered five dollars a week at the Cedar Forks store, hoping to win the jackpot. In between losses, they spent hours discussing how they would spend their winnings when their numbers finally came up. The most popular plan, in Rosie's estimation, was for Poppy to buy a huge ranch with enough houses on it to accommodate the entire Westfield clan.

"If Poppy won the lottery, it'd be really wonderful," Natalie agreed.

"He and Gramps will live in one house, and we'll live in another one." Warming to the subject, Rosie leaned away, her eyes as bright as copper pennies. "And Aunt Valerie will live in hers, and Grammy will live in hers!" She beamed with delight. "And you won't have to sing to people at the supper club anymore."

Natalie tried to imagine her parents living harmoniously as close neighbors and couldn't get the picture to gel. Since their divorce ten years ago, Pete and Naomi Westfield couldn't even do Christmas together without scrapping about something.

"Singing at the club isn't so bad," Natalie said. And she meant it. She'd yearned to be a professional vocalist all her life, and performing onstage at the club was as close to that as she was ever going to get. She found the other aspects of owning a business far more taxing, especially the rapid employee turnover. In a pinch, Natalie could bus tables or fill in as a waitress, but taking over in the kitchen was beyond her. "I love to sing."

Rosie shrugged. "If Poppy wins the lottery, I'll let you sing to me."

Over the top of the child's head, Natalie glanced worriedly at her watch. It was a thirty-minute drive into town, and she had paperwork and books to do before she went onstage.

"Oh, my *goodness!*" She kissed Rosie's chubby fingers as she pried them from her neck. "I have to get my caboose in gear, sweetness. I'm running way behind schedule."

"Maybe Frank can just play the piano, like he did the time you caught the flu."

The Blue Parrot was teetering on the edge of bankruptcy. If Natalie failed to show, the regulars might think twice before patronizing the club again. "No, sweetie. I'm sorry. I won't be gone all that long."

"But I'll be asleep when you get home!"

"I'll sneak in and give you good-night kisses anyway."

"Promise?"

"Cross my heart," Natalie replied.

Zeke couldn't remember the last time he'd been so furious. Standing in his backyard, he took inventory of the damages. His garden was destroyed, his windows were shattered, his ass stung from that damned gander, and, to add insult to injury, his beer had gotten hot from sitting in the truck. *Camp?* What was the woman thinking? Her son had a bitter lesson to learn.

Disgusted, Zeke went to the shed for some cardboard to cover the windows until he could replace the shattered glass. As he approached the broken shed door, his temper kicked up another notch. How had a half-pint kid managed to do this much damage? Zeke looked around for something that the boy might have used as a battering ram to break the one-by-four cross bucks. *Nothing*. As difficult as it was to believe, he decided that Chad must have kicked the door in.

Only rage could give a boy that kind of strength—a mindless, murderous rage. The thought was sobering, and Zeke's anger subsided a little. Maybe, he decided, he should be more concerned about the child than he was about the damage. What drove a kid to strike out like this? Zeke had never even seen Chad until today, so revenge was ruled out. That left—what? Surely the boy hadn't done this solely to get his father's attention.

As Zeke cut pieces of cardboard to fit his windows, he tried to imagine what it would be like to grow up without a father. It was like trying to imagine going through life without arms. His mom and dad had been wonderful parents, both of them devoted. Zeke honestly couldn't remember a single time in his life, even as an adult, when his dad hadn't been there for him.

Not all kids were that lucky. Sometimes, despite the efforts of both parents, a marriage just fell apart. When that happened, a whole lot more than the neighbor's garden could be at risk, namely a young boy who wasn't sure where his loyalties lay anymore and couldn't understand why one of his parents no longer seemed to love him.

At precisely eight o'clock the next morning, Zeke answered the door and found a hostile kid standing on his porch. Today Chad wore an oversize Big Dog T-shirt, sloppy tan shorts that hung well below his knees, and the same dusty Nikes with the laces dangling. He looked like a hundred other boys Zeke had seen in town. All he needed was a nose ring and a tattoo to be totally in vogue.

"My mom says I have to work here to pay you back," Chad said with a sullen glare.

Zeke nodded and pulled the door wide. "Come on in. You had breakfast?"

Chad snorted. "Like my mother doesn't feed me?"

So much for trying to befriend the little shit. Zeke led the way to the kitchen. "I'm having eggs Benedict. If you don't want to eat, you can sit and watch while I do."

Chad shuffled along behind him. "Eggs what?"

"Eggs Benedict," Zeke repeated. "Poached eggs and ham on toasted English muffins with hollandaise sauce on top."

"You cooking it yourself?" Chad asked incredulously

"Of course." Zeke stepped over to turn the flame back up under the eggs. "It's the maid's year off."

Chad flopped onto a chair, skinny legs sprawled. "You a queer or something?"

Zeke slanted the boy a hard look. "The politically correct term for a homosexual is gay, not queer."

"So—are you *gay,* then?" the boy asked with a sneer.

"My sexual persuasions are none of your business."

"That's it, isn't it? You're gay. That's how come you live alone in this big house and cook fancy food."

"Maybe I like living alone and enjoy cooking. Ever think of that?"

"Yeah, right."

Zeke refused to let the kid get his goat. "No long hair in my toothbrush, no nylons hanging on the showerhead, no standing in line to use the john, no fighting over the remote control." He slapped a lid on the Teflon skillet. "Sure you don't want something to eat? It'll be a long time before lunch."

The kid shrugged, which Zeke took as a yes. He stuck two halves of another muffin into the toaster, grabbed more eggs from the fridge, and resumed his position at the stove.

Minutes later when he handed Chad a plate, he said, "When you're finished eating, tie your shoes. We'll be using power tools. I don't want you to trip and get hurt."

"Nobody but geeks tie their shoes."

"You'll be a geek while you're working for me, then."

Chad pushed at the eggs Benedict with his fork. "These are weird."

"Don't eat them. All the more for me." Zeke sat at the opposite side of the table to enjoy his breakfast. "You want some orange juice?"

Chad shrugged again, so Zeke poured him a glass. The kid guzzled the juice, then tried the food. "Yuck," he said, but continued to eat. "We never have eggs this way."

"What kind do you have?"

"Burned scrambled or burned fried. If my mom invites you to dinner, don't come."

Zeke almost grinned. Then he remembered his garden and stifled the urge. "Some people enjoy cooking; others don't."

"My mom enjoys it." Half of the boy's eggs Benedict had already disappeared. "She just sings while she cooks and forgets the food."

Curious, Zeke arched an eyebrow. When Chad wasn't forthcoming with more information, he couldn't resist asking, "What's she sing?"

"Country, mostly. She pretends the spatula or spoon is a microphone and dances around the kitchen."

"Ah. She got a good voice?"

"Poppy says she could've been the next Reba." Chad pushed at his honey-brown hair, which was sorely in need of cutting. "Then she met my dad, got pregnant with me, and had to get married. My dad didn't like her to sing, so she stopped for a long time. Now she's too old to make it big."

"Too old?" Zeke guessed Natalie Patterson to be in her late twenties or early thirties. That wasn't exactly over the hill.

"My mom says lady singers have to make it big really young," Chad explained. "Before their boobs start to sag and their butts get big. She's got cellulite dimples on her thighs."

That was more than Zeke wanted or needed to know. He pushed up from the table, gathered the dishes, and went to put them in the sink. As he scrubbed smears of egg yolk from the plates and utensils, visions of Natalie Patterson's thighs flashed through his mind. Definitely not fat, and if they were dimpled, he hadn't noticed.

"You ready to hit it?" he asked after loading the dishwasher.

"Do I, like, have a choice?"

"No."

Five minutes later, Zeke had Chad lined out for the morning, washing tomato pulp off the siding. The boy worked at tortoise speed, spending more time wiping the sweat from his brow than he did scrubbing.

"Kick it in the butt," Zeke called as he wielded the rake, gathering destroyed garden plants into piles. "You owe me a hundred and forty hours of hard work. If you slough off, I won't give you credit for the time."

Chad sent him a smoldering look. "I'm working."

"You're piddling." Zeke tossed a pile of rubbish into the wheelbarrow. "If you haven't paid off the debt by the time school starts, I'll work you weekends and evenings after school. No sports, no girls, no fun. Choose your poison."

Chad began scrubbing with more enthusiasm. When they'd worked for two hours, Zeke called for a break. They sat in the shade of an oak tree at the edge of the yard and drank nearly a half gallon of ice tea.

"So, seriously, why don't you have a wife?" Chad asked.

"Don't want one."

"Why not?"

Zeke considered the question for a moment. The answer was that he liked being single, but he settled for saying, "Because."

"Like that's an answer?" Chad gestured with his glass. "Why have a garden with no one but you to eat the stuff?"

"I like being the only one to eat the stuff." Zeke pushed to his feet. "The game of twenty questions is over. Back to work."

Chad resumed the task of washing the house while Zeke piled debris into the wheelbarrow and made countless trips to the compost heap. When he'd almost cleared away the mess, Chad tossed the scrub brush into the bucket and turned with a mutinous expression on his face.

"How come I have to work a hundred and forty hours? Once the work's all done, seems to me my debt should be paid."

Zeke forked up some wilted tomato plants and broken cornstalks. "You're forgetting the cost of the damages. New windows, exterior paint, and wood don't come cheap, son."

"I'm not your son."

Zeke straightened and flexed a kink from his shoulder. "True. If you were, you'd have some manners and a better work ethic." He inclined his head at the stained siding. "You'd also have some respect for other people's property. I figured your hours at minimum wage, which is more than you're probably worth, and I shaved off some time, to boot. It's going to cost me a thousand dollars or more to put things right. If you think I'm being unfair, figure it out for yourself, but do it on your own time."

Zeke no sooner finished speaking than he glimpsed a flash of blue at the corner of the cream-colored shop, a cavernous metal building that did triple duty as a garage, work area, and storage room. He turned to see Natalie Patterson stepping into the backyard. Today she looked completely different, more the cute and adorable girl next door than a sexy vamp, her dark hair caught in a clasp at the back of her head, her oval face devoid of makeup. She wore faded jeans and a man's white shirt, the sleeves rolled back to her elbows. The stiletto heels of yesterday had been replaced with smudged sneakers.

"Hi," she said.

Zeke wanted to whistle and say, "Wow." Instead, he laced his voice with studied indifference and said, "Hello."

She glanced around, taking in the mess. "I, um, thought I'd come over and help." Her smile was stiff. "Two for the price of one. This way, the work will get done faster."

And Chad would be able to go to camp. Zeke bit down hard on his back teeth. No way was he backing down on this. The kid had done the damage, and he would pay the debt.

"Can I speak to you for a moment?" Zeke asked.

She stared at him for a long, loaded second before nodding her assent. Zeke led the way to the gravel parking area in front of the shop. When they were beyond Chad's earshot, he turned, settled his hands at his hips, and locked gazes with her.

"I told you last night, I don't think this is a wise idea," he said softly.

She blinked, managing to look both innocent and sexy at once. "You don't think what is a wise idea?"

"You coming over here to help."

"Why not?"

"Because the boy needs to be taught a lesson."

Two bright spots of color flagged her delicate cheekbones. Her lovely brown eyes flashed with anger. In that moment, Zeke was convinced that he'd never seen a more beautiful woman.

"Excuse me? Chad is my son. As long as you receive recompense for the damages, I fail to see how his upbringing is any of your concern."

She had a point, but Zeke chose to ignore it. "Chad is the one who vandalized my property. He should be the one to make restitution. I made my position on that clear."

"True, but you were mad. I hoped you'd be reasonable this morning."

"I'm being perfectly reasonable."

"There are a number of things happening in Chad's life right now that you don't understand."

"I understand that he's too old to be mollycoddled and let off easy."

"I'm not asking you to let him off easy. I'm asking only that you work with me and be fair."

"By doing the repairs myself, I'm shaving off at least five hundred dollars in labor, and I cut him some slack on the hours. That's fair. You can't say it's not."

"My son is going through a *very* difficult time."

"We all go through difficult times. That doesn't give us license to destroy other people's property."

"Who's going to supervise him for three and a half weeks? Don't you have a job?"

"I own a ranch-supply store. I'll juggle the schedule, do the ordering and books at night. I'll be here to monitor him."

Her cheeks grew even redder. "I still fail to see how my helping would be a bad thing. Your place will be put back to rights more quickly that way."

"And Chad will get to go to camp?"

Her eyes sparked with indignation. "You're overstepping your bounds, Mr. Coulter. Whether or not my son goes to camp is none of your business."

"Wrong. It became my business when he threw the first tomato." When she started to speak again, Zeke held up a staying hand. "I've stated my terms. If you don't like them, we can always let Chad's punishment be decided in juvenile court. Is that what you want?"

At the threat, her face drained of color. "You know it isn't."

"Then leave it alone. It won't kill Chad to work off the debt by himself, and he'll learn a valuable lesson while he's at it. If this isn't nipped in the bud now, what'll he do next, rob a convenience store?"

"Don't be absurd! He was just acting out to get attention."

She obviously hadn't been around many teenage boys. If Chad continued on his present course, she would have no control over him in another few years. "Mission accomplished. He definitely has mine."

"Oh, how I wish I had a thousand dollars. I'd pay you off so fast it'd make your head swim! If you're so keen to raise kids, have some of your own."

"It takes a village. You ever read that book?"

Arms rigid at her sides, she gathered her hands into fists. Zeke had a bad feeling that she yearned to punch him. "You're insufferable."

She whirled and stalked away. After taking several steps, she turned back to scorch him with another fiery glare. "Everything else in his world has been taken away—his home, his school, his friends, even his father. Going to camp was the only familiar thing left, and now you'rc taking that away from him, too."

Natalie was so furious when she got home that she slammed the door as she entered the kitchen. Still in her nightshirt, Valerie was at the stove, pouring a cup of coffee from the dented aluminum pot that had served the Westfield family for generations. Dark hair in a lopsided topknot, eyelids smudged with mascara, and mouth still stained red from last night's dress-up lipstick, she looked like a hooker who'd put in a hard night.

"What're you in a snit about?" she asked with a huge yawn.

Huffing from the walk across the field, Natalie stepped to the cupboard to get a clean coffee mug. "That *man.*"

"What man?" Valerie lifted her eyebrows. "If he's under forty and halfway cute, give me five minutes to grab a shower and I'll take him off your hands."

"Is sex all you ever think about?"

Valerie shrugged and smiled. "Getting laid is fun. Maybe if you tried it occasionally, you'd be less acerbic."

Natalie heaped a spoon with sugar and stirred it into her coffee. "I bypassed acerbic and went straight to royally pissed off. He is such a jerk."

"He, who?"

"Zeke Coulter." Natalie went to sit at the battered wood table, which had been painted with light gray enamel in the sixties, had gotten chipped over the years, and was now a mottled mess, with previous layers of paint showing through. Pop refused to get a new dinette set because this one was still serviceable. Natalie waffled between wanting to strip it down to the original wood and wanting to take a hacksaw to one leg. "I went over to help Chad with the work, and he refused to let me stay."

"Why?" Taking care not to spill her coffee, Valerie sat down and crossed her legs, displaying slender thighs tanned to a smooth butternut. "Seems to me he'd be happy to get the repairs done faster."

"Oh, no. He's convinced I'm mollycoddling Chad. Says he needs to learn a lesson. Like it's any of his business how I raise my son? What is it with men, anyway? I've never met one yet who didn't think he was lord of the universe."

Bright-eyed and smiling, Gramps entered the kitchen just then. Up since five, he had already finished reading the *Portland Oregonian* and was eager to start watching television. "What's that you say? Your universal joint went out?" House shoes flapping, he gimped over to the stove to refill his coffee cup. "That'll cost a pretty penny. Too bad your daddy's back is messed up. He could put it on the hoist and have it repaired in nothin' flat. How'd you get home last night? Frank drive you?"

Valerie sighed, looking like a disgruntled raccoon with the smears of black ringing her eyes. "Her car's fine, Gramps. We were talking about men."

Gramps harrumphed and came to sit at the table. "Is that all you ever think about, girl? You only broke up with Keith a few days ago."

"Kevin," Valerie corrected, "and it's been two weeks."

Gramps shook his head. "If he's a geek, why'd you move in with him?"

Natalie took a sip of coffee to hide her grin.

Raising her voice to a near yell, Valerie said, "Turn on your hearing aid! I didn't say he was a geek. I said we've been broken up for two weeks!"

Gramps fiddled with the outdated hearing aid and winced when the increase in volume made the device squeal. "Damned thing."

"You need a new one," Natalie inserted. "Medicare would probably help pay for it."

"That's the problem with you young people. Every durned thing has to be brand spankin' new. Like as if old is worthless? This hearin' aid was good enough for yer grandma, by God, and it's good enough for me." When he had the hearing aid adjusted to suit him, he turned questioning blue eyes on Natalie. "So what's this about your universal joint?"

"My car is fine. I was just grumping about men."

Gramps reached over to pat Natalie's arm. "Stop frettin', honey. Ye're well rid of that bastard."

"She's not stewing over Robert. It's Zeke Coulter next door who's got her dander up today." Valerie cupped her mug in her hands and took a noisy sip of coffee. "She went over to help Chad do the repairs, and Coulter sent her home."

"Why'd he do that?" Natalie's father asked as he entered the kitchen. "Seems like he'd appreciate the help."

Natalie recounted the conversation that she'd had with Zeke Coulter. Just as she finished talking, Rosie joined them at the table. "Little ears," Natalie said to the adults as she gathered the sleepy child onto her lap.

Neither Gramps nor Pop took the hint, and a heated debate ensued. Gramps wanted to go over and show Zeke Coulter how the cow ate the cabbage, an old-timer's way of saying he wanted to kick their neighbor's ass. Pop vetoed that idea by telling the Chihuahua joke again. Gramps took exception. Before Natalie knew it, the exchange had escalated into an argument.

"Do you have to do this?" she cried. "Why can't anyone in this family discuss something without yelling and getting in a fight? You're upsetting Rosie."

Both her father and grandfather fell silent. Then Pop asked, "Are we upsetting you, Rosebud?"

Rosie lifted her face from Natalie's bosom. "Nope."

Pop nodded. "There, you see? *She* understands the difference between yelling and merely raising our voices to make a point."

Getting an honest day's work out of a resentful kid was more difficult than Zeke had expected. Chad scrubbed halfheartedly at the house, leaving smears of tomato pulp in his wake. At first, Zeke pointed out places the boy had missed. But along toward noon, he decided to just let him go. There was no time like the present for Chad to learn that the hours spent doing a half-ass job wouldn't count against his debt.

At twelve sharp, Zeke leaned the rake and pitchfork against the shed and told Chad it was time for lunch. As Chad broke off from work, Zeke suggested that they drive into town and eat at McDonald's, which brightened the boy's mood considerably.

"We need paint, some one-by-fours to fix the door, and I

need to order the window glass," Zeke explained as they walked to the truck. "May as well eat while we're running errands."

En route to Crystal Falls, Chad slumped against the passenger door. To break the silence, Zeke turned on the stereo. His favorite CD, the latest by Garth, began to play, filling the cab with the star's honeyed voice as he belted out ballads about hopes and dreams realized—and loves of a lifetime lost.

After a few minutes, Chad said, "You got anything to play besides sappy shit?"

"Do you kiss your mother with that mouth?"

Chad rolled his eyes. "Do you kiss your mother with yours? You say 'shit.' I heard you."

Guilty as charged. Zeke had gotten a blackberry sticker in his hand that morning and let fly with a few choice words, never once stopping to think that the boy was listening. "I'm an adult."

"Yeah, like, so what? It's okay for adults to cuss, but it's not okay for kids? I don't get it. My grandpa cusses and so does my dad. Nobody even blinks. Let me say one bad word, and Mom acts like the sky split open to rain snakes."

Zeke almost stuck to his guns about his being an adult, but somehow that angle of defense stuck in his craw. The kid was right. If adults set a bad example, no one could really blame a boy for following suit.

"From now on, if I cuss, you can. If I don't, you can't. How's that for a deal?"

Chad looked wary. "You're kidding. Right?"

"Nope. I'm dead serious."

"Yeah, right. If I cuss, you'll tell my mom."

Zeke was determined to clean up his language around the

kid, so that wasn't a worry. "No, I won't. Do I look like a tattletale?"

"All adults are tattletales."

"I'm not about stuff like this. Do we have a deal or not?"

Chad shrugged, but Zeke didn't miss the grin that flirted at the corners of his mouth. "Sure. I got ten bucks that says you'll cuss at least once before we get home."

"You're on."

After stopping for lunch and running all the errands, Zeke drove home in a mild state of shock. "I can't believe how much they charged for that damned window glass."

Chad grinned from ear to ear. "They gotta make a damned living."

Zeke grimaced and reached for his wallet.

"You're really gonna pay up?" Chad asked.

"Of course. A wager is a wager."

Chad accepted the ten spot. A mischievous twinkle danced in his eyes as he stuffed the bill into his pocket. "I got another ten that says you'll cuss again before the day is out."

"You're on." Zeke returned his attention to the road, convinced that he would win the bet. It was a simple matter of watching his language.

By three o'clock, he owed Chad another ten dollars. As he opened his wallet, he said, "Has it occurred to you that this is an inequitable situation? You owe me a thousand dollars in repairs. Why can't my cusswords go against your debt?"

Chad shook his head and held out his hand. "My mama didn't raise no fool. This way, I'm paying off the debt *and* making a profit."

Zeke couldn't help but laugh. He was starting to like this

kid. "If you put it against your debt, it'll reduce the number of hours you have to work."

Chad shrugged. "Working for you isn't so bad. I'm not bored, anyhow."

"Is it boring at home?"

"You ever watched Court TV most of the day?"

"Nope, can't say that I have."

"Big-time boring. Gramps watches trials and shit." Chad cast Zeke a sidelong glance. "I had that one coming. You cussed, remember? That means I can. It was our deal."

Zeke was beginning to regret having made that bargain. "What kind of trials does the old man watch?"

"All kinds. He especially gets off on murder trials. Somebody he doesn't know killed somebody else he doesn't know, and he hangs on every word. It totally sucks. He's fascinated by forensics. Blood splatter patterns and stuff. It's kind of creepy."

"Takes all different kinds to make the world go round, I guess." Zeke tugged a tape measure from his belt. "You ever used a circular saw?"

"You want me to saw boards?" Chad cast a worried glance at the lumber. "I don't think so. I'd better just wash the house and stuff."

"I'm the boss on this job," Zeke said firmly as he handed Chad the safety goggles. "If I say you're going to cut boards, you'll cut boards. You can scrub the house later."

The boy eyed the saw as he might a scorpion. "You don't know what you're getting into. I'm real clumsy."

"Who says you're clumsy?"

"My dad. He says I was born with ten thumbs and two left feet."

Zeke didn't think he would like Robert Patterson. "Bullshit. If you're clumsy, I haven't noticed it."

Chad grinned and thrust out his hand. "That's another ten to me, bucko."

"No, it's not. We didn't bet last time."

"Too bad. I would have had you."

Scarcely able to believe he'd transgressed again, Zeke shook his head. "I never realized I cuss so much." He arched an eyebrow. "Let it be a lesson to you. Get in the habit, and sooner or later you'll slip up in front of your mother."

Chad nodded solemnly. "Yeah, probably. It really upsets her, too, so I'd better watch it."

"Enough said. Back to you using the circular saw. It doesn't take a rocket scientist to handle one. I'll show you how."

"I'm not good at learning new things," Chad warned him.

Zeke had a sneaking hunch that his father had convinced him of that as well. "No one is good at anything the first few times. It takes practice."

"I'll ruin your boards."

"No, you won't. They're long. You can practice on the ends."

Chad donned the goggles and proved to be a fast study. Lending assistance when needed, Zeke stood over him, intoning all the warnings and safety precautions that his father had once given him.

"Set your blade on the long side of the line, or you'll cut the board short."

"Which side is the long side?" Chad asked.

Zeke explained and then touched the penciled line. "You need a board exactly this long. If you cut right here or slightly on the inside, you'll be a fraction off in length. It's always better to cut on the long side. Most times you'll end up with a board just the right length. If you do cut it long, it's a whole lot easier to shave off a little more than to buy more wood."

Chad lined up the blade as Zeke had shown him. The saw screamed, and halfway across the board, the teeth got stuck. Zeke quickly grasped the saw handle. "No problem. You just slacked off on the power a little."

"It tried to buck back at me," Chad said shakily.

"That's because the teeth grabbed. You did fine. You had control of the tool and didn't let it get away from you." Zeke helped jerk the blade free. "Just start over. Don't slack off on the power this time. You can do it."

The saw screamed again as it bit back into the wood. Chad clenched his teeth, gripping the tool with all his strength. When he had cut the width of the board, he flashed a huge grin. "I did it!"

"You sure as hell did."

"That's another ten dollars."

Zeke laughed. "I've created a monster."

Chad nodded. "A rich monster."

"We didn't bet," Zeke reminded him, "and we aren't going to until I break this habit."

"That's positive thinking—that you can break yourself of it, I mean."

"I do have it bad, don't I? I can keep a clean mouth around ladies and children, no problem, but around other men, I forget myself."

"I'm not a man."

"You're doing a man's work. Way I see it, that makes you a man."

Chad straightened his shoulders. "Yeah, I guess."

"Just don't pick up my bad habits. Your mom'll scalp me with a dull knife."

"She thinks I'm still a baby."

"That's typical. May as well get used to it."

"Does your mom still think you're a baby?"

"Absolutely, and I like it that way. Whenever I visit her, she makes my favorite pie. Can't beat that with a stick."

Chad grimaced. "If my mom baked a pie, I'd run."

"Ah, well. When you grow older, she'll think of something special to do when you go see her."

"She makes really good oatmeal treats. They're chocolate, and you just cook them on the stove. I really like them, and they only take three minutes. Even Mom can pay attention that long."

Zeke chuckled. "Better not let her hear you talking that way. Women are funny about their cooking."

Chad shrugged. "Not my mom. She knows she's an awful cook. She's a good mom, and she's a good singer. That's all she really cares about. She says that's why they invented TV dinners, fish sticks, and stew in a can, for moms like her."

A good mom and a good singer? From a purely practical standpoint, the lady had to be good at something else in order to earn a living. "What's her profession?" Zeke asked.

Chad looked mildly exasperated. "One guess, and she isn't a cook."

"She sings for a living?"

The boy nodded. "At the Blue Parrot. It's a supper club."

Zeke had never patronized the place, but he'd heard good things about it. "Ah. That explains why she pretends the spatula is a mike. She's practicing."

"Nah. Trust me, Mom doesn't need to practice. She just

loves to sing." Chad shrugged. "That's why she bought a supper club, so she could sing to a real audience."

"She *owns* the place?"

The boy nodded.

"If she can't cook, why in the hell did she buy a supper club?"

"You just cussed again."

Zeke thought back over what he'd said. "I'm sorry. I just find it amazing that a woman who can't fry eggs would buy a restaurant."

"She hires the cooking done. Mostly, that works."

"Mostly?"

"Sometimes the chef gets mad and quits. Then there's trouble until she can find someone else."

"What does she do in the interim?"

"In the what?"

"In the meantime—until she can hire a new chef?"

Chad laid a new board across the sawhorses. "She has to do the cooking until she can find somebody new. That's why the Blue Parrot's almost bankrupt."

Zeke grabbed the try square. "It must be hard for her to support you kids if the club isn't doing well."

"My dad would send her money if she didn't harp at him all the time. Every time she sees him, she starts running at the mouth and ticks him off."

The way Zeke saw it, no matter how ticked off a father became, he was still morally obligated to support his kids. "Your mom must have reason to harp at him."

"She pretends to be mad about all kinds of things, but the truth is, she's just jealous. Dad has always had girlfriends. For a long time, she didn't seem to care, and then, all of a sudden, she divorced him. Now she's, like, a complete witch every time she sees him." Chad's brown eyes grew suspiciously bright behind the goggles, and his cheeks turned an angry red. "I don't know what her deal is. She was fine with it for a long, long time, and then, bang, she went ballistic. Nothing's the same anymore, and I never get to see my dad."

The picture forming in Zeke's mind of the Pattersons' marriage wasn't pretty. "Your father can see you any time he chooses to, Chad. Your mother says he lives right here in town."

"What do you know about it?" Chad backed away a step. "He travels all the time on important business, and when he's in town, he's got meetings and stuff. He wants to see me. He just can't! And my mom doesn't help matters."

Zeke held up a hand. "Whoa. I didn't mean to step on your toes."

"Then don't bad-mouth my dad. You don't even know him."

"That's true," Zeke agreed, "and I didn't intend to bad-mouth him. I'm just trying to point out that things aren't always the way they appear on the surface. Maybe your mom has other reasons for being mad at your father, reasons she hasn't shared with you."

"My dad is a good dad, and he loves me! He *does.*"

"I'm sure you're right," Zeke said carefully. "If I had a son like you, I'd be proud as punch."

That took the wind out of Chad's sails. He blinked away tears and bent his head to kick at a sliver of wood. "You're just saying that to make me feel better."

It was true. Zeke did want to make Chad feel better. But that didn't mean he hadn't sincerely meant the compliment. "You're a good-looking young man, and you're sharp as a tack."

Chad looked up. Tear tracks glistened on his cheeks below the goggle cups. "I'm not smart. All's I ever get is B's. My dad got straight A's in every subject without even studying, and he was good at sports, too."

"And you're not, I take it."

"I suck at sports."

"Maybe you just haven't found the right one yet."

"I've tried everything." He kicked at the wood again. "I'm not too bad at baseball, but I'm nowhere near as good as my dad was."

Zeke was beginning to actively dislike Robert Patterson. "When I was your age, I sucked at sports, too. It wasn't until I started riding horses and roping competitively that I found my real niche. Don't cubbyhole yourself. Keep trying new things. Sooner or later, you'll find where your talents lie, and you'll excel."

Chad made a face. "Who wants to be good at riding and roping? You can't get a varsity letter for that."

"No varsity letters, that's true," Zeke agreed. "But if you get good on a horse, there are plenty of buckles and trophies to win. My sister, Bethany, was the state champion three years running in barrel racing and would have gone to the nationals but for a riding accident. She has more championship buckles than anyone I've ever known, and you can wear those all your life. A varsity letter—" Zeke broke off and shrugged. "Well, hey, a grown-up would look pretty silly wearing a letterman's sweater to town."

"I guess." Chad glanced at Zeke's belt. "That a championship buckle?"

Zeke turned up the ornate oval of silver and gold for the boy's inspection. "Roping, my specialty. It'll separate the men from the boys in nothing flat."

Chad pursed his lips. "I used to ride horses."

"Too bad you've lost interest. I have a couple. We could have done some riding and roping. Much as I enjoy my horses, it's not as much fun alone."

"I haven't lost interest."

After studying Chad's tear-streaked face for a long moment, Zeke concluded that he'd never met a boy in more serious need of a friend. "Hmm," he settled for saying. "I'll keep that in mind. No better way to relax than to throw a few lassos and go for a ride. Gives a man time to reflect on things and clear his head."

Chad straightened his shoulders. "I hear you." Then he frowned. "If you've got horses, where are they?"

"Rented pasture. Best roping horses you'll ever clap eyes on." Zeke handed Chad the tape measure. "I showed you how last time. Your turn to mark the board."

Chad bent to the task. Zeke stood over him, giving instructions as needed. "Okay," he said, when the board was marked. "Which angle should you cut, a right or a left?"

Chad studied the board. Finally, he said, "It shouldn't matter. I just have to cut the opposite angle at the other end to make it work for a cross buck."

Zeke grinned and patted the kid on the shoulder. "Just like I said, sharp as a tack. I know grown men who can't figure angles to save their souls."

While setting the saw blade, Chad asked, "So when will you bring your horses here?"

"As soon as the fences are up," Zeke replied.

"When will they be up?" the boy asked.

"As soon as you get them built."

Chapter Three

That afternoon Natalie had to leave for work before Chad got home, so she called the house later to check on him. She expected Chad to be upset when he got on the phone, but he greeted her with a cheerful, "Hi. What's up?"

"I just called to see how you are."

"I'm good."

Chad had been sullen and difficult for weeks. "My goodness, did I dial the wrong number?"

"Jeez, Mom, cut me some slack, why don't you?"

"Sorry. It's just so nice to hear a smile in your voice for a change."

Natalie's piano player, Frank Stephanopolis, struck the first chord of a new song. They were supposed to be practicing before the supper crowd came in.

Natalie cupped her hand over the portable phone and called, "I'll be right there, Frank." She returned her attention to the conversation with her son. "So how did it go today?"

"All right, I guess. Mr. Coulter's teaching me some stuff."

"What kind of stuff?"

"Just *stuff,* okay? Nothing you'd know about."

Natalie had grown accustomed to Robert talking down to her. He thought all women were mentally impaired. But it hurt, hearing condescension in her son's voice. For too long, Chad's only point of reference had been his father's bad example. "I was just curious, sweetie."

Chad relented with, "I used a circular saw, is all, no big deal."

"A circular saw?" she echoed.

"What? You don't think I'm old enough or something?"

Could she say or do anything right? "You're old enough. It's just that power tools can be so dangerous. I hope you were very cautious."

"No, I, like, sawed off all my fingers on purpose."

Natalie closed her eyes briefly. "Was Mr. Coulter nice to you?"

"Get real. What reason does he have to be nice?"

"If he's being awful, Chad, I'll figure out a way to pay him back."

"Yeah, right. What'll you do, take it out of petty cash?"

She hadn't punched in the wrong number, after all. This was definitely her son. Natalie yearned to make things better between them, but somehow, no matter how she tried, she only made things worse.

"Did you call Dad to tell him I'm in trouble yet?" Chad asked.

She had left messages on Robert's office and home lines and on his cell phone as well, but so far, Robert hadn't bothered to call her back. He was probably too busy bonking Bonnie Decker, his latest girlfriend, to complicate his life with parenting problems.

"No, I haven't called him yet," Natalie lied. "I'm sorry, Chad. I just haven't had time."

"You *never* have time for things that are important to me."

Natalie wanted to defend herself. She hated taking the heat for Robert's failings. But if she told the truth, Chad would know how little Robert cared.

"I'm sorry," she said, feeling heartsick and so angry with Robert that she could have strangled him. "I rushed off to work last night and never found a second to spare until my shift was over."

"What about today?"

"I got sidetracked doing the laundry and paying bills."

"You always get sidetracked, Mom. Then you blame Dad for not coming through for us. How can he be there for me if he doesn't know I need him?"

Good question. And it took all of Natalie's strength to paint herself as the villain. *Again*. But this wasn't about her.

"I'm sorry, sweetie. I'll call him tomorrow, I promise."

"Yeah, sure."

"I will. Honestly. I just get so busy sometimes."

Long silence. Then Chad sighed. "It's okay, I guess. I tried to call him myself. He didn't call me back. Grandma Grace says he's probably out of town, looking at development property or something."

Grace Patterson was in denial where her son was concerned. Robert, the big-time wheeler and dealer, lived in fear of missing a business call, so he picked up his voice messages no matter where he was. Natalie's anger toward him intensified. *The selfish jerk*. Maybe he'd die of a coronary while ejaculating. On his headstone, she'd have the dates of his birth and death engraved, along with, "He came, he went, and who cares?" Only that wasn't precisely true. Her son cared.

Natalie was grateful that Rosie hadn't been around Robert very much, a result of his incessant late hours at the office before their divorce. *Ha*. In truth, he'd been with his mistress all those nights. But that was beside the point. Rosie hadn't formed a strong attachment to her father, and Natalie prayed it remained that way. Chad was another story. He'd always yearned for Robert's approval, always craved his attention.

"I love you, Chad." It was all that Natalie could think of to say. "More than you'll ever know."

During the ensuing silence, she blinked the sting of tears from her eyes, wishing—oh, she didn't know what she wished. She knew only that she loved her son, and she couldn't seem to talk to him anymore without running face-first into this thick wall of resentment.

"I know you love me, Mom," he finally said.

Natalie's heart leaped with gladness at his change in tone, and she waited, hoping he might say he loved her, too. *Dumb*. Chad saw things with a boy's perspective. Someday, when he grew older, he might come to understand what a lousy husband and father Robert had been, but for now, he was furious with her for destroying his world.

"I'll call your father tomorrow. I promise."

"Never make promises you may not keep."

"That's my line," Natalie teased. Then she tried for another note of humor by saying, "Hey, if all else fails, I'll put a rubber band on my finger to remind me."

"You can't play the guitar with a finger missing. Knowing you, you'll forget the rubber band and get gangrene."

Natalie knew that she was hopelessly forgetful sometimes, and she burst out laughing. She was pleased to hear Chad reluctantly join in. "Hey, mister, I can play a guitar with my toes, and don't you doubt it." Another silence fell between them. Frank pounded on the piano, making impatient noise expressly to distract her. Natalie chose to ignore him. A woman might own many businesses, but, in her case, at least, she would have only one son. "I'm glad to know that it wasn't too awful with Mr. Coulter today. If it gets to be too much, just tell me. I'll figure out a way to settle the debt and just ground you for six months."

Again, Chad laughed, sounding more like her little boy. "Six *months.* How about six weeks?"

"Not!" Natalie retorted with a chuckle. "You totally ruined that poor man's garden, *and* his shed door, *and* his house, *and* his windows. You've got to do some serious time before you get probation."

"I guess that's fair. I was kind of shocked when I saw what I did. It didn't seem like that much while I was doing it. I was so mad, I must have zoned out or something."

Natalie felt partly responsible for Chad's anger. Right before the boy left for Coulter's place, he had tried to call his father. As usual, Robert hadn't answered the phone, and Natalie had muttered something nasty under her breath about Robert, sending Chad into a rage.

"Maybe, when Dad hears my message, he'll pay for the damages."

Natalie knew that Chad's hopes hung on that. "Maybe," she said faintly.

"Do you have to say it like that? Every time you talk about him, you get that sound in your voice, like he's a total loser or something. He's my dad, all right? Hate him all you want, but don't try to make me."

"I don't hate your father, Chad. We've had our differences, I admit, and sometimes I feel angry with him, but I certainly don't hate him."

"Yeah, sure."

In truth, Natalie *was* coming to hate Robert, not because of the things he'd done to her, which were legion, but for all the things he was failing to do for his children. It struck her as being grossly unfair that a wealthy man's kids should be one step away from going on welfare.

Did the bastard even care? Hell, no. He was having the time of his life, single at last, taking his girlfriends to four-star restaurants, putting fancy hubcaps on his new Corvette, and buying himself snazzy suits. He probably looked at their divorce settlement and laughed, giving his friends the high-five, proud of himself for beating the system and coming through a divorce financially unscathed. Most men lost some money to their ex-wives. Instead, Robert had taken her to the cleaners.

Natalie still didn't know how Robert had hidden the giant's share of his assets. She suspected that he'd transferred some of the funds into overseas accounts and the rest into corporate subsidiaries that weren't easily traced, the result being that he'd appeared to be dirt poor when they went before a judge. Natalie's attorney had been unable to disprove the financial depositions. The judge had had no choice but to make his rulings on the evidence provided, and Natalie had left the courtroom an impoverished divorcée, indebted to Robert for his rightful half of her supper club.

To save the business, her only source of income, she'd been forced to lay off employees, run the inventory to dangerous lows, nearly empty her operating accounts, and do a constant juggling act with the remaining funds to hold the creditors at bay. If she dropped one ball—just one—the debts would domino and the club would plummet into bankruptcy.

Did she hate Robert? Yes. But that was her secret, something not to be shared with her son, whose heart was already breaking.

"Mom?"

Natalie blinked and came back to herself. "I'm sorry. Did you say something, sweetie?"

"No," Chad replied softly. "You just stopped talking." As if he sensed her distress, he added, "It's really not that bad, working for Mr. Coulter. If Dad doesn't come through, I'll hang tough and be okay with it."

Natalie swallowed hard.

"He even made me eggs Benedict for breakfast. I think he's a gourmet cook. You ever had them that way?"

"A few times."

Frank pounded on the piano again, and Natalie waved a placating hand at him. She pictured Zeke Coulter—with his chiseled features, dark skin, thick sable hair, and rippling muscles. She couldn't imagine him in the kitchen, fussing over a fancy recipe.

"Would you bounce that ball somewhere else, Rosie?" Chad cried. "This is a kitchen, not a basketball court. You're such a *pest.*" Then, to Natalie, he said, "I kind of like working for him, actually. He doesn't treat me like a kid, unlike other people I know."

Natalie smiled wearily. It figured, didn't it? The man next door communicated with her son better than she did.

"Maybe, if I work with him till school starts, I'll get good enough with a saw to fix Poppy's fences."

Natalie wouldn't hold her breath. It took an Act of Congress to get Chad to take out the garbage. Nevertheless, there was a definite note of pride in his voice, and she couldn't help but rejoice. She had tried to build Chad's confidence, but for some reason, her opinion didn't carry as much weight as his father's. Maybe he needed an adult male friend to give him the reinforcement that she couldn't.

After Natalie said good-bye to her son, she tapped the phone antenna on her chin, wondering if she'd misjudged Zeke Coulter. Her son didn't sound as if he were being mistreated. Just the opposite. He sounded uplifted and proud of himself. Maybe Zeke was a whole lot nicer than she'd judged him to be.

"You gonna make love to that phone all night or come practice this number?" Frank yelled.

Natalie laid the phone on a table, removed her imaginary Mom hat, and walked to the raised stage. "I'm ready," she said as she grabbed her guitar. "Hit it."

Zeke was about to kick back with a beer when he heard a faint tapping noise. Sipping the head from a freshly drawn glass of ale, he moved through the house, wondering if he had mice. *Wonderful thought.* He was just putting traps on his mental shopping list when the tapping came again. He turned toward the kitchen door that opened onto the side porch. One of his brothers, maybe? Hank was as unpredictable as the Oregon weather. Tucker and Isaiah were almost as bad.

When he opened the portal, he nearly missed the tiny visitor who stood on his stoop. Then he glanced down and saw one of the sweetest countenances he'd ever clapped eyes on, framed by a mop of curly black hair.

"Oh! Hello. I thought I was imagining things."

Ethereal in the twilight, the child moved closer. "Hi. I'm sorry for coming over so late, but it was the only time I could leave without Aunt Valerie noticing. She bribed Gramps to let her watch *The Planet's Funniest Animals.*"

At first glance, Zeke had judged the child to be about four, but now that he'd heard her talk, he decided she must be older.

She thrust out a tiny fist. "I'm Rosie Patterson. I came to help pay for what Chad did."

At a loss, Zeke accepted the offering. When the coins were dumped onto his palm, he counted fifty-three cents—two quarters and three pennies—which clearly constituted a fortune to his caller.

"What did you say your name is?"

She pursed her lips like a miniature schoolmarm. "I'm Rosie, Chad's sister. That's Rosie with an I and an E, not a Y."

Zeke noted that she was a dead ringer for her mother. Fascinated, he stared at her perfect little face. "Hi, Rosie," he said, striving to keep his expression solemn. Did all preschoolers know how to spell their names?

Without waiting for an invitation, she started inside. "Mommy says you're mean and noxious."

Zeke struggled not to laugh. He had already concluded that he wasn't high on Natalie Patterson's popularity chart. "Is that so?"

"Yep. I want to know how come. It can't be very fun."

There was a thought. As Zeke shifted to get out of her way, he almost slopped beer on her curly head. He righted his mug just in time. "I, um—hmm."

She nodded as if he'd just said something profound as she invaded his kitchen. "Nice," she pronounced. "Pretty wood floors, and everything's tidy." She turned slowly, taking in the oak cabinetry with a critical eye. "You need some stuff on your walls, though."

That was a sentiment shared by his mother and sister. He guessed it was a female thing. The only thing he'd tacked to a wall so far was a Les Schwab Tires calendar, and he liked it that way. "I just moved in."

"You've been here almost four months. Poppy's been counting. He says you must be stuck up, never coming over to say hello until you have a bitch."

All Zeke could think of to say was, "I've been busy."

She tapped her foot. "Even so, it's important to make your space feel homey. My mommy says."

"She's probably right. I keep meaning to buy some wall hangings, but I never seem to find time."

"You need some magnets for your 'frigerator, too. Maybe, then, it won't look so naked in here."

Magnets? His mother's refrigerator was covered with them, and the thought made him shudder. "I don't like clutter."

"Some potholders, then," she suggested. "When I find time, I'll color you a picture, too. It's always nice to have kid stuff hanging up. Mommy says it makes people feel at home."

Potholders, he could handle. The kid stuff he could do without. She rested her tiny hands on her hips and turned to face him. "Gramps wants to come over here and show you how the cows can eat the cabbages."

Zeke had heard that expression and couldn't help but smile. "Uh-oh."

She pressed forward, forcing him to retreat a step. Her dusty little feet sported bright pink toenails and red sandals with straps held together with duct tape. Hands still at her waist, she looked up at him, the glint in her eye reminiscent of the fire he'd seen in her mother's. "We need to have a talk."

Zeke never argued with a lady who had butterflies on her sundress. He glanced outside to make sure Miss Rosie had no entourage before he closed the door.

"What, exactly, do we need to talk about?" he asked.

"Well, first of all, it isn't very nice to be noxious to your neighbors. Don't you want us to like you? There's nothing worse than having no friends."

"That's true, I suppose."

Dark curls afire in the fluorescent light, she tipped her head to study him. "You got any cabbages in your garden?"

"A few."

"You don't want our cows to eat them, do you?"

Zeke lost his heart right there on the spot. He'd never clapped eyes on a cuter child. Every time she spoke, a dimple flashed in her cheek. And she was so tiny. The top of her head barely grazed his thigh, and yet she stood with her shoulders erect, her chin jutted, ready to take him on.

"No," he replied. "I'd rather your cows stayed at home."

"Cows in the garden are a very bad thing. Daisy and Marigold can eat a lot. They got in Poppy's onion patch last week and ate so many our milk tasted funny."

Setting his beer aside, Zeke sat on one of the kitchen chairs and motioned for her to join him. She was a tad short, and sitting on a chair took a bit of doing, but she finally managed after a good deal of standing on her tiptoes and twisting. When she was properly perched, she covered her smudged knees with her faded skirt, patted her tousled curls, and said, "I hope you'll excuse how I look. I haven't had my bath yet. Until bedtime, Aunt Valerie says it's an effort in futility."

"You look fine to me," Zeke assured her, and meant it.

She folded her hands and fixed him with an imploring gaze. Somehow she reminded him of his little sister, Bethany, as a child, all big brown eyes and innocence. Only he couldn't remember Bethany ever talking like this. The kid had an amazing command of English.

"How old are you, Rosie?"

"Four. My birthday is February twenty-fourth. This month, I'll be four and a half."

"I take it that I'm not very well liked at your house right now."

She pursed her bow-shaped mouth again. "No, not very. My mommy's really glad Chester bit you on the butt."

Zeke gulped down laughter again. "Ah."

"Most times, my mom likes everybody," she said solemnly. "But she doesn't like you very good 'cause you're not being nice to my brother."

"I'm not?"

"No, and that needs to get fixed before Gramps lets our cows eat all your cabbages."

"I see."

She glanced at his hand. "That's all the money I've got. I've been saving for a dune buggy for my Barbie." She rolled her saucer-shaped eyes and puffed at her bangs. "I guess she'll have to walk everywhere a while longer. That's okay, I suppose. Walking is good for the cardigan vascular system." She lowered her voice slightly to add, "That's your heart, in case you didn't know."

Right then, his cardigan vascular system was in serious danger of developing a ravel. His palm burned where the coins rested. He couldn't take this child's Barbie doll savings.

"I know it's quite a lot of money," she went on, "but maybe not enough for paint. Poppy says he's going to win the lottery tonight, but he tells me that every Saturday." She shrugged her narrow shoulders, then leaned forward to whisper conspiratorially, "Aunt Valerie says he's got about as much chance of winning the jackpot as a pig does to fly. If she's right, he may not be obscenely rich anytime soon."

"That's too bad."

"Oh, well." She shrugged again. "It makes Poppy happy to think he might hit the big one. With his back hurting all the time, it's a nice distraction. Mommy says there's no harm in hoping, just so long as he doesn't spend his egg money before the chickens lay."

Zeke nodded. "There's wisdom in that."

"Mommy's real smart about stuff like that. She was raised on the farm." She bent over to scratch one brightly painted toe. "Here's the problem. If Poppy doesn't win tonight, we won't have the money to pay you off until Mommy's ship comes in."

Zeke found himself wondering what this child's IQ was. It was like conversing with a tiny adult. He held out his hand, trying to return her quarters and pennies. "I've made arrangements with your mother for Chad to work off the debt, Rosie. You don't have to pay me anything."

She shook her head, refusing to take the change. "Chad can work, just like you arranged, only he can't work as long as you want. He's got to go to camp. It's extremely important. Mommy says it's vital."

So they were discussing camp again, were they? Zeke settled back to listen. Judging by the determined glint in

Rosie's eyes, he was going to hear her out whether he wanted to or not.

"Chad has been real unhappy since the divorce. My dad hasn't come to see him one single time since school got out."

Zeke was appalled. "Not even for a short visit?"

"Nope. And he hasn't sent Mommy any money for us, either." She heaved another sigh. "It's a very long story. Mommy doesn't think I know about most of it, but I've heard her talking to Grammy when she thought I wasn't listening."

Zeke rubbed his jaw. "I see."

"My daddy ripped her off."

"Ah." He was trying to think of a way to stop this disclosure when Rosie wrinkled her nose and said, "Like before the divorce? Daddy told Mommy that the development company was short on cash and talked her into taking out a second orange on our house."

"A second what?"

"*Orange*. That's where the man at the bank gives you lots of money for your home kitty, and then it's not your kitty anymore."

Zeke slowly deciphered that information. "A second mortgage on the home equity," he translated.

She shrugged. "Anyhow, that's what they did. Only Daddy didn't really need the money. He just told Mommy that so she couldn't take his suits to the cleaners after she divorced him." She lifted her small hands. "Every cent, gone, just like that, and then Daddy hid all his asses so the judge wouldn't make him pay Mommy lots of money."

Zeke shifted uncomfortably on his chair. "Rosie," he inserted, "I don't think your mother would approve of you telling me this."

"She wouldn't care. It's as plain as the nose on her face that she's broke and the club's about to go bank ruptured." She fiddled with the duct tape on one of her sandal straps. "That's why she can't buy me new shoes and Chad couldn't take swimming lessons this year. On Monday she's taking us to Goodwill to shop for school clothes. If it weren't for Poppy letting us live with him, we'd be SOL." She arched a questioning look at him. "Do you happen to know what that stands for? Aunt Valerie says it a lot, and Mommy won't tell me what it means."

Zeke could understand why. Thinking quickly, he said, "It means sadly out of luck."

"Hmm." She scratched under her ear. "That's us, sadly out of luck. And Chad is saddest of all. When he broke his bike frame, Mommy couldn't afford to get it fixed, and riding his bike was the only fun thing he had to do all summer. He can't play with his friends. They live in town, and we don't have gas for extra trips."

"That's too bad," Zeke said softly, and for the first time he was actually starting to understand Chad's rage. Natalie hadn't been exaggerating when she'd said the boy had lost everything.

"At camp," Rosie went on, "Chad will be able to see his church friends and have fun for one whole week, which isn't very long when you compare it to the whole summer. We have to switch schools this year 'cause we moved, so it's real, *real* important for him to keep his church friends. They're all he's got until he gets to know some new kids at South Middle School. Plus, he washed cars and worked at bake sales to make the money. It'd be awfully sad if all the other boys got to go, and he didn't."

"I guess it would, at that."

Rosie arched her dainty eyebrows. "Anyhow, unless you want our cows in your cabbages, we have to work out a deal."

"I definitely don't want your cows in my cabbages."

She nodded as if that went without saying. "Here's my idea. My mom and I can come help Chad get the work done. That way, you'll get everything fixed faster, and Chad will be done paying you back before camp starts. You got a problem with that?"

Zeke remembered the look on Chad's face when he'd picked up the circular saw, all fear and lack of confidence. His heart squeezed, followed by an unpleasant ache. Maybe Chad's father was a neglectful deadbeat, but his mother was there for him—and so was his little sister. Zeke understood family loyalty. The Coulters had invented it.

"No," he pushed out. "I don't have a problem with that."

"Then how come you sent my mom home this morning? She was really, *really* mad."

"I don't know what I was thinking."

Rosie seemed to find that to be an acceptable excuse. "Okay. Tomorrow we'll come help, then. That way, Chad won't miss camp, Gramps will get over being mad at you, and our cows won't eat your cabbages."

"That sounds like an all-around fair deal to me," Zeke replied. Then he couldn't resist asking, "If Chad couldn't take swimming lessons or ride his bike, what has he done all summer?"

"He read his Harry Potter books twice. Now he just lays on his bed, listening to Aunt Valerie's rap. Mommy says it's going to rot his brain, and she worries all the time." She sighed again. "Chad wanted us to go to Disneyland like his friend Tommy, but Mommy says we've got to wait for her ship."

Zeke found himself struggling not to smile again.

"It's a money ship," Rosie elaborated. "When Aunt Valerie says it sank at sea, Mommy tells her to put a sock in it. I'm in total agreement. I really want to go to Disneyland next year and meet Mickey Mouse—the real one, not a fake."

Zeke recalled Chad's saying that he was bored at home, and little wonder if he'd been listening to rap all summer. Rosie's direct, honest gaze made him feel ashamed. He'd been furious about the damages that Chad had inflicted, and he'd gone off half-cocked, hell-bent to teach the kid a lesson. It shouldn't have taken a little girl's honesty to make him step back and question the wisdom of that. Sometimes even tomato throwers needed a break.

"You can keep my money," Rosie went on to say, "and me and Mommy will come every day to help Chad fix stuff. When we've worked long enough to pay for everything, you can tell us, and then we'll stop."

How could Zeke look into those huge brown eyes and argue? "Okay."

She slid down off the chair, a miniature powerhouse who would probably never realize that a glass ceiling existed. She thrust out her tiny hand. "We gotta shake on it. Poppy says no deal is final until you shake."

Zeke agreed. When he made a bargain and shook on it, the terms were written in stone. Her hand felt impossibly small and fragile when he encompassed it with his fingers.

After sealing the deal, she withdrew her arm, fussed daintily with her skirt again, and then beamed a smile at him. "I'm a real hard worker. You'll see."

Zeke tried to picture her carrying boards bigger than she was. "What have you done for fun this summer, Rosie?"

She smiled broadly, flashing her dimple. "Lots of stuff. Aunt Valerie always thinks of something when Mommy's at work. Chad doesn't like the stuff we do, though. He says it's dumb."

"What do you do?"

She frowned. "Sometimes we paint our fingernails. Other times we play Go Fish or checkers. When those things sound big-time boring, Aunt Valerie makes caramel corn and steals the remote control from Gramps so we can watch kid movies. She still likes them 'cause she hasn't ever grown up. She says she's never going to. Being a grown-up is dull, dull, *dull.*"

Zeke tried to imagine sexy Valerie watching children's films. Maybe, he decided, a heart of pure gold was concealed behind all that makeup and hair gel. "Watching movies sounds fun."

"Everything is pretty fun with Aunt Valerie," the child assured him. "Just not as much fun as it is with my mommy." She turned to take inventory of his kitchen again. "My brother says you're a really good cook."

"I try."

She wrinkled her nose. "My mommy likes to cook, too, but she's not very good at it. She tried to make you a welcome cake. Poppy said we should get out the syrup and pretend it was a flapjack. Mommy got mad and said she'd never bake a cake again. We're kind of glad 'cause they're never very good." She turned toward the door. "I gotta go. Aunt Valerie might notice I'm gone and start to worry."

"Uh-oh. I hope you don't get in trouble."

She sent him a surprised look over her shoulder. "From Aunt Valerie? She won't be mad. She'll just want to know what your house looks like. She thinks you're cute. Chad says she's in for a big disappointment because you're gay."

Zeke's eyebrows lifted. Before he could think of a response to that revelation, Rosie was out the door. She paused on the porch to say, "I'll see you tomorrow. Okay?"

"Okay."

The door closed, and Zeke sat there in the quiet kitchen, wondering if he'd imagined the visit. Then he opened his hand and stared at the coins resting on his palm. They were sweaty from Rosie's fist. He smiled and put them on the table. A Barbie dune buggy? He wasn't familiar with Barbie accoutrements but wished he were. He'd head for the nearest department store and buy Rosie's doll some wheels.

Chapter Four

Shortly after Rosie's departure, Zeke returned to town and visited the ranch-supply store that he'd purchased on contract from his father. After getting updated by the night manager and making the rounds to chat with his employees, he stocked shelves until closing time at eight. When everyone had left, he spent a couple of hours in his office doing that day's books, juggling work schedules to cover his shifts for the next three weeks, and making out orders for Monday.

He was yawning by the time he set the security alarm and left the building. En route to his truck across the dark, empty parking lot, he thought of Rosie Patterson and the deal he'd struck with her. He should at least inform her mother of that conversation. He also owed the lady an apology. He cringed when he remembered saying that she mollycoddled her son. Like he was an expert on kids? He'd made some rash assumptions, bottom line. Chad had some problems, no question, but that didn't mean Natalie had caused them.

Zeke checked his watch. It wasn't yet eleven. The Blue Parrot was only a few blocks away. He wasn't dressed for a supper club, but what he had to say would take only a couple of minutes. Why not drop in and get it over with? He might even order a drink. The crow might go down easier with a shot of bourbon.

A few minutes later, Zeke stepped inside the Blue Parrot. He expected a run-of-the-mill gin joint, fancied up with a grill and limited menu. Instead, it was so nice that he almost pulled a U-turn. Jeans and a work shirt definitely weren't appropriate. The few customers at the white-draped tables were dressed to the nines, men in suits, ladies in cocktail dresses, and there wasn't a bar in sight. Dark blue wallpaper and elegant chandeliers complemented the brass wall hangings. Candles adorned each white-draped table, the blue tapers ensconced in holders that gleamed like burnished gold. *Tasteful.* He felt like a weevil in a flour sack.

Then he saw Natalie, and he forgot to feel self-conscious. She was Rosie, but all grown up, standing on a raised platform in a sequined red dress that glinted like a banked flame in the dimly lighted room. Above her, an open-faced sound-system platform supported amps, speakers, spiral lights, and flush spotlights, strategically aimed to spill golden illumination over her as she performed. *Reba, take a backseat.* The sounds coming from her throat were pure honey. The guitar fit over her hip as though it had been carved for her, and she moved with graceful confidence as she belted out a country ballad about a determined woman who never gave up on her man.

Zeke had never seen anyone more beautiful—or more talented. No longer even aware of where he was, he sank onto a chair at a back table. Between numbers, Natalie laughed and chatted with her patrons as if they were old friends, as comfortable onstage as Zeke might have been at a family gathering. Every time she moved, the dress glimmered, shooting ruby daggers. Her eyes intensified the effect, large orbs of shimmering brightness in the delicate oval of her face. With her ample curves and graceful carriage, she made a man ache.

"Before my break, I'd like to sing a special song," she murmured into the mike. Then she laughed and smiled flirtatiously at a gentleman to her left. "It's a little sappy. I wrote it many moons ago when I still believed in happy endings."

Thanks to Rosie and Chad, Zeke already had a fair idea of what had disillusioned her. He settled back to listen. She bent her head, sending her cloud of black curls forward to cover her face. The sudden silence was electrical, and Zeke tensed with anticipation. With the first emission of sound, she snapped erect, revealing a countenance to break men's hearts. From that second on, the lady was pure dynamite, the explosion of voice and guitar so mesmerizing and perfect that no one in the audience even moved. The piano was a barely noticed and unnecessary accompaniment.

"Why do I love you?" she sang. "Why do I care?" She lifted her gaze above the crowd, singing from her heart, seemingly oblivious to those who listened. "When everything could be so perfect, why, in the dark of night, is my pillow wet with tears? We had it all, but you threw it away."

A waitress approached Zeke's table. He waved away the list of available beverages. "Jack and Coke, please."

"Single or double?"

He had to drive home. "Single."

Zeke just wanted the waitress to go away so he could hear Natalie's song. When he could finally refocus on the words—and the woman singing them—the number was nearly over. When Natalie raised her arm on the last note, he felt almost bereft. His heart sank a little when she bent her head and lowered her right hand to her side. The room went absolutely silent again.

She stood there for a full second, body motionless, head still bent. No one applauded until she looked up. It was if she had to release them from her spell before they could think or even move.

Instead of curtsying and nodding to acknowledge the applause, she laid the guitar aside and leaned over her piano player's shoulder. Together, they went through some sheet music. Then she patted his arm and left the stage, a brilliant flame that drew the gaze of every man in the room. As she headed for a door to the right of the platform, she hesitated midstep and looked directly at Zeke. Her shoulders sank slightly. The pianist began playing something bluesy as she wove her way through the tables.

Zeke stood and pushed back a chair for her.

"Hello, Mr. Coulter," she said softly. "Small world, or has my son vandalized your property again?"

"What the hell are you doing in Crystal Falls?" Zeke asked. "You should be taking Nashville by storm."

The question popped out of his mouth of its own volition. She was a phenomenon with a voice that went beyond fabulous and a stage presence to go with it. She should be captivating thousands, not entertaining a few country bumpkins in a ranching community.

She sank wearily onto the chair. "Flattery, Mr. Coulter?"

"Forget flattery. With a voice like that, you could write your own ticket."

"My days of chasing rainbows are over, I'm afraid."

He didn't miss the note of resignation in her voice. No bitterness, only flat acceptance. That struck him as being so sad. If only she had made different choices earlier in life, the world could be her oyster. Instead she struggled to keep her daughter in decent shoes.

She rubbed the nape of her neck and flexed her shoulders. "That guitar weighs a ton toward the end of a shift."

Zeke had a feeling that the guitar was the least of her burdens.

"So what brings you to the Blue Parrot? You don't strike me as the supper-club type."

The waitress returned just then. Zeke accepted his drink and said, "Bring the lady her usual, please, and put it on my tab."

"Water," Natalie said with a flippant smile that Zeke suspected had been practiced to hold admirers at bay. "Charge the gentleman five bucks. He's loaded."

Zeke sat back to regard her. He had stepped on her toes, and she was letting him know right up front that she wouldn't easily forgive him. He shot from the hip himself and admired that about her.

She directed her attention to the table, centering the candle, smoothing the cloth. "I talked with Chad this evening. He seems to like you." She looked back up, her gaze sharper this time. "I have no clue as to why, but that's my thing. It seems that you were right, and I was wrong. This experience is good for him. Working with you today bolstered his confidence. He needs that right now."

His fingers skimming beads of condensation, Zeke turned his glass. "I came here to apologize. Don't give me an out. I'm notorious for never saying I'm sorry."

"I believe you."

He gave a startled laugh. "I have that coming, I guess."

"Yes," she agreed.

"I apologize for making rash assumptions and acting like an ass."

Her expression guarded, she continued to study him. "May I ask what brought this about?"

"Your daughter paid me a visit tonight."

Her expression went from guarded to surprised. "Rosie?"

"Do you have two daughters?"

"No, thank heavens. One's a handful. Why was she at your place?"

"She came to negotiate." Zeke grinned, remembering. "I am now in possession of her life's savings, earmarked for a Barbie dune buggy."

"Oh *no.*"

"Oh yes, and she drives one hell of a bargain. I didn't know whether to shit or go blind." Zeke winced and glanced around, hoping no one else had heard him. "Pardon my French."

"Don't blame the French. My mother's maiden name is Devereaux."

No wonder she had gorgeous legs. French women were famous for them. "My Irish, then."

Her eyes started to twinkle, warming him as they had yesterday afternoon. "Ah. That explains the stubborn streak."

Zeke chuckled. "It's the Scots who are stubborn."

"With the Irish running a close second."

He conceded the point with a shrug. "I wasn't quite stubborn enough to come out on top with your daughter."

"Few people do. My Rosie is indomitable and too cute for her own good."

"True. After she asked why I'm mean and obnoxious, she informed me that Gramps and the cows have nefarious plans for my cabbages. Being a smart man who has no desire whatsoever to get his ass kicked by a geriatric, I quickly agreed to her terms."

Natalie's lovely and very kissable mouth twitched. "Which are?"

"You and Rosie are welcome to help Chad work off the debt. I don't want to be responsible for his missing camp and getting brain rot from Valerie's rap."

She burst out laughing. The sound wasn't quite as magical as her voice in song, but close. "My daughter. She repeats everything she hears."

"And quite eloquently, I might add."

"I'm sorry she bugged you. Chad's right, I guess. She can be a pest."

"I'm glad she came. Trust a child. I *was* being mean and obnoxious. I began to realize that this afternoon when I got to know your son a little better."

"So you're coming to like Chad as much as he's coming to like you?"

Zeke nodded. "He's a troubled boy, but not a bad one. I was wrong to take such a hard line, threatening to bring the law into it." He took a sip of his drink to compose his thoughts. "I also want to apologize for suggesting that you mollycoddle him. Before he left today, I wanted to make things better for him myself." He picked up a complimentary book of matches, studied the Blue Parrot logo, and then said, "I can see his heart in his eyes, and it's a broken one. What the hell's going on with his dad?"

Her eyes went bright with what he suspected were tears. "Nothing." The smile that had touched her mouth a moment ago vanished. "When it comes to being a father, Robert *isn't*. I can't think of another way to say it."

"I gathered as much."

She fiddled with the midnight-blue cloth napkin in front of

her. "I sound like a bitter ex-wife. It's so dead boring to be typical, but I can't help myself."

"You're concerned about your son. There's no crime in that."

Her brow pleated in a thoughtful frown. "I don't mean to paint a black picture of Robert. He's just—well, being Robert. His parents never paid any attention to him, and that's all he knows."

"Don't make excuses for the bastard."

She laughed softly, then puffed air at her bangs, reminding him strongly of Rosie. "There *is* no excusing Robert. I only meant that it isn't really his fault. He's being as good a father to Chad as his father was to him. All too often, we become our parents."

Zeke guessed there was a lot of truth in that. He'd been told countless times that he was a Xerox copy of his dad. "Your son doesn't think he's good at anything. When he actually does something without screwing up, he's amazed."

"Robert is a little critical."

"A little?"

"It's complicated." For a moment, Zeke thought she would leave it at that. "I think he feels inadequate, actually. He hides it very well. If you met him, you'd never for a second believe that he has self-esteem issues. Robert is one of those people who are smarter than everyone else and better at everything. Sports, academics, business, you name it. Poor Chad never quite measures up."

Zeke doubted that Chad had been Robert's only victim. He had known men like that, and in his experience, they took shots at everyone around them.

He felt himself becoming lost in Natalie Patterson's swimming brown eyes and experienced something akin to fear. The lady packed a wallop. Just like her daughter, she tugged at his heartstrings in a way he didn't understand. He disliked the feeling, and he suddenly just wanted to get out of there.

He raised one hip to fish for his money clip, then tossed a twenty onto the table. It was more than enough to cover his drink and the five-dollar glass of water. He hoped Natalie would pay his tab and keep the rest. Judging by her daughter's clothing, she needed the money a lot more than he did.

"I've said what I came to say." *Brilliant, Zeke.* "I, um—" His mind went blank. "I have to go."

She pushed erect before he could shove back in his chair. "Thanks for stopping by, Mr. Coulter. I appreciate the apology and your change of heart. Chad needs a little leniency right now. Camp is important this year."

He stood, nudged the chair back under the table with the toe of his boot, and hooked his thumbs over his belt.

"Now that I've gotten to know him better, I agree with you. He should go. If the damages aren't worked off in time, I'll give him a week off and let him work after school."

She picked up the twenty, sidled around the table, and moved close to tuck the bill into his shirt pocket. The musky scent of her perfume filled his senses. The warmth of her body, moving a scant inch from his, seared him like a brand. "The drink is on the house."

Recalling the duct tape on Rosie's sandals, Zeke wished she would take the money. Instead he stood there like a dumb cluck and watched her walk away. Or, to be more precise, he watched the sway of her hips. Natalie Patterson was not a thin woman. Her body was soft and well rounded in all the right places.

Not a mere flame, he decided, but a wildfire, and only a fool would get burned.

* * *

The following morning when Zeke opened the front door at eight o'clock, he found the same sullen helper standing on his porch, the only difference being that today his shoes were tied.

"'Morning," Zeke said, pulling the door wide.

Chad offered no response. Mouth thinned to a bitter line, he stepped over the threshold. Zeke was bewildered. They'd parted on good terms yesterday.

"So how's it going?" Zeke tried.

"The same way it always goes." Shoving his hands into his pockets, Chad hunched his shoulders and kicked at the carpet.

"Hungry?"

"Not really."

"That's good," Zeke replied. "I'm feeling lazy this morning. All I'm having is cereal."

"Does that mean we don't have to work?"

Zeke chuckled. "Not an option, bucko. Sorry."

"People shouldn't have to work on Sunday."

"You a churchgoer?"

"Not anymore. We used to go every Sunday, but now that we live way out here, we can't afford the gas."

Zeke knew how that went. His parents had seen some really tough times when he was a kid. "I'm sorry things are so difficult right now."

"Why should you feel sorry? It's no skin off your nose."

Chad preceded him into the kitchen, flopped onto a chair, and stared glumly at the floor. *Okay,* Zeke thought. *Back to square one*. He'd foolishly hoped that he and the boy were becoming friends.

As Zeke filled a bowl with Cheerios and milk, he said, "You want to talk about it?"

"Talk about what?"

"Whatever happened that has you feeling so low?"

Chad tossed his head to get the hair out of his eyes. "What good would that do?"

Zeke wasn't much for talking about things himself. "Sometimes it helps."

"It won't help me."

Zeke accepted that with a shrug. "Fine. Just thought I'd offer."

Chad stared out the window, his expression revealing nothing but anger.

"I tried to call my dad again last night," he finally revealed.

"Ah."

"All I get is his voice mail on every phone. I think he's screening my calls because he doesn't want to talk to me."

Zeke had no idea what to say. The only sounds were the ticking of the wall clock and an occasional faint crackle as the cereal absorbed milk.

"Maybe he's just very busy right now," Zeke suggested.

Chad's throat worked as he swallowed. "Maybe."

Zeke grabbed the sugar dispenser and generously sprinkled the cereal. He wished he could think of something more to say. This boy was hurting, and his pain might get worse before it got better. He busied himself with eating.

Between bites, he said, "I had a visit from your sister last night."

"I heard. Aunt Valerie says she convinced you to let her and Mom help work off my debt. You don't have to do that." Chad turned the cereal box to stare blindly at the list of ingredients. "I'm not a baby. I don't need my mom to bail me out." He shot Zeke a burning look. "She doesn't know the first thing about power tools and fence building. All she'll do is screw things up."

Zeke had his own reservations about the new arrangement, namely that he'd be seeing more of Natalie than he wished, but he refrained from saying so. "With power tools, there's a learning curve for everyone." Chad had never touched one himself until yesterday. "I'm sure she'll get the hang of it."

"Hello. She's a female. My dad never let her do anything. He told her to go paint her fingernails and keep out of the workmen's way."

"That's your dad, not me. I grew up on a ranch."

"What's that got to do with it?"

"Everything. If not for my mother, my dad would have been sunk. There wasn't anything on the spread that she couldn't do as well as a man."

"My mom isn't like that. All she can do is sing."

Zeke felt fairly sure that Chad was selling his mother short, but for the moment, at least, he chose to let it slide. "We'll be nicely entertained while we work, then."

Anger flared in Chad's eyes. "Maybe I don't want to spend that much time with her. Did you think of that?"

Careful, Zeke. "Don't the two of you get along?"

Chad's jaw hardened, and his dark eyes went bright with tears. "I *hate* her. My dad won't come see me or answer my phone calls. It's all her fault."

Zeke lost his appetite and shoved away the bowl. A smart man would keep his mouth shut. He was no child psychologist, and he didn't want to say the wrong thing. On the other hand, he couldn't erase from his memory the things Rosie had revealed to him last night.

"I don't think you're giving your mom a fair shake, Chad."

"What do you know?"

"She can't be blamed for the choices your father is making right now."

"He's making those choices because of her. She's a total bitch to him."

In for a penny, in for a pound. "Your dad doesn't have to deal with her. He could make arrangements to pick you up for visitation at the end of the driveway or in a store parking lot. He's also entitled to talk to you on the phone several times a week without interference."

"Tell that to my mom."

"It's the law," Zeke retorted, "and I'm sure your mother is aware of it. After a divorce, animosity between parents is common. The courts protect a noncustodial parent's right to see his kids without a hassle. If your mother causes trouble, your father has legal recourse to make her stop."

Chad brushed at his cheek. "If that's true, why hasn't he done it, then?"

"I don't know. Maybe you should ask him."

"Yeah, like, when?" A muscle in Chad's cheek twitched as he clenched his teeth. "How can I talk to him about anything when he won't take my calls?"

Zeke had no answers. He only knew that he was coming to detest Robert Patterson without ever having met the man. Chad's anger and bitterness toward his mother spelled nothing but trouble. Zeke had seen the results—a sturdy door that this boy had broken with a kick of his foot, signifying a consuming, helpless rage that couldn't be contained.

On what or on whom would the boy's anger be unleashed next?

Chapter Five

Two hours late. Natalie couldn't believe she'd slept until after nine. She had set the alarm for seven, hoping to be up and ready to go when Chad left the house, but the buzzer hadn't gone off.

"It's okay if we're late, Mommy," Rosie said. "Mr. Coulter won't be mad."

For Chad's sake, Natalie hoped not.

Bending to pick some blue lupine, Rosie launched into a one-sided discussion about wildflowers. Trudging beside the child, Natalie barely attended the discourse. Absurd as it was, she felt nervous about seeing Zeke again. When they'd been at odds, she'd had no problem ignoring how attractive he was. But that had changed with his visit to the club last night.

His apology had caught her off guard, and his compassion for Chad had disarmed her. The next thing she knew, she'd been talking with him about Robert's failings as a parent. Normally, she was a very private person. It wasn't like her to reveal family secrets to a man she barely knew. Even more alarming was the inescapable fact that he'd made her pulse race when he looked at her.

Not good. She needed to get control of these feelings before they took control of her. Only for some reason, she couldn't tamp down this girlish sense of excitement. It was similar to the way she'd felt when she first met Robert, and just look where that had gotten her.

It takes two to tango, she reminded herself. *I'm perfectly safe.* How likely was it that Zeke Coulter was attracted to her? After slathering on makeup and stuffing herself into a flashy dress that hid a multitude of sins, she could look pretty good under the right lighting. But that wasn't the real Natalie. Offstage, without all the makeup and glitter, she was a very ordinary woman with an average IQ, so-so looks, a crazy family, and a hectic, boring life.

She tugged at the shirt she'd filched from Pop's closet. Why hadn't she looked at it more closely before she threw it on? It had grease stains on the front. Even worse, her old jeans were so tight at the waist she could barely breathe, a harsh reminder of the twenty pounds she'd gained with two pregnancies. She must be out of her mind to worry about the impression she might make on the handsome bachelor next door. *Reality check.* Zeke Coulter probably had a little black book filled with the phone numbers of beautiful women. He wouldn't care how Natalie looked, only how hard she worked.

"Are you all right, Mommy?"

Natalie hauled in a calming breath. "I'm fine, sweetie. Just tired from rushing around to get ready."

When they reached Zeke's place, Natalie slowed her pace and pushed at her hair. She wished she'd had time to find a nicer top and put on some makeup. They circled the shop to find Chad and Zeke preparing to take a break. *Fabulous.* The troops had arrived at quitting time.

Zeke looked delicious in scuffed Tony Lama boots, faded

Wranglers, and a red cotton shirt with the sleeves rolled back over his tanned, muscular forearms. Tousled by the morning breeze, his chocolate-brown hair lay over his high forehead in lazy waves. The sunlight played on his face, accentuating the sharp bridge of his nose, the chiseled slope of his cheekbones, and the square angle of his jaw.

Natalie took a deep breath and forced away her tension, a trick she'd learned years ago when she first experienced stage fright. "Good morning!" she called brightly. "Sorry we're so late. I set my alarm, but it didn't go off." She sent her son a querulous look. "Someone forgot to wake me when he got up."

Chad, who'd just finished rinsing out a paintbrush, dried his hands on a red shop rag. "How was I supposed to know you wanted to come with me?"

"You'll know tomorrow," Natalie replied.

She forced herself to look at Zeke. Even from across the yard, his eyes had an unsettling effect on her. They were a clear, sky blue, almost startling in contrast to his burnished skin. His expression revealed nothing as his gaze settled on her face, then drifted slowly downward to take in the smudges on her shirt. "You worked last night. I didn't expect you until around noon." He gestured toward a shady oak at the edge of the yard. "We were about to take a break. I made some punch. Care to join us?"

Natalie preferred to stay busy. "Oh, I don't—"

"I love punch!" Rosie said.

Twinkling amusement warmed Zeke's eyes as he met Natalie's gaze. "It sounds as if you're outvoted."

Natalie stared after her daughter as she scampered across the grass. Zeke reached down to tousle the little girl's hair as she bounced by. "How are you this morning, young lady?"

Rosie spun to a stop, looking adorable in faded floral pants that had grown too short and a pink top with bunnies on the front. "I'm fine. Unfortunately, the same can't be said for everyone else in my family."

Natalie guessed what was coming and frantically searched her brain for something, anything to say that might steer the conversation in another direction.

"Really?" Zeke smiled sympathetically. "Is someone sick?"

"Not sick, exactly," Rosie replied. "Aunt Valerie woke up with the cramps. Poppy says a grumpy old bear would be easier to get along with."

Zeke's expression went from inquiring to deadpan. It was a look that Natalie had seen on the faces of many adults. No one, it seemed, knew quite how to handle her precocious daughter.

"Hmm. I'm sorry to hear she isn't feeling well," Zeke finally said.

Rosie sighed. "She usually gets better in a day or so. Gramps's hemorrhoids are another matter."

Not *that,* Natalie thought. But before she could interrupt, Rosie blurted, "He's very forgetful and misplaces things. This morning he can't find his Preparation H."

Zeke's mouth twitched. "You don't say?"

Rosie rolled her eyes. "Mommy and I looked everywhere. Poppy thinks he got it confused with his jock itch ointment and rubbed it on his cro—"

"Rosie!" Natalie cried.

Her daughter sent her an innocent look. "What?"

"There are some things you shouldn't discuss outside our family."

"Why?" Rosie angled an inquiring look at Zeke. "Haven't you ever heard of hemorrhoids and jock itch?"

Zeke didn't look at all certain how to respond. "I have, actually."

"There, you see, Mommy? It's okay."

Zeke sent Natalie another laughing look. Reluctantly, she followed him and her children to the shade of an oak tree where he'd set out a gallon-size jar of punch and four drinking glasses. He lowered himself to the grass, pressed his broad back to the gnarled tree trunk, and gestured for everyone to join him.

"Sorry," he said. "I haven't gotten around to getting lawn furniture yet."

Before Chad dropped to the ground, he put as much distance between himself and Natalie as possible without sitting in the sun. Then, just in case that was too subtle, he scowled and refused to look at her. Natalie's heart hurt every time she glanced his way. Chad was still furious because he believed she had neglected to phone his dad. Natalie couldn't disabuse him of that notion without telling him the truth, that his father couldn't be bothered with him right now.

Rosie knelt beside Zeke, talking nonstop about things that Natalie preferred she not reveal. Unfortunately, silencing Rosie in chatter mode was nearly impossible. Before the punch had been poured, Zeke knew of Valerie's recent breakup with her boyfriend, Kevin, and her fruitless job hunt, Poppy's problem with his lower back, and Natalie's never-ending battle with her weight.

"Practically all Mommy eats is nonfat yogurt and celery," Rosie expounded. "Poppy's afraid she'll make herself sick."

As Zeke passed Natalie a glass of punch, he skimmed his gaze over her person. "You look just right to me."

The mirror told Natalie a different story. Besides, for her dieting was an economic necessity. Her appearance was a tool of her trade. An extra five pounds looked like twenty in a tight, sequined dress, especially under stage lighting. No way was she going to give some inebriated heckler an opportunity to yell, "The show ain't over 'til the fat lady sings."

Zeke slumped against the oak, one arm resting on his upraised knee, his other leg extended. The position accentuated the breadth of his shoulders. In the dappled sunlight that filtered down through the leaves, the furring of dark hair on his roped forearm and the back of his dangling hand glistened like spun silk. He had long, thick fingers, the knuckles calloused to a leathery toughness. It was the hand of a working man, broad across the palm, thick at the base.

Taking his measure with sidelong glances, Natalie decided he was as different from Robert as night was from day. Robert had his blond hair professionally styled. His manicured hands were as soft as a woman's, and he had developed a potbelly from sitting behind a desk. No one would ever mistake him for a workingman.

With a start, Natalie realized that Zeke had caught her staring. She tried to look away, but the magnetic draw of his eyes wouldn't allow it. For a second that seemed torturously long to her, their gazes locked. Her heart skittered and missed a beat. She couldn't have moved if someone had jabbed her with a pin.

Oblivious to the undercurrents between Natalie and Zeke, Rosie abandoned her punch to chase after a monarch butterfly. A moment later, she returned with her small hands cupped to her chest.

"Guess what I caught, Mr. Coulter!"

Zeke smiled. "A leprechaun?"

Rosie giggled. "No, silly. Leprechauns are only in Ireland."

Zeke arched an eyebrow. "How do you know that?"

"Mommy read me a leprechaun story. You can learn lots of things from books."

"Maybe someone accidentally brought a leprechaun over from Ireland in a suitcase," Zeke suggested.

Rosie pursed her mouth, a habitual gesture that had earned her the nickname Rosebud, which, over time, had been shortened to Rosie. "Maybe, but it's not a leprechaun."

"Hmm." Zeke frowned and pretended to think. "A hummingbird?"

"Nope. I'm not fast enough to catch one of those."

"I'm a lousy guesser. You'll just have to show me."

Rosie moved closer and parted her hands. To Natalie's dismay, a toad jumped out, its fat, warty body hitting Zeke squarely in the face. He jerked so violently that he spilled punch on his Wranglers. "Holy shi—Toledo!" he cried. Then, with lightning-quick reflexes, he recaptured the toad before it hopped away.

Natalie clamped a hand over her mouth to keep from laughing.

"Think this is funny, do you?" He angled her an amused look that promised retribution. Then he returned the hapless toad to Rosie's outstretched hands. "This little fellow eats bugs," he told the child. "When you're finished playing with him, turn him loose in what's left of my garden."

Rosie scampered away to do that. Chad leaped up to follow her, barking orders as older brothers will, all of which Rosie ignored.

"Not *there.* He needs shade. They live in the mud, dumbbell."

"I'm not a dumbbell."

"Are, too!"

"Am not!"

"No name calling, Chad!" Natalie yelled, but the children continued volleying insults as if she hadn't spoken.

Rosie moved through the garden, which now sported more bare dirt than plants, looking for the perfect place to release her captive. "Toads don't *live* in the mud," she informed her brother. "They only burrow into it during the day to keep cool."

"Nuh-uh!"

"Yes, sir!"

And so it went. Zeke attended the exchange for a moment. "I'd almost forgotten," he said softly.

"Forgotten what?"

"How kids love to bicker. I was one of six. From dawn 'til dark, there was never a moment's peace. It's a wonder my parents aren't bald from tearing out their hair."

His friendly, easy manner helped Natalie to relax. She set her glass on the grass beside her and looped her arms around her bent knees. "Six kids? I can't imagine. Chad and Rosie are bad enough. Sometimes I want to knock their heads together."

"Times them by three, and you'll have a fair idea of what my childhood was like. Four brothers and a sister. I'm the second oldest."

"My sympathy is all with your sister," she said with a laugh. "How on earth did she survive five brothers?"

"She was the baby. We went pretty easy on her." His eyes went soft with memories. "Not to hear Bethany tell it, of course. Mostly it was Hank, the youngest of us boys, who gave her a hard time. One against one, she held her own fairly well, giving back as good as she got. I think it was healthy for her, actually. She grew up to be one spunky lady."

His expression told Natalie that he loved his sister deeply. "And your brothers, what are they like?"

He frowned thoughtfully. "A lot like me in looks, and in other ways as well, I guess. Jake and Hank have a cattle ranch. They also raise and train quarter horses. The twins, Tucker and Isaiah, are vets, specializing in large animals. I own The Works, a ranch-supply store on the west side of town."

Natalie's dad had frequently patronized The Works before injuring his lower back. Now he leased out his alfalfa fields to neighboring farmers and lived on the proceeds and monthly stipends from his disability insurance. "I've been to The Works. It's a nice store."

He shrugged. "It provides me with a good living, and selling ranch supplies is right up my alley. My father is a third-generation cattleman. There's some truth to the saying that an apple never falls far from the tree, I reckon."

Natalie found it interesting that all five boys had pursued professions linked to their father's. "And your sister, what does she do?"

"In addition to being a fabulous wife and mother, she recently opened a riding academy for handicapped kids."

"What a great idea. A few years back, I saw a television documentary about a riding academy like that. Seeing the joy on those kids' faces the first time they got in the saddle nearly brought tears to my eyes. It gave them such a sense of freedom. I hope your sister can make a go of it."

"No worries. She's married to Ryan Kendrick."

Practically everyone in Crystal Falls had heard of the

Kendrick family. They were richer than Croesus. "Ah. No worries, indeed."

Zeke smiled. "Ryan's very supportive. In fact, I think it was him who came up with the riding academy idea in the first place. Being married to a paraplegic, he's more sympathetic to the plight of handicapped children than most people are."

"Your sister is a paraplegic?"

"A barrel-racing accident at eighteen. Teaching kids to ride is a wonderful way for her to stay active. She's always loved horses. She was the state champion three years running in barrel racing and had her eye on the nationals."

Now that he mentioned it, Natalie vaguely remembered hearing that the younger Kendrick son had married a woman in a wheelchair. "So Ryan Kendrick is your brother-in-law." Natalie shook her head and laughed. "My, my, you have friends in high places, Mr. Coulter."

"Zeke," he corrected, "and I have plenty of friends in low places as well." His white teeth flashed in a quick grin. "Enough about me. Fill me in on the Westfields."

Natalie grimaced. "Rosie's already done that. Is there anything you *don't* know?"

He threw back his dark head and laughed. It was a warm, rich sound that rumbled up from deep in his chest. "She did cover a lot of ground at a fast clip," he admitted. "I suspect I won't be the first person to tell you that she's darling."

"Thank you. And no, you're not the first person to tell me that. Usually after she's just said something embarrassing. Talking is her strong suit. She shuts up only when she sleeps."

He laughed again. "What amazes me is her command of

English. I can't believe she's only four. She gets a few words wrong, but mostly not."

Natalie released a long-suffering sigh. "She's a trial sometimes. I can't seem to break her of repeating everything she hears. I live in terror of what she'll tell her teacher. She starts preschool this year."

His lips twitched. "I'm sure the teacher will take it in stride. They hear everything. For first grade show-and-tell, I got up in front of my class and graphically described the birth of my sister." Twinkling laughter danced in his eyes. "As I recall, I left nothing out. My teacher didn't faint, but she did sit down."

"Surely you didn't witness the birth."

"I did, actually." He rubbed beside his nose. "My mother had all of us at home with a midwife in attendance. My dad tried to corral us boys and keep us out of the bedroom, but my older brother, Jake, and I were slippery little farts. We wanted to see what all the commotion was about."

Natalie tried to picture him as a little boy with a shock of dark hair and big blue eyes. Somehow, the picture wouldn't come clear. It was difficult to imagine a strong, virile man like Zeke being small and innocent.

His amused gaze rested warmly on hers. "The moral is that you shouldn't worry so much about what your daughter says. Most people won't be shocked. They'll just think she's cute as a button and be captivated."

The topic of their conversation returned just then, and she was in tears. Chad hung back, looking guilty.

"Chad pulled my hair!" Rosie sobbed.

"I did not!" Chad cried.

Rosie's lower lip quivered. Huge tears rolled down her cheeks. "Yes, he did, Mommy. I'm not fibbing."

"So, I pulled her hair. Big deal. I didn't do it on purpose."

Natalie sent her son a questioning look. "How did you accidentally pull her hair, Chad?"

Chad's face flushed with anger. "You *always* take her side."

"It's not a matter of taking sides. I merely asked for an explanation. If it was an accident, just explain, and that'll be the end of it."

"I grabbed her by the shoulder," Chad said sullenly. "She thought I was trying to take her stupid frog, and she twisted to get away. Some of her hair was in my hand. I thought I only had hold of her shirt."

It sounded plausible to Natalie. She gathered Rosie close. "There, you see? It was an accident, sweetie. Chad didn't mean to pull your hair."

"It still hurt!" Rosie cried indignantly.

Natalie kissed her daughter's curls and patted her back. "I know, but since it was an accident, you shouldn't be mad at Chad. Has your scalp stopped stinging yet?"

Rosie nodded but continued to whimper pitifully. "I lost my toad."

"Uh-oh. That's too bad. Maybe you can catch another one."

"I don't want another one. I liked that one."

"Maybe you can find the same toad again," Natalie suggested.

As Rosie raced off to begin her search, Natalie pushed to her feet and smiled at Chad. "It would be a nice gesture if you helped her look, sweetie."

"Don't call me sweetie. I'm not a baby."

Zeke got up to collect the glasses. Then he preceded Natalie back to the house. Most of the tomato stain was in the patio area under an overhang, Natalie was pleased to note. They wouldn't be working in the direct sun.

"We've finished scrubbing away the pulp," Zeke explained. "Now we're to the painting stage."

"I'm ready. Where's a brush?"

Within minutes, everyone, including Rosie, had a paintbrush in hand. Chad stood on a stepladder, painting the siding below the eave. Natalie was happy to see that her son was doing a fine job, using plenty of paint and going back over each section to catch all the drips. She wanted to compliment him on his work, but he'd been so prickly with her over the last few weeks that she feared he might take it wrong.

Zeke solved her dilemma by stepping back to survey the house. "Are you sure you've never done any painting, Chad?"

"Totally sure. My dad always hires this kind of stuff done."

"You're doing an excellent job," Zeke observed. "If I didn't know better, I'd swear you were an old hand. That's union quality."

"What's union quality?" Rosie asked.

Zeke explained about the nationwide painters' union. "The members are professional painters, and they usually get paid top-scale wages. If Chad put his mind to it, he could paint with the best of them."

Chad shrugged off the compliment, but Natalie could tell that it actually meant a great deal to him. He stood taller on the ladder rung and became even more intent on his work.

"How does my job look?" Rosie demanded.

Zeke didn't gush and shower the child with false praise as so many adults were inclined to do with a four-year-old. Instead, he crouched at Rosie's side and carefully examined the patch of siding that she'd painted. Rosie waited solemnly to hear his verdict. Zeke borrowed her brush to smooth out some dribbles.

Finally he said, "Not bad, young lady. Not bad at all."

It was praise enough to make Rosie happy, yet not so lavish as to steal any of Chad's sunshine. *Kudos*. Zeke Coulter was a natural with kids. He was everything Natalie wished Robert could be: firm and exacting, yet patient as well, and always ready to encourage with praise when the children did something right. Chad was blossoming right before Natalie's eyes, seeming to gain more confidence with each stroke of the brush.

This truly was good for him, she realized. Being around Zeke was bolstering the boy's self-esteem in ways that Natalie couldn't.

As noon approached, the sun moved high overhead, sending down a blanket of sweltering heat. Natalie was grateful for the overhang that covered the patio. Even in the shade, she was hot. Her mouth and throat were cottony with thirst, and she yearned for another glass of punch.

She was painting the drainpipe at the edge of the patio when Zeke approached and lightly touched her shoulder. Natalie straightened from her work to give him a questioning look. He braced a hand above her head and leaned close.

"We have company, and it's not anyone I know."

Natalie hadn't heard a car pull up. She peeked around the corner of the house and nearly groaned when she saw her ex-mother-in-law, Grace Patterson, climbing out of a new silver Lexus. "Great. It's Robert's mother."

Zeke arched a dark eyebrow. "Not one of your favorite people, I take it."

"Perceptive of you."

"She come around a lot?"

"Rarely, thank goodness." Natalie sighed. "Something must be wrong."

Zeke held out a hand for the paintbrush. "Go see what she wants. I'll keep the kids occupied."

Natalie rubbed her hands clean on her shirt as she crossed the gravel parking area. Even at sixty, Grace was a tall, slender, elegant blonde who carried herself with regal grace. In the early years of her marriage Natalie had trembled with nerves in Grace's presence, ever fearful of doing or saying something gauche. Now she just braced herself for unpleasantness.

"Dear God," Grace said when she saw Natalie's clothes. "What are you doing over here?"

"Painting." Natalie quickly explained about the vandalism. "Mr. Coulter kindly agreed to let me and Rosie help work off the damages so Chad will be done in time for camp."

Grace got that haughty, ice-queen look that had once made Natalie cringe. "This won't do. It won't do at all." The woman opened her purse. "How much do you owe the man?"

"I don't want your money, Grace. It's kind of you to offer, but no."

"Don't be absurd. You're married to a wealthy and very important man. You can't grub around over here, painting some stranger's house."

"Robert and I are *divorced,* remember?"

"There are still appearances to keep up. Working off the debt?" Grace shuddered delicately. "It's so blue collar."

Natalie gestured across the field at the house where she'd grown up. "I'm from blue-collar stock, Grace. Always have been, always will be."

A look of distaste moved across the older woman's perfectly made-up countenance. Grace had never liked any of Natalie's relatives. Their connection to the Patterson family had always been a source of embarrassment to her. "You're the mother of my grandchildren. You must set a proper example."

"In my opinion, that's exactly what I'm doing. Both my kids are learning what it means to take responsibility for their actions."

Grace slipped the checkbook back into her handbag. "I didn't come here to spar with you, Natalie."

"Good. I'm tired." Natalie tried a smile. "So, why have you come?"

"It's Robert."

Natalie noticed then that the older woman was trembling. "What's he done now?" she asked resignedly.

Grace's faded blue eyes filled with tears. "You've got to *do* something, Natalie. His behavior is so scandalous that people are starting to talk."

Natalie translated that to mean that Robert's sexual escapades were raising eyebrows at the country club. "I'm sorry to hear that, Grace, but there's nothing I can do."

"Go back to him! At least he tried to be discreet when he was married."

Natalie thought of the countless nights she'd paced the floors, wondering where Robert was, only to have him come home at dawn, smelling of another woman. "He wasn't discreet enough, I'm afraid. I'll never live like that again."

Grace hugged her Coach handbag to her chest. "It's not as if he's the first man on earth to stray. Smart women weather the storm."

The storm, as Grace called it, had begun shortly after the

wedding and had never stopped in almost eleven years. "I guess I'm not very smart."

"I stopped by his house this morning, hoping to talk with him." Grace got a calculating look in her eyes and leaned closer. "He was with that little tramp, Cheryl Steiner."

The last Natalie had heard Robert had been dating a blonde named Bonnie Decker. Not that it mattered. His girlfriends were interchangeable, all of them young and voluptuous with bleached hair and room temperature IQs.

"I walked in and found them together in *your* bed," Grace added, clearly expecting a horrified reaction.

The bed in question was a Patterson family heirloom, handed down to Robert by his father. Originally it had belonged to Helena Grant Patterson, Robert's great-grandmother.

"It's not my bed, Grace. It never really was."

"The judge determined differently."

Natalie couldn't argue the point. Robert's insistence during the divorce that all their assets be divided equally by a judge had ended just as he planned, with Natalie being fleeced financially, but it had also resulted in a chaotic misappropriation of possessions, with both of them being granted ownership of or interest in things that weren't rightfully theirs. They had finally reached a settlement out of court, each of them forgoing all interest in the other's family heirlooms and inheritances, nullifying Robert's half interest in the Westfield farm, which Natalie had inherited from her grandmother during their marriage.

"Who owns the bed is beside the point." Natalie folded her arms. "Robert and I are divorced. I no longer care what he does or with whom he does it."

"He's shaming you!"

"No, he's shaming himself. Robert's choices are no longer my concern."

"How can you say that? If nothing else, his actions reflect on the children."

Natalie shook her head. "Chad and Rosie aren't responsible for their father's behavior, reprehensible as it may be."

Grace dabbed at her cheeks with a tissue, taking care not to smudge her makeup. "When I walked in on them, Robert was furious and ordered me out of the house. He says I'm no longer welcome there without an invitation."

Natalie's heart caught at the pain she glimpsed in Grace's eyes. Being a mother herself, she understood how that must have hurt. "Ah, Grace."

"I'm his *mother!*" she cried. "After everything I've done for him, how could he treat me that way? And in front of that little tramp? It's the last straw for me, Natalie. I was so furious. You just can't imagine. If I'd had a gun, I would have shot him, I swear."

Natalie patted the older woman's shoulder. "You don't mean that. Robert is your son. You're angry right now, and with good reason, but it'll pass."

"No," she said softly. "Not this time." Hopeless bewilderment clouded her eyes. "I don't know what's gotten into him."

Natalie had long since stopped trying to understand Robert. He could seem warm and compassionate and wonderful when it suited him, but beneath the surface, he was a shallow, selfish, and dishonest man who lived by his own set of rules. *All veneer and no underlay* was how Pop described him, and that pretty much said it all. Unfortunately, Natalie had been too young and naive at eighteen to realize that.

"I called my attorney on the way out here," Grace said

flatly. "I'm cutting him out of my will. When I die, everything will go to Chad."

Eventually Robert would apologize, and his mother would forgive him. That was the way it always went. "I'm sorry you're so upset, Grace, but this will blow over. You'll see."

"Not this time." Grace squared her shoulders. "I'd like to tell my grandson that he's just become my heir."

Natalie had known Grace to use her money as leverage against Robert countless times, her goal always to jerk him back into line and make him toe the Patterson mark. She wasn't about to let Chad get caught in the middle.

"No," Natalie said firmly. "I'm sorry Robert has disappointed you, Grace, and I can understand your need to express your displeasure, but leave Chad out of it."

"But it's fabulous news for him!" Grace smiled tremulously. "He'll be a very wealthy man someday."

"You can tell him when he's older. He has enough to deal with right now."

"I would never tell him *why* I revised my will. Surely you know that."

"I don't want it mentioned to him at all. There's enough negativity in his life right now."

Grace finally nodded, albeit reluctantly. "If I promise to say nothing about it, will you at least let him come to visit me?"

A knot of anger formed in Natalie's chest. In Grace's eyes, Chad was more important than his sister because he was a male and would one day carry on the Patterson name. "What about Rosie?"

"Oh, her, too, of course."

Never in Natalie's life had she wanted so badly to deny a

request. But she couldn't, in good conscience, deny Chad and Rosie the opportunity to know their grandmother.

"Of course they can visit."

"When?" Grace pressed.

"Anytime soon would be difficult. We'll be busy working here until Chad goes to camp. He'll get home only a few days before school starts."

"In September, then?"

Natalie could only hope that Grace's sudden bent to be a grandmother would pass. "Sure. September will work."

"I'll call ahead to make arrangements."

Natalie nodded.

Grace wasn't usually given to displays of affection, but she hugged Natalie now. "My son is a fool," she whispered. "He'll live to rue the day and beg you to come back to him, mark my words." She patted Natalie's back. "Ultimately, that would be best, you know. They're Robert's children. The two of you should raise them together."

Hell would freeze over first. Natalie loosely returned Grace's hug, but her heart wasn't in it. Long after Grace had backed her Lexus from the driveway, she remained there, staring at the road. She jumped when Zeke's deep voice sounded behind her.

"You okay?"

"I'm fine." Sweating under the hot burn of the sun, yet feeling oddly cold, she chafed her arms as she turned to face him. "Grace is pretty upset."

"I heard." He raked a big hand through his hair, leaving the sable strands furrowed by his fingers. "I just wonder at her reason for coming."

"Her son is misbehaving. The only punitive measure within her power is to cut him out of her will. It's a game they've played often over the years." Natalie rubbed her sleeves again. "This time, she wanted to take it one step further by telling Chad that he's now her sole heir. Up the stakes for Robert, so to speak, by making it official."

"You're kidding."

"Grace's parenting techniques are a blend of power and manipulation. If Robert thinks his son may inherit the fortune that's rightfully his, maybe he'll straighten up. If his wife will only go back to him, maybe he'll be more discreet." Natalie sighed. "When you haven't worked to earn your children's respect, it's difficult to exert any control once they become adults."

"Go back to him?" he echoed.

"When Robert and I were married, he sneaked around to see his girlfriends. Now he doesn't bother. Grace's friends are gossiping, and she's mortified."

Zeke's gaze sharpened on hers. "Is there a possibility of that?"

"Of what?"

"Your going back to him."

Natalie laughed bitterly. "Absolutely none. Why do you ask?"

Mischief danced in his blue eyes, and a smile flirted at one corner of his mouth. "Just curious."

Natalie recognized masculine interest when she saw it. A shiver ran up her spine—a lovely, delicious little shiver—and for just an instant, she felt young and pretty and desirable. The moment didn't last.

"I didn't intentionally eavesdrop," he assured her. "I took over painting the drainpipe, and some of the conversation carried to me on the breeze." He arched a dark eyebrow, a gesture she was quickly coming to realize was a habit of his. "Did she mean it, do you think?"

"Which part?"

"That she would have shot him if she'd had a gun."

Natalie chuckled. "Robert has that effect on people sometimes. She'll get over it. She always does."

He nodded, leading Natalie to wonder just how much of the exchange he had overheard. "I'm sorry she came over here," she said. "Someone at the house must have told her where I was. Nothing like airing our dirty laundry in the neighbor's driveway."

"It isn't your laundry." He fixed her with a sympathetic gaze. "It's a shame you're still having to deal with it."

"I'll be dealing with it until my kids turn twenty-one, I'm afraid. Robert's their father."

He squinted against the sunlight, accentuating the crow's-feet around his eyes, which, she guessed, had been etched there by exposure to the elements. Deep creases bracketed his lips, which shimmered like satin, the upper one thin, the lower one full yet firm.

Natalie found herself wondering how it might feel if he kissed her—to feel those big, hard hands moving over her—to be held close in his strong arms. When she realized the direction her thoughts had taken, she gave herself a hard mental shake.

She had enough problems in her life without asking for more, and Zeke Coulter had trouble written all over him.

Chapter Six

That evening, shortly after Natalie and the kids left for the day, Zeke found a woman's wristwatch lying next to the foundation of the house. Fascinated, he held it on his palm, studying the dainty band, the small stem, and the way the fading sunlight glinted off the crystal face. It was only a cheap Timex, and in places, the gold was wearing off. Nothing special. So why was he staring at it?

The answer was simple. It wasn't the watch that intrigued him, but its owner. She was fascinating, coming off as a sexy seductress in sequins one time, as wholesome and sweet as apple pie the next. He enjoyed watching her in candid moments—the way she swayed while painting the house, as if she had music playing inside her head, the gentle manner she had with her children, always smiling at Rosie, looking bewildered and sometimes hurt when she interacted with Chad. She had soulful eyes, large, thickly lashed, and a deep, rich brown flecked with amber. They revealed her every emotion, filling with shadows when she felt sad, sparkling when she felt happy. Every time he looked into those eyes, he got the strangest feeling, a sense of connection and rightness that he'd never experienced before, not with anyone.

After checking the time, he slipped the piece of jewelry into his pocket. It was going on six o'clock. Natalie was probably rushing around to leave for work, and she'd probably feel lost without her watch. If he broke a leg, he might catch her before she took off.

As Zeke crossed the field, he saw an old farmer leaving the Westfield property by a back gate. Zeke waved and breathed deeply, taking in the pungent scent of alfalfa almost ready for a second cutting. Over the summer, he'd noticed that someone else was working Pete Westfield's land, and he surmised that Pete's back problem had forced him to lease out his fields, a common practice when a man couldn't raise any crops himself.

At the edge of the field, Zeke lost his courage and almost went back home. This was stupid, a poorly veiled excuse to see Natalie again, bottom line, and he wasn't sure how he felt about that. The lady had two kids and a crazy family. Did he really want to get involved with her?

Maybe his brothers were right, he decided, and he was way too serious about everything. A lot of men his age dated women who had kids, and practically everyone had a crazy relative or two. Natalie was a beautiful lady, both on and off the stage; he was strongly attracted to her, and he greatly enjoyed her company. If it felt right, why not go for it?

When he reached the Westfield house, he circled around back where they parked their cars, the better to catch Natalie on her way out. To his surprise, the patchy backyard was lined with flowers, the borders so thick that blossoms spilled over onto the grass. Zeke suspected Natalie was responsible for all the color. Her father seemed to have back problems,

Gramps was too feeble to work outdoors, and Valerie was probably far too busy primping.

Just as Zeke reached the rickety back porch, he heard Natalie burst into song somewhere inside the house. He paused and grinned as he listened to the words, something like, "And I shaved my legs for this?" Damn, but she had a beautiful voice. He almost hated to knock and interrupt her.

As he ascended the wooden steps, he saw that the screen door opened onto the kitchen. Through the wire mesh, he could see Natalie in front of an old-fashioned gas range. Just as Chad had described, she was pretending the long-handled fork she held in one hand was a microphone. Bending slightly at the knees and throwing her other arm wide, she belted out the song's refrain. Zeke became so engrossed in her performance that he just stood there. The lady didn't need stage lights and sequins. She was pure dynamite without props.

He finally collected himself and rapped his fist on the wood. She jumped so violently that she almost shoved a fork prong up her nose. "Oh!" She clamped a hand over her heart. "Zeke! You scared me out of ten years' growth."

"Sorry." He swept his gaze over her. She'd changed into pink shorts and a flowery blouse that was faded and wash worn, the thin cloth clinging softly to her full breasts. Her hair lay loose around her narrow shoulders, an ebony cloud of curls. "You forgot your watch. I thought you might need it at work."

She laid aside the fork and came across the kitchen, tugging self-consciously at the shorts in a futile attempt to cover her legs. Zeke fixed his gaze on her face, not wanting to make her feel uncomfortable.

"I don't go in tonight," she said. "I take Sundays and Mondays off."

"Ah." Fishing in his pocket for her watch, Zeke stepped to one side as she pushed open the screen door. "You didn't mention that today."

"Our busy nights are Thursday through Saturday," she explained. "Frank, my piano player, holds down the fort for me on Sunday and Monday, and I return the favor on Tuesday and Wednesday. It gives us each a break."

Zeke put the watch on her outstretched palm. She had gorgeous legs—not that he was looking. "That's good—you getting a little time off, I mean."

She held the screen ajar with her left elbow while she donned the watch and fastened the clasp. "Thank you for bringing it over. I took it off while I was painting. I can't believe I left it."

"Not a problem."

She pushed the screen wide. "I just made some ice tea. Won't you come in and have a glass?"

Zeke hadn't intended to stay, but the lady issuing the invitation tempted him in a way he couldn't understand and didn't want to resist. "I'd love to."

As he stepped inside, she sniffed the air and got a horrified look on her face. "Oh *no,* the chicken!"

The screen slapped Zeke on the ass as she rushed back to the stove. She grabbed a potholder to take the lid off a big cast iron skillet. Smoke billowed upward. She waved her hand and coughed.

"*Darn* it!"

From somewhere at the front of the house, Gramps or Pop, Zeke wasn't sure which, yelled, "Nattie, have you gone and burned supper again?"

She made a face and whispered, "*No*. It's just well done." As she retrieved the fork and turned the meat, she added, "Crispy on one side, that's all."

Zeke grinned and sank onto a chair at a battered gray table, which reminded him strongly of the one in his grandparents' kitchen when he was a boy. Slanting a long look at the stove, he watched the lid bounce on a pot that sat over a back burner. Judging by the smell, she was boiling potatoes.

"Might better turn that rear flame down. I think your spuds are about to spill over."

She adjusted the knob, then wiped her hands on her blouse. "Tea!" She hurried over to the refrigerator. "I'm sorry. Organized, I'm not."

Zeke thought she was adorable, distracted by his presence and all aflutter with nerves. When she bent over to take a pitcher from the fridge, he was afforded a fabulous view of her bottom and the backs of her bare thighs. If she had cellulite dimples, he couldn't see them. Not that he had anything against a few dimples here and there.

"Lemon?"

He jerked and fixed his gaze on hers. "Pardon?"

She'd caught him looking. Two bright spots of color flagged her cheeks. "Do—you—want—lemon?" she asked with exaggerated slowness.

He liked his tea the same way he liked his women, sweet with just a hint of tartness. "Yeah, a little lemon will be great."

She plucked a small bowl of lemon wedges from the shelf, rinsed her hands, and then shoved a wedge over the edge of his glass. She fetched a spoon from a drawer before advancing on him with the tea. Zeke fleetingly wondered if he was going to drink it or wear it.

"Thanks," he said when she set the glass on the table with a decisive click and slid the sugar toward him.

"You're welcome." She returned to the stove to check the chicken. Every time she turned a breast, she tugged at the legs of her shorts. "Can you stay for supper? We have plenty. Valerie and the kids aren't here tonight."

Zeke preferred his breasts plump and tender. "Where are they?" he asked as he stirred two heaping teaspoons of sugar into his drink.

"Valerie worked for an attorney who recently retired and closed his office. She got her severance pay in the mail yesterday. She's springing for pizza and a movie tonight."

"That's sweet of her."

"Yes. My kids don't get many treats these days." She slipped the lid back over the chicken, adjusted the flame to simmer, and went to pour herself a glass of tea. When she joined him at the table, she said, "Sweet as it is, though, I can't help but wonder where her head is. She went to a community college for two years to become a legal secretary, which is great, but now she's hell-bent to do nothing else. There are no jobs in her field at present. I keep hoping she'll take something else, a regular secretarial position or a job as a receptionist, but she won't even consider it. And in the meanwhile, she's out blowing money she can't afford to blow. Next week, she'll be broke and wonder how on earth it happened."

Zeke plucked the wedge of lemon from the edge of his glass and squeezed the pulp into his tea. He'd had similar thoughts about his younger siblings more than once. "I hear you. You're wondering if she'll ever grow up."

She looked a little startled. Then her sweet mouth, which

he found himself wanting to kiss more and more by the moment, curved into a slight smile. "Yes. How'd you know?"

"One of six kids, remember? And I'm the second oldest." He touched his temple. "See the gray? I earned every white hair."

"What gray?"

"It's there, trust me. First off, it was Bethany. When she got hurt, I thought it was the end of the world. Then came Hank. He's finally straightened out, thank God. Now the twins are driving me nuts."

"Tucker and Isaiah, right?"

"Good memory."

"So, what are the little darlings doing to push you over the edge?"

Zeke chuckled. "The little darlings will be thirty-three in December. They're only ten months younger than I am."

"My goodness, your poor mother."

His chuckle deepened to a rumble. "Another story. Don't distract me. I stopped by unannounced at their town house the other night. Not a good plan."

"Uh-oh." Her eyes sparkled with laughter. "Let me guess. A toga and Wesson Oil party, minus the togas."

Zeke grinned, trying to picture her in a toga. He decided she'd be beautiful in anything. "Nope. Tucker was entertaining a lady."

"Hmm." She raised her eyebrows and dimpled a cheek at him. "That sounds pretty tame. There must be something more. If not, get a life."

At that precise moment, he thought that sounded like damned good advice. He could go for getting a life, especially if it included a curvaceous vocalist with eyes he could get lost in. "Oh, there was more."

"Do tell. Were they—? Well, you know."

Zeke touched his tongue to the squeezed lemon rind. The sweetness and tartness made him look at her mouth. "Nope. Tucker was mixing drinks at the bar, and the lady was hanging all over him, but nothing else was going on."

"What, then?" Her eyes reflected genuine interest. "I'm dying here. Get to the good part."

"She was calling him Isaiah."

Long silence. She stared blankly at him for a full second, and then her eyes widened. "Oh, my *gosh!* They're switching places."

"Isn't that juvenile?"

"Juvenile? It's low down and rotten and—and absolutely unforgivable."

"I agree. And now you know why they're driving me nuts."

She clunked her glass down on the table and sank back in her chair. Zeke was glad to have distracted her. She was no longer tugging at her shorts. "That poor woman!"

He peeled the pulp from the lemon rind with his teeth and pocketed it in his cheek, enjoying the sourness as he sipped the tea. "I'm sure that Tucker didn't take it that far. He's a decent guy at heart." He no sooner spoke than he shrugged and added, "Well, I can't be absolutely sure, of course. That's why it bothers me so much, I guess. I didn't blow the whistle on him. How do you tell a woman she's getting cozy with the wrong man?"

"Oh, Zeke." Her tone rang with sympathy.

"I'm sure, in his misguided way, Tucker was only trying to help Isaiah out. But it still bothers me." Zeke lifted a leg to prop a boot on his knee, then immediately lowered it to the floor again. Thinking about the twins agitated him. "Isaiah's the serious, bookish one. Always has been, even as a kid. When Tucker was swinging from curtains and sliding down banisters, Isaiah was off in a corner, totally absorbed in something cerebral. Nothing's ever changed. He's far too busy thinking about a cure for the latest swine virus to connect with reality, thus socks that don't match and two dates the same night."

Natalie's eyes went soft. "You love them."

"Well, of course, I—" Zeke sniffed the air and jumped up to advance on the stove. "If I'm staying for dinner, I'll help get the meal on the table. If you don't mind, that is."

"Not at all. Chad says you're a gourmet cook."

"Not a gourmet, exactly. I just enjoy cooking."

He plucked the lid off the skillet. After pushing at the meat with the fork, he decided it wasn't beyond redemption. More like chicken jerky. Thank God he had strong teeth. He turned off the heat, slapped the lid back on the skillet, and leaned forward to check the spuds. They were as close to mush as potatoes could get.

"How did you plan to fix these?"

"Mashed."

Damned good thing. Zeke turned off the burner. "How's about if we work while we talk?" Without waiting for her assent, he washed his hands and opened the fridge to grab milk and butter. "Where's your masher?"

She jumped up and opened a drawer. Zeke grabbed the utensil, grinned at her, and said, "I hope you don't mind. I can't sit still in the kitchen."

She smiled and shrugged. "Have at it. I'm a disaster waiting to happen."

While Natalie fixed a salad, Zeke cut the chicken into paper-thin slices and created an Alfredo sauce from scratch, which he served over both the chicken and the mashed potatoes. He enjoyed himself immensely, talking nonstop, which was a rarity for him. His brothers laughingly said that he was a man of few words, but around Natalie, he had plenty to say. They discussed gardening, horses, the employee turnover at his business and hers, the alfalfa crop in her father's fields, and different ways to fix chicken.

It felt good. Zeke didn't think about what he said or how he said it; he just turned loose and enjoyed conversing with her. All and all, it was a liberating experience, and, best of all, Natalie seemed to enjoy herself as much as he did.

When dinner was finally served and everyone had gathered around the table, they joined hands and blessed the food before they began to eat. Zeke liked that, too. It reminded him of home.

"For a change, it smells like we got something to eat that we can really be thankful for," Gramps commented.

Natalie flashed Zeke an impish grin. "My reputation in the kitchen is legend."

"Can't cook for squat," Gramps inserted. "Only person I know who can't boil an egg."

"I can so!" Natalie cried.

"Ha. Dad-blamed things bounce off my teeth." To Zeke, Gramps added, "She'll never find her way to a man's heart through his stomach, that's fer sure. Girl's got too many songs in her head to mind the stove."

"It's the new millennium, Gramps," Natalie inserted. "A woman's talents needn't be confined to the kitchen anymore."

"Hmmph. Can't hurt to have *some* talent in the kitchen."

Pop nodded as he sampled the food. "Now *this* is good."

Natalie moaned as if she were in the throes of orgasm when she took a taste. "This is *fabulous,* Zeke."

Gramps made appreciative noises while he chewed. After swallowing, he said, "You oughta marry this fella, Nattie girl. The man can flat cook."

Normally, the very mention of marriage made Zeke nervous, but when he looked across the table at Natalie, he had no inclination to run. "I'm glad all of you like it."

"Mm," she said. "How did you do this with *my* chicken?"

Zeke winked at her. "Good Alfredo can disguise the taste of almost anything."

She laughed. "Thanks a bunch."

Pop dabbed at the corners of his mouth with a paper napkin and slanted a meaningful look at his daughter. "Short of marrying him, you should at least consider hiring him. That chef you got at the club could take lessons."

Natalie flashed Zeke an inquiring look. "You interested in a job?"

Zeke gazed into her beautiful eyes and decided he was interested in far more than that.

The meal ended too quickly to suit Zeke. To his surprise, he enjoyed talking with Pop and Gramps, who'd spent their lives working a farm. Ranching and farming were two different enterprises, of course, but there were enough similarities for Zeke to converse intelligently with them on a variety of topics.

After Natalie's father and grandfather returned to the living room to watch Court TV, Zeke stayed to help clean up the kitchen. On the counter near the sink, he saw a tattered tablet. The top page was filled with chicken scratch. When he looked closer, he realized it was music and verse.

"Songs," Natalie explained with an embarrassed laugh.

"I keep tablets in every room so I can jot ideas down as they come to me." She shrugged. "That way, I don't grab a pen and write on myself."

"Ah." Zeke didn't want to make her feel uncomfortable, so he stopped looking at the tablet. "Makes sense."

A smile lighted her eyes. "Which part, writing stuff down—or taking preventative measures so I don't look like I went to a drunk tattoo artist?"

"Both. It'd be a shame to forget a song that may become a number-one hit."

She made a face. "Not likely. Pop keeps threatening to paper the walls with my songs. I've written hundreds and never sold one yet."

"Ever tried?"

"Not yet. The club and my kids keep me pretty busy." She sent him an apologetic look. "I'm sorry about all the ribbing at dinner tonight." She washed a plate and stacked it in the drainer to be dried. "My family isn't really looking to marry me off. Gramps just didn't stop to think how it sounded."

"I realized that he was only joking."

"Good." She handed him another plate. "I'm really not in the market for another husband. I wouldn't want you to think—well, you know—that I had designs on you or anything."

"No worries." He angled her a questioning glance. "Any particular reason why?"

"Why, what?"

"Why you're not in the market for another husband."

She smiled and grabbed a pot to immerse it in the sudsy water. "The first one cured me for life." Her expression sobered, and she shrugged. "Maybe someday—if I meet a really special man. Then, again, maybe not. Once burned, twice shy, and all that."

"Robert hurt you that deeply?"

She scrubbed on the pot for so long that Zeke almost gave up on getting an answer. Then, in a voice pitched so low it was barely more than a whisper, she said, "A thousand times."

His heart caught at the pain he glimpsed in her eyes. Then, just as quickly, it vanished, and she dimpled her cheek in a mischievous grin. "How about you? Fair is fair. Did some wicked woman break your heart? There must be some reason a guy like you is still running around loose."

Zeke chuckled. "I'm one of those rare birds who's never been in love."

"Never?"

"Well, maybe once, if you count puppy love. When I got older, I just never met anyone who struck me as being that special." Zeke set a drinking glass in the cupboard and then plucked another from the drainer. "I never really wanted to get married. Maybe that accounts for it. Some people are cut out to have a family, others aren't."

"And you're not?"

"It was never high on my list. Came from growing up in such a large family, I guess. As a kid, I felt like a sardine packed into a can a lot of the time. No room of my own, no sacrosanct corner where I could escape to read or be alone with my thoughts. With three younger brothers and a little sister, I couldn't even go for a walk without one or all of them tagging along. When I finally got out on my own, I enjoyed living alone. I didn't really want to get married and clutter up my life with kids." Zeke realized with something of a shock that he was speaking in the past tense. He mentally circled that, wondering what had come over him. Then he looked into her soft brown eyes and knew. "That isn't to say I'll never change my mind. It'll just take a very special lady to get me there."

She nodded in understanding. "You have plenty of solitude now."

"Yes." And it suddenly felt less desirable than it had a week ago. "No background noise when I want peace and quiet. No one to fight with over the remote. No standing in line to use the john."

She laughed. The small diamond studs in her earlobes winked at him through her silky black curls. "Around here, we have to take a number to use the bathroom."

"There's only one?"

"Nothing in this house has been updated. One bath, no dishwasher or garbage disposal. Pop doesn't believe in sparing coin for frivolities."

Zeke doubted that Pete Westfield had much coin to spare, period.

They lapsed into a comfortable silence, and before Zeke knew it, the last dish had been dried and put away. He had no further excuse to hang around.

"Well," he said regretfully, "I guess I better scat."

She looked up at him with those beautiful brown eyes that sucked him under and wouldn't let him resurface to grab for breath. "It was fun. I'm glad you came over."

Zeke seconded that sentiment. He was so damned glad. He wished she'd grab a spoon and sing to him. Anything, just so he wouldn't have to leave. *Nuts*. At the back of his mind, he wondered at the insanity. He tried to think of his empty house, which waited to embrace him with silence.

That was what he wanted. Right? Only when he looked into her eyes, he no longer felt so sure.

She accompanied him to the door and then followed him out onto the porch. Zeke stopped on the bottom rise and turned. She let the screen slap closed behind her and shivered in the chill night breeze.

"One thing," she said softly.

"What's that?" he asked.

Crickets sang in the grass behind him. He heard a cow low in the huge old barn that loomed just beyond the picket fence.

"About Tucker," she murmured.

Zeke's heart sank. He'd been hoping she might ask him to kiss her. Dumb thought. Natalie wasn't that kind. She was too—well, he wasn't sure what. Shy, he guessed, although he hadn't a clue why. She could crook her little finger and have any man she wanted.

"Stop worrying about what he may have done with that woman. The apple never falls far from the tree. Remember? Your brother would never stoop that low."

Zeke's throat went tight. "That's a mighty nice compliment you just paid me."

"Sincerely meant."

"You barely know me."

"Not true. I've seen how you are with my kids."

She chafed her arms, making him wish he could gather her up in a hug and share his warmth.

"Maybe I'm a great loss to the stage," he suggested.

She shook her head. "No act can hold up around Rosie."

"True. She does have a way of dispensing with formality, doesn't she?"

Zeke hadn't felt nervous about kissing a woman in

years—but then, it wasn't often he got an opportunity to kiss someone so beautiful, either. There was also the inescapable possibility that Natalie wouldn't welcome the advance.

To test the water, he brushed a curl from her cheek, then traced the curve of her delicate jaw. She swallowed convulsively. Her lashes fluttered low. He moved closer.

"Zeke?"

"Yo," he whispered, his mouth a scant inch from hers.

"What I said earlier, about being hurt a thousand times? I'm not looking to make it a thousand and one."

He caught her chin on the crook of his finger and moved up a step. "No worries. I'll never hurt you."

"I just—"

He cut her off by settling his mouth over hers. *Warm, moist silk.* She tasted so damned sweet, her lips soft and tremulous, the touch of her hands hesitant and uncertain when she curled them over his shoulders. *Oh, man.* When her lips parted to allow him entry, he felt the punch like a fist to his gut. He cupped his other hand over the nape of her neck, his fingers closing over her thick curls. *Natalie.* Just like that, and he wanted her—wanted her as he'd never wanted anyone.

She moaned softly into his mouth. He felt the nervous tension leave her body. He could have taken her mouth more deeply. God knew he wanted to. But something told him to take it slowly, that a brief, polite, good-night kiss was safer. After getting a taste of her, it took all his self-control to draw away.

She looked up at him with her heart in her eyes, her expression so bewildered and confused and frightened that Zeke wanted to reassure her. He was about to do that when he heard an ominous hissing sound behind him.

"Chester, no!" Natalie cried.

Too late. Zeke's ass exploded with pain. When he whirled to confront his attacker, all he could see was a blur of white. He cleared the porch, cursing and swinging. When his boots connected with solid ground, he was already running, the gander in hot pursuit.

"Oh, Zeke, I'm so *sorry!*" he heard Natalie call after him.

He was already halfway across the field.

Chapter Seven

Falling in love . . .

Over the next week, Zeke experienced for the first time how it felt to fall in love. Accidentally touching hands. Glancing up, only to look into Natalie's eyes and forget what he meant to say. Smiling for no reason at all when he was alone. Lying awake at night because he couldn't get her off his mind. He loved the way she laughed, the sound moving through him like sunlight. He loved the way she wrinkled her nose and rolled her sparkling eyes when she got embarrassed. He loved the little frown that pleated her brow when she grew thoughtful. He even loved the fire that flashed in her eyes when she was perturbed.

A confirmed bachelor, Zeke tried to convince himself that his feelings stemmed from a particularly strong physical attraction—a fleeting fancy, nothing more. But with each passing day, he found himself getting more involved, not only caring more for her, but also coming to care for her children.

Rosie was easy to love—an ebon-haired angel with gigantic brown eyes, irrepressible buoyancy, and a dimple that made Zeke's heart melt every time she smiled. Chad was another story, constantly trying Zeke's patience with his stormy mood swings, sarcastic mouth, and sulky manner, all three traits distinctly more pronounced when his mother was around. Zeke oscillated between wanting to give the kid a hard shake and aching to hug him.

As the week wore on, Zeke discovered that Chad's self-esteem issues were even more serious than he'd originally thought. One moment, the boy could be bursting with pride over an accomplishment, and the next he was convinced that he would fail if Zeke asked him to try something new. The I-suck-at-everything attitude was so ingrained in Chad's makeup that he was constantly fulfilling his own prophecy, screwing up the easiest tasks simply because he knew he would.

When working with Chad, Zeke found himself frequently referring back to his childhood, trying to remember how his father had handled similar situations. Sadly, though, there was no comparison between Zeke as a boy and Chad. Zeke had been around tools and workingmen from infancy. Chad was starting from scratch, not only completely inept at using tools, but also clueless about their names and what they were used for. The poor kid didn't even know the difference between a regular screwdriver and a Phillips. As a result, Zeke found himself spending a great deal of time alone with Chad, playing teacher, while Natalie and Rosie worked together at something else.

Consequently, Zeke developed a bond with three people simultaneously, falling hard for Natalie despite his attempts not to, becoming captivated by her daughter, and developing strong paternal feelings for Chad.

By Sunday evening, one full week after kissing Natalie good night on her back porch, Zeke was beginning to feel as if he'd waded in over his head. Once he'd seen Natalie and the kids off, he sat on the side porch, gazing thoughtfully after them, his mind still shying away from what his heart already knew—that he was falling wildly in love. Given the fact that getting married and having a family weren't in his game plan, he wasn't sure how he felt about that. He knew only that he meant to be damned sure of his feelings before he acted on them.

The following morning, Chad showed up at Zeke's place alone. "Rosie's still asleep," the boy explained. "Mom says to tell you she'll be here as soon as she can."

"No problem," Zeke said. "You hungry? I'm feeling in the mood for French toast."

Chad's eyes brightened. "With powdered sugar and syrup?"

Zeke laughed. "I can swing that."

A few minutes later while they were eating breakfast, Zeke got a call from the glass shop, telling him that his sliding door panes had arrived. "Well, that throws a wrench in the fan blades," he told Chad as he got off the phone. "If I'm going to drive clear into town this morning, I should make the trip count and spend a few hours at the store."

"You got work to do there?"

"I went in late last night and took care of the paperwork, but there's always something." Zeke rubbed the back of his neck. "Monday is a big delivery day. If nothing else, I can put away stock."

"I could help."

Zeke studied the boy's eager expression, silently marveling at the change in his attitude. Was this the same lippy kid who'd stood on his doorstep Saturday morning a week ago? "I appreciate the offer, Chad, but I'll probably get side-tracked doing office stuff afterward. You can't really help me with that, and you'd be bored out of your skull." Zeke reached for the portable phone again. "What's the number over at your place? I'll call your mother and head her off at the pass."

A moment later, Natalie answered Zeke's call. When her sweet voice came over the line, he pictured her face and smiled. "Good morning. How are you today?"

She laughed. "I'm great, just a little sore from swinging that hammer. It's been a number of years since I drove nails."

Zeke glanced out the back window at the compost frame that she and Rosie had worked on together the previous day. "Never know it by the workmanship. I couldn't have done better myself."

"Yes, well, it's a bit difficult to mess up a compost box."

Zeke moved on to the reason he'd called. After explaining the situation, he said, "Anyway, if it's all right with you, I'll send Chad home for the day. Most of the afternoon will be shot by the time I get back."

"That'll be great, actually," she confessed. "I need to take the kids shopping for school clothes, and I'd rather do it on my day off so I'm not exhausted before I start my shift."

Zeke glanced at Chad, who had taken it upon himself to start loading the dishwasher. Pushing up from the chair, Zeke moved into the living room beyond the boy's earshot. "Natalie, about the school clothes. I know you're tight on money right now. I'll be happy to float you a small loan."

"Oh." A long silence ensued. "That's very kind of you, Zeke, but I can manage."

Zeke hated to see her kids dressed in secondhand clothing, but he didn't really know her well enough to press the issue further. "You sure? I've got a nice nest egg in the bank. I honestly wouldn't miss the money. I trust you to pay it back when things get better."

There was a smile in her voice when she replied. "I'm a Westfield. In a pinch, we get creative."

Zeke let it go at that. He had no other choice.

Zeke was stocking shelves early that afternoon when he heard Rosie's voice in the next aisle. He stepped onto an unopened box of oil to look over the shelf and found himself gazing down into Natalie's beautiful brown eyes. Her cheek dimpled in a smile.

"Ah, there you are." She placed a hand atop her daughter's head. "The kids wanted to see your store. There was nothing for it but to bring them by. I hope you don't mind."

"Not at all." Zeke winked at Rosie. "Stay where you are. I'll come give you the grand tour."

Minutes later, after guiding his guests from one department to another, Zeke led the way upstairs via the elevator.

"Pretty fancy," Natalie commented. "Most two-level buildings don't have lifts."

As the door slid open onto the upstairs hallway, Zeke explained, "We had it installed for my sister, Bethany, when she moved down from Portland and went to work here. She's a paraplegic and can't manage stairs."

"She used to work for you?"

"For my brother Jake, actually." Zeke walked with them toward his office. "Long story. The Works has changed hands a few times. My father started the business but had to turn it over to Jake because of his health. Jake ran it for only a year. Then it came to me. I liked it so well, I purchased the business from my dad."

"Oh, look, Mommy!" Rosie cried. "There are horses on the walls!"

Natalie slowed to study the horse photographs. "Are they yours?" she asked Zeke.

"They are." Zeke indicated the first picture with a jab of his finger. "That's Windwalker. The sorrel is named Cinnamon. The little chestnut mare is Jelly Bean."

Chad stepped closer to study the picture gallery, which boasted snapshots of Zeke's family members as well as his horses. "Are these your ropers?" the boy asked.

"Best roping stock in the state." Zeke ruffled the boy's hair. "You can take that with a grain of salt. I love them and undoubtedly think they're more special than they actually are. They're great animals, though."

"Zeke says he'll teach me to rope sometime," Chad informed his mother.

"That would be lovely." Natalie had moved on to look at the family snapshots. When she saw one of Bethany in her wheelchair, she said, "This must be your sister."

"Yes."

"She's beautiful."

"We think so." Zeke joined her and pointed to another picture. "That's Tucker and Isaiah, the day they opened their clinic," he said. "And that's my dad, holding Jake's son at the hospital right after he was born. This one is of Jake and Hank at their ranch, the Lazy J. The pregnant blonde and the redhead you see in the background are their wives, Carly and Molly. The baby is due this coming spring. It's Hank and Carly's first child."

"The family resemblance is incredible," she said as she

perused the collection of snapshots. "All you boys look so much like your dad."

Zeke nodded. When they ran out of pictures to study, he turned to the kids. "How about a soda pop?"

Rosie bounced in place and clapped her hands. Chad shrugged, his standard response to most offers. Zeke directed them into his office. After getting everyone a soft drink, he seated Natalie behind his desk and grabbed a stool for himself.

"We should be going," she said. "We're taking up your time. I only meant to make a fast stop so the kids could see the store."

"I'm glad you came," Zeke said, and he sincerely meant it. It had been nice, sharing this part of his life with her. The realization was vaguely alarming. Normally, he liked to keep his social and private lives separate. With Natalie, everything was different somehow.

She took a sip of her pop and glanced at her watch. "Drink up, you guys," she said to the children. "We have a ton of shopping left to do."

It seemed to Zeke that Chad and Rosie guzzled their soft drinks at record speed, and before he knew it, he was escorting his guests back downstairs. He walked outside with them, loath to say good-bye even though he'd be seeing them again in the morning.

"Have fun shopping!" he called after them as they went to Natalie's car.

Natalie turned to walk backward. "Thanks for the tour. It was fun."

"Anytime."

Zeke remained on the front walkway as they drove off.

Anytime? He had it bad. He wasn't sure how he felt about that, and, even worse, he wasn't sure what to do about it.

That evening, Zeke had been home for no more than thirty minutes when Rosie showed up at his door. The child was decked out in what appeared to be brand-new clothes: a pretty blue top, matching shorts, and cute leather sandals.

"Whoa! Just look at you," Zeke said.

The child pirouetted on the doormat, her thin little arms held out to show off her new summer outfit. "I got bunches of school clothes, too! Mommy says I'll be the prettiest little girl in my whole class."

"Your mommy is absolutely right," Zeke agreed. He just hoped Natalie hadn't put herself in a financial bind to take the kids shopping. "I thought you were supposed to buy clothes at Goodwill."

"We were." Rosie's face fairly glowed. "But Mommy was tired of her earrings and sold them at a shock hop."

"Hockshop," Zeke corrected. He vaguely recalled seeing diamond earrings twinkling through Natalie's curls. It saddened him to think that she'd sold them to dress her kids. "Lucky for you she got tired of them. Looks to me like you scored big time."

"Yep." Rosie tipped her dark head to study him, looking so much like her mother that Zeke wanted to hug her. "Well, I guess I'd better go. I just wanted to show you my clothes."

"I'm glad you did. That is one fine-looking outfit."

His smile fading, Zeke gazed after Rosie as she scampered away. When the child had safely reached her own yard, he closed the door. *Silence*. Zeke had always enjoyed being alone, but now, suddenly, he just felt lonely. He wandered into the kitchen, opened the freezer, and stared at the food on the shelves, wondering what he should fix for supper. Nothing sounded appealing.

He thought of Natalie in the Westfield kitchen last Sunday night, waving the long-handled fork and singing. He wished she were available to burn a couple of chicken breasts for him now. Or better yet, that she'd invite him for dinner again. He had enjoyed visiting with her dad and grandfather. Tonight, with Valerie and the kids there, the conversation at the supper table was sure to be even livelier.

The thought made Zeke slap the freezer door closed. He sank onto a kitchen chair and stared blankly at the gleaming surface of the tabletop. *Time to do some serious thinking.* He was falling, Stetson over boot heels, for Natalie Patterson. Before he took this any further, he needed to be positive it was what he really wanted. Ladies like Natalie weren't made for trial runs.

Problem. How could any man be absolutely sure of his feelings for a lady at the beginning of a relationship? Zeke was cautious by nature, always had been. To even consider making a long-term commitment to a woman was a gigantic step for him, and before he took it, he wanted to be sure he wasn't making a huge mistake. To accomplish that, he needed to spend a lot more time with Natalie and her kids. He also needed to know that he and the lady were sexually compatible. A guy couldn't determine that with only a kiss.

And therein lay the problem, he decided. To be sure of his feelings, he'd be putting Natalie's at risk. If he pressed her to take the relationship to a more intimate level, she might come to expect more from him than he'd feel inclined to give. Rather than take that gamble, it might be better never to go there. He didn't want to hurt her. She'd already been hurt too many times.

So that left him where, exactly? Nowhere, he guessed. He needed to cool it, no question about it.

Throat afire from screaming Chad's name, Natalie walked through the shadowy barn. The dusty smell of the hay filled her nostrils. She stopped to scratch Marigold's broad, bovine nose before climbing the rickety ladder to the loft.

"Chad?" she called. "Are you up here?"

No answer. Natalie was starting to get really worried. Shortly after they returned from town, Chad had placed a phone call, Natalie wasn't sure to whom, and afterward he'd raced from the house as if the devil were at his heels. She hadn't been able to find him since. Glancing at her watch, she determined that three hours had passed since he left the house. This late in the summer, the daylight started to fade around eight. It would be fully dark by nine.

As she descended the ladder, she heard Valerie calling her name. "In here!" she cried, hoping that her sister had news of Chad. "Did he come back?"

"No, not yet." Valerie appeared in the doorway of the dilapidated building. "No sign of him in the fields?"

"No." A tight, suffocating sensation grabbed Natalie by the throat. "I'm getting scared."

Valerie nodded. "Something upset him pretty bad. You don't suppose he called Robert?"

"It's possible, although I can't imagine Robert picking up. He hasn't answered any of my calls. I've dialed his number so many times this last week I've lost count."

Valerie put her hands on her hips and turned to gaze at the fields. "Maybe the shine's worn off his latest love interest and he decided to devote a few minutes to his son. You know

Robert. No staying power. I can see him screwing someone for a week, dropping her, and amusing himself for a few days by playing Daddy of the Year."

Bitterness laced Valerie's voice. She'd disliked Robert for years. One of Natalie's fondest memories was of Valerie backing Robert against a wall with a nail file and threatening to castrate him if he ever stepped out on her big sister again. Robert had taken the threat seriously and stopped screwing around for almost two months, a record for him.

"Do you think Chad might be over at Zeke's place?" Valerie asked.

Natalie had wondered the same thing herself. "I'm sure Zeke would call."

"He might think we know where Chad is."

"That's true, I suppose. Maybe I should give him a ring."

Valerie fell into step beside Natalie as she left the barn. "If Chad isn't at Zeke's, we need to contact the police, Nattic."

Natalie's heart caught. "The police?"

"Chad's been a powder keg waiting to blow for weeks. No telling what set him off. How do you know he hasn't run away?"

Fear made Natalie's blood run cold. "I can't believe that. I know he's confused and unhappy right now, but surely he isn't *that* unhappy. We had such a nice day in town. After we went shopping, I took them for lunch at Papa's Pizza. I even gave him two dollars to play video games. Why would he suddenly decide to run away when I haven't given him a reason?"

"Kids his age need a reason?" Valerie shook her head. "I ran away once because Pop made me wash my face. He was bound and determined that I wouldn't wear makeup until I turned sixteen."

Natalie recalled the incident, and her worry increased.

"On the off chance that Chad has run away, I think we should call the cops," Valerie insisted. "Don't you watch those Amber Alerts on TV? They say it's crucial to find a missing child within twenty-four hours. After that, the chances of a safe return decrease rapidly."

"You're such a comfort," Natalie groused. "Start making funeral arrangements, why don't you?"

"Well, jeez. Don't be so sensitive. I'm not saying he's dead, only that it's important to act swiftly."

A few minutes later, Natalie's hands were shaking as she dialed Zeke's number. He answered on the third ring. "Zeke, here."

"Zeke, this is Natalie."

His tone softened. "Hey."

She swallowed to steady her voice. "Is Chad over there?"

"No, I haven't seen him. He's not at home?"

"No. I'm afraid he's taken off."

"Taken off? How long has he been gone?"

"About three hours." Natalie pressed a fingertip to her throbbing temple. "At first I thought he was out in the fields somewhere. But I've checked all of them now, and the outbuildings as well. I can't find him anywhere. Oh, Zeke, I'm afraid he's run away."

Long silence. Then, "Why would he run away?"

Natalie closed her eyes. "I don't know. Valerie thinks he may have talked to Robert on the phone. I know he called someone, and right after hanging up, he ran from the house." She paused to grab for breath. "Do you think I should call the police?"

"Let's not jump the gun," he said calmly. "I'll take my truck and check the road into town first. If he's run away, he'll be afoot."

Natalie nodded, then realized he couldn't see her. "Good idea." She wondered why she hadn't thought of it. "I can drive the road. I'd rather not trouble you."

"It's no trouble, and it'll be better if I go. If he's trying to run away, he'll recognize your Chevy straight off. He's only been in my Dodge once. It may take him a second longer to recognize it."

That was true. "Thank you, Zeke."

"Don't worry," he said, his voice husky with what sounded like tenderness. "I'm sure he's fine, honey. There aren't many ways for a boy to get in trouble out here. This far out, there isn't even much danger of some weirdo stopping to pick him up."

Natalie nodded again. Then the line clicked and went dead. She slowly lowered the phone from her ear. After relating the conversation to Valerie, she stood at the kitchen window, staring out at the fields, hoping against hope that she'd see Chad walking home.

"I just checked on Rosie," Valerie said, returning from the living room a moment later. "Gramps is letting her watch cartoons, and she's totally engrossed."

"That's good. There's no point in her getting all upset."

"There's no point in any of us getting all upset," Valerie said brightly. "How's about a nice cup of tea?"

"No, thanks." Natalie braced her hand on the edge of the sink and leaned forward, craning her neck to see behind the house. "You go ahead."

"Hey. Cheer up. Zeke's so totally right. What can happen to a kid out here?"

Natalie just hugged her waist and continued to watch for her son.

Zeke was about to climb in his truck and go looking for Chad when a prickly sensation moved up his spine. He spun back around to sweep his gaze over the shop and what he could see of the backyard.

"Chad?"

The boy didn't answer, but Zeke couldn't shake the feeling that he was somewhere nearby. Just in case his instincts were correct, he went out back to check. At first glance, he saw nothing. Then he spotted Chad huddling in the shadows under the oak tree. The kid sat with his back to the trunk, knees drawn to his chest, forehead resting on his folded arms. Even at a distance, Zeke could see that he was sobbing as if his heart were broken.

He walked slowly across the grass. "Hey, buddy," he said softly. "I was about to go looking for you. Your mom just called. She's really worried."

As Zeke lowered himself to the grass, he saw Chad's shoulders jerking convulsively, but he heard no accompanying noise. He realized that the boy was embarrassed to be caught crying and was trying to stop by holding his breath. Zeke knew from experience that nothing he said would make Chad feel better, so he took a page out of his father's book and kept his trap shut.

It took Chad a few minutes to collect himself. When he was finally able to speak, his voice was ragged with pain. "I called my d-dad, and he t-told me to leave him alone."

An ache filled Zeke's chest and moved up from there into his throat. "Why'd he say a thing like that?"

Chad's mouth twisted and his chin quivered. "Because I bawled him out and p-pissed him off."

"Uh-oh. What did you bawl him out about?"

The boy wiped his nose on the sleeve of his T-shirt. "About m-my mom selling h-her earrings. They b-belonged to her g-grandma. Since the d-divorce, she's sold practically everything else, but n-never the earrings 'cause they're so sp-special. Now they're g-gone. She hocked them to buy us c-clothes for school." His voice went shrill, and his face twisted again. "We'll probably never have enough money to buy them back before s-someone else gets them."

Zeke resisted the urge to curl an arm around the boy's shoulders. Instead he just sat there for a while, letting Chad cry himself out. When the boy's sobs began to abate, he said, "Becoming a man is a real bitch. Isn't it?" He nudged Chad over a bit so they could share the tree trunk as a backrest. "One of the hardest things of all is watching our parents make sacrifices for us."

"I'll n-never have to watch my dad make any."

Zeke wasn't about to bite on that. He waited for Chad to say more.

"He d-doesn't c-care if Rosie's sandals are taped together. He doesn't care if I have to go to school in secondhand clothes. I could be dying, and h-he wouldn't care."

"Ah, now."

"It's true! Only my mom really loves me." Chad's face twisted again. "I've been so mean to her all summer. Sometimes I almost h-hated her. I didn't want to believe my dad didn't care about me, so I blamed everything on her." He swiped at his cheeks and sniffed. "Today when she h-hocked Grandma Westfield's earrings, she laughed and pretended it was no big d-deal. Then she spent all the money on me and

Rosie so we'd have nice clothes for school. Rosie d-didn't understand what she was doing, but I did."

Zeke sighed and straightened one leg to get more comfortable. "You're a lot older than Rosie, Chad. She's still just a baby."

"I know. I don't blame her or anything." Chad clenched his jaw. "I blame my dad for letting it h-happen."

Zeke refrained from commenting. Chad was making a very painful journey right now. He needed to complete it in his own way and at his own speed.

"I didn't think my dad knew how bad things were for us," Chad whispered. "Dumb of me. Huh?"

"Not dumb, exactly. It's a pretty reasonable conclusion to reach about your father."

The boy's breath snagged convulsively and stuttered out on a shaky sigh. "Yeah. He's, like, my *dad*. I thought if I told him how h-hard up we were for money he'd take care of it. I figured he'd say, 'S-sure, Chad. Tell your m-mom I'll send her a check.' Only he d-didn't. 'She made her b-bed,' he said, 'and now she can sleep in it.' " He fixed Zeke with a disbelieving, injured look. "He isn't going to give her a dime. If Rosie and I have to do without food, too bad. All he c-cares about is getting even with Mom for leaving him. He says he gave her everything money could buy, and it wasn't enough for her."

Money couldn't buy everything that a woman needed from a man, Zeke thought, but he still chose to say nothing. A long silence followed. Chad gulped and went on. "He was with a woman when I called. I think they were in bed together."

Zeke winced, wishing that particular reality hadn't been

shoved in Chad's face. "Ah," he said softly. "Your father is divorced now. I guess maybe so."

"No maybe to it. He was so busy fooling around with her that he didn't pay attention to half of what I said." Chad's voice cracked. "That was the worst part: knowing, after all this time, that he didn't even care if he talked to me."

Zeke closed his eyes, thinking of his own father, who'd always, *always* loved him without fail.

"It made me hurt inside." Chad pressed a fist to his breastbone. "Like nothing else has ever, ever hurt."

"I'm sorry, partner. That's rough."

Chad made a mewling sound. "I never really understood how bad my mom used to feel when he was with some girlfriend when she talked to him on the phone. I should've been there for her all those times, and I wasn't."

Zeke sighed. "Don't beat up on yourself for that."

Chad sent him a wondering look. "She was hurting. I could've hugged her or something to make it better, and all I did was flip her crap."

"What you're feeling for your mother right now is called compassion," Zeke explained, "and the ability to feel it isn't something most of us are born with. We have to suffer a little ourselves to understand the pain someone else is feeling." Zeke paused to let that sink in. "When I was younger and bad things happened, my dad used to tell me that someday I'd be a better man for the experience. I never understood what he meant until I got to be about your age. The long and short of it is, getting kicked in the teeth every once in a while teaches us never to kick another guy when he's down."

Chad rubbed his cheeks and sniffed. There was a lifetime of wisdom and regret in his tear-filled eyes. "When I heard that lady whispering to my dad and giggling like he was tickling her, I knew the same thing had probably happened to my mom a hundred times." Chad's breath hitched. "I heard the woman tell Dad to get rid of me. Pretty soon, that's exactly what he did." At the admission, Chad went absolutely still and squeezed his eyes closed. "That's when he told me to leave him alone. Then he just hung up."

Zeke didn't know what to say.

"My dad's a terrible person, isn't he?" Chad whispered.

It wasn't really a question, and again, Zeke wasn't sure what to say. "That may be a little harsh. Sometimes, perfectly nice people get off on the wrong track. Only time will tell if your father has what it takes to come out on the other side."

"I hate his guts."

"That'll pass." Zeke dragged in a deep breath, praying for the right words. Never in his life had it been this important to say the right thing. His track record for eloquence was so sorry it scared him. "He's your dad, faults and all. That's what you have to remember. Another hard part about growing up is learning to love our parents anyway. You know what I'm saying?"

"The way my mom loves me?"

Zeke's heart nearly broke at the expression on Chad's face. "Yeah, exactly like that. If you've been mean to her all summer, nobody would know it by watching her. She busted her little fanny over here yesterday, helping to work off your debt so you can go to camp. That's a perfect example of loving someone anyway."

"I think she tried to call my dad all last week and lied to me about it."

"Why do you think that?"

"Because she didn't want me to know he didn't care enough about me to pick up the stupid phone."

"He answered when you called this afternoon."

"Yeah, but, like, *why?* He was probably expecting a business call and doesn't have caller ID in the bedroom."

Zeke was no more inclined to argue the point than he was to criticize the boy's father. "That's possible, I guess."

Chad sighed. Then he puffed out his cheeks, and fresh tears filled his eyes. "I've never, *ever* been good enough for him. Not at school, not at sports, not at anything. All I've ever wanted is for him to love me, but he doesn't."

Zeke grasped the boy's shoulder to give him a light shake. "You get that thought straight out of your head." As reluctant as he was to criticize Chad's father, he couldn't let that slide by. "You're a fine young man. If anyone has a failing, it's your dad, not you."

"Why doesn't he love me, then?"

"Maybe he does, and he just can't or doesn't know how to show it. Showing affection—being loyal—coming through for people when they need us—all those things are learned behaviors, kind of like feeling compassion. You're lucky. You've got a mother who's teaching you all those things. Maybe your father didn't have someone like her when he was growing up."

Chad frowned thoughtfully. "Maybe not. My Grandpa Patterson never paid very much attention to me, and Grandma Grace is, like, totally uptight. If you forget to put your napkin on your lap, she goes off, acting like it's a crime or something. My grandma Naomi—she's my mom's mom—is a lot more fun. She makes cookies, and we play games. If Rosie hugs her with sticky hands, she just laughs. Grandma Grace gets mad."

"There, you see, your mom was raised by warm and loving people. That shows in the way she treats you. Could be it was different for your dad."

"I guess."

"I only know that none of this business with your father is your fault," Zeke went on. "So don't take it onto your shoulders and blame yourself. If you need to take measure of your worth as a son, Chad, look at your mom. Seems to me she thinks you're pretty special."

Chad stared unseeingly at the back of the house. "I couldn't face her after I talked to my dad," he whispered.

"Ah. So that's why you've taken up squatting rights under my tree."

Chad flashed a wobbly grin that vanished as quickly as it came. "What'll I say to her? That I'm sorry for being such a jerk? I've been pissed at her ever since we moved. I've even flipped her crap about the club going under when I knew, deep down, that my dad made it happen by taking half of her operating money."

"I think your mother understands how you're feeling better than you realize."

"I still don't know what to say to her when I go home."

"Don't say anything, then. Just give her a great big hug. She'll get the message."

"I wish I could buy her earrings back. They were supposed to go to Rosie someday. Now some stranger will get them."

Zeke smiled. "Now, there's a problem I may be able to help you with."

"How?"

"By floating you a loan."

"You'd do that?"

"That depends. Are you good for the debt?"

Chad looked uncertain. "She sold them for a lot."

"How much?"

"Three fifty."

Zeke hooked a thumb over his shoulder. "I've got forty acres of unfenced land. It's going to be one hell of a job, digging all those postholes. We'll never get it done in the time you owe me, and I've been toying with the idea of hiring someone. If you're willing to take the job and promise to stick with it until you get me paid back, I'll loan you the money to redeem the earrings."

Chad's eyes brightened. "You will?"

Zeke stretched out a hand. "Put it right there, partner."

The boy flashed another wobbly grin and placed his hand in Zeke's. "You're really gonna buy my mom's earrings back?"

"You're good for the money, aren't you?"

"Yes."

"Well, then, consider it done. Just bear in mind that it may cost you a lot of weekends."

"I don't care. I like working for you."

Zeke ruffled the boy's hair. "I like working with you, too."

Natalie nearly jumped out of her skin when the phone rang. As she raced across the kitchen to answer it, she collided so hard with Valerie that the pair of them almost lost their footing. Valerie swore and fell back, allowing Natalie to reach the phone first.

"Hello?" she said breathlessly.

"Hi, honey. It's Zeke."

"Did you find him?" she cried.

"I did. And he didn't run away. He was sitting under my oak tree."

Natalie sank onto a chair, so relieved that her legs went weak. "He's okay?"

"He's a little upset, but he's okay. He'll be home any minute. You need to listen to me. All right?"

"I'm listening."

"Chad had a nasty conversation with his father. He was pretty upset and needed some alone time to sort his way through it. Don't be mad at him for frightening you. Okay?"

She wanted to wring Chad's neck for scaring her half to death. "All right."

"Promise? I think you're going to like where he's at right now."

Natalie's hand tightened on the phone. "Where's that?"

There was a smile in Zeke's voice when he replied, "In his mama's corner."

Natalie no sooner broke the connection than the back door opened and Chad walked in. Her heart caught when she saw his face. His eyes were red and puffy from crying.

"Mom?" he squeaked.

She gained her feet and opened her arms. For the first time in six months, her son ran to her for a hug. Natalie caught him close. Her chest grew so tight that she couldn't speak. She just rocked to and fro, wishing with all her heart that she'd made wiser choices in her youth and spared Chad this heartache. But then he might not be her Chad, she thought. Robert had helped create this boy. When Natalie thought in those terms, she knew that, mistakes or not, she wouldn't go back in time and change anything.

"I love you," she managed to say.

Chad's arms tightened convulsively around her. "I love

you, too, Mom. I love you, too." He shoved his face so hard against Natalie's shoulder that it hurt. "Thank you for the clothes."

The clothes? Bewildered, Natalie smoothed his hair and patted his back. "You're welcome, sweetie. I was glad to get them for you. That's my job. I'm your mother. Remember?"

He nodded. Then he straightened away, wiping his cheeks and straightening his face. When he met Natalie's gaze, she got the strangest feeling. The eyes looking back at her weren't those of a little boy anymore.

"I'm buying back your earrings," he said.

"What?"

Chad nodded. "You heard me. I'm buying them back for you."

Natalie thought of the cost and knew he'd never be able to get his hands on that much money. Instead of saying that, she cried, "Oh, Chad, that isn't necessary. Grandma would understand."

"No," he said firmly. "They're a family heirloom and very important. Someday they should go to Rosie. I'm buying them back."

Natalie nodded, not wanting to ask how he planned to accomplish that. "Okay. Getting them back will make me very happy."

Chad twisted his neck to wipe his nose on his shirt. "Consider it done."

That said, he glanced at his aunt and exited the kitchen. Valerie shrugged and raised her eyebrows. "Who the hell was that?"

Natalie wasn't sure she knew. She glanced at the phone. After a long moment, she smiled tremulously and made her way to a chair on unsteady feet.

"Chad can't buy those earrings back," Valerie cried softly. "Why'd you act like he could?"

Natalie buried her face in her hands. *Zeke*. She took a trembling breath. "Because he can."

Valerie came to sit at the table. "Coulter?"

Natalie lifted her head and nodded, so choked up she could barely speak. "Yes. It's the only explanation. Chad wasn't blowing smoke. He honestly believes he's going to put those earrings in my hands."

Valerie nodded and gazed off for a moment. Then she grinned. Her eyes danced with mischief when she looked at Natalie again. "Okay, time to level with each other. Am I going to be stepping on your toes if I screw that cowboy's brains out?"

Natalie was too wrapped up in her son to immediately assimilate the question. When it registered, she almost scolded her little sister for being crass. But, then, for the second time in as many minutes, she really looked into someone's eyes and realized she was no longer dealing with a child.

She sat back in her chair, met Valerie's gaze straight on, and said, "Mess with him, girlfriend, and you're dead."

Chapter Eight

True to his word, Zeke postponed work at his place the next morning to drive Chad to the pawnshop in Crystal Falls. Zeke had never done business in such a place and mistakenly thought that they could buy back Natalie's earrings, no problem.

"I'm sorry," the elderly proprietress said. "I'm obligated to hold the earrings for thirty days. I'll take your name and number. If Mrs. Patterson hasn't redeemed them by then, I can let you know."

"You don't understand." Zeke curled a hand over Chad's shoulder. "This is Mrs. Patterson's son. He'd like to buy his mother's earrings back."

The woman smiled sadly at Chad. "I'm sorry, sweetie. Without your mother's permission, I can't let you do that." She opened the drawer of a file cabinet, searched for a moment, and withdrew a one-page contract. "If you'll read the fine print, you'll see that I'm obligated to hold the earrings."

Chad glanced at the paper. "My mom won't care if I buy them back. We'll be taking them straight home to her."

"It's not as if we're strangers in off the street," Zeke inserted.

The woman sighed. "If only you had the receipt," she said. "I'd feel better about bending the rules if I knew for certain that you are who you say you are."

"You think we're lying?" Chad asked incredulously.

"Not really, no." The woman smiled. "I'm sure you're not, dear. And I think it's lovely of you to buy the jewelry back for your mom. I could tell yesterday that it broke her heart to part with those diamond studs."

Chad's expression brightened. "I have an idea. Why don't you call the number she left for you? Ask to talk to Valerie. She's my aunt. She'll tell you I'm me."

The lady laughed and shook her head. Then she focused on Chad, her expression softened, and she reached hesitantly for the phone.

Minutes later, Chad had his mother's earrings in his pocket. As they left the shop, Zeke said, "Whatever you do, don't lose those puppies."

Chad grinned from ear to ear. "I won't." After they were in the truck, the boy turned on the seat to say, "When we get home, I'd kind of like to talk to my mom about some stuff when I give her the earrings. Do you care if I wait an hour before I come to work?"

Zeke had a feeling the conversation that Chad had in mind might take much longer than an hour. He also believed it was a mother-and-son talk that was long overdue. "Take as long as you need."

Zeke had just finished installing the new glass in the slider when someone's shadow fell over him. Crouched to adjust the runner guide, he sat back on his heel and turned to find Natalie standing behind him. Her eyes were puffy and the tip of her nose was bright pink. Through her jet curls, he could see the diamond earrings twinkling.

"Hi, there," he said.

"Hi." She sounded as if a clothespin had been clamped over her nose. "I, um, came over ahead of the kids to thank you, Zeke."

The shimmer in her eyes made him uneasy. She was looking at him as if he'd just hung the moon. "Thank me for what?"

She smiled and touched an earring. "You know very well for what. Chad couldn't have gotten these back without your help."

As Zeke pushed erect, his knee joint popped, a harsh reminder that he was far too old to let hormones do his thinking for him. "Don't thank me. Chad's the one who went into debt to redeem them, and he'll have to work a lot of hours to pay me back."

"Still." She shrugged and caught her full lower lip between her teeth. Zeke had a bad feeling she was about to cry. "You lent him the money. That was very generous of you."

"Not a problem. He's a good kid. I trust him to make good on the debt."

She nodded. "He is a good kid." She went to chewing on her lip again, and there was no mistaking it this time; her eyes were filling with tears. "Thank you so much for whatever it was that you said to him last night."

"I didn't say much of anything."

She rolled her eyes and dimpled her cheek. "It's so wonderful to have my son back again. Talking with you helped him deal with his feelings about his dad. He's disappointed in Robert, but he doesn't seem to be destroyed over it."

Zeke held up a staying hand. "Don't give credit where it's

not due, Natalie. You raised Chad, not me." To his intense dismay, he felt a lump forming at the base of his throat. "You're the one who gave him a blueprint to follow."

Her eyes widened. "Me? But I—"

Zeke cut her off. "I don't deserve credit for anything."

A single tear slipped over her thick lower lashes onto her cheek.

Then, taking him completely off guard, she stepped forward, went up on her tiptoes, and fiercely hugged his neck, pressing full-length against him in the process. "Thank you anyway, Zeke. Thank you so much."

Zeke instinctively slipped an arm around her. "You're welcome," he said gruffly. "I really didn't do much, though."

"Enough. Exactly enough," she whispered shakily.

She kissed his cheek, her intent obviously to strike and retreat. Zeke intended to let her go. Only somehow he turned his head at the last instant and captured her mouth with his. She jerked and gave a startled little gasp. But then her lips parted in tremulous surrender. He angled his head to take control, the warning bells going off in some distant part of his mind too faint to make him release her. *Natalie.* She grabbed for breath, the inhalation momentarily robbing him of oxygen. But then she exhaled in a sweet, ragged rush that teased his lungs just as her softness teased his body.

As if her bones suddenly melted, she sank in to him and knotted her slender hands on his shirt. Her mouth was hot from crying, the flavor of her so sweet and intoxicating that he ached. He cupped his free hand over the back of her head to deepen the kiss. She moaned, the sound a muted cry of pleasure in the hollow of her throat that further inflamed him.

He wanted her as he'd never wanted anything, needed her as he had never needed anyone. It wasn't a decision. It wasn't even really a thought. He knew only that he had to have her, the feeling riding high on a crushing wave of urgency that washed his vision with red.

She moaned again, stepping up onto his boots to kiss him back with such abandon that he lost it. *Sweet. Oh, God.* He couldn't believe this. All his life, he'd prided himself on being cautious and never losing control. Now, suddenly, he had no control at all, and being cautious was the farthest thing from his mind. He feasted on her mouth. He slipped a hand under her shirt to touch her skin, which was warm, satiny, and purely feminine. He growled low in his throat, hooked an arm under her bottom, and turned to press her against the house.

Her breathing shallow and rapid, her teeth nipping hungrily at his lips, she ran her hands over him, touching his shoulders, learning the shape of his arms, every press of her fingertips conveying a frantic need that equaled his own. Holding her aloft with the press of his hips, he cupped her breasts in his hands, hating the fact that two layers of clothing covered them, but so aroused he couldn't think how to remedy the problem. She whimpered when he thumbed her nipples, her pelvis pushing hard against his with every pass.

"What're you doing, Mommy?"

Zeke jumped as if he'd just been poked with a cattle prod. He and Natalie sprang apart like guilty teenagers.

"Rosie!" she said breathlessly. "You startled me."

The child squinched her face. "Were you guys kissing?"

Natalie pushed at her hair and straightened her shirt. "We, um—" She laughed nervously. "Heavens, no."

No? Zeke wondered how she meant to explain her way out of that one.

Rosie looked suspiciously at Zeke. "What were you doing, then?"

"Mr. Coulter was helping me with my earring," Natalie said quickly. "The back came loose, and I couldn't get it back on without a mirror."

"Oh." Rosie still seemed unconvinced. "It sure looked like you were kissing to me."

Zeke turned away, pretending intense interest in the sliding-glass door while he pushed at his fly to reposition a certain part of his anatomy. *Damn.* He was out of his mind. That was the only explanation.

For the rest of the day, Zeke wanted to kick himself. Of all the ill-advised things he'd ever done, waylaying Natalie when she kissed his cheek had been one of the dumbest. Now he couldn't look at her without remembering how fabulous it had felt to have her lush body pressed against him. And every time she looked at him, her cheeks turned a pretty pink, a surefire sign that she was thinking about it, too, which only nudged his blood pressure up and made him entertain notions that he shouldn't.

What bothered Zeke most was that nothing had changed since last night when he'd reached the decision that it would be best to stop this madness before it began. He still wasn't sure beyond any doubt that his feelings for her were the lasting kind or that he'd continue to enjoy being around her kids. And, despite what had happened between them that morning, he still didn't know if they were sexually compatible, either. A fabulous start was no guarantee of a satisfying ending.

That left him precisely where he'd been before, convinced that he should cool it. No more passionate kisses, that was for damned sure. If Rosie hadn't interrupted them, Zeke wasn't certain that he would have had the presence of mind or the self-control to stop.

Natalie wasn't the sort of lady to give herself to a man without her heart being part of the package. Did he want to put himself in a position where he felt obligated to remain in a relationship that wasn't right for him?

Zeke's answer to that wasn't just no; it was hell no.

Cooling it. Zeke discovered it was easier said than done. Each morning, Natalie showed up at his place to work, looking good enough to eat in snug, faded jeans and her father's ratty old shirts, her wonderfully curly hair flying in all directions. He watched her sway her hips to music that only she could hear until he felt sure he'd go mad. At night, he had to take cold showers in order to fall asleep. Then he got up the next morning to go through the same torture all over again.

In short, despite his decision to resist his sexy neighbor, Zeke found himself getting sucked in deeper with each passing day, unable to deny his attraction to her. She was everything he'd ever yearned to find without consciously realizing he wanted to look. *Natalie.*

He longed to hear her sing again and fought a nightly battle to keep himself from stopping by the Blue Parrot after he finished doing paperwork at his store. Sometimes, at unexpected moments, he could have sworn he caught the scent of her when she was nowhere around. He'd even started to dream of her—passionate, white-hot dreams that jerked him awake and sent him running for the shower again.

In the not-so-distant past, Zeke had ribbed his brother Hank about falling hard and fast for his wife, Carly. Now he was muttering the same words to himself. *You're a goner, Romeo.*

In the end, Zeke went to the one person whose advice he trusted above all others. Harv Coulter was picking tomatoes in the kitchen garden when Zeke showed up. Not realizing the importance of his son's visit, Harv asked Zeke to bring him a basket.

"I've never seen so many damned tomatoes," Harv complained when Zeke returned from the garage. "I'll be helping your mother can these sons of bitches for a week."

Zeke had a surefire cure for a bumper crop of tomatoes—a snot-nosed kid with a rotten father—but he refrained from saying so.

"Dad, I have a question I need to ask you."

"Fire off."

"When you married Mom, did you—" Zeke broke off and tugged on his ear. "What I mean to say is—did you have an opportunity to try her on for size before you jumped in with both feet?"

Busy moving tomatoes from the bowl of his shirt to the basket, Harv turned sharp blue eyes on Zeke. "You insultin' your mother, son?"

"No, of course not, Dad."

"You thinkin' she was the kind of woman to let a man sample the milk without buyin' the cow?"

"No, sir."

"Then don't ask such a damned fool question."

Now that Zeke thought about it, he realized it actually was a damned fool question. His mother was as close to being an angel as any woman with six kids could possibly get.

Harv sighed and shook his head. "Your mother was a churchgoer and had herself a fine set of values she wasn't about to compromise for me. To be with her, I had to put a ring on her finger and promise her forever."

"Didn't you have doubts?" Zeke asked incredulously.

"Doubts about what?"

Zeke gritted his teeth and started helping pick tomatoes.

"Don't bruise 'em," Harv cautioned. Then he said, "You always have been my serious one. Ever since you were a little tyke, you've walked a circle around a decision until you damned near wore a rut before makin' up your mind."

Zeke grinned in spite of himself. As unflattering as it was, the description fit him perfectly. "Ouch."

"Well, it's true. You always want to hedge your bets."

"Is that so wrong?"

"Not wrong, exactly. It's just that some of the best things in life don't come with guarantees. You gonna pass on all those things because you're afraid to take a chance?"

Zeke put another tomato into the basket. "When you fell in love with Mom, how did you know it would last?"

"Didn't. I only knew I couldn't walk away. Love's not a decision, son. It hits a man betwixt the eyes, and there's no decidin' to it. Right or wrong, doubts or no doubts, he's standin' knee deep in cement that's about to set." He slanted Zeke a questioning look. "If you can walk away from this woman, grab your hat and make tracks. She isn't the one."

"And if walking away is damned near impossible?"

Harv grinned and winked. "Then get your head out of your ass and do something about it before some other fellow snaps her up."

* * *

That night, Zeke didn't resist his urge to stop by the Blue Parrot after he finished doing the books at the store. He'd even prepared by wearing a white Western shirt and bringing along a sports jacket. When he entered the supper club shortly after nine, Natalie was onstage, just as she'd been the last time he visited. Tonight she wore a shimmering, midnight-blue dress with a slit in the figure-hugging skirt that shot clear to midthigh.

Just as before, she was pure dynamite under the stage lights. She smiled when she saw him, her gaze holding his from clear across the room. She was singing "Up!," a Shania Twain hit. He sank onto a chair, completely captivated and barely aware of the people around him. When a waitress came by the table, he ordered a Jack and Coke. Then he sat back to enjoy himself, indulging in X-rated thoughts about silk sheets and making love to Natalie Patterson until she went limp.

When the song ended, she spoke briefly to her piano player, then returned to center stage. Her next number, "Forever and for Always," was another Twain hit, the words expressing a deep yearning to remain in her lover's arms forever and to never let him go. As she sang, she never took her gaze from Zeke, giving him the feeling that she meant the words only for him.

Minutes later, after informing her small audience that it was time for her break, she wove her way through the tables toward him, the sway of her hips the culmination of every man's wet dream. Ebony curls that fell to her shoulders, eyes that issued a sultry invitation, a smile that made his heart pound against his rib cage like a fist. He loved the way her mouth tipped up at the corners and how her face glowed with gladness at seeing him.

He stood up to pull out a chair for her.

"Hey," she said, her voice throaty yet soft, reminding him of a kitten's purr. "What brings you here?"

"You."

The light and flowery scent she wore surrounded him as she sat down. She glanced back over her bare, elegantly molded shoulder to search his face. "Me?"

She was so beautiful that his tongue stuck to his teeth. He could barely breathe as he sat down across from her. "I wanted to see you," he said, and then immediately felt like an imbecile. "And hear you sing again," he quickly tacked on. "You're an incredible talent, Natalie. I meant it when I said you should be in Nashville."

Her eyes reflected the candlelight that flickered between them. "If wishes were horses, poor men would ride."

It was as close as he'd ever heard her come to admitting that her life wasn't all that she'd like. "What happened, honey? A lot of singers have families. What held you back?"

She smiled wistfully. "One wrong turn." A distant look came into her eyes. "That's all it takes sometimes, one wrong turn." She turned her hands to study her palms. "I feel guilty for even saying that. I've got such wonderful kids, and I love them with all my heart."

Zeke huffed and leaned forward. "Would you stop being a mother for two seconds and just talk to me straight? Of *course* you love your kids. It goes without saying that you don't wish them gone. I just want to know what happened."

"Right after my high-school graduation, I competed at the fair in a singing competition. Robert was in the audience. I guess he thought an eighteen-year-old cowgirl with rhythm would be a nice change of pace." She gestured limply with her hand. "He was charming. I was naive. What else is there to say? I got pregnant. Pop oiled his shotgun and aimed it at Robert's groin. Unfortunately for me, Robert is very fond of his testicles. The next thing I knew, I was married to a man who thought performing onstage was low class and inappropriate for a woman of my social standing."

"Tell it to Wynonna."

"The Pattersons aren't into Wynonna." She smiled faintly. "They're very upper crust, obsessed with appearances and their position in society."

"In Crystal Falls? I didn't know we had a society."

She laughed, and then she grew serious again. "Big fish in a little pond. Robert married beneath himself." She rubbed her dainty nose and flashed a grin that didn't warm her eyes. "Raggedy Ann had to walk the straight and narrow to be worthy of the Patterson name. It took me a few years to toughen up and blow them off."

"And then you bought the club?"

She nodded and glanced around. "I only lease the building. All I needed was start-up capital and enough money to do renovations." She sent him a mischievous look. "I raised calves and pigs on the farm and sold them for a profit, a totally crass endeavor that made my parents-in-law hyperventilate. It took me five years to save enough money."

"Robert wouldn't give it to you?" Zeke winced. "Forget I asked. Upper crust. I can just imagine."

"He threatened to divorce me when I told him I was opening the club."

"What did you say?"

Her eyes fairly danced with devilment. "That I'd really miss him."

Zeke snorted and almost choked on his drink. "Good for you."

"It was enough for me," she went on. "I could finally sing to an audience, what I believe I was born to do. Either that, or write songs." She reached across the table and took a sip of his drink. "I've got music in my head. It never goes away. Tunes and little blips that can be songs if I put them together and smooth them out."

Zeke's heart hurt for her. This was no whimsical desire. She'd called it right. It was what she'd been born to do. "That song you sang the last time I was here. It was beautiful."

" 'Shattered Dreams'?"

Zeke nodded. Until now, he hadn't remembered the title. "You have a God-given gift. To waste it is a crime." He turned his glass, watching the way the ice glistened and bobbed in the Coke. "With music and words and voice, you have the power to reach people in a way most of us never can, Natalie. It's more than just a need within you. It's a responsibility."

Her eyes went suspiciously bright, and she blinked. "Where were you twelve years ago? I'm thirty. It's too late for me now."

"Bullshit. You're not too old." Zeke shoved a hand through his hair. "*Damn* it. I look at you, and all I see is beautiful. You can still do it, honey. All you need is to believe in yourself."

"I've always believed in myself." She shot him a look that dared him to condemn her for that. "Where it involves music, at any rate, I know I've got something special. I knew it at five, and it was a volcano inside me all during my growing-up years. Pop supported me. My mother always did, too. But I didn't choose a husband who would stand behind me."

In that moment, Zeke leaped into that knee-deep cement with both feet. Looking at her sweet face, seeing the yearning in her beautiful eyes, he couldn't have walked away to save his life. She was it for him. He felt it in his bones.

It was frightening as hell. But when that primal shiver of warning ran up his spine, he ignored it this time. When he grew old, he didn't want to look back on tonight and kick himself for making the worst mistake of all, running in the wrong direction.

"I'm falling in love with you," he said huskily. "I think you should know that."

Her face drained of color. "What?"

"You heard me. I'm falling in love with you. It's not what I set out to do. It just happened. I'm scared shitless. I won't lie to you about it. But I'm not walking away from this."

She laughed shrilly, the sound a little hysterical. "But you're a confirmed bachelor. A sardine in a can who likes empty bathrooms. Remember?"

"Not anymore, I'm not." Zeke gulped down the remainder of his drink and slapped the empty glass on the table. "And just so we understand each other, I'm not looking for a short-term deal. If you return my feelings, don't make the decision lightly, because I won't make life easy for you. I don't believe in giving up on dreams. God gives people talent like yours for a reason." He pushed to his feet. "If I have to push and prod you every step of the way, I won't allow you to waste yours."

If Zeke Coulter had been a rodeo cowboy, Natalie would have laughed at his avowal of love and gone home smiling at the absurdity of it all. But he was as steady as a rock, a man who seemed to stand by his word and who never spoke lightly.

He wasn't the only one who was scared. Natalie was shaking with nerves as she set the alarm and left the club. She couldn't be like Valerie, taking her pleasure where she found it, then waltzing away to paint her toenails. And anything more serious than that was terrifying to her. She'd tried the forever stuff, and it hadn't worked out. She couldn't go through that kind of heartbreak again.

Once in her rattletrap Chevy, Natalie sat there with the doors locked, feeling claustrophobic and staring at nothing as she came to grips with an undeniable truth. Just the thought of having sex with Zeke Coulter scared her half to death.

Her hands trembled as she inserted the key into the ignition. Life was okay right now. She loved her family. At night she could throw on an oversized T-shirt, forget to brush her teeth, and make love to her pillow as she fell asleep. There were worse things.

"You look like hell," Valerie said when Natalie walked in the back door a half hour later.

"Thanks. I feel even worse."

Valerie sank down on a kitchen chair and drew up her feet to sit cross-legged. Her nightshirt revealed enviously firm legs from calf to thigh, which made Natalie grind her teeth. She tossed her purse onto the table and went to the sink for a drink of water.

Life wasn't fair. Valerie ate pizza and pigged out on buttered popcorn at the movies. Did she put on weight? Heck no. Natalie could gain five pounds if she even smelled the stuff.

"Well," Valerie said peevishly, "you're in a great mood."

"I'm doing menopause twenty years early and packing a gun. Leave me alone." Natalie downed the water, set the glass on the counter, and turned to face her sister. "You are such a child. Get a wrinkle, and maybe, just maybe, I'll be able to talk to you."

"Well, shit." Valerie jerked her nightshirt up and plucked a pack of Marlboros out of her panties. "*That's* got a man written all over it."

Natalie had never seen her sister smoke. She wondered where Valerie kept the lighter. Her sister answered that question by fishing deeper into her panties and pulling out a red Bic. She tapped a cigarette from the pack, lit up, and blissfully blew out a trail of smoke.

"That's a terrible habit."

"My substitute for sex," Valerie said with an impish grin. "You should try it. God knows you need something to relax you."

"Don't do it around my kids."

Valerie bugged her eyes. "Have I so far? Get off my back. I'm depressed. All right? I'm sending out job apps and résumés every day and getting no responses."

"Why don't you try something besides secretarial positions?"

"Why don't you try something besides singing?"

Natalie was too tired to spar with her sister. She waved her hand and said, "Good night. Go ahead and turn your lungs black. I honestly don't give a rat's ass."

"What crawled up your butt?"

Natalie started from the kitchen. At the archway, she

turned back. "Do you realize that you may have saggy boobs and tapioca thighs in five short years? If you have a kid or two in the meantime, it's guaranteed."

Valerie lowered the cigarette from her mouth without taking another drag. "What?"

"Right now, you think you'll be young and beautiful forever," Natalie informed her. "But that isn't how it works. Every woman gets ten, maybe fifteen years of young and beautiful. That's her allotment, period. One day, she's eighteen and the world's her oyster. The next, she's thirty, and young and beautiful are only a memory." Natalie sighed raggedly. "You don't realize what's happening at first. You kid yourself when you look in the mirror, only studying your best side. You stuff yourself into old jeans that are way too tight and think you still look pretty good. Then, one sad day when you're cleaning your car, you look into the rearview mirror when the sun's beating down on your face, and you see itty-bitty lines around your eyes and on your cheeks and at the corners of your mouth. It's a shock. You're not young anymore. You think there must be a fix, so you rush out to buy moisturizer and wrinkle-concealing foundation. But guess what? It doesn't help."

"Well, *shit.* Cheer me up, why don't ya?"

Tears burned in Natalie's eyes. "Zeke says he's falling in love with me."

Valerie choked on an inhalation of smoke. With tears streaming down her cheeks, she flicked ashes into her cupped palm. When she recovered, she got up to fish in the recycle bin under the sink for an empty food can to use as an ashtray.

When she resumed her seat, she said, "Zeke Coulter's falling in love with you, and that's bad news?"

Natalie braced a hand against the archway to pluck off her shoes. She groaned and wiggled her toes. "*God,* I hate high heels. A man must have invented them."

Valerie took another drag from the cigarette as Natalie made her way back to the table. "Let's castrate the whole bunch of them. Well, maybe we should spare a half dozen or so. A lady needs her fun, after all."

Natalie giggled as she collapsed onto a chair, too exhausted to feel devastated anymore. Letting her head fall back, she stared at the ceiling. A cobweb dangled from the ceiling fixture. "I'm comfortable the way things are right now. I can throw on a dingy old nightshirt and no one hassles me."

"Don't you miss sex?"

"Of course I miss it. I just don't miss all the troubles that came with it. Maybe I'll get a vibrator. An appliance can't make your life miserable. Right?"

"Not all guys are like Robert."

"Maybe not. I honestly don't care anymore." Natalie dropped her chin to look her sister in the eye. "You can have Zeke, after all. I can't do this."

Valerie held up a hand. "No way. Do I have 'dumb' printed on my forehead? I'm not touching him with a ten-foot pole."

"Me, neither." Natalie stretched out an arm. "Give me a cigarette."

"You don't smoke."

"Maybe I'll start."

"It'll damage your voice."

"One cigarette won't damage my voice. Besides, what am I saving it for? I'll never make it big. That's another thing you live with after thirty, that you missed your window of opportunity."

Valerie thought about it for a moment and then reached into her panties again for the Marlboros. As she tossed the pack onto the table, she said, "If we're gonna get wild and woolly, we should do it right. We got any booze around here?"

Natalie glanced around the kitchen. "I don't think so." Then she brightened. "*Gramps*. He keeps gallon jugs of cheap wine under his bed. When I was looking for his Preparation H, I found two full bottles under there."

"Oh, yeah." Valerie grinned. "I could snatch it while I was singing 'God Bless America.' He's deaf as a post."

"Bet you can't."

"Yes, I can."

"Dare ya."

Minutes later, Natalie was doing something unprecedented, getting drunk with her baby sister. Maybe it was only the wine, or maybe it was just a meeting of minds after twenty-five years, but Valerie suddenly seemed to make sense.

"You know what your problem is?" Valerie asked.

Natalie shook her head.

"You worry too much." Valerie lit another cigarette and spewed blue smoke. "A woman's looks are preliminary stuff. A guy scopes you out. If he likes what he sees when you're dressed, relax, babe. Once you unzip his fly, he goes stone blind."

Natalie choked on a swallow of burgundy and laughed until she felt weak. When she finally regained her voice, she said, "Are we even related?"

"I'm afraid so."

"You hate it, don't you? I'm so *boring.*"

"Not boring, exactly. You just always, *always* have your panties in a twist. Like this *thing* you've got about getting old. I think you look great."

"Not without clothes, I don't." Natalie took a huge gulp of wine. "My headlights have gotten stuck on dim."

Valerie snorted.

"It's not funny. You have no idea how it feels to look down and realize that your nipples are looking down with you. And I have this awful tapioca stuff high on thc inside of my thighs. I do squats until my knees turn to jelly every morning, but it doesn't help."

"Like any guy will notice? If he's still thinking at that point, you haven't done your homework, girlfriend."

Natalie sobered, her thoughts on Zeke. "He's so nauseatingly *perfect.* Have you looked at him?"

"Oh *yeah.*" Valerie waved a hand in front of her face. "Totally hot. I get turned on just looking at the dude."

Natalie nodded. "He could have anyone he wanted. Why me? My stomach pooches and I've got stretch marks on my hips. When I even *think* about taking my clothes off in front of him, I want to die."

Valerie jumped up, switched hands with her cigarettc, and jerked her shirt up to display a slender hip. "Stretch marks." She wriggled to pull her panties partway down. "See 'em? I got them from growing too fast. Jeez, Nattie, get a life. You really do worry too much."

"I have a life. I've got a wonderful family and two fabulous kids. Why muck things up with a man who'll break my heart again?"

"Because you're a Westfield, and the odds are good. He's gorgeous. I won't argue the point. But you're not bad yourself. So what if you're not twenty-five anymore? Lots and *lots* of guys like a woman with experience."

"That rules me out, then."

"What do you mean? You were married for almost eleven years."

"And every once in a while when Robert needed some downtime, he honored me with his attention. We didn't have sex very often, and when we did, he didn't put himself out. He saved the good stuff for girlfriends."

Valerie's eyes went sparkly with tears. "Ah, Nattie."

"I didn't have what it took to make him happy," Natalie said hoarsely. "It was only good between us for about a month. Then he started coming home late. I was about six months pregnant with Chad before I realized what was going on."

Valerie sank back down on her chair. "I could kill that creep for doing this to you."

"I did it to myself. I got pregnant and married him, didn't I?"

"You were just a kid, taken in by a thirty-one-year-old predator. How can you blame yourself for that?" Valerie rolled her eyes. "Two months earlier, and he would've done time for statutory rape."

Natalie closed her eyes and just sat there. "I loved him," she finally whispered. "I loved him so much. Right before Chad was born, I'd go looking for him late at night—just drive around town, looking for his car. Most times, I searched in vain. But a couple of times, he was at his office. It was late January and it got really cold at night. I sat out there in the dark, freezing and crying because I knew he was inside with another woman." Natalie swallowed and sighed. "There's no hurt quite like that, Valerie. It tears you apart inside and sucks the life out of you. I never want to feel that way about anyone again."

"I know. But look at it rationally. No woman on earth could have kept Robert at home. He's like a virus looking for a host, and any warm body will do."

"Maybe so. But knowing that doesn't help, somehow. It did something to me. I don't love him anymore. I almost hate him, in fact. But there's a dead place inside of me now. I don't want to love again. I'm not even sure I can."

"If that's true," Valerie said, "then you need to level with Zeke. And you should do it soon."

Chapter Nine

A light knock sounded on Zeke's kitchen door. He rolled over in bed, squinted at his watch, determined that it was after two in the morning, and grunted as he rolled out of bed. After finding his jeans, he hopped on one foot and then the other to shove his feet down the legs. Then he staggered through the dark house, wondering who the hell would come calling at this time of night.

When he swung the door open, he found Natalie standing on his doormat. Bathed in soft moonlight, she was, without question, the most beautiful thing he'd ever clapped eyes on. She still wore the midnight-blue dress with the slit that shot clear to her hip. For a fleeting instant, he wondered if he was dreaming. But then a rush of cool night air washed over his bare chest.

He blinked to clear the sleep from his eyes and stifled a yawn. "Hey."

"I, um—" She gulped and jerked her gaze from his nude upper torso to look him in the eye. "I hope I didn't wake you."

"Nah," he lied. When a midnight-blue vision stood on the

porch, no man in his right mind wanted to sleep. "I was just—about to drift off."

She flashed that fabulous dimple at him and shoved a gallon jug under his nose. "I brought refreshments. You got a few minutes?"

Zeke passed a hand over his face. "Sure. Come on in."

She placed a narrow, delicately boned foot on the metal threshold plate. He glanced out into the darkness. "Didn't you walk across the field to get here?"

"Of course."

"Without your shoes?"

"Those aren't shoes; they're torture devices." She moved into the kitchen, brushing against him and dizzying his senses with her perfume as she sidled by. "I'm a farm girl, remember? I went barefoot half my life."

That explained it, he guessed. Not that Zeke minded bare feet. Watching the sway of her hips, he decided that bare everything would be even nicer. He closed the door and turned to peer through the moonlit gloom, trying to make out her features. He finally woke up enough to reach behind him for the light switch, then winced at the sudden brightness.

"What brings you over"—he glanced at his watch again—"so late, honey? Is anything wrong?"

"Not wrong, exactly." She walked to the sink and started opening cupboards. "Glasses? Ah." She sent him a slightly unfocused look. "Found 'em." She drew out two juice glasses, uncapped the jug of burgundy, which was already partially gone, and poured them each a generous portion of wine. "I came to talk to you, Zeke." She turned to hand him a glass. "What you said at the club tonight, it really worries me. You don't strike me as the tapioca type."

"I don't?"

"No. And that poses an insurmountable problem."

Zeke wasn't following. "I like tapioca, actually."

"You won't like mine."

He nodded as though he understood. Only, of course, he didn't. He was starting to suspect that she was just a little bit drunk. "Are you particularly fond of tapioca or something?"

She made a face. "God no. But I'm stuck with it, so there you go." She took a big gulp of wine as if the alcohol content might fortify her. "I could have surgery, I guess, but what would be next?"

"Why do I get the feeling we're not talking about pudding?"

She sent him a bewildered look. "Pudding? Where'd that come from?"

"Tapioca. I thought—" Zeke scowled at her. "What, exactly, are we discussing?"

Her eyes went suspiciously bright. "My body."

And that posed a problem? Zeke sank slowly down onto a chair. *Dangerous territory.* On a radio talk show the other day, he'd heard the host and a psychologist discussing women's negative feelings about their bodies. In a society that touted young and rail thin as the feminine ideal, with unnecessary cosmetic surgery almost epidemic, many women felt inferior and oftentimes ugly if they weren't a perfect size three with balloons for breasts.

"What about your body?" he asked.

"It's a mess."

"A mess?" Zeke glanced downward. Never had sequins shimmered so enticingly. Natalie wasn't a thin woman, but she was firm, carried her weight well, and every generous curve looked just right to him. "In what way?"

"Do you want me to make you a list? I never had a perfect figure to begin with, and now I've had two kids. I diet and exercise, but it's a constant battle just to look halfway decent. I'm not a young girl anymore."

"It's a damned good thing. I'm no spring chicken myself."

"Men wear better than women do."

Zeke folded his arms. "I think you're beautiful."

She puffed air at her bangs. "You haven't seen me naked."

That could be rectified in damned short order. "That dress doesn't hide much."

She laughed humorlessly. "Oh yes it does. Do you think I just walked into a store and grabbed it off the rack? Not. I tried on dozens of gowns that showed every flaw and looked perfectly awful on me first. Every dress I own was handpicked to flatter my shape."

Zeke gave the dress another long look. He honestly couldn't imagine how anything could look perfectly awful on her. "What flaws does it hide?"

"The most troublesome thing right now is the tapioca stuff I'm getting on my inner thighs." A flush of embarrassment crept up her neck. She took another swallow of wine. Then she set her glass on the counter. "In short, I'm not beautiful from the neck down. Passable, maybe. Why do you think my ex-husband always had affairs?"

"Because he's a jerk?"

"That, too. But it was also because he wasn't happy with what he had at home." She sighed and smiled tremulously. "You are a totally fabulous guy, Zeke, and I'm wildly attracted to you."

That sounded promising.

"And I really, *really* wish—"

Looking distracted, she broke off, and Zeke realized she was staring at his chest again. He considered going to the bedroom for a shirt but discarded the idea almost as soon as it came to him. He needed all the advantages he could get.

"You were saying?" he prompted.

Her cheeks flushing with embarrassment, she jerked her gaze to a cupboard and pretended intense interest in the brass handle. "Just that I wish I was up for another go-around, but the very thought scares me to death."

That didn't sound positive. In fact, it had good-bye written all over it. "Natalie, I—"

She held up a hand. "These feelings I have—and the feelings you say you have—they can't go anywhere."

"Why the hell not?"

"Because." She flapped a limp hand. "Just hear me out. All right?"

"I'm listening."

She fiddled nervously with an earring. "I won't say I'm deliriously happy with my life or that I don't sometimes wish for more. But I am fairly content. I've got a great family and two wonderful kids. If I can get the club back on its feet, I'll have a business that I love." She shrugged. "Why muck it all up with another man? Especially someone like you."

"What's the matter with me?"

"*Nothing*. That's the whole point. Me being passable and you being gorgeous, that isn't a good mix." She shook her head. "All my instincts tell me not to go there." She dragged in a tremulous breath. "I loved Robert when I married him. I would have done anything to save my marriage. Only nothing was enough. You know?" She flattened a slender hand over her heart. "It did something to me, left me empty inside. I can't ever love a man that way again."

"Sweetheart, you're a beautiful lady. I don't know what Robert's problem was, but it sure as hell had nothing to do with you." Zeke pushed to his feet and walked slowly toward her. "If I had you waiting at home, I'd be the happiest man alive."

"Words," she whispered. "Only words. I appreciate your saying them. It's very flattering. But they can't fix what's wrong inside of me." She swallowed convulsively. "I felt that I owed you an explanation. It's not anything personal against you. I just can't go there again."

Zeke stopped a few steps short of her. "I'd like to introduce Robert Patterson's teeth to his asshole for doing this to you."

Her lovely eyes went wide with alarm.

"Just look at you. The most beautiful woman I've ever seen, and you're convinced I'll find fault with you? That's nuts."

Her mouth quivered and turned up at only one corner. "Yes, well, it's very sweet of you to—"

"Sweet, hell. I'm a straight-up guy, Natalie. I don't bullshit people just to make them feel good. You know what I thought the first time I heard you sing? I thought, 'Reba, move over.' You're pure dynamite onstage. I have never, and I do mean never, seen anyone who could make people stop breathing in anticipation. Then you just *exploded,* grabbing everybody by the throat. You blew me away, and I wasn't the only one who felt that way. Every man in the room had his tongue hanging out."

"I know I can sing, Zeke. But that doesn't—"

"You can sing, yes, but it takes a hell of a lot more than

that to create pure magic. It takes the whole package, a fabulous voice, a gorgeous body, a face so beautiful that it breaks men's hearts." He reached out to touch her cheekbone. "Your eyes, your smile, the way you move—everything about you is extraordinary. I couldn't believe such an incredible talent was standing up there on a stage in Podunk, Oregon, with a cheap guitar and a so-so piano player as her only accompaniment. You're a phenomenon, Natalie. You have a gift that is almost, and I stress *almost,* as beautiful as you are."

"Thank you," she whispered.

"Don't *thank* me," he cried, frustration making his tone harsh. "I'm not paying you a compliment. I'm telling you the facts. You should have the world by the tail, darlin'. And there's not a single reason on earth you can't still do it."

She chafed her arms as though with a chill. "Oh, well, I'm not so sure about that."

"I am. You know what your holdback is?"

"No, what?"

"You think too small. Instead of going out there and knocking 'em dead, you're content to own a supper club and sing to a handful of country hicks who wouldn't recognize true talent if it ran up and bit them on the ass. God *blessed* you with an extraordinary gift and you're pissing it away."

Her cheeks flamed with color. "I have two kids, in case you haven't noticed. They're more important than a silly pipe dream."

"A silly pipe dream? *Jesus*. And why does it have to be a choice between your talent and your kids? Take them to the top with you. Stop hiding behind mediocrity and detonate on a stage where it'll count."

A bruised look entered her eyes. "You have no idea what

it'd take for me to even try. I'd have to hit the road and do gigs in a thousand different towns to even have a *shot* at making it. I'd be gone for a month at a time. You can't drag kids from hell to breakfast when they're in school, and being a summertime performer doesn't cut the mustard. I'm a mother *first*, a singer second. I won't give my kids short shrift to chase a dream."

Zeke smiled. "If they had a decent father, couldn't you be gone for a month without shortchanging them?"

"They don't have a decent father."

"Fix the problem. I'm applying for the job."

She rolled her eyes. "I'm out of here. You've only known me for what—three weeks?"

"I'm a Coulter."

"What does that have to do with anything?"

"Everything. I'm my father's son. I'll give my heart to only one woman. It's taken me damned near thirty-four years to find you, but now that I have, it's a done deal."

"I need to go now. We've gotten off track. I came here to be up-front with you. You're not hearing me. I need to go."

"Oh, I'm hearing you. In fact, I was exactly where you're at all last week, frightened by my feelings, wanting them to go away."

She sent him a wondering look.

"Do you think I set out to fall in love with you?" he asked. "Think again, lady. The confirmed bachelor, remember? Falling in love with a woman with two kids was a damned scary proposition, and I tried my damnedest to ignore the feelings."

"You did?"

"Of course. I like silence. I like space. I *like* being single." Zeke paused and pinched the bridge of his nose. He'd never been good with words, and he had an awful feeling that he was saying all the wrong things. "At least I thought I liked it. Rosie never stops talking. And Chad has a load of problems. A part of me wants to run the other way."

She tossed her hair. "Do it, then. No one's stopping you."

"I can't." Zeke dropped his hand. "I just *can't*. This is it for me. You're it for me. I loved this house when I bought it. Now it feels huge and empty. When I look at the refrigerator, I hate the bareness. It needs Rosie's pictures to make it right. I've always loved to cook, and now I don't because there's no one to eat the meal with me. I wish I was over at your place, that you were singing to me with a long-handled fork while you scorch the chicken."

"I didn't *scorch* the chicken. It was just a little too brown on one side."

He laughed and took another step toward her. "I go to the store at night, and right when I'm totally absorbed in paperwork, you know what happens?"

She hugged her waist, a purely defensive posture that wasn't lost on him. "No, what?"

"I smell you. Your perfume, the scent of your hair and skin. It's like you're there in the room with me, only I can't see you." He saw tears coming to her eyes and knew he was getting through to her. "I wake up in a hot sweat from dreaming about you and have to take cold showers. I can't count the times I've driven past your club on my way home at night, wanting to go in, needing to go in so I could see you for just a second."

"Why didn't you?"

"Because I didn't want to feel this way, because it scared the living hell out of me. Falling in love and becoming an instant daddy weren't part of my game plan."

"Then it's lucky for you I'm here to end this before it starts."

"Ah, but I'm not feeling scared now." He took another step toward her. "I can't turn my back on this and walk away. I'm in love with you. No decision to it, no changing it. Done deal."

Her eyes filled with wariness. "Can you just sit at the table while we talk about this? I'd feel a lot safer that way."

"You're perfectly safe, and no, I can't stay at the table. I like to make eye contact when I'm discussing something this important."

"We *were* making eye contact."

Zeke had a feeling it wasn't eye contact that had her worried.

"I, um—" She tried to step around him. "I really should go."

Zeke shot out a hand and caught her wrist. "Oh no, you don't."

She flashed him a startled look.

He firmed his grip on her wrist and turned her to face him again. "Do you honestly think I'll let the best thing that's ever happened to me walk out of my life because Robert Patterson's a prick? No way."

"I can't do this again, Zeke. I just *can't.*"

"Yes, you can. Take a chance on me, honey. I swear to you, you'll never regret it."

Her eyes softened. Zeke knew then that she'd fallen in love with him, just as he had with her, and for the first time since she'd mentioned tapioca, he felt on solid ground.

"Stay with me. There's something special between us, Natalie. Have you ever felt like this before, even with Robert?"

"No," she confessed, but even as she whispered the word, fear shadowed her eyes. "Not with anyone. That's why it's so terrifying to me. The stakes will be higher this time. I survived my marriage. I've come out on the other side. I'm not sure I can do that again. And I don't want to find out. When I look at you, I don't think about how I'm feeling right now. I think about letting myself care and eventually having you walk away."

Still holding her wrist, he drew her slowly toward him. "Do you honestly believe I'd say any of these things to you if I thought there was any chance of that ever happening? I won't walk away, honey. Never."

He could see her wavering. That was his signal to dispense with talking, which had never been his strong point anyway. He slipped an arm around her waist, hauled her snugly against him, and kissed her with all the longing that he felt. For a moment, she went rigid, the heels of her hands pressing hard on his shoulders. But then she sobbed into his mouth, hooked her arms around his neck, went up onto her tiptoes, and returned his kiss. Zeke tightened his hold on her and deepened his thrust, boldly tasting the hidden recesses of her mouth and staking claim. She was just as sweet as he remembered.

When he allowed her to come up for air, she fixed unfocused eyes on his face. He could see her pulse hammering at the base of her throat. The air between them went electric.

"I'm so terrified, Zeke," she whispered raggedly.

"Don't be. I'll never break your heart, honey. I swear it." He trailed soothing kisses along her cheekbone, kissed her eyelids closed, and then claimed her mouth again, gently this time, coaxing her with everything he had and trying to convey with his touch how much he loved her. "Trust me," he whispered. "Please, Nattie? Just throw caution to the wind and take the biggest gamble of your life. I promise you'll never regret it."

Her lips went soft, opening for him. She shyly trailed the tip of her tongue over his bottom lip. Then all the resistance shuddered out of her. She kissed him harder, this time making fists in his hair and stepping up onto his feet to lessen the difference in their heights. Her mouth was warm, and sweet, and hungry. *Moist silk.* Zeke moved a hand from the small of her back to her hip. The contrast between the scratchy surface of her dress and the soft woman underneath set him on fire. He searched lower, found the slit in her skirt, and slipped his fingers through the opening to caress her thigh. Her breath snagged. Then she moaned, the sound a low growl of feminine urgency that further inflamed him.

"It's been so long," she whispered raggedly into his mouth, her breath heady with the wine and another taste that Zeke realized was exclusively her own. "Oh, *God,* it's been so *long,* Zeke."

Zeke wasn't prepared for what happened next. With a muted little cry, she locked her arms around his neck, hitched herself up, and encircled his waist with her legs, hooking her ankles to lock them in place. Startled and caught off balance, he staggered back a step. Natalie seemed oblivious. She captured his mouth with hers again, delving deeply with her quick little tongue, then nipping feverishly at his lips. Every clear thought in his head took a hiatus.

Holy shit.

"*Touch* me," she cried.

From some murky part of his brain, a single, disjointed thought resurfaced. *Not here*. The kitchen was no place to make love to a lady. But, oh, God, never in all his life had he been kissed like this—need and hunger converging their pulses into a single, throbbing beat. She freed one hand to smooth her palm over his shoulder, then dug in hard with her fingertips.

"Please," she whispered.

"The bedroom," he managed to rasp. "I want this to be perfect for you."

Her breathing rapid and shallow, she pressed her forehead to his. "Perfect isn't necessary." She hauled in another shuddering breath. "Just close will make me happy."

Zeke caught her up in his arms and walked through the dark house, drinking in the taste of her as he went. He made it as far as the hallway before he had to stop. Using the wall to support her back, he dipped his head to skim his teeth down the column of her arched throat. "Ah, Natalie," he whispered.

She moaned and found his ear with her hot mouth, using lips, tongue, and teeth to torture him. The sound of her quickened breathing prodded him to move a few more feet. At the doorway of the bedroom, he braced her against the frame, angled his head to deepen the kiss, and barely had the presence of mind to come up for air.

"Last chance," he whispered. "If you're not sure about this, I'll let you go home. We can discuss it later when you haven't been drink—"

She hitched herself higher to silence him with her hungry mouth. Zeke accepted that as her answer and carried her to the bed. He meant to gently deposit her on the mattress, but she loosened her legs from around his hips to fall back, the tight circle of her arms at his neck pulling him down on top of her. The next instant, he felt her hand on his belly. The jolt shot clear to the soles of his feet.

"Whoa," he whispered, grabbing her wrist. "Where's the fire?"

She quivered beneath him. "Inside of me."

Her answer drove him straight over the edge. Feverish to get her naked, he reached around to unzip her dress, but he couldn't find the tab—or a damned zipper, period, for that matter. She assisted him by lifting her hips to tug up her skirt.

"It's stretchy," she whispered breathlessly. "Off over my head."

He twisted onto his knees, grasped her by the shoulders, sat her up, and divested her of the dress with one upward tug. In the moonlight that poured in through the window, her skin shimmered like pearls, pale and flawless. Her bra was a black push-up with lacy half cups and a front clasp. He'd never seen anything sexier in his life. When he unfastened the clasp, her full, heavy breasts spilled out into his hands, her large nipples as dark as copper in the shadows.

"They sag," she whispered.

"What?" Zeke sat back on his heels to make his own assessment. "You're perfect," he said, and meant it with all his heart. She was all the more beautiful to him because she didn't seem to know it. He gently pushed her back onto the pillows and bent to trace a line up her breastbone with the tip of his tongue. "You're absolutely perfect, Natalie."

"But—"

"No arguments. I'm the expert here, and my opinion is the only one that counts."

She shivered and threaded her slender fingers through his hair. "Oh, Zeke. I'm scared."

"Feeling like this would scare the bejesus out of anyone."

She giggled. Then she sobered, her big, luminous gaze

clinging to his. "Let's forget all the heavy stuff. Only for tonight. Okay? No expectations, no strings. Tomorrow we'll just—you know—pretend it didn't happen."

"No way, lady. I have expectations, and I want strings. Tomorrow morning when you wake up, I want to be the first thing you think about—that you're mine, that you'll always be mine." He scraped his teeth over the underside of her jaw and settled in to nibble at the sensitive hollow just beneath her ear. "One time with you will never be enough for me. And if I do my job, it won't be enough for you, either."

That said, Zeke set himself to the task of making this the most fabulous experience of her life, paying relentless attention to detail during foreplay. He kissed his way up the sensitive inside of her arm, then nibbled his way down her side, lingering to tease the outer swell of her breast. From there, he angled across to her navel and inched her panties down with his lips as he tasted the satiny skin of her lower abdomen. Soon she was strung as tautly as a bow, her spine arched, her breath coming in shallow pants, every line of her body begging him for release.

To keep her distracted, he reclaimed her mouth with his while he reached over to tug open his nightstand drawer. When his hand met with open air, he froze for an instant. Then his mind went ice cold with realization.

"Well, *shit.*"

She stiffened and blinked in bewilderment. "What?"

"My nightstand."

"What about it?"

"I sold it when I moved! *Shit*!"

Natalie couldn't see how his nightstand had anything to do with anything. When he pulled away to sit on the edge of the bed, she struggled to sit up, her head spinning from the wine she'd drunk earlier, her body throbbing with unsatisfied needs. It had been so *perfect.* She wanted to slug him. No orgasm in three years, and he had stopped because of a stupid nightstand?

"Shit," he said again. "This is great, just *great.*" He turned to look at her. "That's where I kept the condoms. We're SOL."

SOL? Natalie's brain finally clicked into place. She drew up the rumpled sheet to cover herself. "No condoms?"

"I kept them in the frigging nightstand."

She sat back on her heels and tried to slow her breathing. "Didn't you empty the drawers of the nightstand before you sold it?"

"Yes."

There was hope, after all. "Where'd you put the condoms?"

"In the trash. They were old. I was afraid they might be rotten. I figured I could just buy some more if I ever had occasion to need one."

She swallowed hard. "No protection." She laughed a little hysterically. "You've lived here since May, and you haven't needed a condom in all that time?"

"You find this humorous?"

Natalie didn't think it was humorous at all. But it was revealing. "No, not humorous. I just can't believe you haven't been with someone since you moved here."

"What do you take me for?"

The indignant expression on his dark, shadowed face nearly made her laugh again, and in that moment, all her fears fell away. He was, hands down, the handsomest and most wonderful man she'd ever known, and she was starting to believe he'd be the most loyal, never straying, possibly never even looking at another woman.

"I don't sleep around." His voice was gruff with frustration and unspent passion.

Tears stung her eyes. "Oh, Zeke."

"What?"

"No condoms? That's the sweetest thing anyone's ever said to me."

Sweet? He didn't get it. He couldn't make love to her, damn it. He wanted to tear hell out of something or put his fist through a wall. She'd come very close to walking away from him tonight. Now he'd blown it, and he might never get this chance again.

Since becoming an adult, he'd been as horny as a two-pecker goat more times than he wanted to count, but he'd never felt this kind of need—a knifing pain, low in his groin, the ache spreading up into his belly.

She patted the sheets, looking for her clothes, which made his heart sink even though he couldn't accommodate her if she stayed. When she found her bra, she lifted her beautiful legs over the opposite edge of the mattress and presented him with her back while she donned the garment. When she stood up, she tugged her panties back into place and reached around for her dress. Zeke wanted to weep.

"Will you come again?" he asked. "Next time, I swear, I'll make it worth your while."

After pulling the dress over her head, she wiggled to tug the stretchy material down over her hips. Watching her, Zeke almost came in his Wranglers. Turning to look at him, she raked a hand through her wildly mussed hair and tossed her head. "Of course I'll come again." She flashed him a sassy grin. "I'm not finished with you yet, cowboy."

Relief eased the tension from Zeke's shoulders. He pushed erect, refastened his jeans, and followed her from the room. "When?"

She giggled. "When we can find some time alone. Two kids, remember. They pose a slight problem."

Even in the darkness, her dress sparkled as she walked up the hallway. Once in the kitchen, she spun to look at him. "I've got Sunday night off. How about then?"

"Sunday?" Zeke took a quick mental count. "That's *five* days from now."

She smiled demurely. "I'll keep."

He wasn't sure he would. "Tomorrow night."

She shook her head. "I'm essentially working two full-time jobs right now, coming here during the day and going to the club at night. I really can't afford to stay up late like this again and lose the sleep."

Zeke had seen shadows of exhaustion under her eyes more than once. "Sleep in tomorrow. It's really not necessary for you to be here early."

"But that was our deal. Now, on top of the damages to your place, Chad owes you for the earrings. I can't sleep in and come late. How would that be right?"

Zeke caught her face between his hands and kissed her again. Within seconds they were both breathless. "That's how." He leaned back to find that she'd closed her eyes and was smiling. "Tomorrow night?"

She slowly lifted her lashes. "How late can I sleep in?"

"As long as you need to."

She giggled and went up on her toes to taste his mouth again. "We're assuming I'll be able to sleep. The way I'm feeling right now, I may lie awake all night, staring at the ceiling."

When Zeke awakened the next morning, he felt supercharged. *Natalie.* Her name was like a song in his mind. He wanted to see her face. He *needed* to know that last night hadn't been a figment of his imagination. *Problem.* He didn't have a single good reason to walk across the field to see her at six thirty in the morning and couldn't have brought himself to do it anyway. She needed her rest.

Instead he grabbed a shower, then went to the kitchen to make coffee. The gallon jug of wine still sat on his kitchen counter. He picked up the juice glass she'd used and smiled. She'd actually been there, and they'd almost made love. It had been the most frustrating experience of his life—and the most fabulous.

He scowled as he measured grounds into the coffee filter. *No condoms.* Never had he felt like such a dope. Zeke Coulter, the guy who planned everything down to a gnat's ass.

Well, he'd damned sure be ready the next time, he assured himself. Assuming, of course, that there'd be a next time. She'd been a little tipsy last night. When she woke up this morning, she might thank her lucky stars that nothing had happened.

The thought made it difficult for him to breathe. She was terrified of getting hurt again. He'd seen it in her eyes, heard it in her voice. *Just words,* she'd said. How was she to know that he'd never said them to anyone else?

Lemon-yellow sunlight played over Natalie's face. Luxuriating in the warmth, she bunched her pillow under her cheek and listened to the birds singing outside her open window. *Wake up. Wake up!* they seemed to say. *It's a beautiful morning!* In complete agreement, she smiled dreamily, thinking of Zeke, how the deep rumble of his voice moved through her when he whispered near her ear, how his big, work-roughened hands felt against her skin, how steely his arms felt when he locked them around her. He was so wonderful—a tall, dark, sexy cowboy who could have had any woman he wanted.

And he'd chosen *her*.

She almost laughed out loud every time she remembered the condom debacle. Bless his heart. He'd sat there on the edge of the bed, *whooshing* for air like a surfacing whale, every muscle in his body coiled with frustration. Up until that moment, she'd still had reservations. A woman couldn't live through what she had with Robert and trust another man without questioning her sanity. What if everything Zeke said was a pack of lies? But knowing that he'd been with no one since moving into his house, discovering that the prophylactics in his old nightstand had lain in the drawer for so long that he'd thrown them away, and seeing the indignant look on his face when he'd said, "What do you take me for?" had soothed away her fears.

Well, not all her fears, she decided as she swung her legs over the edge of the bed and sat up. Robert had left his mark on her, and she would always be afraid, way deep down. But the fear was no longer so overwhelming that she felt panicky. She was coming to trust Zeke in a way she hadn't thought possible.

Natalie threw her arms wide to stretch, feeling fabulous even though she'd barely slept a wink. *Tonight*. A delightful sizzle of arousal moved through her at the thought.

A light tap at the door brought her head around. "Who is it?"

Valerie opened the door and poked her head through the crack. "Well?" she asked sleepily. "How'd it go?"

"How'd what go?"

Valerie slipped into the room and eased the door closed behind her. "When you talked to Zeke."

"Oh, that." Natalie smiled happily. "He changed my mind."

"He what?"

"He changed my mind. I'm going to take a chance on him, after all."

Valerie's brown eyes sharpened with curiosity. "You're kidding."

"Nope." Natalie briefly recounted her conversation with Zeke. "Afterward he kissed me, and the next thing I knew, we were in bed."

Valerie plopped down on the mattress. "No shit?"

Natalie laughed at her sister's shocked expression and told her the best part of all, that Zeke hadn't had any protection in the house. "It was *awful*. But wonderful, too. He hasn't been with anyone since he moved here, and no telling how long before that."

"Wow," Valerie said softly, her eyes going dreamy. "A guy like that is hard to find."

So happy she could barely contain herself, Natalie hugged her knees. "I'm falling in love with him, Ree-Ree."

"You haven't called me that in years."

"I haven't, have I?" Natalie tipped her head to study her sister. "Don't laugh. This'll sound really sappy, but I feel as if things changed between us last night—that you all of a sudden grew up or something, and now you're not just my baby sister anymore, but a friend."

Valerie did laugh, but not mockingly. "I've been grown up for a long time, sister dear. You just never opened up to me like you did last night. I'm glad you did. *You* suddenly seem *almost* human."

"Thanks a lot."

"Well, it's true. You've always been so nauseatingly perfect. Beautiful, talented, smart. Except for Robert, I can't remember a single time you screwed up really bad. It hasn't been easy following in your footsteps."

"I never knew you felt that way."

"For, like, *always*. When I was little, I used to practice singing in the barn where no one would hear. I wanted so much to be like you. Mom and Pop were so proud of you, and I never felt as if they were proud of me. I was so-so at everything—okay in school, okay at art, okay at singing. I didn't shine at anything, and I still don't."

Natalie caught her lower lip in her teeth. Then she shifted to hug her sister with all her might. "You *do* shine," she whispered fiercely. "You're wonderful and funny and kind. My kids adore you, and no wonder. You can make me laugh when no one else can."

Valerie returned her hug. "That's nice, I guess, being good for a laugh. But it's not exactly a great talent."

Natalie sat back. "Look at the flip side. Besides singing, what am I good at?"

Valerie frowned thoughtfully. Then she grinned. "Nothing much."

"Exactly. You're proficient at a lot of things. Being really, *really* good at one thing—being obsessed with it like I am—has its drawbacks. I'm forgetful and unorganized. I lose my train of thought and screw up the simplest things because I'm hearing music in my head and not concentrating on the task. You're a good cook. I'm not. You don't turn the white clothes pink. I do. You remember to check the oil in your car. When daylight savings time comes, you remember to reset your watch and all the clocks. I go around subtracting or adding an hour for weeks because I never remember to set my watch."

Valerie giggled. "You do, don't you?"

They fell quiet for a moment, just smiling at each other. Then Valerie said, "Now that we've established a mutual-admiration society, let's get back to Zeke. You're really falling in love, huh?"

"Yes." Natalie hugged her knees again and shivered with delicious delight. "Am I crazy, or what?"

"Not crazy." Valerie playfully punched Natalie's shoulder. "Right *on*. I'm so glad for you, Nattie. If anyone on earth deserves to get a really great guy, it's you."

Tears stung Natalie's eyes. That seemed to happen a lot since she met Zeke. "Thank you. It's so weird, how it happened. Isn't it? I get a divorce, go flat broke, and move home with both my kids. My whole life seems to be falling apart. Then he buys the place next door. Chad vandalizes his house, forcing him to come over and hassle it out with me. If that hadn't happened, I might never have met him. It's almost as if it was meant to be. You know?"

"I believe in that, actually. Some people are just meant to be together. You can tell by the way they look at each other."

"Who do you know like that?" Natalie asked.

"Mom and Pop."

Natalie stared incredulously at her sister for a moment. Then she shrieked with laughter.

"Well, it's true," Valerie insisted. "They still love each other. They just can't stand each other."

Natalie fell back on the pillows, laughing so hard she felt

weak. "A f-fatal attraction," she said with a gasp, "that never r-reached the lethal stage?"

"Sort of." Valerie sent her sister a disgruntled glance. "Name me one time in the ten years since they separated that either of them has so much as *looked* at someone else."

Natalie sobered and suddenly felt sad. "You're right. Mom is so pretty. She could crook her finger and have guys standing in line, but she never dates."

"And Pop is married to the damn television and his backache. He doesn't have a life anymore. It ended the day she walked out."

"Oh, *God*." Natalie sat up. "You're so *right*. They still love each other."

Rosie bounded into the bedroom just then. Natalie threw her arms wide. The child catapulted onto her lap, giggling and squirming. Valerie met Natalie's gaze over the top of her niece's head.

"Meant for each other," she said as she pushed to her feet. "I've got twenty that says they get back together someday."

"It'd take a miracle." Natalie gobbled like a turkey as she nibbled her daughter's neck. Between gobbles, she said, "They fight like two cats in a burlap bag."

"My point exactly. People don't go for the jugular every time they see each other unless some very powerful emotions are at work. They don't just dislike each other. They *detest* each other. Gotta be a reason for that."

Zeke was on his third mug of coffee when he saw Natalie come out the back door of the Westfield house, carrying a bag of trash. Even though she was far away, he identified her by her trademark walk—an unintentionally sexy sway that Valerie lacked. He nearly growled in frustration when she left the porch and became obscured by bushes. He glanced at his watch, saw that it wasn't quite eight o'clock, and wondered why she'd gotten up so early. She was supposed to sleep in this morning, damn it.

As she exited the yard to reach the trash cans, she walked out into the open again. He settled back against the steps, never taking his eyes off of her as she dumped her burden in the garbage can. She wore something pink—a nightshirt of some kind, he decided, because her legs looked bare. At such a distance, he couldn't make out any details, much to his regret. But where vision failed him, imagination took over. In his mind's eye, he envisioned her shapely calves, the slender turn of her ankles, and the way the nightshirt would hike up in back as she bent over. He wished she were there with him. That he could run his hands over her softness and bury his face in her hair.

Soon, he promised himself. Now that he'd made up his mind about Natalie, he wanted her in his bed every night. With two kids in the mix, that meant marriage, the sooner, the better. It was his responsibility to set a good example for her children, after all, especially for Chad, who'd be a walking, talking hormone before they knew it. Zeke wanted the boy to respect girls, and teaching that trait required more than lip service.

Not long after Natalie went back in the house, Chad emerged. As the boy cut across the field, Zeke lifted an arm and waved. Chad spotted the movement and waved back.

"Morning," Zeke called when the kid was within earshot. "Going to be a scorcher today."

"It's already getting warm," Chad shouted back.

When the boy reached the porch, Zeke pushed to his feet. "You eat breakfast?"

"Cereal and toast."

Zeke swirled his cup and dumped the dregs. "May as well get to work then."

"What are we gonna do today?"

Zeke led the way to the shop. "Build fences."

"You got the lumber?"

"Yep," Zeke said as he opened one of the shop doors. He slanted Chad a meaningful look. "Got it a couple of months ago. Would have finished some stalls and a corral by now if it hadn't rained tomatoes and rocks on my house."

Chad blushed. "I'm real sorry I did that now."

Zeke laughed and ruffled the boy's hair. "I know you are. Wouldn't needle you about it, otherwise."

An hour later, Zeke and Chad were digging the fourth posthole when Natalie and Rosie showed up. Wiping sweat from his brow with his shirtsleeve, Zeke turned to greet them. He meant to ask Natalie why she'd come so early, but as it happened, he never even got a chance to say hello. Chester had followed the ladies across the field. When the gander spotted Zeke, he went into instant attack mode, lifting his wings, extending his neck, and hissing.

"Chester!" Natalie cried.

"Bad boy!" Rosie screeched.

Zeke wasn't about to be chased off his own property by a silly goose with a bad attitude. This time, instead of running, he lifted his arms, yelled, and met the gander's charge. Accustomed to victims that fled, Chester clearly didn't know how to react. With a panicky quack, the huge bird banked his wings sharply to the right, turned, and ran, honking with every step. Determined to teach the gander a lesson, Zeke continued the chase until Chester had crossed the field and reached his own driveway.

"That'll show you," Zeke yelled for good measure as he slowed his pace and turned back for home. In the distance, he could see Natalie cupping her hands to her mouth and yelling something, but he was too far away to distinguish her words. Rosie began waving her arms and jumping about. "What in blazes are they hollering about?" Zeke wondered aloud.

An instant later, Chester pinched Zeke on the ass, providing him with a startling and painful answer to that question. "Ouch!" Instinctively breaking into a run so the gander couldn't bite him again, Zeke yelled, "You no-good, rotten, miserable excuse for a—*ouch!*"

Zeke picked up speed. When he'd put a good ten feet between himself and the vengeful gander, he wheeled to press a frontal attack again, waving his arms and yelling to frighten the bird. Chester honked frantically and fled, Zeke once again right on his ass.

Looking on, Natalie started to laugh. Her children cast her appalled glances, which only made her laugh harder. Ten minutes later, she had tears streaming down her cheeks and was holding her sides. Every time Zeke gave up the chase, Chester doubled back and tried to bite him. In all her days, Natalie couldn't recall ever having seen anything so funny. Even the kids finally started to giggle.

"How long is Mr. Coulter going to chase Chester, Mommy?" Rosie asked.

"Until Chester stops trying to bite him, I guess."

Thirty minutes later, Zeke walked home with far less energy and enthusiasm than he'd shown when leaving. Chester waddled behind him, quacking unhappily but no longer attempting to bite.

"I think we have an understanding," Zeke said when he

reached them. "Crazy, stubborn bird." He swiped sweat from his forehead and gave Natalie a lazy grin. "You have an odd sense of humor, lady."

Natalie nodded and brushed tears of mirth from her cheeks. "I'm sorry," she pushed out. "It just looked so comical. From now on, I'm calling you 'Dances with Ganders.' "

His twinkling blue eyes narrowed in threat. "You'll pay for that one."

The growl in his voice made Natalie's insides tighten. "Promises, promises."

He ran his gaze slowly over her. "I'm a man of my word. Do you stand behind yours?"

A sizzle of desire tightened her chest. "You'll soon find out." She glanced meaningfully at her kids. Zeke followed her gaze. Then he clapped his hands. "Time to get cracking," he said, his tone suddenly brusque.

Chester sat in the shade of the shop, quacking softly, his tone reminiscent of an old man muttering under his breath. Natalie went over to scratch his head. "Poor baby. You wore yourself to a frazzle."

"That poor baby darned near took a hunk out of my backside."

Two hours later, when the four of them stopped working to take a break, Natalie sat with Zeke in the shade of the building, their backs braced against the metal siding. After draining a glass of ice tea, he settled those amazingly blue eyes on her, his expression thoughtful, his firm mouth solemn.

"You didn't sleep in."

"I barely slept at all. I finally drifted off about five, and only a few minutes later, Lothario started crowing."

"Lothario? The rooster that I hear crowing every blasted

morning?" Zeke chuckled at the name. Then he sobered. "You didn't get your rest."

"Nope."

Zeke studied her face. Those damned shadows were under her eyes again. He couldn't, in good conscience, insist that she lose more sleep tonight. "Sunday," he whispered. "I can wait."

Her eyes danced with pure, unadulterated mischief. "No way, buster. I'm not staring at the ceiling all night again. I can think of more productive ways to spend my time."

Chapter Ten

That evening, Natalie left for work a half hour early, no easy feat when she had only thirty minutes to get ready after leaving Zeke's place. She took the fastest shower in history, pulled her hair up on top of her head, slapped on makeup, shimmied into a dress, and left the house in a mad dash, blowing kisses to the kids on her way out.

Her first stop when she reached town was at a drugstore. When her business there was concluded, she stashed her purchase on the back floorboard and drove straight to Robert's posh new home on Eagle Butte, Crystal Falls's equivalent of snob hill. She ground her teeth when she pulled into the driveway, which encircled an elaborate stone fountain, a feature befitting the stately house with its pillared front portico, expansive front doors, and cathedral windows. The place was a mansion. It had probably set him back a couple of mil. How could he sleep at night, living in such opulence when his children were doing without?

Doing a slow burn, Natalie parked her old Chevy dead center in the drive, cut the engine, and then sat there, taking deep breaths to calm down. She wasn't here to argue with Robert about money. Ever since the earring incident, she'd moved beyond that, her concerns more centered on Chad and how this mess between her and Robert was affecting him. Let Robert hoard his wealth. She honestly didn't care anymore.

Zeke was largely responsible for Natalie's change of heart. Loving him and knowing that he loved her had set her free of the past. Tonight when she made love with him, she wanted no ties binding her to that past. She needed to start over fresh, with no old grudges or grievances weighing on her heart. With Zeke behind her, she would see to her children's needs without Robert's help. If the club went under, so be it; she'd get a job. Chad and Rosie might not have the best of everything for the next year or so, but they'd have the essentials, and they would know they were loved, not only by their mother but hopefully by their father as well.

That was the reason for Natalie's visit here today—to talk with Robert about his failure to telephone or visit his children. A truce of sorts was her aim. To encourage Robert to exercise his visitation rights and keep in touch with the kids, she would forgo all child support, past, present, and future. No more snide remarks, no more hassles, no more threats to take legal action when she spoke to him on the phone. She couldn't force her ex-husband to be a responsible, loving father, but she could at least encourage him to go through the motions. Just an occasional phone call would make Chad feel better. Even if Robert's heart wasn't in it, he could spare ten minutes a week to play the concerned, interested dad.

Natalie swung purposefully from the car. Her heels tapped sharply on the flagstones as she made her way up the wide, curved steps. When she reached the ornate double doors, she could hear the faint strains of Chopin coming from inside—the Berceuse, if she remembered correctly.

The melancholy, Italianate sweetness of the piece almost made her shudder. On the rare occasion when Robert had deigned to have sex with her, he'd always played Chopin on the stereo.

Five years ago, Natalie would have trembled and felt heartsick, knowing he was inside with another woman. Now she was just glad it was Cheryl or Bonnie putting up with him. She leaned heavily on the buzzer, then rapped the brass knocker a few times for good measure.

For almost three minutes, Natalie cooled her heels waiting for Robert to answer her ring. She knew he was home. He never would have left the stereo on when he left the house; he was anal about things like that. She'd also called his office on the way into town, and his secretary had informed her that he was taking care of business at the house this evening.

Business, ha. Since when did bonking a blonde qualify as work? Growing impatient, Natalie grasped the ornate door lever. She meant to speak with Robert whether he wanted to see her or not. He could forgo a few minutes of playtime to talk with her about the emotional welfare of their son.

To her relief, the door wasn't locked. Riding high on nerves and determination, she barely noticed the gorgeous entry hall as she stepped inside. "Robert?" she called. "It's Natalie! Can we talk for a couple of minutes?"

No answer. Natalie might have turned to leave, but the music playing on the piped-in stereo system emboldened her. Her ex-husband was somewhere in the house. She would have bet what remained of the Blue Parrot's assets on it.

"Robert!" she called again, trying to inject a syrupy sweetness into her voice so he wouldn't dread talking to her.

"This won't take long, I promise. I just want to talk to you about Chad for a few seconds."

It was a huge house. If the interior walls were soundproofed, maybe he couldn't hear her. Gathering her courage, Natalie decided to check the downstairs before she left. What could he do, have her arrested for unlawful entry? Not even Robert would be that petty, and this was a discussion long overdue.

Half expecting to walk in on a tawdry scene as she entered each room, Natalie quickly covered the first floor, calling her ex-husband's name every few steps. The more she saw of his home, the more outraged she became. Robert wasn't just selfish; he was without conscience. He had spent a fortune on furnishings alone. The place was so flashy it bordered on tasteless. He'd really gone all out. Grace undoubtedly hated it. *Nouveau riche,* she would say with a sneer.

As Natalie entered the study, she saw some papers lying on the edge of a vast cherrywood desk. No longer even mildly curious about Robert's business dealings, she gave them only a cursory glance. The plush sitting area to the left of the desk did catch her attention, however. Two glasses of partially consumed wine sat on the glass coffee table, yet another sign that Robert had been in the room recently.

Her gaze coming to rest on the goblets, Natalie froze. Her grandma Devereaux's crystal? Just like that, and her temper reached boiling point. She'd looked *everywhere* for those goblets, thinking that they'd been put in an unmarked box by the movers Robert hired and were in her storage building somewhere. She'd asked Robert countless times if he'd come across the glasses, and he'd said no. The rotten *bastard.* That crystal was a Devereaux family heirloom, mid-eighteenth century, straight from Bayel. The delicate fleur-de-lis pattern on the French-footed goblets was unmistakable.

Natalie stepped around the cushy leather sofa to pick up a glass. How dare he serve wine to some two-bit tramp in her grandmother's irreplaceable crystal? She swirled the wine, took a sniff, and wished Robert were standing there so she could throw it in his face. Where, she wondered furiously, did he keep the rest of the set? She had a good mind to wrap the goblets in dish towels and take them with her now. Otherwise she might never see them again.

And why not? They were *hers*. Someday they should go to Rosie. If left in Robert's possession, they might get broken. Decision made, Natalie collected both goblets and marched to the kitchen. After dumping the wine down the sink, she gave the glasses a cursory rinse, dried them, and began pulling open drawers, searching for clean towels. *Bingo*. Then, in the drawer below the towels, she found paper sacks, one of which would serve her purpose perfectly.

So mad she didn't care if Robert came in and caught her, Natalie went on a crystal search. She finally found the other six goblets behind his wet bar. Carefully gathering them into her arms, she returned to the kitchen, wrapped each glass in a towel, and gently deposited them in the sack before spinning to leave the room with her loot. *Ha*. If Robert was hiding upstairs with his current flavor of the month, this would teach him. Next time he played these stupid games with her, maybe she'd swipe the silver.

As Natalie returned to the entry hall, she could have sworn she heard a door latch click. Her heart tripped and stuttered. *Caught red-handed*. She whirled and clutched the bulging paper bag to her chest, prepared to do battle. *Nothing*. She glanced upstairs. If he was up there, pretending not to hear her, the joke was on him this time.

Feeling like a common thief, Natalie rushed from the house.

At precisely nine thirty that evening, Zeke stepped into the Blue Parrot. Natalie was in the middle of a number, and the glare of the stage lights made it difficult for her to see beyond the bright pool of light that surrounded her. The rear tables, cloaked in shadows, were especially difficult for her to see. Nevertheless, she felt the air change when Zeke entered, almost as if a surge of electricity had come in the door with him.

She continued to sing, never missing a beat, but the same couldn't be said for her heart. Straining to make him out, she followed him with her gaze as he walked to a table. He had the lazy, loose-hipped stride of a man who'd spent years in the saddle, the heels of his boots lightly scuffing the floor with each step. He wore the Western-cut brown sports jacket again tonight, this time over a dark blue shirt. The brim of his chocolate-colored Stetson cast his face into shadow, making it impossible for her to see his features. Not that she really needed to. Somehow, in a very short time, each plane and angle of his countenance had been engraved on her memory.

He sat at a back table, just as he had the other times. After settling on a chair, he propped one boot on his opposite thigh and removed the hat. Raking his fingers through his dark hair, he hooked the Stetson over his bent knee. His every movement was deliciously masculine. In Natalie's estimation, he was the handsomest man in the place.

When he realized that she'd spotted him, his firm mouth tipped into a slow, lopsided grin. He touched two fingertips to the sable forelock that lay in waves over his high forehead, the mock salute serving as a silent hello.

Natalie wasn't due to take a break yet. She had four more numbers to get through before she could go to him. *Agony.* She wanted to be sitting across from him. She wanted to hear the deep, husky timbre of his voice. She wanted to see his eyes light up with laughter or glint with teasing mischief.

To get through her routine, she sang directly to him—songs about love and forever, her heart in every word. Last night, she'd foolishly believed she could shut down her feelings for him, and she'd desperately wanted to do just that. Madness. She'd been waiting for him all her life. And he was right; this magic between them was very special. He couldn't turn his back on it, and neither could she.

As she ended her last song, Natalie took a sweeping bow, laid aside her guitar, and went down the stage steps. Zeke pushed to his feet as she approached his table. "Hey, cowboy," she said with a glad smile.

"Hey, yourself." He leaned around to draw out a chair for her. "Have I told you today that you're the most gorgeous creature I've ever seen?"

"Yes. But don't let that stop you."

He grinned and sat back down. The waitress delivered his drink just then. Natalie glanced up. "Next time out, could you bring me a water, Becky?"

"Sure."

The slender blonde cast a curious glance at Zeke as she sidled away. Natalie gazed after her and smiled. "My employees are starting to whisper about you, Mr. Coulter. If I walk into the bar or kitchen, everything goes absolutely silent for a second."

"There's a bar here?"

She pointed to a closed door to the left of the front entrance. "Right through there. I wanted the dining room kept separate, so I had a wall put in when I leased the place. The atmosphere in here is more dignified that way."

He studied the door, frowning thoughtfully. Then his expression cleared and he smiled. "I'm sorry. You were saying?"

"Just that my employees are wondering about you."

"Uh-oh."

"This is your third visit, and I've always sat with you during my break. They know something's up."

He arched a thick, winged eyebrow. "Does that bother you?"

"I'm here, aren't I?"

He chuckled. "You are. I just hate to make tongues wag. I have employees myself. I understand the importance of keeping your private life private."

Natalie sighed and took in the room. More tables were empty than not, and she'd had a particularly stressful time earlier in the evening, trying to juggle funds to pay for tomorrow's deliveries. "The way things are going, I may not be open that much longer. Let my employees speculate."

"Are things that bad, honey?"

Natalie fiddled with the drape of the tablecloth. "Take a gander at the crowd, and you tell me." She let the linen slip from her fingers and straightened her shoulders. "But enough about that. It's a special night. I don't want to ruin it, fretting about business slumps and money problems."

A smoldering heat flashed in his eyes. "It is a special

night," he agreed. "And I don't want to ruin it any more than you do."

"Do I hear a 'but' at the end of that sentence?"

His mouth twitched. Then he settled his sharp gaze on the crowd again. "Business before pleasure, as the old saying goes. If the club is in that much trouble, you need to act quickly."

"And do what? I've cut back on the menu. I'm operating with a skeleton crew. I'm buying cheap sour mash and refilling popular-brand bottles so people think they're drinking the good stuff."

He flicked a glance at his glass. "This isn't Jack Daniel's?"

Natalie touched a finger to her lips. "Don't tell anyone. I come in once a week to pull the switches when no one else is here. Not even my help knows." She shifted nervously on her chair. "I think it's against the law. I don't want my liquor license pulled."

Zeke tasted the drink. His blue eyes danced with laughter. "You little crook."

"Needs must. I'm barely managing to pay my suppliers as it is. You can't operate on credit in this business. You either settle up front, or you go under."

"That's rough."

"It's the nature of the business. Do you have any idea how many restaurants and bars in this town go bankrupt each year? The wholesalers would go down with them if they extended credit."

"Have you considered making a few changes to increase your clientele?"

"What kind of changes?"

"If I step on your toes with what I'm about to say, just tell me so. All right?"

"Uh-oh. That doesn't sound good."

He didn't smile. "Correct me if I'm wrong, but this club seems to have the Patterson stamp all over it."

"The Patterson what?"

"Stamp," he repeated. "It's classy all the way—formal dining, tasteful decor, complete with a first-class entertainer dressed to the nines in an evening gown or cocktail dress. The usual country-western joint has a relaxed atmosphere, and the entertainers are far more likely to be wearing jeans, riding boots, and a Western shirt."

"Your point?"

"That maybe, just maybe, you compromised when you opened this place, trying to please your husband and in-laws."

Natalie swept her gaze over the room again. It was true, she realized, though she'd never consciously thought about it at the time.

"The piano player, for instance," Zeke went on. "Piano's fine, don't get me wrong, but that highbrow shit he plays during your breaks is a total shock after the songs you sing. What is that he's pounding out right now, anyway?"

Natalie listened for a moment. "That's Beethoven's 'Moonlight Sonata.'"

He nodded. "It's not 'Boot Scootin' Boogie,' that's for damned sure."

The disgruntled look on his face made Natalie laugh. "I guess I did aim for a classier atmosphere to pacify Robert and his mother. It seemed like a good plan at the time—a one-of-a-kind country-western club, a place where enthusiasts could enjoy both the music and fine dining."

"You still worried about pacifying Robert?"

"No. Why?"

He plucked his hat from his knee to put it on the table and sat forward on his chair. That serious, down-to-business expression suited him, she decided. Dark brows pleated in a slight frown, his eyes razor sharp on hers. Little wonder he'd just purchased a lovely home and still had money to make loans to the neighbor kid. She had a feeling that he was a force to be reckoned with in retail.

"I think you have a fabulous idea going here—great entertainment, fine dining, classy atmosphere. But what if you toned it down just a hair and offered something more middle of the road?"

"Then the club would be ordinary. I wouldn't have anything special to offer."

"I'm not talking about making it ordinary. Keep it fancy enough to pull in Yuppies who like country-western, but relaxed and reasonable enough price-wise to appeal to working-class guys as well. Shit kickers who want to put on the dog for their ladies but can't afford filet mignon once a week."

"Go on," she said softly.

He rested his folded arms on the table. "The ordinary Joe can't come in here on a regular basis, and if they splurge for dinner, they'll go elsewhere afterward for entertainment—someplace where they can shuffle their boots on a dance floor and get cozy with a main squeeze."

Natalie glanced around again. "Too stuffy, huh?"

"Not stuffy, exactly, just a hair too ritzy. For mass appeal, you should knock out that wall so people in the bar can enjoy the live entertainment, too. What are they, second-class citizens because they prefer a beer and some smoke in the air? You can slap in a good filtration system if you don't already have one. Offer a few inexpensive entrées on the menu. Hold karaoke competitions a few nights a week. Move the tables back to make room for a dance floor. Don't turn it into a honky-tonk. Crystal Falls is crawling with those. Just make it friendlier, a place where people from all walks of life can enjoy themselves. I think you'd be packed every night of the week."

A thrill of excitement moved up the back of Natalie's throat. She turned on her chair to better survey the room. "You know, it just might work. Karaoke is a lot of fun. I never thought of that. A lot of people go from bar to bar, just so they can get up and sing to an audience."

"Damn straight. And you'll be providing a first-class place for them to do it. People love to make fools of themselves."

She laughed again. She seemed to do a lot of that around this man.

"Karaoke a few evenings a week would give you more breaks between numbers to take care of orders and paperwork. You might even find some time to write some new songs."

She threw him a wondering look. "Like anyone will ever buy them."

"You ever tried to sell one?"

Her face went hot under his searching gaze. "Well, no. I'm not even sure how to start."

"By starting," he said simply.

Natalie laughed again. He made her feel as if she could do almost anything. "Cheaper entrées, huh? I'm *terrible* at doing menus."

"I'll help. And don't change the subject. I want you to

pick your favorite out of all the songs you've ever written and give it to me, no questions asked. Will you do that?"

"Why?"

"That's a question. Just do it, and keep your focus on this club before it goes tits up."

Natalie chewed on her bottom lip. "I can't afford to have that wall knocked out, Zeke. It'll cost a small fortune."

"Nah. Give me a crowbar and hammer, and I can have it down in no time. You added it when you leased the place, right? It doesn't look like a bearing wall."

"You've been scoping out my club, thinking of structural changes?"

Looking sheepish, he rubbed his jaw. "The place isn't exactly hopping. I can testify to the fact that it's not the entertainment. The businessman in me can't help but ask himself why, and once I start doing that, I think of ways to remedy the problem."

"I did all right until Robert siphoned off half my working capital."

"I've offended you."

"No!" Natalie protested. "Not at all. It's just—well, there's a space deficiency, for one thing. How can I keep all the tables and have room for a dance floor? And I have to observe the fire regulations. I have a capacity limit of two hundred in here, fifty in the bar."

He took a quick head count. "Sweetheart, you presently have twenty people in here."

"It was busier earlier. After dinner, a lot of people leave."

"My point exactly. That's what you do in a restaurant, eat and shag. You don't want to occupy the table all night when you've finished eating, no matter how much you're enjoying yourself."

He was right; she knew he was. Only his suggestions would cost money—money she didn't have.

"You don't need a large dance floor," he speculated. "You might lose a few tables, but not many. Just put them closer together. If you're worried about overcrowding, have a cover charge, maybe five bucks a head. Almost anybody can afford that. You'll make money the instant they walk through the door, and people won't be inclined to leave once they get here. Clubs turn most of their profit on drinks. Right?"

"Yes." She stared dubiously at the wall.

"It's no big deal," he assured her. "I can slap up some trim to hide where it was, fix the floor somehow, and it'll be done. Do you have enough money to do a little advertising to bring new people in and rent some karaoke equipment?"

Natalie's heart sank as she recalled the mess her books were in. "No, not really."

"How much do you think you'll need? I have some extra stashed away."

"No way, Zeke. Don't even go there."

"Why not? I've got the cash just sitting in the bank. You can pay me back with interest. How's that?"

"At what rate?"

"A garter belt and nylons once a month."

She burst out laughing. "You're *terrible.*"

"I'm hornier than a teenage boy on prom night, is what I am." He arched a dark eyebrow. "Nothing else. Just the garter belt and nylons. Heels, of course."

Natalie saw the twinkle in his eyes and knew he was teasing. "Do you really like garter belts?"

"Not really, but we're bargaining here. You're a hard-headed woman."

"It's sweet of you to offer, Zeke, but I'd feel funny."

"Better to feel funny than go broke."

Natalie shook her head. "I don't want to muddy the water between us by borrowing money from you." She tried for a lighthearted smile. "I'd feel like a kept woman."

"Works for me." The smoldering glint returned to his eyes. "I'll have a vested interest, that way, until I can snub you down with a ring and promises."

Natalie gaped at him.

He grinned and lifted his glass to her in a mock toast. Winking at her over the rim, he said, "Close your mouth, honey. You're gonna catch flies."

Natalie was almost giddy with nerves by the time she started across the field to Zeke's place later that night. She was still wearing her work clothes, the black dress she'd had on the first time she met him and the same high-heeled sandals. It was treacherous walking. When her spikes weren't sinking into the dirt, she was stepping into holes. She thought about going barefoot, but she didn't want to show up at his door with dirty feet. *Not sexy*. It was extremely important to look her best tonight.

When she reached his driveway, she stopped to fluff her hair, which she'd let down before leaving the house. Then she smoothed her dress. Her stomach squeezed and butterflies fluttered at the base of her throat. All of a sudden, she no longer felt certain this was a good idea. Maybe she should just go home, call him on the phone, and tell him she'd changed her mind.

"What's that you're carrying?"

His deep voice came unexpectedly from the inky shadows and made her jump a foot.

"I'm sorry," he said. She heard his boots crunching on the gravel, the sounds growing louder as he approached. "I didn't mean to startle you."

Her heart hopped around in her chest like a frog on hot cement. "What're you doing out here?"

"Waiting for you." He emerged from the shadows into the moonlight, taller than she remembered and broader across the shoulders. His dark hair looked frosted in the silvery moonbeams, and his eyes gleamed like polished pewter. "Do you have any idea how long a minute seems when you've got to wait two hours for someone?"

Some of the tension eased from her body. "Sorry. I got here as soon as I could."

"You were in the house for fifteen minutes. I was starting to worry that you'd changed your mind."

She ran her fingers through her hair. "Last-minute touch-ups. I didn't want to look shopworn."

"You worry too much."

Her sister had told her exactly the same thing last night, giving Natalie cause to wonder if they both weren't right. She did worry a lot, especially about her appearance. Maybe it came from being onstage five nights a week, with people staring at her from all angles.

"I'll happily take you any way I can get you." He stepped so close that she could feel the heat coming off his body. "What's that you have in your hand?"

She glanced down at the drugstore sack. Then she smiled as she handed it over. "A gift for you."

"A gift?" He opened the bag, tipped it toward the light, and squinted to see the contents. Then he threw back his dark head and barked with laughter. "A whole carton?"

"Just so you'll have plenty on hand."

He gave her one of those heart-stopping grins. "That's two."

"Two what?"

"Cartons. I went to town, too."

It was Natalie's turn to laugh. He slipped a strong arm around her waist and led her to the kitchen steps. "No more repeats of last night. We're well equipped now." He bent his head to nibble the side of her neck and then her shoulder. "I remember this dress, by the way."

"You do?"

"Yeah." He kept a firm hold on her as they ascended the steps, then leaned across in front of her to throw open the door. "You had it on the first time I ever saw you. You were so beautiful, I damned near swallowed my tongue, and then, for the life of me, I couldn't remember why the hell I'd gone over there."

"Huh-uh."

"God's truth, I swear. All that saved me was seeing tomato pulp on the toe of my boot. You weren't what I was expecting to find when I rounded the corner of the house. I wanted to touch you"—he dipped his head to kiss her cleavage—"right there."

Liquid heat pooled in her belly. Her legs went a little wobbly as she stepped ahead of him into the kitchen. He tossed the sack onto the table, caught her by the elbow, and swung her back around into his arms, his mouth hot and hungry on hers before she could even gasp in surprise.

She'd expected to feel tense the first few minutes after she arrived, imagined that they'd make stilted conversation and ease their way into this. *Not*. His arm was like a band of steel around her, his large hand splayed over her back to press her firmly against him. No preliminaries. No opportunity to feel nervous. He just took control.

He kissed her as if he never meant to stop. Searing heat. His hands skimmed her dress, setting her nerve endings afire. His tongue teased her lips, making her quiver clear to her toes. As he tightened his embrace and molded her body to his, she felt as if she were going to melt right on the spot. He delved deeply into her mouth with his tongue, his body quivering, desire evident in every hard line of his torso.

He drew away with such suddenness that Natalie was startled. Taking her face between his hands, he trailed his lips over her cheek, then kissed her eyelids closed. "You're so beautiful." His voice had gone husky with need. He ran his hands into her hair and bent his dark head to feather his lips down the column of her neck to the V of her collarbone, then lower to the swells of her breasts just above the bodice of her dress. "So damned beautiful."

His breathing had become more rapid, shuddering from his chest, warm and steamy against her skin. He hooked an arm under her bottom, lifted her as if she weighed no more than a child, pulled her against him, pelvis to pelvis, and went at her mouth so feverishly that she thought he was going to take her right there.

And she was ready. More than ready. She'd never ached like this in her life. Her desire for him went beyond feverish. It was a primal need deep within her. She ran her hands through his hair, pulled his head down so she could more thoroughly take his mouth with hers, and absorbed the heat of him, pulsating into her like shock waves.

He drew his lips from hers. In a dizzying rush, she felt him move with her. The next thing she knew, she was sitting on the kitchen counter, Zeke standing between her parted legs. Breathing rapidly and whispering nonsensically, he rained kisses over her hair and face, his hands lightly caressing her bare thighs, his body held slightly apart from hers. Natalie blinked back to awareness and realized that he was trying to slow things down.

She became lost in his fabulous blue eyes. *Zeke.* He was her everything in that moment. She needed him, yes. But she loved him even more for wanting to slow the pace and make this special for her. Following his example, she cupped his dark face between her hands and trailed light kisses over his lean cheeks, soothing him, pulling him back.

"I've never wanted anyone the way I want you right now," he whispered raggedly. "But I want this to be perfect, something that you'll remember."

He couldn't have said anything that meant more to her. She was accustomed to a man who thought only of his own pleasure. She could feel the yearning that coursed through his large frame, sense that he rode a dangerous edge. That told her more than he could know.

"How about a drink?" he asked out of the blue.

"Sure," she managed to push out through kiss-swollen lips.

She no sooner spoke than he slipped an arm under her knees, caught her around the back, and swept her up against his chest. She wished that he'd carry her straight to his bed, but instead, he carried her to the family room, carefully deposited her on a stool, and asked, "What's your pleasure?"

Her imagination ran away with her. Sex on top of the bar sounded fantastic at that moment.

"Surprise me," she said, using the husky, come-hither voice she'd perfected for the club.

He gave her a long, thoughtful look and mixed her a sloe

gin tonic. "Why did you choose sloe gin?" she couldn't resist asking.

He flashed a lazy grin. "It's supposed to get you in the mood."

She squirmed on the bar stool, crossed her legs, and then quickly uncrossed them because the pressure at certain points was more than she could handle. "If this is supposed to get me in the mood, what was that in the kitchen?"

"Just the icebreaker, sweetie. The main course is yet to come."

What ice? She'd never wanted anyone the way she wanted him—right *now*. She curled her hand around the tumbler that he slid across the bar, shifted on the bar stool, set her feet on the floor, and gave him her most seductive smile. Switching into performance mode, she walked toward the archway to the hall, swinging her hips as seductively as she knew how. When she reached her destination, she turned, lifted her glass, and flashed him a smile that she hoped would send an unmistakable message.

"I'm ready for the main course now, Zeke."

As she turned to lead the way, he made it across the room with Olympic speed. "I wanted to make this romantic for you."

Any more romantic, and she was going to rape him. She reached up, grabbed him by the front of his shirt, and led him down the hall to the bedroom, both of their drinks sloshing over the edges of their glasses. Natalie didn't care. It wasn't her carpet. And at the moment, she wouldn't have cared if it had been.

She pulled him over to the bed, set her glass on the floor where his blasted nightstand should have been, turned, relieved him of his tumbler and placed it beside hers. With tense fingers, she began unbuttoning his shirt and unfastening his belt buckle. When she had him satisfactorily undone, she placed her hands against his broad chest and shoved with all her might. He landed on the mattress with a *harrumph* that made her grin. She hiked her up her skirt and followed him down, bracketing his hips with her thighs.

"What about foreplay?" he asked raggedly.

"That was last night." She bent down and began planting kisses on his face and bare chest. "I want you. *Now.* I haven't had sex in three years, and it was lousy even then."

Zeke lay there for a moment, enjoying the feel of her warm, moist lips trailing over his skin. Her hair tickled his chest—light, silken curls still warm from her body that sent electrical zings coursing through him. Her fingertips danced over his shoulders, pushing back his shirt, igniting him with needs he couldn't deny or resist. Without conscious thought, he whipped up from the bed, caught her around the waist, and rolled with her to get on top. As he paused to look into her brown eyes, which shimmered in the moonlight coming through the window, he knew beyond a shadow of a doubt that she was the love of his life.

He gently reached up and took hold of the straps of her dress, slipping them down over her slender shoulders. Natalie arched her back and reached behind to pull down the zipper, her gaze fixed on his. He smiled, tugged the dress down to below her hips, and bent to kiss the upper swells of her breasts. She trembled when he nibbled lightly at the lace cups of her bra.

Natalie wished that her nipples were bare.

"I love you," he whispered.

Looking into his eyes now, she believed he meant it. He made her feel as if she were the center of his universe, more important, even, than breathing. She'd never imagined a man looking at her this way, never even thought it was possible.

"Oh, Zeke."

"I love you," he professed again, his voice husky with emotion. "I don't know how it happened. I only know it did."

She understood. Loving him had crept up on her, too. She wasn't sure exactly when. That first day, when he'd stood in her yard, boots spread and arms akimbo, his eyes flashing with anger? Or later when they'd stood in his driveway, nose to nose? Or maybe it had been when Chad had come to her, holding her grandma Westfield's earrings on his palm, his eyes beaming with pride because he'd been able to buy them back for her, compliments of Zeke Coulter.

"Oh, Zeke, I love you, too. I love you so much."

He slid his hands up her rib cage and unfastened her bra with a masterful flick of his fingertips. Natalie felt her fullness exposed, the elastic and lace springing away, only to be replaced by Zeke's warm, hard hands. He caught her nipples gently between his thumbs and fingers. One roll, and she gasped, arching up off the bed, totally lost to the sensation. He was there like a wall above her, his hardness encased in denim, his chest like white-hot fire against her bare skin, the coarseness of his chest hair abrading her nerve endings.

"Zeke!" she moaned breathlessly. "Kiss me there. *Please.*"

Zeke didn't want this to be over before it started. He wanted to make her reach heights that she'd never experienced. Instead of taking her breasts into his mouth, he trailed kisses around her aureoles, glorying in the fact that her nipples went rock hard. As she moved beneath him, feverish for what he wouldn't give her, he lightly flicked their throbbing tips with his tongue and shifted his weight to lie beside her. Using one hand, he trailed his fingertips in a featherlight path from her navel to her pelvis.

Hooking his thumb under the elastic of her panties, he jerked them and her dress down to below her knees with one motion. She lifted her hips to accommodate him, and with a swish, most of her clothing fell to the floor. Only her bra remained, still caught beneath her, the trailing ends winging out like parenthetic marks, drawing his gaze back to her generous breasts.

He couldn't resist those dark, erect nipples, which pleaded so sweetly for attention. He curled his tongue around one and gently teased the other with his fingers, glorying as she moaned in delight and jerked at every sensation. She began rotating her hips in unmistakable invitation. He met her thrusts with his hand, dipping a finger into the wet, slick heat of her. She gasped and froze, her lips parted in breathless anticipation. He laved her with moisture and lightly stroked her, watching her face as she climaxed.

Afterward she grasped his neck with a quivering arm and tugged him toward her. "I want you inside of me."

He was beyond resisting her any longer. He sprang from the bed, shed his clothes as fast as was humanly possible, and went to the bathroom where he'd left the condoms he'd bought. After taking care of matters, he returned to the bed. Bracing his arms to catch himself, he fell back over her and situated himself between her thighs.

As he pushed slowly into her, he almost lost it. She was so wet and warm and ready. *Dear God.* She felt good. A sudden tightness knotted his lower abdomen, and pain radiated out from there, snapping his whole body taut. He wanted to hold back, to make this last, but it was pure hell. Being sheathed in her hot, moist softness, feeling her muscles convulsing around him, he couldn't control the urges of his body any longer.

With rapid thrusts of his hips, he drove into her. She quickly learned his rhythm and met him, thrust for thrust, her legs locked around his thighs. *Faster and deeper.* He felt her body jerk slightly, and then her inner walls started to spasm. He went into overdrive, his groin exploding with sensation. She sobbed and held on to him, her breath coming in short, shallow gasps. They peaked together, a frenzied, desperate completion that left them both drained.

Afterward, he collapsed against her, trying to support his weight to keep from crushing her.

"Oh, Zeke," she said tremulously.

He rolled to one side and gathered her into his arms, kissing her hair, lightly stroking her damp skin.

"That was lovely," she whispered.

He tucked in his chin to narrow an eye at her. "Lovely, hell. That was fabulous, sweetheart."

She giggled weakly and placed a small hand over his pounding heart. Zeke turned his cheek against her hair, feeling sated and absolutely content. "Give me five, and we'll go again."

"Five minutes?" she asked incredulously.

"You got a problem with that?"

She nipped the underside of his jaw and turned to lie facing him, her breasts like firebrands where they touched his chest. Cupping a hand over his jaw, she smiled beatifically. "I'm so happy, Zeke. I never want this moment to end."

He kissed the tip of her elegant nose. "The moment will pass, but the feeling never will."

They rested then, limbs intertwined, heartbeats slowing to a more normal pace. He heard her stomach growl and opened one eye. "Sweetheart, are you hungry?"

"I usually have some yogurt when I get home. I passed tonight."

"Did you eat dinner at the club?"

"Good grief, no. I'd get fat if I did that every night."

He slapped her bottom. "Up."

"I thought we were going to make love again."

"Nourishment first, fun later. You worked your little tail off all day and put in a full shift tonight. I don't want you getting sick."

Zeke lent her a shirt, then led her to the kitchen. When she offered to help as he collected the ingredients for an omelet from the fridge, he handed her a wooden spoon, bent to kiss her, and said, "Sing to me."

"That wouldn't be a help."

"I don't want my teeth to bounce off these eggs."

She sighed in exasperation. "I'm not *that* bad a cook. Gramps was only teasing when he said that."

Zeke doubted it. "Sing me 'Forever and for Always,' " he coaxed.

She tapped her chin with the spoon and dimpled a cheek. "I'd feel silly."

Zeke began singing the words himself. That got her started, and once she got into the song, nature took over. She did what she'd been born to do while he manned the stove.

She looked so adorable, wearing nothing but his shirt, with her hair going every which way and her lips swollen from lovemaking, that he almost turned off the burner to carry her back to bed. He resisted the urge, wanting to get some food into her first.

Later, after she ate her omelet, they returned to the bedroom. The second time was even better than the first, in Zeke's estimation. He was able to go more slowly, savoring every sweet inch of her and bringing her to climax several times before he reached completion himself.

Afterward they slept for a while, clasped in each other's arms. Then he slipped from bed, threw on his clothes, gently nudged her awake, helped her to dress, and walked her home. Once at her back door, he kissed her good night, a long, lingering kiss filled with promise.

"Oh, Zeke, I don't want to go in."

One arm locked around her, he cupped his other hand over her bottom and swayed with her. "I know," he whispered. "I don't want to let you. But it'll be daylight soon. We don't want the kids to see you sneaking home."

She clung to his neck. "It's silly, I guess. But I feel like we'll only get this one night, that something will happen to ruin this for me."

Zeke tightened his arms around her. "No way, lady. We're going to have a million nights just like this one. That's a promise."

He kissed her forehead, released her, and backed away. "Go!" he called softly. "I want to see you safely inside."

She hurried up the steps. After opening the door, she turned to give him one last look, her heart shining in her eyes. With a saucy smile, she said, "Be sure to look in that drugstore sack before you throw it away."

"What's in there besides condoms?"

She giggled. "That's a question."

A feeling of warmth moved through Zeke. "You gave me one of your songs? I thought you had forgotten."

"When it comes to my music, I have a mind like a steel trap."

He smiled. "I can't wait to look it over."

"If you don't like it," she qualified, "it's no big deal. I'm not sensitive."

"Oh, I'll like it," he assured her.

She ran her gaze slowly over him. "Later, cowboy. I'm not finished with you yet."

Zeke was banking on it.

Chapter Eleven

The following morning, a frantic pounding on Natalie's bedroom door interrupted her sleep. She jerked erect, blinked bewilderedly, and came instantly awake, thinking that something was wrong with one of the kids. "Come in!"

The portal opened. Her kimono hanging crooked from her shoulders, the sash barely knotted, Valerie stood in the doorway. "The *cops,*" she croaked, her eyes as round as nickels. "They're at the front door, asking for you."

"Who?"

"The *cops*. Holy Moses, Nattie, what did you do?"

"I didn't do anything." Natalie grabbed her robe and finger combed her hair as she hurried downstairs with Valerie at her heels. "Don't be silly."

"They look grim," Valerie whispered. "Something's really wrong."

When Natalie entered the living room, she saw two police officers framed in the open doorway. Valerie had called it right. They stood on the front porch like navy bookends, not returning her smile as she moved toward them. She straightened her shoulders, trying to look innocent, which struck her as being the greatest absurdity of all. She hadn't done anything. Right? Then a horrible thought hit her. If Robert had noticed the missing goblets, he would know who took them. What if he had pressed charges against her?

"Good morning, Officers. My sister says you want to speak to me?"

One policeman flashed his credentials. "Are you Natalie Patterson?"

"Yes."

"Formerly Mrs. Robert Patterson?"

"Yes." Natalie didn't like the way the two men looked at her—as if she'd committed a heinous crime. "Did I forget to pay a parking ticket or something?"

"Something far more serious than that, I'm afraid," the tall, thin officer said. "Brace yourself for sad news. Mr. Patterson was found dead in his garage at around midnight. Can you get dressed and come down to the station with us for a while? We'd like to ask you a few questions."

All the blood rushed from Natalie's head, and black spots danced in front of her eyes. She heard Valerie bleat in horror behind her.

"What?" Her body going watery with shock, Natalie held up a hand. "Would you—" She gulped and grabbed for breath. "What did you say?"

"Mr. Patterson was found dead in his garage last night," the younger, stockier policeman repeated.

"Oh, my God," Natalie whispered. "Oh, my *God.*" She turned to see Chad standing behind Valerie in the archway. The boy had turned as white as milk.

"Mom?" Chad said, his voice quivering.

Natalie sent a smoldering look at the policemen. "You'll have to wait a few minutes. My son needs me."

"Mom?" Chad said again. "Dad's *dead*? How can he be dead?"

Natalie ran to catch her son in her arms. Over the top of his head, she met Valerie's gaze. "Call Mom. Tell her I need her to come as quickly as she can." As Valerie wheeled to run to the phone, Natalie began rocking her sobbing child. "It's okay, sweetie. I'm here. You're okay."

From that moment forward, Natalie felt trapped in a fog. Nothing seemed real. She couldn't make her brain function properly. This couldn't be happening.

Zeke had just poured a second cup of coffee when his phone jangled. He caught it on the third ring. A hysterical female voice came over the line. For a moment, he thought it was Natalie. Then he determined that it was her sister.

"Valerie, slow down. I can't make heads or tails of anything you're saying."

Valerie's breath hitched and spewed wetly into the receiver, nearly blasting out his eardrum. "Robert—is—*dead.* Is that slow enough for you? The cops are here, and they're taking Nattie away."

"What?"

"I think someone murdered the son of a bitch," Valerie whispered. "Oh, *God,* someone killed him, sure as shit, and they think Natalie did it."

Zeke slapped down the phone and left the house at a dead run. Moments later when he reached the Westfield yard, he saw that there was indeed a cop car parked in the drive. He circled around to let himself in the kitchen door.

"Not without a lawyer, she ain't answerin' no questions," Gramps was yelling. "You hear me, Nattie? Don't you say a word until you got an attorney present."

"Mr. Westfield," an unfamiliar male voice said calmly, "there's no need for Mrs. Patterson to have an attorney present. We only want to ask her some questions."

"That's what they always say!" Gramps cried. "Then they slap ya with charges, Nattie. Keep yer lips zipped."

Zeke followed the voices to the living room. Natalie stood just beyond the archway, holding Chad tightly against her. Her tousled black hair fell in a rippling veil over one of the boy's shoulders. Her face was drawn and pale, her eyes huge and dazed. If she saw Zeke, she gave no sign of it.

Valerie immediately came to him. When Zeke noticed how badly she was shaking, he curled a steadying arm around her waist. Valerie grabbed his other hand and dug in hard with her fingernails.

"Robert's really dead," she whispered. "They won't tell us anything. But it doesn't look good."

Zeke agreed. And Gramps was only making things worse. He released Valerie to enter the living room. With a pointed look at Pete, he grasped Natalie's grandfather by a frail elbow. "There's no need to get all upset, Charlie," Zeke cajoled. "Come in the kitchen. We'll have a cup of coffee. How does that sound?"

Rosie came bouncing down the stairs just then. The child came to a dead stop when she saw the two policemen. She turned questioning brown eyes on her mother. Zeke handed Gramps off to Pete and reached over the banister to pluck the little girl off her feet.

"Hi, gorgeous!" he said as he settled the child on his hip and followed the two older men to the kitchen. To drown out Gramps, who was making dire predictions about Natalie's fate if she didn't get a lawyer, Zeke spoke in a booming voice. "How's my favorite girl this morning?"

"I'm fine." Rosie looked back over his shoulder. "Why are those cops here?"

The child was too smart for her own good. "I think they want to talk to your mom for a little bit," Zeke replied.

"What about?" Rosie pressed. "Did she break the law?"

"No, of course not. I have no idea what they want to talk to her about," Zeke lied.

He yearned to stay with Natalie, but someone had to care for her daughter, and it seemed he was the only someone available. He went to the refrigerator and hauled out a pitcher of milk. Then he sat the little girl on the counter while he filled a glass for her. "What do you usually eat for breakfast, kiddo?"

"Cereal."

Zeke left her to sip the milk while he searched through the cupboards.

"What do they want to talk to my mommy about?" Rosie asked again.

"Well, now, I'm not sure." Zeke filled a small bowl with frosted flakes. "When your mom comes home, I bet she'll tell us."

"Where's she going?"

Zeke did his best to flash a broad smile. "I think she's going to go for a ride with them."

"In their cop car?"

"Yes."

Rosie's eyes gleamed with interest. "I want to go, too."

Zeke returned to the child and smoothed her black hair. "I don't think you're invited, sweetheart." He leaned down to get at her eye level. "Have you ever had a morning picnic outside?"

"No."

"You *haven't?*" Zeke lifted the child down from her perch, handed her the glass of milk, and gestured at the porch. "You don't know what you're missing. A morning picnic is more fun than a barrel full of monkeys."

"Won't I just eat?"

"Heck no. We'll do all kinds of exciting things."

Zeke's words proved to be prophetic. He'd no sooner parked his keister on the stoop than he heard Chester let loose with a war honk. Rosie's eyes widened with horror. Zeke leaped to his feet. He heard masculine cries of distress coming from the front yard, confirming his worst fears.

"Chester, no!" Rosie yelled.

Zeke knew from experience that remonstrative shouts wouldn't slow the gander down one iota. He'd just reached the front corner of the house when a police officer vaulted over the veranda rail, a flurry of white, honking feathers going airborne behind him.

With amazing speed, the cop raced for his car. Big problem. He stopped momentarily to wrest the door open, giving Chester opportunity to nail him on the ass. Zeke winced. The officer jumped, his shiny black shoes clearing the ground by at least a foot.

"Ouch!" he yelled. "Goddamned bird!"

The cop jerked off his hat and turned to swat at the gander. Chester was no faint heart, to be sent running by anything so insubstantial as a flapping hat. The bird hissed, extended his neck, and chomped the closest target, which just happened to be the fly of the police officer's pants. The poor man folded at the knees as if he'd been drop-kicked, hands cupped over his crotch, face buried in the grass. Luckily, Chester became momentarily distracted by the officer's hat rolling across the lawn.

Zeke flew into action to protect the fallen officer before Chester decided to press further assault. Unfortunately, before Zeke could reach the gander, the other cop came running out onto the grass to assist his partner. He had his hand on his firearm and murder in his eye.

"Don't shoot him," Zeke called. "He's a family pet."

"Pet, my ass. He attacked my partner!" the stocky fellow cried.

"I'll get him," Zeke promised, and then set himself to the task of doing just that, spreading his arms wide and racing in to do the "Dances with Ganders" thing again. He chased the blasted goose in circles around the yard for at least five minutes before finally getting him herded to the barn.

Zeke had been outside with Rosie for about thirty minutes when a blue Honda came bouncing up the gravel driveway and circled the police car to reach the back parking area. A raven-haired woman swung out. She was dressed in a skintight black leather skirt that rode well above her knees, a bright red knit top that showcased curves to knock a man's eyes out, and black heels that gave a whole new definition to the word spike. Zeke needed no introduction to know that this was Natalie's mother. She had the same sexy twist to her walk, the same flair with clothes, and almost the same face, except that hers had seen a little more wear.

When she entered the backyard, Rosie gave a delighted laugh and raced across the grass. "Grammy!" she cried. "You aren't doing hair today?"

"No, I'm taking the whole day off to be with you!" Naomi Patterson hooked her black purse over one arm and crouched down to catch the child in her arms. "How's my precious girl?"

"I've been better," Rosie replied in that tiny but very adult voice that had so astounded Zeke at first. "The policemen are here to see Mommy, and Chad is crying. I think something very unpleasant has happened."

So much for shielding the child. She seemed to know almost as much about what was occurring inside as Zeke did.

"Then, as if that weren't enough, Chester bit one of the policemen once on his butt and the next time in the very worst place."

Naomi's brown, heavily lined eyes widened in dismay. "Oh *no*. Is the policeman okay?"

"He's still walking sort of funny, but I think he'll be all right." Rosie sighed theatrically. "Chester almost got it good, though. The other policeman nearly shot him."

"Good grief! He's only a silly goose."

"Mr. Coulter saved him," Rosie went on. "And now we're having a morning picnic outside." Rosie scrunched her nose. "I don't think he wants me to hear what those policemen are saying to Mommy."

Naomi sent Zeke a worried look. Zeke guessed her to be in her mid-fifties, but even at close range, she was still a knockout with cameo-perfect features, beautiful brown eyes, and the body of a much younger woman.

Lifting Rosie to ride her hip, she managed to teeter across the uneven lawn with commendable grace. Zeke would have broken his neck on level ground trying to walk in those damned heels.

"Mr. Coulter." Juggling both the child and her purse, she held out a slender hand. "As I'm sure you've already gathered, I'm Naomi Westfield, Natalie's mother."

He clasped her delicate fingers. "Good to meet you, Mrs. Westfield. I'm sorry it's under these circumstances."

"Please, just call me Naomi." She kissed her granddaughter's curls and then handed the child back to Zeke. "I have to go inside, sweetie. You stay out here and finish your morning picnic. Okay?"

"My cereal's all gone," Rosie protested. "Why can't I go back in?"

Zeke tickled the little girl's ribs. "You promised to introduce me to Daisy and Marigold."

"Oh. I forgot." Rosie squirmed to get down. Then she grabbed Zeke's index finger to lead him to the barn. "We'll be right back, Grammy!" she called.

"Take your time," Naomi replied. "And whatever you do, don't let Chester out."

Never in Zeke's life had he lived through a longer day. After Naomi arrived, Natalie got dressed and left with the police officers. After her departure, Naomi gave Chad a Benadryl and hustled him up to bed. Within an hour, the boy had fallen into an exhausted sleep.

When Naomi came back downstairs, Zeke was sitting at the table, holding Rosie on his knee. Pop and Gramps sat across from him, the pair slumped over their coffee mugs, their faces haggard with worry.

"Valerie's sitting with Chad." Naomi stopped at the center of the room and put her hands on her shapely hips. To Pete and Charlie, she said, "Aren't you a sorry-looking pair?"

"Don't start with me," Pete growled.

"Better I should let you sit there, looking like death warmed over? Go wash up and shave, for heaven's sake. I can smell you from here, Pete, and I'm standing upwind."

Pete's blue eyes sparked with anger. "Don't come into my house and start ordering me around, woman."

"It's technically Natalie's house," she shot back. "Your mother left it to *her,* if you'll remember. And if you don't want to be ordered around, stop moping and do something productive."

"For Christ's sake!" Pete shot up from his chair with amazing agility for a man with a painful lower back. "Our daughter is—"

"Having a lovely time," Naomi cut in, casting a meaningful glance at Rosie. "It's not every day she gets to go for a ride in a police car." She smiled sweetly and fluttered her bejeweled hand at the doorway. "Run along, Pete. Get cleaned up while I fix you some breakfast." Naomi's gaze softened when she looked at Charlie. She came around the table to give the old man a hug. "Hi, Dad. Goodness, it's nice to see you."

Gramps twisted on the chair to return her embrace. "How's my favorite girl?" he asked.

"Fat and sassy," she said with a laugh.

"I can testify to the sassy part. You always gotta needle him. Don't ya?"

Naomi patted the old man's shoulder. "Of *course!* He'd think I was sick if I acted nice." She rasped her red acrylic nails over Gramps's bewhiskered jaw. "Go scrape that grizzle off your face, you ornery old codger, so I can give you a proper kiss. Breakfast will be waiting when you're done."

Gramps sighed resignedly and pushed back on the chair. "What're ya fixin' us?"

"I'll surprise you." Naomi ruffled Rosie's hair as she swept away. "Time to get dressed, little girl. Chop-chop. Breakfast will be done shortly."

"I already ate!" Rosie protested.

Naomi smiled as she donned an apron. "Oh, that's a crying shame! I'm going to make Easter-bunny flapjacks. You don't want any?"

Rosie was off Zeke's knee in a flash and running from the room. Naomi's smile faded after the child left. She turned a worried gaze on Zeke. "Robert either killed himself or was murdered," she said without preamble. "They found him out in the garage, dead in his 'Vette. He'd been asphyxiated."

"How did you learn that?"

"I called Grace Patterson on my way here. They rang her doorbell at three this morning and asked all kinds of questions. Who Robert's been dating. Who his last girlfriend was. If he had any enemies. If he and Natalie were still having problems."

"So they believe there was foul play?"

"Looks that way." Natalie took a mixing bowl from a shelf and began adding ingredients for flapjacks. After measuring in baking powder, she brushed off her hands and turned to look at him again. "Are you involved with my daughter?"

Zeke saw no point in denying it. "Yes."

"Do you love her?"

He nodded.

Naomi cut right to the chase. "I think she'd going to need a lawyer. How much money can you get your hands on? I've got only two grand. If a lawyer so much as farts, it costs more than that."

Moments later, Zeke was on the phone with his brother-in-law, Ryan Kendrick, asking if he knew of a good attorney. Ryan gave him the names of two, both of whom he highly recommended.

* * *

When Natalie reached the police station, she fully expected to be ushered into a gray room furnished with only a table and chairs. That was how it happened in the movies. Instead, a nice older detective named Monroe invited her into his office where she was comfortably seated. His desk was gray metal, but that was as close to her expectations as it came.

"Can I get you anything? Coffee? A breakfast pastry?"

Natalie was too upset to swallow anything solid. "Coffee, please. Black."

The pudgy detective brought her a steaming Styrofoam cup. Then he sat at his desk and rocked back on his chair, his gray head cocked slightly to one side as he studied her. She felt like a bug he was about to pluck legless.

"What happened to Robert?" she asked shakily. "The officers who brought me here weren't forthcoming with much information, only that he was found in the garage."

Detective Monroe nodded.

Natalie waited. When he said nothing more, she cried, "How did he die? Did he fall, have a coronary, what?"

"He was asphyxiated."

For a moment, Natalie couldn't think what that meant. Then it sank home with sickening clarity. "Asphyxiated?" she repeated stupidly. "How on earth did that happen?"

"He was found in his vehicle. The engine had been left running. The exhaust fumes killed him."

A picture popped into Natalie's mind of Robert slumped over the steering wheel with his face all pasty. Her head went dizzy. Her stomach lurched. She set the coffee on the corner of the detective's desk. "Sick. I'm going to be sick," was all she managed to say.

He sprang to his feet and shoved a wastebasket under her nose just as she vomited. "Oh, God," she rasped out, groping frantically with a hand. "Something—for—my—mouth."

He gave her some tissues. Shaking violently and gulping down her gorge, Natalie moaned and tried to apologize. The detective patted her shoulder. "Don't worry about it. The can's lined. Easy cleanup."

Natalie was still so embarrassed she wanted to crawl in a hole and hide. "I'm sorry, so sorry. Such a shock. Robert dead. I can't *believe* it. I just can't believe it."

The detective resumed his seat. "Keep the basket close. Sometimes it hits people this way."

Natalie nodded and tried to stop her hand from shaking so she could wipe her mouth. The taste on her tongue was so awful that her stomach rolled again. She sat for a moment with her head hanging over the trash receptacle, too weak to even consider finding a bathroom where she could be sick in private.

"I'm sorry," she said again. "Just—give me a second." A few minutes passed before she was recovered enough to talk. "I was sound asleep when the police came," she explained. *And dreaming the most fabulous dreams.* "The next thing I knew, they were telling me Robert was dead. It's a nightmare. My son, Chad, is devastated."

"I'm sorry the news has upset you and your family. Given the fact that you and Mr. Patterson were divorced, we assumed—" He rustled some papers and sighed. "I guess no one stopped to think that you might take it this hard."

Natalie sank back on the chair. She wanted Zeke. Needed him so badly that she ached. "Robert is, *was* the father of my children," she said. "My son didn't file for a divorce. I did."

"Point taken."

"Chad was in the room when I was informed of his death. The officers just—blurted it out in front of him. Of *course* I'm upset. Wouldn't you be?"

Detective Monroe ran a hand over his balding head. "Were you still in love with your husband, Mrs. Patterson?"

"Ex-husband," she corrected, "and, no, I wasn't in love with him. I hated his guts." Natalie no sooner spoke than she wanted to call back the words. If the police had reason to believe Robert was murdered, statements like that might get her arrested. "That isn't to say I ever wished something like this on him." Natalie pictured her blond ex-husband slumped over the wheel of his Corvette again and clamped a hand to her waist. "He was only forty-three," she said thinly. Then an even more awful thought struck her. "Oh, *God.* His *mother*. Does she even know yet?"

"Grace Patterson has been notified, yes."

Tears filled Natalie's eyes. That sounded so cold and impersonal. "Notified?"

"Shortly after the body was discovered, two officers went by her home to ask her a few questions."

Natalie envisioned Grace going through the same experience she had just gone through. "Questions? She's his *mother,* for heaven's sake. Robert was her only child, all she had left of her family. What's wrong with you people?"

Seeming not to hear her question, Monroe stroked his chin. "To your knowledge, did your ex-husband have any enemies, Mrs. Patterson?"

Natalie's pulse started to race. *Me,* she almost blurted out. Wariness turned her skin icy. She stared stupidly at the detective. "Can I take that to mean you think he was murdered?" When the detective didn't reply, Natalie asked,

"How do you know he didn't do it himself? That's a common way to commit suicide, isn't it?"

"Interesting that you should point that out. I believe that whoever killed your ex-husband went to a great deal of trouble to make it look like a suicide."

Oops. Natalie thought of Gramps and decided she might do well to follow his advice and keep her lips zipped.

As though he guessed her thoughts, Monroe smiled sourly. "I'll ask the questions, if you don't mind. You just do your best to answer them."

The air in the room suddenly seemed too thin. Natalie grabbed for breath, but her lungs wouldn't inflate properly. "Am I a suspect?"

The detective regarded her solemnly. "If my suspicions are proved correct, and there was indeed foul play, everyone who knew your ex-husband is presently a suspect." He arched a brow, his expression inquisitive. "Do you have reason to think Mr. Patterson might have killed himself? Was he depressed, having financial problems, jilted by a lover?"

"No, not that I'm aware of," Natalie replied. "Robert wasn't the type to get depressed." *He was too shallow.* "And if he'd been in financial trouble, his mother would have bailed him out. She's very wealthy."

"Back to my original question, then. Did he have enemies?"

"Of course he had enemies. Doesn't everyone?"

"Anyone who might have wanted him dead?"

"No." Natalie rubbed her aching forehead. "Possibly, I suppose. I haven't lived with him for over a year, Detective Monroe."

"Just answer the question to the best of your knowledge."

"Robert was very—ambitious." Greedy described it better, but Natalie was growing more guarded by the moment. "Sometimes he pulled fast ones in his business dealings. That didn't earn him many friends. He was also—" She ran a hand into her hair. "How can I say this? Inconstant in his personal relationships?"

"Inconstant. With women, you mean?"

Natalie nodded. "Lots of girlfriends. He was very polished and charming. Every woman he ever dated thought she was his one and only until someone new caught his eye. Hc didn't stay long in any one relationship, and he thought nothing of two-timing. Needless to say, the women involved were often bitterly angry when he dropped them."

"Is that why you divorced him, because he was stepping out on you?"

"That was part of it, a large part of it. In addition to that, he was a rotten father. I finally had enough and filed for divorce."

"Did you hate the man enough to kill him?"

Natalie tried to curl her hands over the arms of the chair but was shaking so badly her fingers wouldn't work. "I've never hated anyone enough to do murder, Detective Monroe. Divorcing the man suited my purposes well enough. He was out of my life. Why would I kill him?"

"No beefs?"

"Of course there were beefs."

"About?"

"He neglected our children—no phone calls, no visitations. He refused to pay child support. I was angry with him much of the time. That doesn't mean I wanted him dead."

The detective jotted something in a notebook. "Do you know the names of any of the women your husband dated?"

Natalie felt as if an ice pick were being shoved through

her sinuses and pressed a fingertip to her temple. "Bonnie Decker was his last girlfriend, but Robert's mother recently told me that he dropped her and was with someone new. A girl named Cheryl, I think."

"A girl? How old are these women?"

"Early twenties, I'd guess. I saw Bonnie only from a distance one time, but she looked young. Robert's friends are—*were*—always young."

The detective jotted more notes. Then he looked up at her, his eyes as sharp as knife blades. "When did you last see Robert Patterson?"

"Months ago. He and I didn't get along. That goes without saying, I suppose, or we wouldn't be divorced. Right?"

The detective nodded. "Where were you yesterday evening between five and eight?"

Burglarizing Robert's house and stealing my wineglasses back. A bubble of hysterical laughter tickled the back of her throat. She'd gone all over the ground floor of Robert's home, opening cupboards and china cabinets, looking for her goblets. Had Robert been in the garage, even then, dying of asphyxiation? *Oh, God. Oh, God.* That explained why his stereo had been left on.

The trembling of her body turned to violent shudders she couldn't control. She remembered hearing a door latch click as she was about to leave the house. Had the killer been in there with her?

"Mrs. Patterson, it's not a difficult question. Where were you between five and eight last night?"

She returned the detective's piercing regard for several endless seconds. "I'm sorry. Before I say any more, I'd like an attorney present."

Monroe sniffed and tossed his pen down on the desk. The

gesture conveyed his impatience. He rested his folded arms on the desk blotter, which had notes written all over it. "Here's the scoop, Mrs. Patterson. We believe your ex-husband was drugged and carried out to the garage by his killer." He glanced pointedly at her body. "I don't think you have the muscle for that." His mouth quirked. "Or the stomach for it, as far as that goes."

Natalie's lips felt numb. "Drugged, you say? What makes you think that?"

"Preliminary findings from the coroner. Along with high levels of alcohol in the bloodstream, there's evidence that Mr. Patterson had been given a strong sedative prior to death. The contents of his stomach back that up. We found no prescription bottles for sedatives or sleeping pills in the house to indicate that he might have taken the drug voluntarily."

Natalie's head felt light. "Robert wasn't a pill popper."

The detective watched her closely as he said, "Another strange thing. The alcohol Mr. Patterson consumed shortly before his death was wine. A rather expensive brand, judging by the bottle in the trash and a partially empty one we found in the library. Only there were no glasses sitting out. We believe the killer must have cleaned up afterward and put the goblets away."

He scratched his head. "Odd, that, don't you think? Patterson was no lightweight. I automatically lean toward thinking a man killed him. It would have been difficult for a woman to carry someone that large out to the garage and put him inside the car. On the other hand . . ." His voice trailed off. He picked up his pen and tapped it on the blotter. "A man would be more inclined to just wipe off the goblets to remove his fingerprints. A woman would be more likely to wash the glasses, dry them, and put them away."

The goblets hadn't been washed and put away. She had them on her dresser in a paper sack.

The detective pushed up from his chair, came around the desk, and grasped her elbow to help her stand. "Speaking of which, we'll need a set of your prints before you go. It'll take only a few minutes."

Her legs grew so weak with terror that she feared they might buckle.

Flashing a bright smile, she said, "Fingerprints? Sure. No problem."

Zeke went to pick Natalie up. When she emerged from the police station, she hesitated on the walkway, her face so white that her eyes looked like large dark smudges. Zeke climbed out of his truck, circled the front bumper, and called her name. Her gaze jerked to him. Then she moved forward robotically. He met her on the sidewalk.

"How'd it go?"

Instead of answering, she looped her arms around his waist and flattened her face against his chest. "Hold me," she said, her voice so muffled he strained to catch the words. "Just hold me."

Zeke complied, his gaze sweeping the station windows as he rested his cheek on her hair. "You okay?"

"No. I'm in big, *big* trouble."

Zeke guided her to the truck, got her deposited inside, and hurried around to climb under the steering wheel. "Sweetheart," he said in a reasoning voice, "no one in his right mind is going to believe you killed Robert."

She sent him a terrified look. "Oh, yes. You just don't *know.*"

"Okay, so tell me."

Zeke started the engine, shifted the truck into first, and pulled out into traffic, fully intending to drive her home. He hadn't quite reached the highway entrance when she finished telling her disjointed story about going to see Robert yesterday evening and searching his house to find her grandma Devereaux's wine goblets.

"Holy shit, Natalie. Your prints will be all over the place."

She nodded and mewled. "Even worse, I stole the evidence."

"Jesus."

Zeke pulled a U-turn, not caring if he got a traffic ticket.

"Where are you going?"

"To the attorney's office. You need legal counsel."

"But I need to be with my kids."

"To ensure that you are for the next twenty years, you need an attorney *now.*"

The next thing Natalie knew, she was sitting on the interrogation side of another desk, a mahogany one this time, being grilled by an attorney who could have passed for Gramps in a fancy suit and spectacles. To Sterling Johnson's credit, he never once said, "You did *what?*" He was obviously a criminal lawyer. Nothing Natalie said seemed to shock him.

When Natalie finally finished talking, Johnson interlaced his hands and gave her a piercing look. Zeke tightened his hold on her hand, trying to comfort her, she felt sure, but right then, not much could.

"They're going to find your fingerprints all over the house," the attorney said.

Zeke had paid him a five-hundred-dollar retainer to have him tell her that?

"Here's my advice," Johnson went on. "I think we should call Detective Monroe, go back to the police station, and make a clean breast of it. You technically did nothing criminal. Aside from stealing the crystal, of course, and even that is understandable, since it was yours in the first place. This is a classic case of being in the right place at the worst possible time. It happens. I think Monroe will appreciate your honesty, and your coming forward with the information may direct his attention toward someone else."

Natalie wasn't so sure. Sterling Johnson had never sat across from a suspicious detective and been asked if he'd hated his wife enough to kill her.

"I think he's right, sweetheart," Zeke said softly, squeezing her hand again. "Let's go see Monroe. You have a plausible reason for going to see Robert yesterday. Everything you did after ringing the doorbell makes perfect sense to me." He paused. "Well, sort of."

Natalie shot him a fearful look.

He tugged on his ear, his expression sheepish. "You have to admit, it was pretty dumb to go in uninvited." He held up a hand. "Understandable, though. And once inside, I can see why you took the goblets. If it all makes sense to me, it probably will to Monroe."

The trash can in Detective Monroe's office had been emptied since Natalie's last visit. That was the only improvement. The detective sat with his elbows propped on his desk blotter, his chin resting on his folded hands while he listened to Sterling Johnson give an account of Natalie's story. Every once in a while, Monroe's eyebrows wiggled, and he looked at Natalie wonderingly, making her feel like a nutcase who shouldn't be allowed loose on the streets.

When Johnson had finished talking, Detective Monroe sighed and passed a hand over his eyes. "I'm very glad you came in. We just matched your prints to about fifty sets our crime team lifted from the house."

Natalie's stomach dropped to somewhere around her ankles. "Yes, well, I had to look for a while to find my grandma's crystal."

"You heard nothing as you were going through the rooms?" He leafed through some papers, studied something for a moment, and said, "The kitchen is right off the garage. Are you saying that you stood at the sink, rinsed the two wine goblets, wrapped the entire set in kitchen towels, and never heard the sound of a car engine?"

"No."

"Do you know how a Corvette engine rumbles at idle?"

"No."

"Do you honestly expect me to believe you walked into a house during a murder in progress, searched every room on the ground floor, and saw *nothing* suspicious?"

Natalie gulped. "I, um—have you ever heard the saying that the truth is stranger than fiction?"

Monroe swore under his breath and rocked back on his caster chair. He leafed through his notes again. "No paperwork was on the desk."

Natalie sat more erect. "I'm sure there were papers on Robert's desk."

"Did you look closely at them?"

"No. Why would I? It wasn't my intention to snoop."

"But you went through all his cupboards and hutches."

"That was after I saw Grandma Devereaux's goblets and realized Robert had lied about having them." Natalie took a shaky breath. "There was one odd thing that happened."

"What?" Monroe asked, his eyes glinting with interest.

Natalie told him about hearing a door latch click as she was leaving. "I thought at the time that Robert might be hiding upstairs, trying to avoid me. Now—" Natalie's voice quivered and broke. "Now I wonder if someone was hiding in a closet or something."

Monroe excused himself for a moment. While he was gone, Sterling Johnson patted Natalie's shoulder. "You're fine," he assured her. "He believes you. I can tell."

"Really?"

The lawyer nodded. "Who would dream up a story like this?"

When Monroe returned, he said, "A car is being sent out to your home to pick up the wine goblets."

Natalie sent him a worried look. "Why do you need them?"

"To have them examined for prints and trace elements."

That seemed reasonable. Nevertheless, Natalie said, "I do hope the people in your lab will be *very* careful with them. Those goblets date back to the seventeen hundreds, straight from Bayel, a village in Basse Champagne on the banks of the Aube."

The detective pushed his eyeglasses up his nose. "To me, they're just evidence in a murder case."

Chapter Twelve

Before taking Natalie home, Zeke stopped by a diner to get something in her stomach. It was going on five o'clock. She'd been running on nothing but nerves all day. Once she reached the house, he knew she'd be too upset, trying to comfort her children and deal with her zany family, to think about food.

"I'm really not hungry," she insisted when he opened a menu and pushed it into her hands. "Maybe a glass of milk."

"Eat," Zeke ordered. "They serve breakfast all day. How about some poached eggs on toast?"

She peered at him over the menu. "Poached eggs when I'm a murder suspect?"

"Monroe just questioned you, honey. That doesn't mean you're a suspect." Zeke reached across the table to lay a hand over hers. The circles of exhaustion under her eyes worried him. "You need to calm down. Making yourself sick won't help the situation."

"What will help the situation? I left prints all over the place. I didn't hear the car running in the garage." Panic flared in her eyes. "If I were Monroe, I'd think I was guilty."

"I know you're scared, but try to look at it from his point

of view. First off, you don't have the necessary strength to carry a full-grown man out to the garage and stuff him in a car."

"I could do it if my adrenaline were up," she insisted.

"But a man could do it more easily," Zeke argued. "Secondly, the very fact that you left prints all over the house points to your innocence. You clearly weren't worried about leaving evidence behind. How many murderers do you think he's run across who made no attempt whatsoever to cover their tracks?"

Her shoulders relaxed slightly. "You're good for me. You know that?"

"I'm just pointing out the obvious. Monroe has to take evidence into account when he's working on a case. I won't argue the point. But he'll also go with his instincts. You obviously aren't a dim-witted woman. If you had killed Robert, would you have stolen a set of crystal while you were at it? It makes no sense that you'd commit cold-blooded murder, then go into Neiman Marcus mode before you left the house."

She sighed. "You're right. The case against me doesn't hold together very well when you look at it like that."

"Damn straight it doesn't, and if they're dumb enough to think it does, Johnson will rip it apart in court."

"Court?"

Zeke squeezed her hand. "Sweetheart, it'll never come to that. Where's your motive? Women don't kill men for back child support. That'd be tantamount to killing the goose that lays the golden egg. You had no plausible motive."

"Who did?" she asked in a hushed voice.

"Good question, one that we should probably be asking ourselves." Zeke studied his menu for a moment. "Maybe draw up a list of people who might have had reason to want Robert dead."

"Just the thought exhausts me. There are so many people who might have had it in for him." She laid her menu aside. "My mom, for instance."

Naomi Patterson had had murder in her eyes when she looked at Pete that morning, but Zeke didn't have her pegged as a killer. "Nah. Why would she have wanted Robert dead?"

"Mom *detested* him. I can't count the times she said she wanted to kill him."

"That's only a figure of speech."

"You don't know my mother. Robert hurt me a thousand times if he hurt me once. Mom is very protective of her kids and grandkids. And then there's Valerie. She once backed Robert against a wall with a fingernail file to his crotch."

Making a mental note never to cross her mother or sister, Zeke rested his elbow on the table and propped his chin on the heel of his hand. "As far as I know, Robert's manhood was still intact."

"You know what I'm saying."

He conceded the point with a nod. "I just don't think either of them has a violent streak."

"Neither do I. But they did have reason to hate my ex-husband. So did Pop. He threatened Robert with a shotgun after I got pregnant with Chad, and he never really forgave Robert for 'preying on his little girl,' as he so succinctly put it. Even Gramps got into it with Robert once. And that's not counting all the people Robert screwed in business deals. Or all the women he did dirty. Even his mother threatened his life the last time I saw her. I could draw up a list of at least twenty people who might have wanted Robert dead."

Zeke tossed his menu down on top of hers. "You're right. I guess there are a lot of people we could put on a list."

Natalie shivered. "And one of them did something about it."

Zeke searched her worried brown eyes. "Any educated guesses?"

"If it weren't for the strength issue, my first suspect would be Bonnie Decker, Robert's last girlfriend. I've never met her or anything, but if I know Robert, he led her on, making her think she was the love of his life. She was probably devastated when he dumped her. Most of them usually are." She unrolled the napkin from around her silverware. "I can't count the times a hysterical girl called the house, sometimes to talk to Robert, other times to plead with me."

"Plead with you? About what?"

"To let him go—to stop being unreasonable and give him a divorce." She began rubbing her temple as though it ached. "Robert wasn't very original. He told the same old clichéd story that adulterous men have been telling for centuries, that he was married to a heartless witch, miserably unhappy, and couldn't get a divorce. Some of the girls grew desperate when he dumped them, so desperate that they followed him around, or telephoned the house at all hours, or even lied, claiming to be pregnant so he'd go back to them. What's to say one of them didn't go completely off the deep end and murder him?"

Until that moment, Zeke hadn't really understood all that Natalie had been through during her marriage. He gave her fingers a squeeze, wishing that he could go back in time and rewrite the story of her life. Only then she might not be sitting across from him now.

"Exactly how young is Bonnie Decker?" he asked.

"Early twenties would be my guess."

"Wasn't Robert over forty?"

"Yes, but that never stopped him. Remember when I told you I thought he had an inferiority complex? One of the reasons I believe he preferred young girls is because they're easy to impress. Robert liked to play the big shot, and he needed the mindless adoration that only a young woman without much experience is likely to feel."

Zeke had known men like that, and he had little, if any, respect for them. He ran his thumb over her knuckles, vaguely aware as he did of how delicately she was made. "Did you hear what you just said?"

She gave him a questioning look. "That Robert liked to play the big shot?"

"And needed to be worshiped. It can't have taken you very long to realize that your prince was actually a toad. Has it ever occurred to you that the reason Robert repeatedly had affairs wasn't due to any physical flaws you may have had, but because you no longer mindlessly adored him?"

A tiny frown pleated her brows. "No. In the early years, I still thought I loved him, and he was having affairs even then."

"Ah, but love is different from adoration, Natalie. We can love someone in spite of his faults. Instead of love, maybe what Robert really needed was for you to make him feel like a god, and after the new wore off, you no longer did that. Think about it. He flitted from one young woman to the next. Isn't it possible he always bailed out because his lovers began to see the cracks in his veneer?"

A confused, incredulous expression entered her large, dark eyes. Then, as if an invisible hand moved over her face to alter her expression, her mouth softened, and her lips curved up at the corners in a tremulous smile. "Maybe so," she agreed. "Probably so. There were a lot of cracks in his veneer. It didn't take long for me to start seeing them."

"Exactly, and suddenly his interest in you palled. One moment he loved you—or at least you thought he did—and the next, he was with someone new. I can't even start to imagine how that must have hurt. If you suddenly stopped loving me tomorrow, I'd drive myself nuts wondering why, and I'd automatically assume it was something that I did—or failed to do. I can see how it could really mess with your mind."

"I got through it," she said faintly. "I had my family to support me, and I had my kids to love. If I'd had to go through it alone, heaven knows what I might have done. Sometimes I felt such rage." She ran the tip of her tongue over her bottom lip. "An unreasoning rage that led me to do things I never would have done otherwise. I once cut all of his silk boxers into ribbons with a pair of manicure scissors."

"Good for you."

She smiled. "Yeah, right. I was over the edge. When I remember doing that—when I recall the state my emotions were in at the time—I can easily imagine one of his girlfriends totally losing it."

"It could have been a jilted lover, but I'm more inclined to look at men."

"Chopin was playing on the stereo," she murmured.

Zeke didn't see how that pertained until she added, "Robert liked to play Chopin when he had sex. My first thought when I rang the doorbell and heard the music was that he was upstairs with his girlfriend. But when I went inside, no one was there, not Robert, not the girlfriend, *no one*.

At the time, I thought Robert was hiding somewhere in the house, pretending not to hear me. Only now I know that wasn't the case at all." She leaned closer. "So why was Chopin playing on the stereo?"

Zeke realized he was gripping her hand too hard and forced his fingers to relax. "Are you saying he only played Chopin when he had sex?"

"As far as I know, yes. That's why I keep coming back to the killer being a woman." She turned her wrist to curl her fingers around his. "What if Bonnie—or one of the others—came to the house to confront Robert and caught him with Cheryl, the new girlfriend? Maybe there was a scene. Robert might have asked Cheryl to leave for a while so he could calm Bonnie down. Maybe, after Cheryl left, Bonnie grew distraught and killed him."

Zeke shook his head. "Someone slipped a sedative into his wine. You have to plan ahead to pull something like that off."

"Maybe Bonnie or one of the others went there, intending to kill him. She could have deliberately caused a scene to get Cheryl out of there."

"Did you mention any of this to Monroe?"

"No. I was afraid to start pointing the finger at anyone. That's what guilty people do."

Zeke chuckled even though the subject under discussion wasn't humorous. "You need to stop worrying about stuff like that and give the man all the information you can. On the surface, the type of music playing in the house doesn't seem important, but if it's true that Robert only played Chopin when he had sex, it could be extremely important."

The waitress came to take their order. Zeke asked for poached eggs on toast. Natalie ordered a three-egg omelet.

She blushed when Zeke looked questioningly at her. "I'm feeling a little better."

"Good. You need to eat."

"I'll skip lunch tomorrow to make up for it."

"Over my dead body."

"Don't *say* that. It gives me cold chills."

It was just turning dusk when Zeke parked the Dodge truck in his driveway. Natalie sat huddled against the passenger door, her face still pale, her eyes still haunted. After cutting the engine and releasing his safety restraint, Zeke turned to cup a hand over her shoulder.

"You going to be okay?"

A tiny muscle under her eye twitched. "Yes. I just wish—"

"What?" he asked.

"I just wish you could come home with me."

Zeke rasped his fingertips lightly over her blouse, acutely conscious of how small and delicate her bones felt under the layer of cotton. "I wish I could, too, sweetheart."

She reached up to lay her hand over his. It was unnecessary for either of them to say more. Her children had lost their father. Chad, especially, was going to need her undivided attention tonight and possibly for several days to come.

"If there's anything I can do, I'll be a phone call away."

She unbuckled her seat belt and reached for the door latch, her movements jerky. As she pushed the door open, she turned to look at him. Then, without warning, she launched herself into his arms, the tension in her body conveying a desperation and need that made his heart hurt for her.

"It's going to be okay," he whispered against her hair. "Everything, all of it. You'll see."

She nodded, her arms still locked around his neck. "I wish I could sneak over after the kids are asleep, but they might wake up and need me."

Zeke ran his hand slowly up her spine. "Maybe I'll pay you a surprise visit instead. How would that be?"

"Fabulous," she murmured.

"Which window's yours? I don't want to surprise the wrong person."

She answered his question, then sat back and smiled. "Up the drainpipe and through my window? I'm afraid you'll break your neck."

Zeke trailed the pad of his thumb lightly over her cheek. "Not to worry. I became an accomplished second-story man as a teenager."

"You sneaked into a girlfriend's house?"

He grinned and kissed the tip of her nose. "No, I sneaked out of my own."

She laughed. "Is that what lies in store for me when Chad becomes a teenager?"

"Probably. Not to worry, though. I'll know what he's going to do before he thinks of it and head him off at the pass."

Her mouth curved into a wondering smile. "Say that again."

"Say what again?"

"That you'll still be with me when Chad becomes a teenager."

He bent his head to kiss her, a sweet, lingering kiss devoid of passion, yet full of promise. "Count on it, Nattie girl."

* * *

When Natalie got home a few minutes later, her mother was in the kitchen, cooking dinner. The smell of simmering beef and onions wafted warmly on the air. Naomi had kicked off her heels, wore a faded bib apron over her skirt and top, and had her hair pulled back in a ponytail. The scene was so reminiscent of days gone by that Natalie rested her back against the door for a moment, memories of her childhood and happier times moving through her like a caress. The worn speckled linoleum, the scarred gray table, the nicked white cupboards, the ugly green countertop—over the years, this room had never changed. Natalie couldn't count the times as a child that she'd walked into the kitchen and found her mother cooking in her bare feet, wearing an apron similar to the one she wore now.

"You're here!" Naomi cried when she saw her daughter. She wiped her hands and hurried across the kitchen to give Natalie a hard hug. "I've been so worried! How did it go?"

Natalie returned her mother's embrace. "It went. That's all I can say."

"The police were here. They asked to go upstairs and get something from your room. Charlie pitched a holy fit and wouldn't let them inside the house until they had a search warrant."

"Oh, no. Did they go get one?"

"Yes. They weren't upstairs for long. They left with a paper sack full of stuff."

Natalie drew back to look into her mother's eyes. "It's okay, Mom. I knew they were coming out to get the bag."

"What was in it?"

"Grandma Devereaux's crystal."

"What? I thought it was lost in storage."

As briefly as possible, Natalie told her mother about her

visit to Robert's house the previous evening. During the recounting, Naomi's face drained of color. "Oh, dear God. You were in the house at the time of the murder?"

"They estimate time of death between five and eight. I stopped by on my way to the club, sometime around six thirty."

"Oh, my *God.*"

Natalie put her pursc on top of the refrigerator, an ancient Frigidaire gone yellow with age that her father continually repaired. "That's why I'm so late. Zeke took me to see a lawyer, a man named Sterling Johnson who looks like a corpse propped up in a chair. He insisted that I return to the station and make a clean breast of it." Natalie went on to recount the rest of the story. "For better or worse, Detective Monroe knows everything now."

"He didn't press charges. That's a positive sign."

"Yeah. Now it's a wait-and-see game."

Naomi bussed Natalie's cheek. "I called the club. Frank says he'll manage without you tonight and not to worry."

Thc club. Natalie hadn't given it a thought all day. In a twinkling, all her money worries came crashing back over her. She sighed and rubbed the back of her neck. "Where are the kids?"

"Rosie's watching a movie Valerie rented for her. Chad's upstairs."

"How are they doing?" Natalie asked.

"Rosie's great. When I told her the news, it was almost as if we were talking about a stranger."

"And Chad?"

"He's not handling it as well. I gave him a Benadryl this morning, and he slept for several hours. Now he's just lying on the bed, staring at the ceiling."

"Thanks for being here, Mom. I worried less, knowing you were here with them." Natalie patted her mother's shoulder. "I better go up to see him."

"When supper's done, I'll fix him a plate and bring it up."

"That'll be great." At the archway, Natalie turned back. "How's it going with you and Pop?"

Naomi rolled her eyes. "Don't ask."

After giving Rosie a hug and telling her all about the ride in a police car, Natalie went upstairs to Chad's room, one of two small gable bedrooms at each end of the second floor. Both rooms had been used for storage until Natalie moved home with the kids. Now all the boxes had been moved to an outbuilding, and the rooms were being used as sleeping quarters. Natalie had done her best with a limited amount of money to personalize the rooms for her children, but they were still sadly lacking compared to the rooms they'd had while living with their father.

When Natalie opened the door, Chad didn't stir. He just stared sightlessly at the sharply sloped ceiling as if he hadn't heard her. His twin-sized bed was unmade, the spread, blanket, and sheet rumpled beneath him. Natalie quietly closed the door behind her.

"Hey, big guy. I'm home."

Chad didn't move. Natalie walked slowly to the bed, her sneakers making funny squeaky sounds on the hardwood floor. As she sat on the edge of the mattress, Chad squeezed his eyes closed. He lay with his arms at his sides, his hands knotted into fists. When Natalie touched him, his body was rigid.

"Oh, sweetie."

Chad swallowed convulsively. "I thought maybe—you'd never come back. That they'd k-keep you in jail or something."

Natalie smoothed his honey-brown hair from his forehead and bent to kiss his cheek. "Why on earth would they put me in jail? I've done nothing wrong."

Chad lifted his lashes. The pain in his eyes made Natalie want to weep. "I was just afraid. They aren't going to put you in jail, are they, Mom? Me and Rosie, we'd be all alone."

Natalie straightened away. Her first impulse was to pretend Chad's fears were groundless. But that wouldn't have been completely true, and she wasn't going to lie to him. "No matter what happens, Chad, you and Rosie will never be left alone." She tipped her head to listen to the sounds coming from downstairs. Then she smiled. "Hear that?"

Chad listened for a second. Naomi was griping at Pete about something, and he was rumbling back. Between exchanges, Valerie's and Gramps's voices rang out faintly.

"That's your family," Natalie said softly. "They're all a little crazy—no argument from me about that. But you know what?"

Chad shook his head.

"They're like the old wallpaper that was on the walls in here. Remember earlier this summer, how I peeled and sanded, trying to get all of it off?"

Chad nodded.

"I finally ended up having to texture over it before I painted the room. The darned stuff wouldn't come off, no matter what. All those people downstairs are like that, stuck to you with so much glue that you'll never pry them loose.

That's what family is, people who'll always be there for you, no matter what."

"Dad's really and truly dead, isn't he?"

Natalie's heart squeezed. "I'm afraid so."

"And someone killed him?"

"The police think so."

"Why would someone do that, Mom?"

Natalie remembered her conversation with Zeke at the diner and stared at the worn floor planks. "All I can do is guess, Chad," she said honestly. "I don't really know."

"Somebody would've had to hate Dad a lot to kill him."

"Yes." No man could live as Robert had without making some dangerous enemies. "But let's not focus on that."

Chad's face crumpled, and he turned to hide his face against his pillow. In a muffled voice, he said, "I wanted to make him proud of me. Now, if I ever get real good at sports and stuff, he'll never know."

Natalie lay down beside her son and gathered him close. He resisted for a moment, but then he clamped his arms around her neck and clung to her almost desperately.

"I'm already proud of you," she whispered. "I'm not your dad, and I understand that it's not exactly the same. But I am so very proud of you, Chad. I always have been, and I always will be. Just you remember that."

Natalie felt totally drained by the time Chad drifted back to sleep and she carried his empty supper plate downstairs. She found her family gathered in the kitchen. Naomi had baked sugar cookies, and Valerie was helping Rosie decorate them. Pop and Gramps were snitching the cookies almost as fast as Rosie could get them frosted and sprinkled.

Natalie smiled and leaned a shoulder against the kitchen

archway, her heart swelling with love and more gratitude than she'd ever be able to express with words. What she'd told Chad was true; these people were far from perfect, but they stuck like old wallpaper. Even Pop and Mom were doing their best to tolerate each other.

"This one's Grammy," Rosie said, scrunching her face as she pushed on the handle of the icing tube. "I'm going to make her *very* beautiful."

Pete sent Naomi a long look. "Better put her in a short black skirt and tight sweater, then."

"Eat your heart out," Naomi purred. Then she arched her ebony brows, smiled sweetly, and said, "Absolutely, Rosebud. No grandma clothes for me. When you do Poppy, put him in holey overalls and give him gray whiskers."

Natalie's gaze shifted to her father, who was freshly shaved and in rare form, wearing a clean pinstripe oxford shirt and black Wrangler jeans. It was a bit of a shock for Natalie to realize that her father was still a handsome man when he cleaned up. She wondered what the occasion was and glanced at Valerie, who winked conspiratorially.

Gramps harrumphed and said, "Why don't the two of ya just step outside and settle yer differences? I get damned tired of hearin' ya go on at each other."

"No way, Charlie. I might hurt him." Naomi stepped to a cupboard. Natalie felt fairly sure her mother stretched higher than was necessary to show off her legs as she fetched a wineglass from the top shelf. "I'm having some burgundy. Anyone else care to join me?"

"You can't have wine, Naomi," Pete said. "You have to drive home."

"I'm staying the night. Did I forget to mention that?"

Pete's eyebrows shot up. "You're what?"

Naomi dimpled her cheek in a saucy grin. "You heard me. I took the week off so I can be here to help Natalie."

Pete looked as if he'd just swallowed an ice cube. "You ever think to ask the man of the house if you're welcome?"

"Am I welcome here, Charlie?" Naomi asked her ex-father-in-law.

"Are as far as I'm concerned," Gramps replied. "Just go easy on my wine. Dad-blamed girls already raided my stash this week. I got only that one gallon."

Pete's face had gone almost as red as the burgundy. He pushed up from his chair and stalked outside, slamming the kitchen door behind him with a wall-shuddering *thwack.* Natalie was accustomed to her parents' sparring, so she took the tiff in stride. What amazed her was that her dad had just crossed the kitchen without hunching over and holding the small of his back.

Naomi scraped her bright red thumbnail over the outside of a goblet. "This is disgusting. How long has it been since someone used these wineglasses?" She stepped to the sink to run some water. "I swear, there's ten years of scum on this thing."

Valerie glanced up from the cookie that Rosie was frosting. "Nattie and I used juice glasses for our wine the other night. Why wash them if we aren't going to drink from them?"

"This place needs a good cleaning," Naomi grumped. "I can't believe that man lives like this."

From outside, Pop yelled, "You don't like the accommodations, feel free to leave anytime."

Naomi chuckled and called back, "I'll just muck out a corner and take my chances, thanks."

Pete grumbled indistinguishably, a sure sign that he was

cussing a blue streak under his breath so Rosie wouldn't hear. Natalie made her way across the kitchen to get another goblet. "Give this one a scrub while you're at it, Mom. I'll join you in self-defense. Can't you and Pop do *one* evening without being unpleasant? I don't need the added stress right now, and neither do the kids."

Naomi's smile faded. "I'm sorry. You're right. Bad timing. I'll go out and apologize."

"Don't bother," Pop yelled through the door. More muttering followed.

Naomi called back, "If you want to exchange insults with me, you washed-up old fart, come back in here and say it to my face."

Natalie grabbed the wet goblet from her mother's hands. "Better idea. *You* go outside. The two of you can fight to your heart's content that way, without subjecting the rest of us to your childish exchanges."

Naomi grabbed the goblet back and filled it to the brim with wine. "With a mouth like that, little girl, you can wash your own glass."

With the scent of Calvin Klein's Obsession trailing behind her, Naomi left the kitchen to join her ex-husband on the porch. Within seconds, she and Pete were engaged in a heated argument. Natalie sent Valerie a hopeless look.

Gramps shook his white head. "Damn foolish nonsense. Why don't he just say he's sorry, kiss the woman, and be done with it?"

Natalie and Valerie riveted their gazes to their grandfather and simultaneously asked, "Sorry for what?"

"For bein' a jealous idiot. That girl out there ain't never looked crosswise at another man. He was out of his everlovin' mind for thinkin' she did, and he should've ate crow ten years ago. Stubborn, that's what. Damn Westfield pride's gonna be the death of him."

Valerie's eyebrows lifted toward her hairline. "Pop thought Mom had a thing for some other guy?"

Gramps settled a disgruntled frown on Rosie. "Worse'n that. Got it in his head she was doin' the backseat tango after she left the shop every night."

Rosie glanced up from the cookie she was decorating. "What's the backseat tango?"

Gramps's neck went ruddy red. "Just never you mind, Rosebud."

Natalie sank wearily onto a chair and took a huge swallow of wine. "So that was it."

"No wonder everything was fine one day and over the next," Valerie mused. Then she frowned. "How could Pop think that of Mom?"

"Green monster ridin' his shoulder. Wasn't thinkin', period. She'd just finished hairdressing school and started to work, makin' her own money for the first time in their marriage. She went a little wild at first, buyin' herself pretty clothes and fixin' up. She took to comin' home late 'cause she had ladies who came in to get their hair or nails done after they got off work. Yer dad got it in his head that she was triflin' on him." Gramps glanced at the back door. "Now he's too damn proud and stubborn to admit he was wrong for the things he said and done, and she rubs his nose in it every time she sees him. They need their heads knocked together, that's what."

Natalie listened to her parents' voices for a moment, then took another sip of wine. *Not tonight,* she wanted to yell at them. As if they'd hear her. They were so intent on fighting that Natalie doubted she could get their attention if she fired the shotgun over their heads. Her stomach knotted. With every hateful word her parents uttered, her nerves drew tighter.

Finally, when she could bear it no longer, she marched to the back door, jerked it open, and cried, "Enough!"

Sitting side by side on the step, Pete and Naomi swiveled their heads to stare at her, shocked into silence by the fury in her voice.

"Not another word," Natalie said. "If you have so little consideration for me after the day I've been through, then at least have some consideration for your grandson. He needs you to be strong and united right now. Do you think he doesn't realize that I may be arrested?"

"Ah, honey," Pete said. "We're just going on. We don't mean anything."

"Well, I've had it up to my eyebrows," Natalie cried. "My kids lost their father today, in case you've forgotten."

Light from the kitchen bathed Pete's and Naomi's faces. Both of them looked ashamed. Natalie didn't realize that Rosie had joined her in the doorway until the child piped in with, "Grammy never did the backseat tango with anybody, Poppy. You should just say you're sorry, then kiss her and make up. Gramps says the Westfield pride is going to be the death of you. I don't want you to die."

Natalie's parents called a temporary truce for the remainder of the evening, but no apologies were extended by either of them. Pop went off to bed. Gramps adjourned to his living room recliner to snore while he supposedly watched CNN. Naomi remained in the kitchen, pretending, for Rosie's sake, that the quarrel with Pete had never occurred.

After getting her daughter to bed an hour later, Natalie

felt as if her spine had turned to Jell-O. She sat slumped on a kitchen chair, so exhausted that just the thought of climbing the stairs again nearly overwhelmed her. "Where are you going to sleep tonight, Mom?" she asked sleepily.

Naomi glanced at the ceiling. "With my favorite granddaughter. She's so small, the twin-sized bed will do for both of us." She reached over to smooth Natalie's hair from her brow. "Ah, sweetie, I'm sorry you've had such a bad day. You look as if you've been flattened by a train. Leave it to me and your father to make matters worse by getting into a fight. I don't know what comes over me around that man."

Valerie rocked back on her chair. "You're still crazy about him. That's the problem. When you're around him, your brain takes a hike."

Naomi puffed up like a little toad on a lily pad. "I am not crazy about him."

"Give it up." Valerie took a sip of wine. "Nattie and I both know you're lying, that you never stopped loving him. We just didn't know why you left him until tonight."

"Charlie has a big mouth."

Natalie yawned and patted her lips. "It's not as if we're children, Mom. What's the big deal? You can't talk to us honestly about our own father?"

Naomi glanced uneasily over her shoulder. "He might hear me."

"He went to bed," Valerie replied. "And I think we deserve an explanation. Our family got destroyed. You and Pop used to be so—well, perfect together, and all of a sudden, you left him. I didn't get it then, and I don't get it now. How could you throw away all those years of marriage over a silly misunderstanding?"

Naomi's cheeks went pink with indignation. "He said

horrible things—called me filthy names. I'd never been with anyone else, never even entertained the notion. There's only been one man for me in my entire life."

"Jeez, that sucks."

"Valerie Lynn!" Naomi looked at Natalie. "Where did she come from?"

Valerie peeled her hair back from her forehead. "Recognize this mug, Mom? I'm you all over again."

"I was referring to that smart mouth of yours."

"Like you don't have one?" Valerie darted another look at Natalie. "You heard her ripping on Pop tonight. Does she, or does she not, have a smart mouth?"

Natalie stifled another yawn. " 'Fraid so, Mom. No offense intended, but you aren't exactly reticent."

Naomi played with the sugar shaker. After licking granules from her dampened fingertip, she flashed the dimple in her cheek and fluttered her long eyelashes. "Well, I swan, I just don't know what y'all are talkin' about."

"Buh-ruther," Valerie said with a groan. "It's a lost cause, Nattie. Let them be miserable for the rest of their lives." She took another swig of wine. "It's your funeral, Mom. So what if he was a jerk? He was a good, faithful, loving husband for, what, twenty-two years? I can't believe you left him because he had a brain fart. Didn't he have one screwup coming to him?"

Naomi's eyes went shiny with tears. "A screwup, yes. He had a dozen coming, as far as that goes. But he has yet to say he's sorry for all the things he said to me. And, excuse me, little Miss Know It All, after twenty-two years of being a loyal and faithful wife, I didn't deserve that from him!"

Naomi shot to her feet. Valerie rocked forward so suddenly that the chair legs struck the linoleum with a loud *whop*. From the downstairs master bedroom, Pop yelled, "Quiet it down out there! Damn fool women, getting drunk and raisin' sand. Go to bed, why don't you?"

"Mom, I'm sorry," Valerie tried.

Naomi waved her hand as though erasing a chalkboard. "Take his side. See if I care. I will *never* forgive him for the things he said until he gets down on his knees and *begs* me. And even then I'll have to think about it!"

Chapter Thirteen

Natalie thought she would fall asleep the moment her head hit the pillow, but instead she followed Chad's example and stared at the ceiling, her mind racing with concerns about the supper club, her chest aching with sadness for her son. Given her mom and dad's behavior, how could she fault Chad for being terrified at the thought of being left parentless? In her heart of hearts, Natalie knew her folks would always be there for her kids, no matter what. But it might be a rough road to adulthood for Chad and Rosie, with Pete and Naomi acting like such idiots.

What if she did end up in jail? Natalie wondered. She wasn't really afraid for herself. She'd survive, no matter what. But her children needed her. How could she possibly go to sleep while their future lay in the hands of Detective Monroe and his gut instincts?

A thumping sound brought Natalie upright in bed. Her first thought was that one of the kids had rolled off the mattress onto the floor, and she expected to hear a muffled wail. But then she heard another whisper of noise that jerked her gaze to the window. She saw the hulking black silhouette of a man coming through the opening. For an awful instant, she thought it was a burglar. Then she remembered the handsome second-story man next door, and her heart lifted with gladness.

"Zeke?" she said softly.

A raspy laugh, so faint she could scarcely hear it, drifted to her. "Who else are you expecting, the mailman?"

Natalie was so pleased to see him that she just opened her arms. He tiptoed across the room in his bare feet, put one denim-clad knee on her mattress, and caught her close to his wide chest. His arms locked around her, muscle and tendon tightening to a relentless hardness that made her feel indescribably safe. One of his big, work-roughened hands splayed over her back, the tip of his thumb nudging her shoulder blade, his pinky extending well below her bottom rib. When he shifted, he drew her along with him, seeming to expend no effort to lift her.

She pressed her face against his neck, loving the smell of him, a masculine blend of denim, leather, woodsy cologne, and another underlying scent that was exclusively masculine, a light muskiness that made her want to melt and be absorbed by him.

"Oh, Zeke, I didn't expect you to actually come."

His silken lips traced the shape of her ear. "Of course I came. Nothing could have kept me away."

Coming from someone else, that avowal might have been meaningless, but Natalie sensed that Zeke meant it from the bottom of his heart. She'd needed him, so he had come. It was a simple thing—yet so beautiful it brought tears to her eyes. Robert had never been there for her, and over the years she'd come to believe that no man ever would be. Now, suddenly and inexplicably, she had Zeke.

"This has been the longest night on record," he whispered.

"I can't *believe* you climbed up the drainpipe."

His warm mouth did incredible things to the sensitive hollow beneath her ear. "Drainpipe, hell. It'd never hold my weight."

"How'd you get up here, then?"

"My secret."

He fell back against the pillows with her clasped in his arms. A big hand settled over her head, and he applied pressure to nestle her cheek on the hollow of his shoulder. Then he tugged up the blankets to cover her.

"I love you. All evening long, I've been trying to remember if I thought to tell you that today."

"Say it again," she whispered.

He brushed his lips over her hair. "I love you, Nattie girl. I love you so much my bones ache."

He felt so wonderful, so big and solid and *durable*. Natalie trailed her fingers over his hair, testing its thickness, loving the slightly coarse texture of the strands. At his nape, springy tufts tickled her fingertips. She ran her thumb down his neck, tracing the cords of muscle that bracketed his throat. Warm to the touch, his skin reminded her of silk when she ran her hand against the grain.

She sighed and closed her eyes, content to just lie there and let him hold her.

"How are you bearing up?" he finally asked.

"Fair, I guess. Just feeling stressed out and worried."

"Worried about what?"

"How long have you got?"

She felt his mouth curve into a smile. "Forever."

She liked the sound of that. *Forever*. It helped immensely, knowing that she'd never face life alone again. "I'm worried about the club, for starters. On the surface, it seems peripheral, I know. But it is paying my bills. Business will fall off if I'm not there, but I can't see my way clear to leave the kids tomorrow night."

He toyed with a curl at her temple. "Maybe we should put the downtime to good use."

"How?"

"Close the doors for a few nights while I rip that damned wall out. I can get my brothers to help me. Get some advertising started. Get a karaoke machine brought in. When you can go back, the place will have had a face-lift, and your time spent at home won't be wasted. You'll have to close the doors during renovations, anyway."

"You'd do that?"

"Give me the go-ahead, and it's as good as done."

"But the money."

"Don't go there. We'll discuss the financial aspects later. I'll stop by in the morning for your keys."

It was amazingly easy to snuggle deeper into his arms and leave it at that. He stroked her hair, his touch soothing the knots of tension from her muscles and making her feel deliciously languorous.

"How'd it go with the kids tonight?"

"Awful. Chad is having a terrible time. And my parents acted like total idiots."

"How's that?"

Natalie related the events that had occurred in the kitchen. "It's so *stupid*. How can two people who love each other so much throw it all away over a misunderstanding? No wonder Chad is feeling so insecure."

"Insecure?" he echoed.

Natalie told him about the conversation with her son. "I assured him that he and Rosie will never be left alone, no matter what may happen to me, but I can see why he worries. My parents aren't exactly the epitome of love's unshakable devotion."

"I'll talk to him," Zeke whispered.

"About what?"

"About never being alone. I'm going to marry his mother. That isn't a worry."

Natalie stiffened. As deeply as she yearned to spend the rest of her life with this man, she wasn't sure now was a good time to broach the subject to Chad. "Oh, Zeke, he just lost his father. Maybe we should keep our relationship under our hats for a while."

"Trust me," he said huskily. "I won't upset him. Don't worry about that. Okay?"

If any other man had told her that, Natalie might have argued. But Zeke had a wonderful way with kids. He seemed to understand Chad in a way even she couldn't. If anyone could talk with her son about the future without upsetting him, it had to be this man.

Natalie lifted her head. "Excuse me, sir, but I don't recall your asking me to marry you."

"Can't."

That wasn't the answer she expected. "What?"

"Can't ask. Not yet. I have to ask your son for your hand first."

"What?"

"He takes precedence over your father," Zeke said matter-of-factly. "I have to ask him for your hand. If he says yes, we're home free."

"That's archaic. Men don't ask for a woman's hand anymore."

"This man does."

"But what if Chad says no?"

"Then we're sunk."

"What?"

He chuckled and kissed her temple. "He won't say no. And it's important for him to feel he's got a vote. Just trust me, all right?"

She trusted him. She'd never thought to trust anyone so completely again. She sought his mouth with hers. They shared another soft, incredibly gentle kiss that worked on her nerves like a balm. She hitched herself higher. As exhausted as she was, she knew he hadn't scaled the roof of a two-story house to take a snooze in her bed.

When she kissed him again, more deeply this time, he made a hard fist in her hair and said, "Not tonight, sweetheart. I have a headache."

Natalie almost strangled on hysterical laughter and weakly punched his shoulder. His chest jerked on a silent chuckle.

"Sleep," he rumbled near her ear. "You need to rest. I just want to be with you."

Natalie couldn't just blink out with six feet plus of sexy cowboy stretched out atop her coverlet. After three years without lovemaking, it would be a shameful waste. "I want you," she whispered.

"No," he replied. "That isn't why I came."

She tightened her arms around his neck and kissed him again. When she drew up for air, she said, "Changed your mind yet?"

"No. You've been through one hell of a day. No expectations. I just want to be with you." In the moonlight, she saw his eyes warm with a smile that didn't touch his mouth. He lightly ran his fingers over her cheek. "Here's some news to distract you. I looked your song over, and I absolutely love it." He softly hummed part of the tune and whispered a few of the words. "The lyrics are fabulous."

Natalie leaned her head back to stare at him in surprised wonder. "You can read musical notes?"

"What? Do you think you're the only musician on earth? I can't write lyrics or create my own tunes, but I do play a fiddle. I'm damned good, too, if I do say so myself. I played all the music at my sister, Bethany's, wedding."

"How fun. Someday we'll have to jam together."

"It's a date," he promised. "Although you may be too busy and have to stand me up. It truly is a fabulous song, Nattie. Snappy and catchy. I know it'll sell if I can find an agent to shop it around."

"How will you find an agent?"

"The same way writers and actors do. Agents are listed in publications. If our local library is a dead end, I'll get on the Internet and find you one."

"The trick will be in finding one who'll bother with my work."

He grinned and kissed the tip of her nose. "Piece of cake. Any agent who won't jump at the chance doesn't know pure gold when he sees it."

"Oh, Zeke."

Knowing that he believed in her enough to try to find her an agent touched Natalie deeply, and in her opinion, it was too romantic for words, making her want to make love with him even more. When she tried to convey that to him with a searching kiss, he broke the contact.

"Behave yourself. I'm just here to hold you, remember?"

As much as Natalie appreciated the thought, she wanted more, needed more. She'd been having difficulty falling asleep. He could cure that problem. She trailed the tip of her tongue over his bottom lip and pressed her pelvis against the bulge of hardness behind his fly. "Please. I'm so uptight. You could help me relax."

His breath hitched in his chest when she nipped his chin and then licked the sting away. "You sure? I honestly didn't come over expecting—"

"Shush." Natalie tasted his mouth again, wanting him as she'd never wanted anyone. "Please?"

Zeke could only withstand so much persuasion. He consoled himself with the thought that he'd do more than help her to relax. He'd love her until she went limp and couldn't connect one thought to another. He'd just settled in to savor the taste of her mouth when she pressed a hand to his shoulder. He drew back to give her a questioning look.

"Are you carrying protection?"

"What do I look like, an idiot?"

She smiled, her face as sweet as an angel's in the moonlight. "I thought you only came to hold me."

Zeke just grinned and kissed her again.

After making love to Natalie until she lay in a sprawl, Zeke tugged his britches back on and slipped into bed with her. Daylight wouldn't come for a few hours. He meant to spend every minute until dawn holding her in his arms. He'd sneak back home before the kids awakened, he promised himself.

That was his last conscious thought. The next thing he

knew, a light tap on the door brought him awake to discover that it had turned broad daylight. "Mommy?"

Zeke vaulted off the bed, grabbing his shirt as he went. Before he could dash to the window, the bedroom door pushed open. He dove for the floor, catching his upper body with the flat of his hands. Scooting in close to the bed, he turned onto his back.

"Mommy?" Rosie whimpered. "I had a bad dream."

Zeke could almost feel Natalie's confusion. She'd surely felt the bed shake when he jumped out. He heard her sit up and straighten the covers. He was damned glad now that he hadn't pulled her nightshirt off. At least she was dressed.

"Oh, sweetie." A patting sound on the mattress drifted down to Zeke, and he imagined Natalie indicating the place beside her. "Come here. We'll cuddle."

Zeke winced. Natalie clearly thought he'd left. *Shit.* How did he get into messes like this? He should have just let Rosie see him and come up with a plausible reason for being there. Too late now. If the kid discovered him, what the hell was he going to say, that he'd come over to collect dust bunnies from under Natalie's bed?

While Natalie and Rosie snuggled down together under the blankets, Zeke struggled to slip his shirt on, no easy feat while lying full length on the floor. But he was motivated. Under no circumstances did he want that precious little girl to find him half-dressed in her mother's bedroom.

"What's that?" Rosie whispered.

Zeke froze with one arm stuck partway down a sleeve.

"What's what?" Natalie asked.

"I heard a noise."

The mattress creaked, and the next instant, Rosie's darling little face appeared just inches above Zeke's nose. Her eyes went wide with surprise. "Hello. How come you're on Mommy's floor?"

Zeke told the first lie that popped into his head. "I've been trying to catch a mouse."

Rosie sprang to her knees and leaned farther over the edge of the mattress. "A mouse?"

"A mouse," Zeke confirmed. "Your mom called me for help. It ran under her bed, and she didn't know what to do."

Rosie got a speculative gleam in her big brown eyes. Not for the first time, Zeke decided the child was too smart for her own good—or his, for that matter.

"There's no phone in here," Rosie pointed out.

Natalie's face appeared beside her daughter's. Her brown eyes round with dismay, she said, "Cell phone. I called him on my cell phone."

Rosie looked at her mother. "Where is it?"

"Where's what?" Natalie asked.

"Your cell phone."

"Here somewhere." Natalie lifted the covers. "I've misplaced the darned thing again."

Zeke sat up.

"How come your shirt is off?" Rosie asked.

Because he was a blithering idiot. "I was going to catch the mouse in it."

"How?"

"Throw it over the top of him—kind of like a net."

"Did you?" Rosie asked.

"Nope. He got away."

"Where'd he go?"

Zeke thought quickly. "In the closet."

Rosie scampered off the bed. Zeke pushed to his feet, finished buttoning his shirt, and glanced hopelessly around for his boots. Then, with a sinking heart, he remembered stripping down to his bare feet for better traction on the roof.

To Natalie, he said, "If you see that mouse again, don't hesitate to call me."

Natalie's eyes danced with laughter. "Absolutely. Thank you so much for coming, Zeke. I know it's silly, but mice terrify me."

Zeke turned toward the window and stopped dead. He couldn't possibly leave that way, not without arousing Rosie's suspicions. So instead he exited through the bedroom door, tiptoed down the old staircase, through the living room, and into the kitchen.

Naomi and Valerie sat at the table, sipping morning coffee. The instant they saw Zeke, their startled gazes dropped to his bare feet.

"'Morning," he said, doing his damnedest to act as if his presence in their kitchen was a perfectly normal occurrence.

Valerie tugged her nightshirt down. Naomi was already dressed in the clothes she'd worn yesterday. She arched one eyebrow. "Good morning," she said. "What brings you over so"—she glanced at her watch—"bright and early?"

"A mouse."

"A *mouse?*" Valerie repeated.

"Under Natalie's bed." Zeke felt like a total imbecile. Heat crawled up his neck. "Rosie's searching the closet for it as we speak. It's a quick little bugger."

Naomi smiled. "Coffee?" she offered, lifting her cup.

Zeke reached up to smooth his hair and almost groaned. It was standing straight up in spikes. "No, thanks. I'd better get on home."

With as much dignity as possible, he padded across the

kitchen floor. When he reached the door, Valerie said, "That's dangerous, you know."

"What is?" Zeke asked.

"Hunting mice in your bare feet. They bite."

Once outside, Zeke could find only one of his boots. He'd left both of them next to the back stairs. Bewildered, he did a slow turn, searching the yard. Beyond the fence, he spotted Chester. When Zeke walked closer, his suspicions were confirmed. The damned gander had confiscated one of his Tony Lamas.

"Good-bye!" a feminine voice called.

Zeke turned to see Natalie leaning out her bedroom window. She looked so beautiful with her hair all mussed and her nightshirt slipping off one shoulder that his embarrassing trek through the kitchen seemed almost worth it.

Zeke grinned and shook his head. "Coffee's on. Your mother and sister are already up."

She cringed and touched her fingertips to her mouth to stifle a laugh. "Sorry."

Zeke tapped his watch. "Next time, I'm using the alarm function."

"Good plan." She took a deep breath of the sun-warmed morning air. Then she grinned and said, "Just so long as there *is* a next time."

Zeke nodded. "I have it on good authority that mice are creatures of habit. He's sure to come back. When he does, I'll be there."

Rosie appeared in the window, her small face barely visible above the sill. "Good-bye, Mr. Coulter!"

Zeke waved and went to retrieve his boot, knowing with every step that he was leaving a big chunk of his heart behind.

* * *

Natalie had just gotten the kids' breakfast on the table when the phone rang and a knock came on the back door at precisely the same moment. Naomi had gone into town to pack some essentials for her stay at the farm, Pete was in the barn milking the cows, Gramps was snoozing, and Valerie was grabbing a shower. Natalie raced to open the door, glimpsed Zeke's dark face, and dashed away without saying hello, hoping he'd let himself in.

Grabbing the phone, she breathlessly said, "Hello?"

"Mrs. Patterson, please."

Natalie recognized Detective Monroe's voice and sent Zeke a panicked look as he stepped into the kitchen. "This is she."

"Good morning, Mrs. Patterson. Detective Monroe, here. Some new information about your husband's business affairs has come to light. I'd like you to come in and field a few more questions this morning."

Natalie tried to slow her breathing. "I, um—certainly, Detective Monroe. I'll happily come in. But I really wasn't kept abreast of my ex-husband's business affairs. I'm not sure what, if anything, I can tell you."

"I feel fairly sure you can shed some light on this," the detective insisted.

Natalie glanced at the clock. "Do you have a particular time in mind?"

"Eleven?"

"Sure," Natalie agreed. "Eleven is fine."

"Mrs. Patterson?"

Something in the detective's tone raised goose bumps on Natalie's arms. "Yes?"

"Be sure to bring legal counsel."

Natalie was shaking when she broke the connection. She

glanced meaningfully at the kids and then sought Zeke's gaze. "That was Monroe. He has some more questions."

"About?"

Natalie led the way into the living room so Chad wouldn't overhear. Turning back to Zeke, she said softly, "Something about Robert's business affairs. I didn't like his tone, especially at the last. He told me to bring my attorney."

Zeke frowned. "What can you possibly tell him about Robert's business affairs?"

That was a question Natalie couldn't answer. "I only know something's up."

Zeke glanced at his watch. "I can go with you."

"That won't be necessary. Sterling Johnson will be there. I'll be fine."

"You sure? I came over to get your club keys. A couple of my brothers are going to meet me there and have a look at your wall. But it's no problem for me to postpone."

Natalie managed to smile. "No way. Free manpower? I'd be crazy to pass on that. Let me get you the keys."

When Natalie met with Monroe at eleven, she felt a little more self-assured than she had yesterday. She'd had time to dress nicely, for one thing, and she'd done her hair and wore makeup. As she sat beside Sterling Johnson in front of the detective's metal desk, she tried to look relaxed and blithely unconcerned.

Monroe wasted no time on pleasantries this morning. No offers of coffee. No friendly smiles. He slid a sheaf of papers across the blotter to Natalie. "You forgot to mention this when we chatted yesterday."

Natalie barely glimpsed the paperwork before Sterling

Johnson commandeered it. The old attorney settled his glasses on his nose and quickly skimmed the document. Only then did he hand it over to Natalie. "Were you aware of this?" he asked.

Natalie started to read. At first the legalese made no sense. Then she realized it was an earnest money agreement of some sort. Robert had been in land development and frequently acquired or sold large parcels, so that didn't strike her as strange. Then her gaze landed on the address of the property.

"Old Mill Road?" she whispered incredulously. She glanced at the detective. "There must be some mistake. This is my father's farm."

"The deed on record says otherwise," the detective replied. "That land is in your name, Mrs. Patterson."

Natalie's fingers convulsed over the edges of the document. "Well, yes, technically, it does belong to me. My grandmother Westfield left me the property when she died. It was originally Mitchell land. Her father gave it to her as a wedding gift with the stipulation that it should be passed down to her eldest daughter. My father was her only child, so the property came to me instead. My grandfather worked the farm all his life, and then my dad took it over. I'll never actually take possession until both of them pass away."

The detective interlaced his fingers. "I don't care about your family arrangements, Mrs. Patterson. Bottom line, that property is yours, it was in your name before you got a divorce, and your ex-husband was granted fifty-percent interest in the decree. You must have been mighty upset when you discovered he was finagling to sell your inheritance and take his half of the proceeds."

Natalie's blood ran ice cold. She let the papers fall to her lap. Robert had been working a deal to sell Pop's home? She couldn't believe it.

Monroe rocked back on his chair. "Do you expect me to believe you knew nothing of this until now?"

It was all that Natalie could do to remain calmly seated. She began reading the document again. The amount of money mentioned, three and a quarter million, made her head go dizzy. A section of land surely wasn't worth that unless it could be subdivided into lots. She skimmed through the pages until she found what she was looking for, a contingency that the buyer could get the land rezoned as residential.

"Is this final?" she asked her lawyer. "Surely it can't be final. I can't let Pop's home be sold out from under him."

"The sale can't go forward now," the detective assured her. "All of your ex-husband's assets, including his interest in that land, will undoubtedly go into probate."

Natalie realized the implications of that and sent her attorney a worried look. Sterling Johnson touched the sleeve of her suit jacket. She laid the papers back on the desk blotter and rubbed her hands over her skirt as if to decontaminate her fingertips.

"My client obviously wasn't aware of this transaction," Johnson told the detective.

"Ah, come on, Mr. Johnson," Monroe said impatiently. "Robert Patterson was moving forward with the sale. She must have been aware of it. The man was no fool, surely. That's a legally binding contract, and she had half interest in the land."

"You're making an erroneous assumption, Detective. In the state of Oregon, an earnest money agreement does not require the signature of more than one seller. In the case of married couples selling a home, for instance, only the signature of one of them is necessary on an earnest money agreement. Mr. Patterson could have transacted to sell the land without my client's knowledge."

"To what end? She'd have had to agree to sign later. If she refused, it would have blown the deal."

Johnson removed his eyeglasses and slipped them into his shirt pocket. "Another assumption. I haven't reviewed the Patterson divorce settlement, but a clause to prevent either party from unreasonably hindering the liquidation of commonly owned assets is standard. Otherwise a husband or wife could stonewall an ex-spouse at every turn, preventing the sale of the marital home, vacation homes, and myriad other possessions."

"So Patterson could have proceeded this far in the land sale without ever mentioning it to Mrs. Patterson?" the detective asked.

Johnson nodded. "As I said, I haven't reviewed the terms of dissolution, but I will be very surprised if an unreasonable hindrance clause isn't included in the fine print."

Natalie felt sick to her stomach. Robert had been wheeling and dealing behind her back, conniving to sell her inheritance. This went beyond greedy. It was downright evil. He'd signed a written agreement never to touch the farm.

"Robert was way out of line, doing this," Natalie said. "We had a written agreement, a settlement out of court, that said we both got to keep our family heirlooms and inheritances. A lawyer drew it up."

"What was his name?"

Natalie rubbed her forehead. "Baskin, I think. Yes, that was it, Harry Baskin."

Sterling Johnson frowned. "Was he here in Crystal Falls?"

"Yes."

"I've never heard of him," Johnson said, "and I know every lawyer in town. Did you check him out, make sure he was legit?"

Alarm mounting within her, Natalie stared at her attorney. "Of course he was legit. I went to his office, saw the gold letters on his window. He was even a notary public and authenticated the contract for us. Robert hired him."

Monroe asked, "Did you have the contract reviewed by your own counsel?"

Natalie doubled her hands into fists over her skirt. She'd been flat broke at the time and grateful that Robert had offered to pay the attorney fees. She'd had no money to have another attorney look at the documents. "No," she whispered.

Johnson cleared his throat, removed his hand from Natalie's sleeve, and sat back on his chair, looking deflated for a second. Then he recovered, straightened his shoulders, and smiled as if they'd stopped in to pay a social call.

Detective Monroe smirked. "It seems obvious to me, if you've never heard of Harry Baskin, that Mrs. Patterson got the wool pulled over her eyes. The contract that she and her ex-husband signed probably wasn't worth the paper it was written on, meaning that the divorce decree took precedence. Robert Patterson could have forced the sale of that farm." He slanted a speculative look at Natalie. "If Mrs. Patterson discovered what he was up to, what could she have done, save grow angry?"

Johnson's lips thinned. "If my client had refused to cooperate, Mr. Patterson would have had legal recourse under the unreasonable hindrance clause in the decree to sue. Eventually, the land would have been sold."

"Whether Mrs. Patterson liked it or not?"

Johnson cleared his throat again. "Precisely."

Detective Monroe settled a piercing gaze on Natalie. "Correct me if I'm wrong, Mr. Johnson, but doesn't that give your client a compelling motive for murder?"

Chapter Fourteen

On the off chance that she'd find Zeke at the club, Natalie drove past there before leaving town. On a rational level, she didn't know why she so desperately needed to see his face, or why she yearned with such urgency to feel his arms around her. She'd been financially independent for nearly two years and emotionally independent for much longer than that, the key to her survival an ingrained confidence that she could make it alone, no matter what. But now, suddenly, like an addict hooked on a chemical substance, she absolutely had to be with him.

She wasn't surprised to see the front door of the Blue Parrot standing open and Zeke's Dodge parked at the curb. Rather than fight traffic to grab a parallel parking space, she drove around to the side lot. *Zeke.* Recalling the meeting with Monroe, her insides quaked with fear. She needed Zeke to hold her close and assure her that everything would be all right. *Madness.* He had no magic wand. Against the system, he'd be powerless to protect her if Monroe decided to arrest her for Robert's murder.

When she entered the building a moment later, she saw Zeke hunkered down in front of an electrical socket in the wall he planned to remove. Dressed in his standard Wranglers, a chambray work shirt, and the chocolate-brown Stetson, he was studying an odd-looking gadget he held in one hand that had two wires with metal probes attached to it.

Still quivering with trepidation, Natalie stopped just inside the door to gather her composure. She didn't want to project herself as a needy, clinging basket case who leaned on him every time something went wrong. She owned this business. She'd scraped and saved and worked her ass off to make a go of it without any man to support her in the endeavor. She needed him, yes, but she needed to maintain her dignity almost as much.

A playful, teasing approach might be best, she decided. After the initial hellos, she could tell him about the meeting with Monroe—calmly, stating only the facts, coming off as mildly upset, not frantic.

To that end, she crept up behind him, bent low, and lifted the brim of his hat to kiss the back of his neck. He jumped, spun, and almost fell over backward.

"Sweet Christ!"

"I'm sorry. I didn't mean to startle—" *Wrong man.* Natalie gaped in astonishment. He looked enough like Zeke to be his twin. Her heart did a funny flip and squiggle in her chest when she realized what she'd just done. A stranger? It was one of the most embarrassing moments of her life. "Oh *dear!*"

The man nudged up the brim of his Stetson to give her a lazy once-over with sky-blue eyes so similar to Zeke's that Natalie could scarcely credit it. Then he flashed a slow grin. "You must be Natalie. I'm Hank, Zeke's younger brother."

"I'm sorry. You look so much like—"

"You taking a nap out there?" another deep voice called from the kitchen. "Did I throw the right switch or not?"

Natalie glanced up to see another sun-bronzed, blue-eyed cowboy in a chocolate-brown Stetson in the kitchen doorway. He stood exactly like Zeke, one hip cocked, his opposite knee slightly bent—a tall, well-muscled cowboy, every inch of him honed to a rugged toughness. Only he wasn't Zeke.

"That's Jake, the oldest," Hank said. Then he startled her half to death with a shrill whistle. "Yo, Zeke!" he yelled. "Your lady's out here!"

Zeke appeared in the doorway that led to the bar. He flashed her a slow, lopsided grin that she was quickly coming to realize must be the Coulter male trademark. "Hi, sweetheart. What're you doing here?"

"Kissing perfect strangers," Hank replied. "You'd best marry the lady and keep a closer eye on her, or some lonesome cowboy's gonna snatch her up."

Natalie's face went fiery hot. "I thought—" She looked helplessly at Zeke. "You mentioned a family resemblance, but I had no idea—" She broke off again, feeling too stupid for words. "I thought it was you."

Zeke chuckled. "You're not the first person to make that mistake. And don't let Hank nettle you. He's an incurable tease." He glanced at his brother. "Show your manners and stand up, little brother. I want you to meet my lady."

This was the second time in as many minutes that she'd been referred to as Zeke's lady. For a fleeting instant, Natalie wasn't sure how she felt about that. She wasn't a possession, after all. But then she looked into Zeke's laughing blue eyes and knew the handle fitted her perfectly. She did indeed belong to him, just as he belonged to her. And she wouldn't have changed that for anything.

"The lady and I have met," Hank replied as he pushed to his feet. He sent Natalie a twinkling look and drew off his Stetson. "Hank Coulter," he said with a grin and extended his hand. "Don't believe a word he says about me, by the way. He lies through his teeth." With a wink, he added in a stage whisper, "It's the bane of my existence, being the handsomest one of the lot. They're all jealous and pick on me."

Zeke elbowed his brother's arm, a not-very-subtle signal for Hank to behave himself. Hank staggered sideways, exaggerating the impact. "He's mean, too. Don't cross him."

Natalie felt herself relaxing. Their brotherly razzing reminded her of the way she and Valerie teased each other. She shook Hank's hand. "I'm pleased to meet you, Hank. Zeke says you raise and train quarter horses?"

"Only when I'm not volunteering to do carpentry work," Hank replied.

Jake sauntered from the kitchen, exhibiting the same, loose-jointed stride that Natalie had so often admired in Zeke. As he extended his hand to her, he said, "Good to finally meet you, Natalie. Now I know why Zeke's been chasing his tail for a month."

Like Hank, Jake had a friendly smile and warm blue eyes. Natalie immediately liked him. "We're here to tear out your wall," he explained, "and the electrical circuits aren't clearly marked. Hank's using the voltage tester to tell when I get the power shut off."

"Ah." Natalie glanced at the little box Hank held. "I really appreciate the two of you coming to help."

"Not a problem," Hank assured her. "That's what family is for."

He hunkered back down in front of the electrical socket. Jake tipped his hat to her in farewell and returned to the kitchen. Zeke curled an arm around Natalie's shoulders and led her into the bar. After closing the door behind them, he caught her close in his embrace and soundly kissed her. By the time he released her, Natalie was breathless and hated to spoil the mood by telling him why she'd come.

"What?" Zeke said when he saw her face.

She wanted so badly to be strong and matter-of-fact. Instead she sank against him. "Oh, Zeke," she whispered, "I'm so scared. The most *awful* thing has happened."

He ran his hand over her back, his fingers gently massaging her muscles. "What, honey? What did Monroe say?"

"Remember yesterday when you said I had no motive to kill Robert?"

"Yes."

"I do now."

Zeke led her over to the bar, caught her at the waist, and lifted her up to sit on a stool. Even as upset as she was, Natalie marveled at his strength. When he searched her gaze, the most wondrous feeling moved through her, a sense that he would be there for her, steady as a rock, no matter what. She could see the love he felt for her in his eyes and in his expression. *Not Robert.* She had to remember that. Posturing and facades weren't necessary with this man. If she had weak moments and needed to lean on him, he wouldn't mind or think less of her.

"You acquired a motive since yesterday?"

She nodded. "A really, really *compelling* motive."

Zeke sat on a stool beside her as she filled him in on her

visit with Detective Monroe. "He believes I knew about the land sale. Before we left, he even said, plain out, that he feels this gives me a strong motive for murder."

Zeke swiveled on the stool to face her, his squared knees bracketing hers, his big hands enveloping hers in leathery warmth. His grip was as steady as his character, strong yet not punishing, dependable but not oppressive. "Robert was trying to sell your dad's farm?"

"Technically it belongs to me." She explained the terms of her grandmother's will. "Someday it should go to Rosie. It was in my name when I divorced Robert, making it a part of our joint assets. Robert understood that it was Westfield land, only mine on loan, so to speak, and we signed a contract, agreeing to leave each other's family property alone. Only it was a hoax." She explained about Harry Baskin, who'd posed as an attorney and notary public. "Sterling Johnson says I could have been forced to sell the farm."

"That doesn't mean you killed Robert."

"No, but it gives me a very good reason to have wanted him dead. In fact—" She broke off, sighed, and let her head fall back to stare at the ceiling. "Oh, Zeke, this is terrible of me, but had I found that contract two days ago, I might have considered killing him. Knowing he would stoop that low—that he wanted to toss Pop and Gramps out of their home without a thought for their welfare—it makes me so mad I could spit."

Zeke grasped her chin and forced her to look at him. "You can't think a man to death, darlin', and that's as far as you would have taken it. No cop in his right mind will try to pin this on you. Monroe may be sniffing at your back trail right now, but he'll eventually circle around to where he was yesterday. You didn't do it."

"I'm scared, Zeke. I don't think I've ever been this scared."

"I know." He hooked a hand over the back of her neck, slid off the stool, and enfolded her in the safe circle of his arms. As he tightened his hold, Natalie found the solace she'd been seeking—an indescribable sense of rightness and peace. "But don't worry, all right? If that detective is crazy enough to come after you, I'll fight him with everything I've got."

Natalie pressed her nose against the collar of his shirt. As much as she enjoyed feeling his strength curled so warmly around her, she loved the essence of him even more. "Fighting him would cost a fortune. I can't let you do that. You'd lose everything."

"Try stopping me. Five years ago, all I had was a pocketful of dreams. Easy come, easy go. I'm not hung up on material things. Never have been. Fortunes are made and lost in a day. You can't let possessions rule your life."

"And what if, despite everything, they still convict me?"

He slid his hand into her hair and made a tight fist. "We'll run," he whispered huskily. "How do you feel about Brazil?"

"Where?"

"Colombia, then. Where is it criminals go? Someplace tropical where we can live like kings and lie under a palm tree, sipping drinks with little umbrellas in them. Rosie will love it—hundreds of parasols for Barbie."

Natalie laughed in spite of herself. "Would you really do that for me?"

His voice gravelly with heartfelt sincerity, he said, "In a bronc rider's minute, darlin'."

It was a silly response, and yet, for reasons beyond her, it was all she needed to hear. "What, exactly, is a bronc rider's minute?"

"You ever been on a bronc?"

She giggled again. "No."

"Well, you are flat anxious for sixty seconds to elapse, let's put it like that. If a bronc rider were to watch his own clock, he'd shave off seconds, thus the term. In short order, in other words. Before you could take a deep breath and yell howdy, we'd be out of here."

Natalie felt better just knowing he loved her that much. "I am so lucky to have met you," she whispered.

"I'm the lucky one," he replied. "Just don't hit on my baby brother anymore. Okay?"

Natalie dissolved into a fit of laughter. It made no sense. She'd been terrified when she came. But that was the miracle of it, she decided, being with someone who could make her laugh when her whole world was falling apart.

"If that bastard wasn't already dead, I'd castrate him and hang him from a hay hook," Naomi vowed when Natalie told her the latest news.

Pete slapped his coffee mug down on the kitchen table. "To hell with castrating the son of a bitch, I'd blow his goddamned head off."

For once over the last ten years, Natalie's parents seemed to be in perfect agreement on something, that being that they'd both love to do Robert physical injury if he were still alive. Natalie sat at the table, too drained to add a word to the exchange. She was just glad her kids were out of earshot, Chad in the barn feeding Chester, and Rosie upstairs playing with a new Barbie dune buggy that had mysteriously appeared on the back stoop. No one in Natalie's family had confessed to buying the doll accessory, which led Natalie to suspect that the second-story man next door might be responsible.

"Well, don't you worry, honey," Pop said as he patted Natalie's shoulder. "We Westfields stick together. If those damned cops think they're going to pin this on you, they've got another think coming."

"That's exactly right," Naomi seconded. She looked at Pete and smiled. "They won't know what hit them."

Valerie entered the kitchen just then, waving her freshly painted fingernails. "Well, now, ain't this a cozy picture of family unity."

"Oh, be quiet," Natalie's parents said in unison. Naomi added, "This is no time for smart-aleck remarks, Valerie. Your sister is in trouble."

Valerie plopped down on a kitchen chair. "For once it's her and not me. That's cause to celebrate." She grinned at her folks. "It's good to see you guys teaming up on the same side for a change."

"Be quiet," Naomi and Pete said again. Then they promptly dispersed, Naomi to the sink where she'd been peeling potatoes and Pete to the stove for another mug of coffee. "It's the Westfield blood in her veins," Naomi said over her shoulder to Pete. "No one on my side was ever so lippy."

"Westfield blood, my ass," he shot back. "Girl's the spittin' image of you, inside and out, and she came by the smart mouth naturally. Just look at her mama."

Valerie fluttered her eyelashes. "Maybe I'm a changeling, dumped on the stoop, kind of like the dune buggy. Is that how it happened, Pop?"

"Shut up," he grumbled.

Valerie flashed Natalie a mischievous grin. "That had to be it. Don't you agree, sis? We must have been dropped on the porch by the stork." Valerie propped her elbows on the table to blow on her nails. The color of the day was psychedelic purple with silver and red glitter. "I can't imagine the two of them actually—well, you know—*doing* it. They'd kill each other first."

"Valerie Lynn!" Naomi cried, chucking a half-peeled potato across the kitchen.

Valerie ducked and laughed. "Was that a potato that just sailed past my head? No wonder I'm a mess. My family is completely dysfunctional."

Naomi's mouth twitched. She quickly showed her daughters her back to hide her smile. "I'd have nailed you if I meant to hit you, you little twerp. Ask your father about my aim. He'll tell you."

Pete turned from the stove and gave his ex-wife's backside a meandering appraisal. "She can definitely hit her target with deadly accuracy," he said with a reminiscent smile.

Naomi giggled. "Right between the eyes, if I remember right."

"Damn near coldcocked me."

"Served you right. Came home drunk and feeling your oats. I told you to sleep it off in the barn, and you refused."

Pete winked at his daughters. "Had her jealous up. Thought I'd been squeezing the fruit down at Chester's Hideaway. When I walked in the door, she bonked me with a spud before I could say hello and what's for supper."

Natalie leaned back on her chair. "Were you guilty as charged, Pop?"

Pete grinned. "Hell no. But there wasn't no convincing her of that."

Naomi turned from the sink. In one hand, she held another partly peeled potato. "You want to test my aim again, Pete Westfield?"

"No, ma'am."

Pete made a hasty retreat to the living room, once again exhibiting a miraculous recovery from his back pain. Natalie sent her sister a wondering look. Valerie grinned and puffed on her nails again. Naomi turned, caught her daughters smiling, and said, "Wipe those smirks off your faces."

Valerie's expression went dead serious except for the dimple in her cheek. "So, Mom, is that how we came to have a gander named Chester, because Pop was fond of squeezing the fruit down at Chester's Hideaway?"

"Damn bird," Naomi said under her breath. "He named him Chester just to get my goat. Knew very well I'd grind my teeth every time I came out here."

Valerie waggled her eyebrows at Natalie. "Men," she said with a theatrical sigh. "Can't live with 'em, and can't live without 'em."

"You can't live with them, that's for darned sure," Naomi replied. She rinsed the potato she'd just peeled and tossed it in the colander. "I'm much happier in my nice condo. Would you just look at this kitchen? Hasn't changed one thing in the last ten years, and it was ugly as sin back then." She grabbed another spud. "Valerie Lynn, get off your fanny and help me."

"My nails are wet."

"Run them under cold water. The chicken needs flouring."

Valerie groaned and touched a nail to test it for dryness. Then she pushed up from the chair to advance on the chicken, which was already cut up and waiting on a board.

"This is enough to make me become a vegetarian." She touched a slippery thigh. "I like precut frozen. It doesn't gross me out."

"You'll survive. Flour the damned chicken."

Natalie smiled and rubbed her aching forehead. Naomi dried her hands and came to the table with the jug of burgundy. "You look like you need some happy juice, sweetie."

Natalie sighed. "I don't think it'll help, Mom. My mind is circling. Nothing seems real. I honestly can't believe this is happening to me."

Valerie glanced over her shoulder. "I can believe it. Robert's been messing up your life ever since you met him. This is his coup de grâce, delivered from beyond the grave. He couldn't rest in peace knowing you might live happily ever after."

Naomi took three goblets from the cupboard, all of which had been freshly scrubbed, and set them on the table. "Get the spuds and chicken on, Valerie Lynn. While supper's cooking, the three of us will share a nip or two."

Valerie came to the table, waited for her mother to pour a glass of wine, and then took it with her to the counter. "When all else fails, get drunk."

Natalie accepted the wine her mother pushed toward her. "I just want all of this to go away."

Naomi took a sip of wine. "Can't blame you there. Drink enough of this, and it will."

"That's no solution," Natalie said hopelessly. "I don't think there is a solution. Monroe has his sights trained on me. Unless something happens to make him suspect someone else, I'm going to be toast."

Naomi grabbed a notepad and pen from the telephone

stand. "Let's give him another suspect, then. Who, besides you, had a reason to want the son of a bitch dead?"

He came to Natalie that night as if in a dream—slipping silently into the bed beside her, running his fingertips lightly over her body, then kissing her throat and upper chest until she moaned and surfaced from sleep. She tried to say his name, but he covered her mouth with his and laid claim to her with hard, masterful hands that seemed to know every secret of her body. She went from black oblivion to ecstasy before her head could clear, then drifted with him on sensation, quivering at his every touch.

"I love you," he whispered as he plunged deep and filled her with his hardness. "I love you, Nattie girl."

She clung to his broad shoulders, her mouth trembling beneath his, her body undulating to meet his thrusts, her mind exploding in a kaleidoscope of fragmented color as her body pitched in the throes of orgasm.

Afterward he held her against him and stroked her trembling body until she melted contentedly into his heat and once again became lost in the swirling black veils of sleep. *Zeke*. She took him with her into her dreams and felt safe even when Detective Monroe's face leered at her from the shadows.

Toward dawn, Natalie was roused from sleep by a faint beeping sound. She lifted her lashes to see Zeke sitting up and pushing at a button on his wristwatch. She smiled and ran a hand down his bare back. He didn't speak, and neither did she. He just kissed her deeply and then vanished into the predawn gloom as if he'd never been there.

*   *   *

Late the following afternoon, Natalie got a call from Grace Patterson. Immediately after ending the conversation, she went to find her son. Chad was nowhere to be found inside the house, so Natalie broadened her search, combing the yard first, then venturing farther afield to check the outbuildings.

The August heat lay over the farm like a blanket that sucked all the moisture from the air. Normally Natalie appreciated the low humidity in Central Oregon, but today even her throat felt parched when she took a deep breath, and her skin felt scratchy where her clothing touched. She missed having central air, she decided. Pop didn't believe in air-conditioning. When the house grew hot and stuffy, his only solution was to open the windows and use a fan.

Natalie squinted against the slanting afternoon sun as she passed the chicken coop. "Chad?" she called.

"Out here, Mom."

She circled the barn and spied her son behind the building, sitting forlornly on a dilapidated section of fence that had once served as a paddock. Dressed in jeans and sneakers, her usual at-home attire, Natalie swung up to sit beside him. Sensing his morose mood, she didn't speak for a while. Grasshoppers whirred in the tall grass clumped around the fence posts. Hens clucked and fluttered in the lean-to behind them. Occasionally Daisy and Marigold added lowing to the mix.

"I used to sit out here when I wanted to be alone," Natalie finally said. "I hope I'm not intruding."

"No, not really. I just like it out here sometimes."

Chad bent his ebony head and swung his feet. Natalie remembered all the hours she'd spent teaching him how to tie his shoes. Now his laces dangled like drool from a hound's jowls, and the crotch of his shorts drooped between his knees. She didn't understand the fashions nowadays, but then she doubted that her parents had appreciated her look as a youngster, either.

"I, um, need to talk to you, Chad," Natalie began. "Your grandma Grace just called."

"What did she want?"

Natalie stared off at the towering pines that bordered the back quarter of their land. As a girl, she'd often gone walking in those woods on hot summer days, craving the silence and deep shade that only the trees could offer.

"She's very upset," she replied honestly. "Your dad was her only child. Grandpa Herbert is gone now, too. I think she's very lonely."

"Maybe I should call her," Chad said huskily.

"That would be nice."

"I don't like her very well."

Natalie shared that sentiment, but she refrained from saying so. "She has her good moments."

Chad gave her a sidelong glance. "When?"

Natalie laughed softly. "Okay, not often, but she's your grandmother. I don't want to say bad things about her."

Chad nodded. "I shouldn't either, I guess. It's just—"

"Just what?" Natalie pressed gently.

"I don't know. Take Gramps, for instance. All he does is gripe and carry on about one thing or another, but I love him anyway. Every once in a while when he stops grumping to take a breath, he'll pat me on the arm or give me a hug, like he's telling me not to take him seriously."

Natalie smiled. She'd seen her grandfather hugging her kids. "He does gripe a lot," she agreed. "That's just his nature, I guess."

"Grandma Grace never gives hugs like that. Only when she says hello and good-bye, and then she's all stiff, like she's afraid I'll get her clothes dirty. And she never kisses me. She just makes smacking noises in the air."

"She does have a formal way about her," Natalie conceded.

"When I go see her, I wish she'd be more normal. I can't relax when I'm with her. Even when she offers me a treat, I'm nervous about making a mess on her tablecloth. One time I laid out paper towels around my bowl of ice cream so I wouldn't have to worry about it, and she got all bent out of shape, turning it into this big thing about practicing my manners so they'd be second nature."

"I'm sorry she's that way. You don't have to call her if you'd rather not."

Chad sighed. "I'll call her. It's not like I hate her or anything. Maybe it'll make her feel better."

Natalie's heart filled with pride. "That would be very kind of you. She needs to feel loved right now."

He straightened his legs to stare at his shoes. "She called once, right after we heard about Dad. It was while you were gone to the police station. All she wanted to talk about was me inheriting the Patterson money someday."

"I suppose you will inherit now that your father's gone."

"But she's, like, totally stuck on it," Chad replied. "She cried a little about Dad, but mainly she wanted to talk about the responsibility that had fallen to me and how I should take more pride in the Patterson name now." He began swinging his feet, his movements agitated. "It's like—I don't know. This will sound really mean, but she acts like she owns me now or something."

Natalie couldn't count the times that she'd seen Grace

and Herbert use the Patterson wealth as leverage against Robert to make him toe the mark. She hated to see her son go through that, but she could do nothing to stop it. Chad was a Patterson, and he was next in line to inherit. She couldn't prevent Grace from making Robert's son her heir.

"A large amount of money is a wonderful blessing," Natalie said carefully. "It enables those who have it to please themselves in ways other people can't. You can own a beautiful home and wear fine clothes and drive fancy cars. You can help the disadvantaged by giving generously to charities. In some instances, money can even buy you prestige and power. But there's also a downside."

"What's that?" Chad asked.

"Money can become a god to some people, and it's more important than anything else." Natalie looked over at her son. "I can't tell you how to feel about one day inheriting the Patterson money—or how to deal with your grandma when you feel that she's trying to control you. But I can tell you that people are seldom happy if they let money become the most important thing in their lives."

"It's not that important to me," the boy replied. "I never want to be like that."

"Then don't be. Own the money, but never let it own you. Does that make sense?"

Chad nodded. "And don't let Grandma Grace own me because she has control of the money I'll inherit someday?"

Natalie felt the tension ease from her shoulders. "Exactly. When she brings up your inheritance, one way you might handle it is to say you don't want to think about losing her someday. That will make her feel nice, and it will let her know in a very kind way that her money isn't that important to you."

Chad smiled faintly and nodded. "That'd work, and it's how I feel, too. I don't want to think about her dying someday."

"Just tell her that, then."

Chad released a long breath. "What did she call about today?"

"Your father's funeral service was supposed to be tomorrow."

"And now it's not?"

"The coroner's office won't release his remains just yet."

"How come?"

"In cases like this, it isn't uncommon." Because Robert's body was a piece of evidence. She couldn't bring herself to say that to her son, not about his father. "Red tape, lots of paperwork. It's no big deal. Sometime next week, maybe a bit later, they'll release your dad's remains, and we'll be able to say our farewells properly."

Chad swallowed, his larynx bobbing. "I'm not in any hurry. Are you?"

Natalie would have given a lot to close this chapter of her life. "No. It'll be a very sad occasion."

Chad gave her a searching look. "Will it? For you, I mean. I know you didn't love him anymore—that in a way, you even hated him."

She moved her hands on the weathered rail. "I didn't hate your father, sweetheart. I hated the things he did. Can you understand the difference?"

Chad nodded. "Why was he like that, Mom? My blood is partly from him, and I'm not like that. Rosie's not like that, either. What happened to make Dad so weird?"

In that moment, Natalie was finally able to turn loose of her bitterness toward Robert. "Maybe his mom was always stiff when she hugged him," she said softly. "Maybe she never kissed him and only made smacking noises by his ear. Maybe he never got to make a mess on the tablecloth when he ate ice cream." She took a deep breath and slowly let it out, feeling cleansed. "Maybe, for your dad, it was always about clothes and manners and shining at school, and never about being loved just because. All of us need to be loved just because, Chad. If we're not, we grow up feeling second-rate."

"You loved him that way once. Didn't you?"

"I loved him very much," Natalie confessed. Mindlessly, foolishly, with all the devotion an eighteen-year-old heart could feel. "But I think it was too late for him by then. He'd gone so many years without getting a real hug that he no longer even realized he wanted one."

"That's sad."

Natalie ruffled his hair. "Yes, very sad. When you wonder about your father and feel hurt because he didn't give you hugs when you needed them, remind yourself that he never got hugs himself."

"Zeke said the same thing almost, that maybe my dad never learned how to love because no one ever really loved him."

Zeke. Natalie could almost feel his arms around her. "Well, then? There you go."

Silence fell between them again. Then Chad asked, "When do you think the funeral will be?"

"At this point, no telling. Next week sometime, I imagine, which was my original reason for coming out to talk to you. Camp starts on Monday."

"I'd forgotten all about camp."

"You're all paid up to go, and I think you'll have a lot of fun. But you'll be gone all week."

"What about Dad's funeral?"

"That's the wrinkle we need to iron out. If you'd like, you can go to camp, and if the funeral happens next week, I'll drive up to the lake to get you the evening before."

Chad gazed off across the field. "I think I'll just skip camp this year."

"I'd love to see you go and have a good time. But I also understand that you're feeling very sad right now. It might be difficult, being around friends who don't really understand."

Chad moved his hands on the rail, pushing farther forward with his upper body. His shoulder bones poked up under his T-shirt, their expanse broader than Natalie remembered. Someday soon he'd be a man, she realized with a sharp tug on her heart.

"I do feel sad," he said, "but I'd probably still have fun."

"Then go."

"I think I need to be home this week," he insisted. "Just in case anything happens, I want to be here for Rosie."

Natalie couldn't think what to say. With a sinking heart, she realized that her son knew far more about what was happening behind the scenes than she'd hoped. She felt so bad. Chad would not only miss camp, but would also forfeit the money he'd earned and put on deposit to pay his way.

"How come the cops think you did it?" Chad asked. "I just don't get it. You get upset when Gramps puts out poison for the barn rats. You'd never kill anybody, especially not Dad. Why do they suspect you?"

Natalie swallowed hard and tightened her grip on the railing. If Chad was old enough to ask, he was old enough to get a straight answer, she decided.

"It's a really long story," she began.

At a quarter of six that evening, Zeke's phone rang. He answered to find Naomi Westfield on the line. After the usual pleasantries, she said, "I know this is late notice, but I wanted to invite you over for dinner tonight. Nothing fancy, just pot roast, but I thought you might enjoy the company."

Zeke had just taken a steak from the freezer. He glanced at the package on the counter. "I'd love to," he said.

"Good," Naomi replied. "Show up anytime. If dinner isn't ready yet, we'll chat while we wait."

"Five minutes."

"Great. And Zeke?"

"Ma'am?"

"Wear your boots this time."

Zeke grinned. "Yes, ma'am. Is there anything I can bring?"

"No, nothing, unless you happen to have some red wine on hand. Gramps's burgundy does in a pinch, but it tastes like drain cleaner."

Less than ten minutes later, Zeke stood on the Westfield back porch with two bottles of merlot cradled in his arm. At his knock, Naomi appeared at the opposite side of the screen in blue jeans, a clingy pink top, and white running shoes. Somehow, even in casual dress, she managed to look classy. Zeke wondered what Pete had been thinking to let a woman like her slip off his hook.

He searched the kitchen for Natalie when he stepped inside, but she was nowhere to be seen. Naomi took the wine, thanked him prettily, and gestured toward the living room.

"Natalie doesn't know you're coming. She and Rosie are playing with Barbie. I thought having you over would be a nice surprise for her, something to cheer her up."

"Is she feeling pretty down?"

"Not down, exactly." Naomi smiled wistfully. "But she's worried. Every time the phone rang today, she jumped a foot."

Zeke lowered his voice. "I spoke to Monroe today."

"You did?" Naomi set the wine on the counter. "About what?"

Zeke told her about the Chopin playing on Robert's stereo system when Natalie visited his home. "Natalie meant to tell him herself, but given the curveball he threw her with that damned earnest money agreement, I had a sneaking hunch she forgot. I ran it by Sterling Johnson before I made the call. He feels that any leads, no matter how small, should be passed on to Monroe."

"So you told him about the Chopin?"

"He's wasting time trying to pin it on Natalie. I told him as much."

"Is he going to question all the girlfriends?"

"He's already questioned Cheryl Steiner, Robert's most recent significant other. And Natalie guessed right. Cheryl left Robert's house around five thirty that afternoon, about an hour before Natalie got there." Zeke hung his hat on a hook on a horizontal coatrack by the back door. "Cheryl says she and Robert had a cozy evening planned and were about to go upstairs when the phone rang. After talking with the caller, Robert gave Cheryl a credit card to go shopping and asked her to come back around ten. She was the one who found him in the garage."

"She heard the car running?"

"No, actually. Not for a couple of hours, anyway. Around midnight, the Corvette engine started to cough and sputter. She noticed the odd sound and went to investigate."

Naomi shivered and chafed her arms. "If she was in the house for two hours without hearing the car, why does Detective Monroe find it odd that Natalie didn't hear it in the space of a few minutes?"

"That's exactly what I asked him."

"And?"

"He says he has to double-check everyone's story. That he asked Natalie about it mainly because Ms. Steiner claimed not to have heard the car running until the engine coughed."

"But Natalie is still up there on his suspect list?"

Zeke glanced toward the living room. "I think that earnest money agreement is the biggest reason for that. So far, she's the only person with a motive."

"There *has* to be someone else."

Zeke nodded. "Do you suppose Robert's mother would be willing to talk with me?"

"Grace?" Naomi rolled her eyes. "Do you run with the country club set?"

"No."

"She probably won't be bothered then. The woman has a fixation about social standing."

"I do have a very influential connection, though. Maybe I can get in to see her, riding on his shirttails."

"Who might that be?"

"Ryan Kendrick."

Naomi's eyes widened. "Of the Rocking K Kendricks?"

"One and the same. Ryan's my brother-in-law."

Naomi crossed her arms and smiled. "My, my. That's definitely a name to get Grace's attention. May I ask why you want to talk to her?"

"I'm hoping she can give me a list of people with whom Robert recently did business."

"Surely Monroe has already done that."

"Probably. But maybe he didn't ask the same questions I will. I'm not so much interested in people with whom Robert completed transactions. I'm more interested in finding out about deals that fell through for one reason or another."

Light dawned in Naomi's eyes. "People who may have been done dirty, in other words."

"Exactly. The guy who walks away with money in his pocket isn't usually so unhappy that he'll contemplate murder." Zeke shrugged. "I may turn up nothing, but I'd really like to talk with Robert's mom. If anyone will know about his affairs, it'll be her."

Holding Barbie in one hand, Natalie was flirting outrageously with Ken in a high-pitched voice when she sensed Zeke behind her. She jumped with a start and went hot with embarrassment when she looked into his laughing blue eyes.

"What have we got going here?" he asked in that deep, resonant voice that did such strange things to her nerve endings.

"We're playing Barbie!" Rosie informed him. "I got a new dune buggy today!"

Zeke looked far more amazed than the announcement warranted, telling Natalie she'd guessed right about who'd left the package on their porch. Her heart went soft and achy watching him interact with her daughter. Even though he looked silly handling the brightly colored dune buggy, he pretended intense interest as Rosie pointed out all the features of the miniature conveyance.

"Wow," Zeke said. "Barbie has some nice wheels now." He inclined his head at Ken, who'd been cast aside in a sprawl by the child. "Is that young fellow a safe driver?"

"Oh, yes. He's got a license and everything." Rosie retrieved Ken and straightened his swimming trunks. "He's very safe."

"That's good. If I were Barbie's dad, I'd make him take a driving test to make sure my little girl would be safe with him."

Rosie gave Zeke a speculative look. "Do you want to be her dad?"

"Rosie," Natalie interjected, "Mr. Coulter probably—"

"Mr. Coulter is just plain old Zeke from now on," Zeke interrupted, "and I'd love to be Barbie's dad."

He smiled at Natalie, one of those bone-melting grins that never failed to make her knees feel weak. Then he sat cross-legged beside them on the hardwood floor, gave Barbie's string bikini a long look, and said, "First things first. If I'm going to be Barbie's dad, she needs to get some clothes on, or I'm going to ground her for the rest of her natural life."

"It was the most awful moment of my life!" Naomi said, tears of mirth streaming down her cheeks. "Poor baby. Standing there on the stage in nothing but her underwear, with her poppy costume in a puddle around her ankles."

Holding Natalie's hand under the table, Zeke gave her slender fingers a squeeze to let her know he was very much aware of her sitting beside him. The meal was long since over, and the plates had been removed to the sink. Now only the adults remained seated, their wine goblets thrice filled and subsequently emptied. Zeke's two bottles of merlot had been drained, and Gramps's rotgut burgundy was presently under attack, the contents of the gallon jug diving at an enjoyable rate.

"The most awful moment of *your* life?" Valerie cried. "I was the one on display, Mom, not you!"

Naomi wiped her cheeks. "Finally the poor little thing had the presence of mind to duck behind the curtain. Then she ran. Pete went to find her. He looked for thirty minutes, had almost given up, and then heard her sobbing in a closet in the dressing room. Opened the door, and there she was, huddled under a Santa costume from the Christmas play, her yellow blossoms sitting crooked on her head."

Valerie lazed back on her chair, turning her wine goblet in her fingers, her smile nostalgic. "My one chance at fame, and my mother blew it by gluing my costume together."

Naomi started to laugh again. "Oh, that was a horrible year. I was stretched so thin, helping Pete in the fields, that there weren't enough minutes in a day. After I got the costume cut out, I decided to use Stitch Witchery and a steam iron to put it together, thinking it'd hold just fine for one performance. It didn't, and my daughter has never forgiven me. I think what bothered her most was that she was wearing Tuesday panties on Friday."

Pete winked at Valerie. "Didn't bother her a bit to flash her fanny at three hundred people. Oh, no. She was just fit to be tied because she was wearing the wrong day of the week."

"Nothing has ever changed," Valerie said, lifting her wineglass to her dad. "Put me in fancy enough underwear, and I'll walk down Main Street in broad daylight."

Naomi groaned. "Anyway, such is the Westfield family's tawdry past." She sent Zeke an expectant look. "Your turn."

"I have five siblings," Zeke began. "If I even *touched* on all the crazy things that have happened in my family, we'd be here all night. Besides, none of my stories would be half as entertaining as yours."

"Ah, come on," Naomi said.

"What would you like to hear about first, my brother Hank's brush with the law when he and some friends carried a teacher's Triumph into the gymnasium after a game? Or about the time Tucker got in a fight, and all the Coulter boys ended up in a rumble to defend him? Or about the time my sister, Bethany, was getting ready for the prom, and Hank did her makeup?"

Chin propped on her fist, Naomi grinned broadly. "I want to hear all three stories. But first tell something on yourself."

Zeke chuckled. "Caught that, did you? In all honesty, I was a pretty boring kid. I can't really recall any funny stories about myself."

"Really." Naomi arched one elegantly penciled eyebrow. "Do you lie your way out of sticky situations frequently, or only occasionally?"

Zeke burst out laughing. "Okay. A story about me." He thought for a moment. "There was the time I loaded my father's cigarettes with those little explosives you can buy at joke stores."

Naomi's eyes warmed with amusement, and she nodded. "That'll do."

As Zeke began the tale, he lightly trailed his thumb over the back of Natalie's hand. "I was about sixteen, I think, and I was really put out with my dad because the doctor had warned him to quit smoking, and he was still puffing away.

As an incentive, I got the bright idea to load his cigarettes. I only tampered with three, and being a smart kid who didn't want to get caught, I put them toward the back of his pack before I left for school one morning. My father chain-smoked, most times two to three packs a day, so it was pretty much guaranteed that he'd light the loaded cigarettes while I was gone. Or so I thought. Come to find out, even though he hadn't actually quit yet, he was trying to cut back, so he'd slowed way down on his consumption.

"That evening when I got home, he never said a word about his cigarettes being loaded. After dinner, he always sat in his recliner and smoked while he watched the news. I noticed that his pack was about half gone. I spent the whole night on pins and needles, expecting a cigarette to blow up in his face. It never happened until the next morning, as luck would have it when he visited the bank. He'd gone in to see about getting a loan to keep the ranch afloat. The bank manager invited him into a private office and asked Dad if smoking bothered him. Dad said no and lit up himself. Murphy's Law, of course. *That* was the cigarette that blew."

"Oh, of *course,*" Naomi inserted in a voice gone thin with suppressed laughter.

"Dad swears to this day that I must have double loaded the thing because the blast was deafening and sent tobacco and paper flying everywhere. It startled the bank manager pretty badly, and he had a weak bladder."

Naomi started laughing so hard that she slid down on her chair. "Oh *no!*"

Between chuckles, Pete asked, "Did your old man get his loan?"

Zeke grinned and looked at Natalie. "He did, actually. The bank manager had teenage boys himself, and one of his sons had pulled the same thing on him only a few months before."

A few minutes later, Zeke was about to launch into an account of his sister's senior prom when the doorbell rang. Everyone at the table straightened on their chairs. Gramps frowned. "Who'n hell might that be, do ya think?"

"It's only twenty 'til eight," Naomi pronounced.

Chad came in from the living room where he and Rosie had been watching the animal channel. "It's two guys in suits," he said in a hushed voice. "I think maybe they're cops."

A moment later, with all his dinner companions gathered in the kitchen archway behind him, Pete opened the door to find two of Crystal Falls's finest standing on the porch. The plainclothesmen flashed their badges and then a search warrant. Pete had no choice but to let them enter, a fact that Gramps begrudgingly stated countless times over the next two hours as the detectives systematically destroyed the household with gloved hands, upending cereal boxes and drawers, rifling closets, stripping beds, flipping over the mattresses, and just generally wreaking havoc. It appeared to Zeke that the two men were searching mainly for prescription drugs, which they ferreted away in a clear plastic bag, regardless of the bottle labels.

When practically every room had been gone over with a fine-toothed comb, Zeke made a fast trip to the barn to lock Chester in the tack room. When he returned to the house, he assured Natalie that he would release the gander when he went home later.

"I think they're almost done," she told Zeke. "They even searched the attic."

The two detectives came tripping down the stairs just

then. At the sound of their footsteps on the wooden risers, Natalie and Zeke moved into the living room. Wide-eyed and pale, the kids huddled together on the sofa.

"You gonna clean up yer mess?" Gramps demanded as the two detectives moved toward the front door to let themselves out.

"No, sir," the older fellow replied. "That isn't part of our job."

"It part of the job for you to be a smart-ass?" Gramps popped back.

The detective smiled with strained politeness. "I apologize for the inconvenience. I know it's unsettling to have your home searched."

Gramps puffed out his chest. "Unsettlin'? Ye've turned the whole place topsy-turvy."

"Our superiors will be in touch tomorrow," the younger detective replied. "And, again, we apologize for the inconvenience."

Gramps followed them onto the porch. "Wait a minute! That's my blood pressure pills you got there!"

The older detective glanced down at the clear evidence bag he carried in one hand. "After these medications are examined at the lab, they'll most likely be returned to you, sir."

"How long will that take?"

"A day or two."

"And what am I supposed to take tonight? If I die of a stroke, my son will sue yer fancy britches off!"

The detective lifted the sack higher. "Which bottle contains your blood pressure medication, Mr. Westfield?"

"That one," Gramps replied, indicating the bottle under discussion with a jab of his index finger.

The detective drew a pair of plastic gloves from his

pocket, slipped them on, carefully removed the bottle from the sack, read the dosage directions, and shook three of the tablets onto his palm. After giving them to Gramps, he returned the bottle to the bag. The younger man made note of the exchange in a black notebook.

"Three doses will get you by until the prescriptions are returned to you," the detective holding the sack said.

Gramps shook his head. "What's this country comin' to?" he blustered. "I never in all my days seen the like. You got any idea how much those damned pills cost? Way over a hundred bucks for a month's supply, that's what. I can't afford to go buyin' more of 'em!"

"I understand, sir, and I assure you that the prescription will most likely be returned to you. I'll make a special note regarding the blood pressure pills, telling our lab techs to put a rush on them."

As Gramps stepped back in the house and closed the door, Zeke felt Natalie's body go heavy against him where he held her tucked under his arm. He glanced down and saw that her face was as white as alabaster, her eyes huge and luminous in her pale countenance.

"They were searching for sedatives," she said, her voice reedy with tension and exhaustion. "They think I'm the one who drugged Robert."

Zeke had already determined that. He glanced at Rosie, who sat so close to Chad she was almost on the boy's lap. First things first, he thought, and left Natalie to go upstairs and right the child's bedroom. As he shoved clothing back into drawers and put the little girl's bed to rights, he clenched his teeth, furious beyond bearing that the law of the land allowed such invasions. There wasn't a single room in the Westfield home that hadn't been rifled. Zeke under stood that the detectives had only been doing their jobs, but it seemed to him that they could have at least tried not to make such a mess.

Just as Zeke smoothed the coverlet on Rosie's bed, Natalie appeared in the doorway, her daughter draped over her shoulder. "Out like a light, thank goodness."

Zeke jerked the covers back. "I'm sorry this happened, honey."

Natalie laid her daughter on the bed and spent an inordinate amount of time arranging the sheet and blanket over Rosie's small form. Never had Zeke seen such pain in anyone's eyes.

"It's my fault," she said. "Of all the stupid things to do, going into Robert's house takes the prize. None of this would be happening if I hadn't been such an idiot."

"You had no idea he'd been murdered. If not for that, what would have come of it? At the worst, Robert would have missed the goblets and confronted you about taking them. No real harm done, and you would have your grandmother's crystal back."

"He has been murdered, though," she whispered. "And now, because I went in there, they're convinced I killed him."

Zeke couldn't argue the point, and the fact made him heartsick. This woman had suffered enough at Robert Patterson's hands, yet it seemed she was fated to endure more.

For the first time since Robert's death, Zeke believed there was actually a chance that Natalie might go to jail for the man's murder.

Chapter Fifteen

After Zeke left that night, Natalie joined her mother for a cup of herbal tea before heading upstairs for bed. When she entered her room a bit later, she leaned heavily against the closed door and stared at the mess the detectives had made of everything. Clothing still hung from her drawers and lay in heaps on the floor. Earlier she'd remade the bed and put things back on their hangers. The rest would have to wait until tomorrow.

Exhausted, yet brittle with tension, Natalie moved farther into the room. Now she could understand how people felt after their homes had been burglarized. Those detectives had gone through everything, even her lingerie drawer. Shoe boxes of keepsakes lay strewn across the floor, the contents jumbled by careless hands. Natalie crouched down to straighten her mementos. She smiled when she came across a lock of Chad's baby hair. Tears stung her eyes when she reached to close Rosie's baby book and saw her tiny footprint.

By the time Natalie had the boxes righted and returned to their place on the closet shelf, she was so tired she could barely move. Even so, she didn't expect to fall asleep very quickly after she donned a nightshirt, slipped between the sheets, and flicked off the lamp. She lay on her back, the feather pillow arranged just so beneath her head. As always, the night sounds that came through the open window soothed her. She listened to the whir of a nighthawk as it dove for mosquitoes, the cheerful trill of crickets in the field grass, and the throaty voices of frogs out in the irrigation pond. The old farmhouse groaned and creaked in the light breeze, the noises as familiar and comforting to Natalie as a lullaby.

Staring through the moon-silvery shadows at the ceiling, she let her thoughts drift to Zeke. He'd said nothing about sneaking over to see her tonight, but she still hoped he would come. Feeling his arms around her had been all that had held her together over the last few days.

Zeke. Over dinner, he'd told her that the wall between the bar and dining room at the club had come down today. Tomorrow he and his brothers would begin fixing the floor and putting up wood trim to hide where the framing had been attached to the intersecting walls and ceiling. According to him, the cosmetic facia boards would look as though they belonged there, a delineation between bar and dining room that would be stained to match the laminate wood floor. Natalie was anxious to see it for herself, and she'd been hoping to drive into town tomorrow. Now the entire day would be spent putting the house back in order.

Her eyelids began to droop. She relaxed in the cozy warmth of her comforter, grateful in a distant part of her mind for the cool summer nights in Central Oregon. No matter how hot the day, the night winds brought relief.

Natalie had just drifted off when a loud, raucous honking noise brought her awake. Startled, she was out of bed before she could think clearly. The honking sound came again. *Chester? Oh, no!* Still bleary-eyed, she rushed to the open window. As she leaned out over the windowsill, she heard a man curse. Then it sounded as if he collided with the sheet metal that Pop had leaned against the pump house. *Zeke.* That dad-blamed gander was after him again.

"Zeke," she called softly. "Is that you?"

She wanted to yell at Chester to behave himself, but she was afraid she'd wake everyone in the whole house. Out by the cars, which were parked at random between the picket fence and barn, Natalie saw a ghostly flurry of white, which she suspected was the gander, flapping its wings. Then she saw the indistinct figure of a man running toward the back of the barn. She leaned farther out the window, trying to see better.

The gander honked again, clearly in hot pursuit of someone. Natalie imagined Zeke, circling the barn and vaulting over fences, trying to escape Chester's vicious pinches. She wanted to grab her robe, race outside, and lock the bird in the barn again.

"What the Sam Hill is going on?"

Valerie's whispered question startled Natalie so badly that she jerked erect and cracked the back of her head on the bottom rail of the window frame. *"Ouch!"* she cried in a hushed voice and grabbed the smarting spot.

"Sorry." Valerie moved farther into the room. "What on earth is Chester all upset about?"

Natalie dropped her hand. "I think he's after Zeke."

"Uh-oh." Valerie snickered. "As if scaling the roof to see you isn't bad enough? That dumb bird. I thought he was getting used to Zeke."

"Maybe he didn't recognize him in the dark."

"Zeke's going to get mad one of these times and wring that gander's neck." Valerie yawned and rubbed her eyes. "If that's all it is, I'm going back to bed."

" 'Night," Natalie said softly.

Valerie tiptoed quietly from the room and eased the door closed again. Natalie turned back to the window and peered through the darkness. She saw no sign of Zeke—or of Chester, either. With a sigh, she retraced her steps to the bed and flopped down on the mattress. *Dumb gander.* If he ruined her chance to see Zeke tonight, she might lose patience and wring his neck herself.

Zeke crawled through Natalie's window at three o'clock in the morning. When he slipped into bed with her, she stirred awake, smiled sleepily, and said, "You came back."

"Of course. Sorry I'm so late."

She slipped her slender arms around his neck. "I'm the one who's sorry. Is Chester still in one piece?"

Zeke gave her a bewildered look. "Why wouldn't he be?" he whispered.

"I'm surprised you didn't murder him," she said with a sleepy laugh. "I can't believe he chased you like that again."

Zeke didn't know what she was talking about. "Chester didn't chase me again. When I let him out of the barn after I left, he was a perfect gentleman."

Natalie tucked in her chin to study his face. Her eyes were so damned beautiful in the moonlight. Zeke started to kiss her. She stopped him dead with, "It wasn't you he chased off the property earlier?"

"Tonight?" Zeke glanced at the window. "Chester chased someone off the property tonight?"

"A man, judging by his size, or maybe a teenage boy. He was out by the cars. Chester took after him. It wasn't you?"

Zeke shook his head. "After I left here, I drove to town to do my books and make out some orders. I ran into a few wrinkles and ended up having to stay longer than I expected." Zeke swung off the bed. "You got a flashlight? I'd better go check on things."

Natalie rose onto her knees. "I'm sure everything is perfectly fine. It was probably some kid trying to siphon some gas. No big deal." She opened her arms. "Come back here."

Zeke glanced at the window. "What if someone stripped the cars?"

"Then someone stripped the cars. Whoever it was, he's long gone now. If anything's missing, we'll worry about it in the morning."

She looked so sweet and inviting that Zeke was back on the bed before he consciously made the decision to move. He knelt in front of her and gently claimed her lips in a lingering kiss. She sighed and went soft against him.

He promptly forgot all about the damned cars and made love to her.

The following morning Natalie woke up bright and early. When she got downstairs, she found Valerie already up, dressed, and drinking a cup of coffee.

"Wow. What lit a fire under you?" Natalie asked.

Valerie sank onto a chair. "There's a lot of work to be done around here today if we're going to get the house put back together. I thought I'd hit it early before it gets too hot."

"Good plan." Natalie stepped to the door. "It wasn't Zeke that Chester was chasing last night."

"It wasn't?"

"No. I'm going to check the cars, just in case something was stolen."

Moments later, Natalie was circling the automobiles. It didn't appear to her that anything was missing. Valerie's boom box was still sitting on the front passenger seat of her Mazda, Naomi's factory-installed stereo system was still in the dash of her small sedan, and Pop's tools were still in the bed of his pickup.

"If he was a thief, he ran before he could snatch any good stuff," Natalie told her sister when she returned to the house. "Kids, trying to siphon gas, I'll bet."

"With Chester standing guard, they probably didn't get any fuel, either," Valerie observed with a laugh.

"Thank goodness. I can barely afford to keep my tank full as it is."

Natalie stepped to the cupboard to get a coffee mug. The counter was littered with spilled cereal. She pictured the detectives upending the boxes onto the drain and then scooping the contents back in with their hands. *Disgusting.* Every box of cereal was going in the trash. She wasn't about to let her kids eat it now.

"Man, this gripes me," she said as she grabbed a dishcloth to wipe the countertop. "How can the police get away with muscling their way into people's homes and doing stuff like this? I even saw one of them sifting through the flour bin. Who wants to eat food that strangers touched?"

"They wore gloves."

"How do we know they were clean gloves? The only reason they wore them was to keep from putting their fingerprints on any possible evidence. For all we know, they wear the same ones, over and over. Heaven only knows what filth they've touched. Toilet tank covers, for instance. They always look under tank covers in the movies."

"Oh, nasty, yucka." Valerie curled her lip. "I guess you're right."

"The flour and cereal have to go. I'm not eating it, and my kids aren't, for sure."

Valerie nodded. "I see what you're saying, but there's no point in getting pissed off about it. They were only doing their job." She crossed her slender legs. She wore jeans with strategic slits in the legs, one so high on her thigh that her pink underpants showed. "If you were guilty of Robert's murder, you wouldn't hide the sedatives in the medicine cabinet, would you?"

Natalie sighed. "No, of course not. I'd have thrown them away or hidden them in the most unlikely place possible."

"Like, maybe, the flour bin?"

"Not now, I wouldn't. Seeing that detective going through the flour is emblazoned on my brain forever." Natalie poured herself some coffee. "Sorry I'm so cranky. I wanted to drive in and check on things at the club today. Zeke says it looks great with the wall gone. Thanks to last night's raid, my whole day is screwed up."

Valerie yawned and took a sip of coffee. "Doesn't have to be. Mom and I can take care of this."

"I can't waltz off and let you guys do all the work. It's my fault it even happened."

"It'd be better for the kids if you got them out of here. Poor little Rosie doesn't understand any of this. Did you see her eyes last night? She was scared to death of those guys."

Cradling the steaming mug in her hands, Natalie turned to rest her hips against the stove. "This whole mess has been hard on both of them."

"Then get them out of here," Valerie urged. "I don't mind. Honestly. And I know Mom won't either. Take the kids to town and make a day of it. You haven't been to church in weeks. They'd both enjoy that. Afterward, take them by the club with you. When you're finished there, treat them to something really fun to get their minds off everything."

"Are you sure?"

"Positive. Just remember you owe me one."

Natalie glanced at her watch. Then she hurriedly finished her coffee, hugged her sister, and went upstairs to roust her kids out of bed. As the children raced around to get ready for church, Natalie yelled, "New clothes today."

Rosie slid to a stop in the hall and planted her tiny hands on her hips. "I thought we couldn't wear them 'til school starts!"

"Church is more special than school," Natalie insisted. "Pick out your favorite new outfit."

Rosie shrieked in delight and raced off to her bedroom. Chad grinned and said, "I'm wearing my new Nikes."

"Go for it, my man."

A few minutes later, Natalie joined her children at the kitchen table for a fast breakfast of toast and milk, neither of which had been handled by the detectives last night. The moment they all finished eating, they said their good-byes and made for the door. En route to the car, Natalie announced, "After church, we're going to stop by the supper club to see what it looks like with the wall removed."

"Cool," Chad said as he climbed into the back.

"Cool!" Rosie, the parrot, said as she joined her brother on the rear seat and searched for the ends of her safety belt.

After fastening her own safety restraint, Natalie started

the car. "When I'm done at the club, we're going grocery shopping."

"Big-time boring," Chad said.

"Yeah, Mommy. That's no fun."

Natalie smiled at them over the seat. "But then . . ." She let her voice trail off to get their attention. "*Then* we're going to do something really special."

"What?" Chad asked.

"Well, we can go to Papa's Pizza or, if you'd rather, we can see if there's a good movie showing. Or we can go to that huge indoor place with the miniature golf and stuff."

"Fun Village?" Chad asked incredulously.

"Yeah, Fun Village." At the end of the drive, Natalie turned left onto Old Mill Road, which got very little traffic this far out. After making the turn onto the asphalt, she waved her arm above her head and yelled, "Hurray! We're on our way!"

"Hurray!" Rosie shrieked. "I get to go to Sunday school in my pretty new top and pants!"

"And then maybe to Fun Village!" Chad cried.

Natalie settled back to devote her attention to driving. After adjusting her mirrors, she accelerated to fifty-five, the rural speed limit in Oregon, and began the long trip to town, slowing down only for the occasional curve. She was going to make this a special day, she thought with a smile. Chad needed a distraction and so did Rosie. After Fun Village, she might even take them to the park to feed the ducks, a fairly inexpensive activity that both kids enjoyed.

That was Natalie's last rational thought. The next instant, she came upon a sharp curve, and when she pushed on the brake, the pedal offered only momentary resistance before it went clear to the floor. She tried to pump it back up and got a little pedal back, but then it vanished.

She gripped the steering wheel in both hands and focused completely on taking the curve at high speed. The tires of the old Chevy screamed as they grabbed the pavement.

"Mom?" Chad said.

"Our brakes are gone," Natalie replied in as calm a voice as she could muster. "Keep your belts on and lie sideways on the seat."

"But—"

"Just *do* it!" Natalie ordered.

After that there was no more time for talking. As they came out of the curve, they came upon a slow-moving cattle truck. Natalie had mere seconds to react. From the darkest reaches of her mind, a memory of Pop's voice came to her. *If your brakes ever fail when you're driving an automatic, gear down and grab the emergency brake.* Using all her strength, Natalie jerked downward on the gearshift. The transmission of the Chevy grinded down, metal groaning as gear teeth caught and tried to hold. *Not enough.* She leaned sharply forward to grasp the emergency brake lever, a prayer on her lips as she pulled back on it and the tires locked up. At the sudden deceleration, the rear end of the Chevy fishtailed, sending the car into a sideways skid. It took all Natalie's skill as a driver to regain control of the car.

In that instant, the world around her seemed to vanish. All she could see was the back of that truck coming at them with horrifying speed. She sensed rather than saw Chad still sitting up behind her.

"Lie down!" she shrieked. "Now, Chad! Drop!"

* * *

Zeke dialed Natalie's home number. When Naomi answered, he said, "Hi, Naomi, this is Zeke. My brothers and I are about finished up here at the club for today. They both have families and, this being Sunday, they want to lay off early. Natalie said she planned to stop by, but she still hasn't come. Before I locked up, I thought I'd call to see if she still plans to show."

"Oh, Zeke."

The tremulous note in Naomi's voice told Zeke that something was horribly wrong. "What?" he said.

"Natalie and the kids were in an accident."

Zeke's stomach dropped. "Oh, God. How bad?"

"Bad," Naomi said shakily. "Hit the back end of a cattle truck and rolled into a ditch. The car's totaled."

Zeke didn't give a shit about the damned car. "How are Natalie and the kids?"

"They're at the hospital. That's all I know. Pete already left for there. Valerie and I were just leaving when you phoned."

Zeke didn't even tell Naomi good-bye. As he raced from the supper club, he tossed the door and alarm keys to Jake. "Natalie and the kids have been in a wreck!"

Once inside his truck, Zeke was shaking so badly that he couldn't get the key into the ignition. *Natalie and the kids* Oh, God. He didn't know when he'd come to love the three of them so much, but the thought of losing one of them made his heart feel as if it were being ripped from his chest

Waiting. Zeke had never been particularly good at it, bu now it was sheer torture. Mindlessly counting specks on th gray-green floor tile, he sat on a green vinyl chair in the E lounge beside Pete and Naomi. A nurse had come out to se them a few minutes ago. There was a strong possibility that Rosie had a concussion, and Chad had been taken to X ray to see if he had broken ribs. By some miracle, Natalie had escaped with only a few scrapes and bruises, the worst of them on her chest where the steering wheel had struck her breastbone.

Valerie paced back and forth in front of Zeke, biting her nails.

"I *hate* this," she complained. "Why can't we just go in and be with them?"

"The cubicles are small. They need room to work," Naomi replied calmly. "Natalie will update us the moment she knows more."

"Well, this totally sucks," Valerie cried. "Why don't they have someone who comes out to tell the family something on a more regular basis?"

"Stop chewing those acrylic overlays," Naomi said. "If you tear them off, you'll ruin your natural nails."

"Like I care?"

Zeke lost his train of thought and had to start over counting dots. Madness. He didn't know why he'd started counting the damned things in the first place, but now he couldn't make himself stop. *Three, four—please, God—five, six—let them be all right.* He'd never been a praying man, but he was praying now. Rosie was so tiny. Zeke cringed every time he thought about her fragile little skull hitting something hard enough to give her a concussion. And Chad. Broken ribs were not only painful but also dangerous sometimes. As a boy, Zeke had seen a man almost drown in his own blood from a broken rib that had punctured his lung.

"We can thank our lucky stars," Pete said for about the

hundredth time. "I saw the car on the way into town. I'm telling you, Zeke, it's a miracle they weren't killed."

Zeke only nodded. He couldn't speak. He wished he could see Natalie—that he could be with her and hold her hand. But that wasn't possible. Only a member of the immediate family could invade the inner sanctum, and he was only a friend.

Never again, he vowed to himself. He was marrying that lady before her bruises faded. He'd never again sit in a waiting room while Rosie and Chad lay on gurneys in the ER. What if Rosie slipped off to sleep and never woke up? Or what if she developed a blood clot on the brain? Zeke had heard of that happening after a severe blow to the skull.

He kept remembering the evening he'd first seen Rosie—how she had invaded his kitchen, all big brown eyes and curly black hair, chattering like a little magpie. He remembered thinking then that he could do without kid drawings on his fridge. Now he would happily wallpaper his whole house with them.

And Chad. The boy had been through so much over the last few months. He didn't need a physical injury on top of everything else. He'd just lost his father, for God's sake.

Zeke wondered yet again how the accident had happened. According to Pete, Natalie had said something about the brakes going out. *Damned old rattletrap.* From now on, she'd have a decent vehicle. He'd make sure of it.

Just when Zeke thought he could bear the waiting no longer, he heard the shuffle of boots at the ER entrance. He glanced up to see Jake and Hank coming through the glass revolving door. Behind them were his parents.

Zeke pushed to his feet. *His family.* Just seeing their faces made him feel calmer and more centered.

"How are they?" Jake asked as he entered the lounge. "On the way over, I called to check, but the gal at the desk wouldn't tell me much."

"Natalie will be fine," Zeke replied, hugging each of his brothers in turn. "The jury's still out on the kids. Rosie may have a concussion, and they think Chad could have some broken ribs."

"Ah, dear heart," Zeke's mother crooned as she went up on her tiptoes to kiss his cheek. "We came the moment we heard. Thank God they aren't seriously hurt."

After hugging his mom, Zeke hooked an arm around his father's shoulders. "Thanks for coming, you guys."

"Of course we came," Mary exclaimed in a scolding voice. "Surely you didn't think we'd let you go through this alone."

In truth, Zeke had assumed exactly that. He hadn't gotten around to taking Natalie over to meet his folks yet. Jake and Hank had met her only by chance.

Remembering his manners, Zeke introduced his parents and brothers to Natalie's family. Within seconds, Naomi and Valerie were off in a corner with Zeke's mother Mary, the three of them chatting like old friends about broken ribs, concussions, and car accidents. As upset as Zeke was, he couldn't help but smile. Mary Coulter and Naomi Westfield were as different as night from day. Zeke's mom was a short, buxom little lady with merry blue eyes and an angelic smile who spent all her time crocheting stuff for her grandbabies. Naomi was flashy by comparison with a well-preserved figure and a flare for style.

When Zeke turned his attention back to the men, he heard his father say, "Pete Westfield, huh. Have we met? Can't think where or when it was, but the face and name ring a bell."

"We've never actually met," Pete replied. "But we've rubbed elbows a few times at meetings and the like. I have a farm out on Old Mill Road."

From there, the two older men fell into a discussion about the similarities between ranching and farming. Hank and Jake joined Zeke across the room, asking questions about the accident that Zeke couldn't readily answer.

"Natalie said something about the brakes going out. According to her dad, she plowed into the back of a cattle truck and rolled the car into a ditch."

Jake winced.

"Luckily," Zeke went on, "the truck held steady on the road. If it had jackknifed, it could have been much worse."

Hank laid a hand on Zeke's shoulder. "They're alive. That's the important thing."

Zeke expressed his concerns about Rosie's possible concussion and Chad's injured ribs. Jake shook his head. "You're letting fear do your thinking, Zeke. If they aren't even sure the little girl has a concussion, a blood clot on the brain is probably unlikely. I think there'd be some unmistakable symptoms with something that serious."

Zeke released a tight breath. "Maybe you're right."

"I know I'm right. You're just scared and imagining worst-case scenarios. The rib thing, for instance. They'll keep the boy's torso immobilized until they know what they're dealing with. If he didn't come in with a punctured lung, he isn't likely to get one now."

More of the tension eased from Zeke's body. "God, I'm glad you're here. You're right, absolutely right. I'm blowing this way out of proportion."

Hank lifted one foot to rest a boot on his knee. "Damn straight. Relax, big brother. Next time Natalie comes out, she'll bring good news. Your kids'll be fine."

Pete overheard Hank's comment and looked at Zeke. "Your kids, huh?"

Zeke met his future father-in-law's gaze straight on. "Yes, sir. Do you have a problem with that?"

Pete smiled and shook his head. "Nope, no problem at all."

By the time Natalie emerged from the ER, Zeke's whole family had arrived at the hospital. The small waiting room was packed with people, and the noise level was almost deafening. Zeke leaped to his feet and quickly closed the distance to the doorway.

Chapter Sixteen

Natalie swayed on her feet and clutched Zeke's shirt-sleeve for balance.

"Sweetheart, are you okay?"

"Fine. Just a little light-headed."

Zeke smoothed her hair back from her face. "Are you hurting anywhere?"

"A little achy." She leaned her shoulder against his chest. "I'm fine, otherwise, I think. The doctor says I'll be right as rain in a couple of days."

Zeke wasn't so sure. "How are the kids?" he finally found the courage to ask.

The room around them went suddenly silent. Zeke followed Natalie's bewildered gaze as she took in all the curious eyes that had been trained on them. "Who are all these people?" she asked softly.

"My family," he replied. "Jake and Hank were with me when I heard about the wreck. Everyone else came as soon as they heard."

She nodded, but her expression remained confused. "Most of them don't even know me."

Mary Coulter smiled from her chair in the corner. "Don't

mind us, honey. I know I speak for everyone in the family when I say we don't expect you to stand on ceremony. We'll save the introductions for another time."

"Oh, God, that's your mom, isn't it?" Natalie squeaked.

Zeke bent to whisper, "Forget my family. Just pretend they aren't here. How are the kids? That's the important thing."

She passed a tremulous hand over her eyes. "The doctor says the kids can go home. We should watch Rosie tonight and wake her up every couple of hours. He still hasn't ruled out a slight concussion. He was pretty worried about Chad's ribs, too, but it turned out that they're only bruised."

Zeke almost whooped with relief. "Did you hear that?" He glanced around the lounge, flashing a happy grin. "Both the kids are going home!"

The noise level in the waiting room went up again, with members of both families expressing relief. "Thank God!" "What fabulous news!" "Bless their little hearts."

"They wrapped Chad's ribs to ease the pain," Natalie went on. "And the doctor's going to give me a prescription to keep him comfortable over the next couple of days." She frowned and pressed a fingertip to her temple. "I'll need to stop somewhere to get the prescription filled, I guess."

Gazing down at her drawn face, Zeke's concern for her increased. To hell with the ER rules. She'd been through enough and needed to lie down herself.

Zeke sent Pete a look rife with meaning. Natalie's father hurried over to take his daughter by the arm. "Come sit down, honey," Pete said softly.

"I can't, Pop. I need to—"

"Your mother and Zeke will take care of the kids now."

Pete's voice grew sterner. "You need to sit, no arguments. Let them handle it now. You've done enough."

Natalie allowed her father to lead her to a chair. Zeke motioned to Naomi. Seconds later, they invaded the ER together. A short, redheaded nurse spotted Zeke almost instantly and came out from behind the station. "May I help you?"

"We're here with the Patterson children," Zeke said. "Their mother was in the accident with them, and she's about to collapse. We're taking it from here."

"Are you a relative, sir?"

Zeke held the woman's gaze with unwavering intensity. "I'm their stepfather." He gestured to Naomi. "She's their maternal grandmother."

The nurse seemed satisfied with that response and smiled. "They're in five and six. We've drawn the curtain back between their beds." As she led the way to the cubicles, she went on to say, "The doctor will be in soon with home-care instructions." She pulled back a blue curtain. "I'll get another chair. Just a second."

Zeke saw the kids, and moved between the hospital beds. Rosie had a nasty bruise on her forehead, but she was smiling. Chad's face was ghostly pale, and Zeke could tell by the way he lay that he was in pain, but he looked all right otherwise. Zeke kissed Rosie and gave her a careful hug. Then he handed the little girl over to Naomi while he concentrated on Chad.

"Hey, partner. I've been pretty worried about you."

Chad tried to smile, but the result was more a grimace. "I'm okay. The doctor says I'm just bruised up real bad."

"Hurts like hell, though, doesn't it?" Zeke took the boy's hand and gave it a hard squeeze. "Been there. For the next week, I promise not to make you laugh, and I won't allow any pepper on your food. The last thing you want is to sneeze."

Chad's second attempt at a smile was more successful. Zeke knew the boy would be all right when he said, "My shorts and jeans are in a sack under the bed. Will you help me put them on, Zeke? I don't want that nurse to see me naked."

A cow was sitting on her chest. Natalie put the flats of her hands on its rump and pushed with all her might, but the stupid bovine refused to budge. It was hard for her to breathe. Expanding her lungs hurt. She pushed at the cow again, wanting it off of her.

"Natalie, sweetheart? Honey, wake up. It's time for your pain medication."

Natalie blinked awake and saw Zeke leaning over her. When she realized that she'd been pushing at his shoulders, she said, "Oh. I thought you were a cow."

He chuckled and lifted one of her hands to place a soft kiss on her palm. Then he sat back and curled her fingers around it. "Hold tight to that. It's the only kind of kiss you're going to get for a few days, I'm afraid."

It hurt to breathe, even now that she was awake. Natalie swallowed hard. "My chest."

"According to the doctor, that steering wheel rammed you pretty hard. You're going to be really sore for a while." He reached for a glass on the nightstand. "He prescribed some pain reliever. The shot he gave you in the ER is wearing off now. That's probably why you're uncomfortable." He slipped a hand under her head. "Don't try to sit up. Let me do the work. All right?"

Natalie nodded weakly and swallowed the pills he gave her. Her skin was moist with sweat by the time he settled her back against the pillows. "Where are the kids? Are they—?"

"They're just fine. Your mom and dad and sister are taking great care of them."

Natalie's stomach clenched with worry. "Are they waking Rosie every two hours?"

Zeke chuckled. She loved the sound of his laugh, a deep, rich sound that rumbled up from his broad chest. "Rosie has yet to close her eyes. Valerie rented her movies, *George in the Jungle,* or something like that, and another one about a horse. She's ensconced on the sofa like a little princess with her royal subjects running at her beck and call."

Natalie stifled a yawn and smiled. "And Chad?"

"Valerie got him the new Harry Potter book. He's too doped up to read by himself, so she's in his room, reading it aloud to him."

Natalie closed her eyes. "She couldn't afford to buy that book. What'll I do with her?"

"Just love her and lend her money when her car insurance comes due."

Natalie wanted to laugh, but her chest hurt too much. She lifted her lashes and settled for smiling again. "You're pretty special. You know that?"

"So are you. Did you know that?" He trailed a fingertip along her cheek. She loved the warm rasp of his skin against hers. "I nearly died when your mom told me you'd been in a wreck. Until that moment, I knew I loved you, but I didn't realize how much I loved your kids."

A stinging sensation washed over Natalie's eyes. "Oh Zeke."

"Seriously. I was so scared I couldn't shove the damned

key in my truck ignition, and it's a damned miracle I made it to the hospital without having a wreck myself." He moved his fingertip to her mouth. "I've decided that you have to marry me. No long engagement, no messing around. I want it done yesterday. They wouldn't let me in the ER until I lied and said I was the kids' stepfather."

Natalie felt her lashes drooping. She blinked and tried her best to wake up. "I'm sorry. I can't seem to keep my eyes open."

"Don't be sorry. Just say yes."

She couldn't quite remember the question. "Yes," she whispered, and slipped back into her dreams, lovely ones this time about a dark-faced man with eyes the color of a summer sky.

Zeke lay beside Natalie atop the covers. He'd left the bedroom door ajar but had turned out the light so it wouldn't disturb her rest. Occasionally Naomi came in to check on her daughter. Zeke's response to her questions had been the same each time. Natalie seemed to be sleeping peacefully.

It was going on midnight now. Zeke listened to the night sounds drifting in through the open window. Frogs, crickets, and the occasional low of a cow out in the barn. He closed his eyes and thanked God that Natalie and her kids were okay—that he could lie here now, at peace and happily contemplating a future with them. Pete's descriptions of Natalie's car were frightening. It had been a close call, a very close call. In the blink of an eye, Zeke could have lost her and the kids. Just the thought made his guts clench.

Brake failure. Zeke kept coming back to that, not quite able to believe her brakes could go out like that without any prior warning. Most times, when the fluid got low or the shoes started to wear, there were signs of trouble long before the brakes completely failed. Pete thought it was strange, too. He claimed that he'd put the Chevy on a rack and given it a thorough going-over before Natalie bought it last winter. The brakes had been like new then.

Zeke sighed and closed his eyes, growing drowsy from the sound of Natalie's slow, even breathing. He'd almost drifted off when Chester honked somewhere outside. The sound jerked Zeke back awake. He listened for a moment. The gander raised no further alarm, an indication that the initial honk had meant nothing. Even so, Zeke swung to his feet to approach the window. Gazing out into the shifting shadows of darkness, he recalled Natalie's story of a midnight prowler last night. Someone out around the cars, she'd said, a man or teenage boy, judging by his size.

An awful suspicion slithered into Zeke's mind. It was so preposterous that he quickly shoved it away. Robert's death was playing with his mind, he decided. Who would have it in for Natalie? And if someone did, why would he tamper with the brakes of her car? Anyone with half a brain would realize that such an act might endanger her children or other passengers.

Zeke raked a hand through his hair and returned to the bed. He tried to stretch out and snooze for a while, but the suspicion wouldn't leave him alone. Sudden brake failure. Robert had been killed only a few days ago. Natalie had been in his home at or around the time of the murder. What if she'd seen something that could incriminate the killer—something she hadn't realized was significant at the time?

If someone killed once, he could kill again—especially if a certain pretty lady had seen something that could put a noose around that person's neck.

Zeke swung off the bed again. This time, he bypassed the window and went downstairs to discuss his suspicions with Pete.

"Do you think I'm whacked?" Zeke asked Pete a few minutes later.

Pete poured each of them another measure of bourbon, a private stash he kept in his bedroom closet. Gramps, it seemed, enjoyed having a nightly tipple, and Pete didn't want the old man to develop a taste for the hard stuff.

"It is strange that the brakes failed that way," Pete acknowledged. His blue eyes darkened with worry. "The truth? I don't want to believe someone tampered with her car. It scares the livin' hell out of me. But, having said that, I can't rule out the possibility. When brakes fail suddenly like Natalie described, something's usually gone haywire with the brake lines."

"Which occasionally happens under completely ordinary circumstances. But it's not common." Zeke downed his whiskey in one gulp and set his glass back on the table. "Here's my train of thought. I think we should visit the wrecking yard and have a look at her car."

Pete inclined his head. "I'm game. No harm in looking. If we find nothing peculiar, then we can both rest easy in our minds."

By nine thirty the following morning, Zeke was lying on his back under Natalie's demolished Chevy. He'd checked the brakes on the other side of the vehicle and found nothing out of the ordinary. As he started to check the right rear side, he called out to Pete.

"Well, it looks like I was whacked, after all. Nothing's

wrong, as far as I can see. The damned brakes must have just failed on their own."

"Don't apologize." Pete was hunkered down next to the tire. "I'd just as soon be on a wild-goose chase as to find out someone tried to kill her."

Zeke was about to slide back out from under the car when he remembered to check the bleeder valve. "Son of a *bitch*!"

"What?" Pete went down on his knees to peer under the car. "You find something?"

"Sure as shit. Someone loosened this bleeder valve."

"What?"

"The bleeder valve is open," Zeke repeated. "Every time she touched the brake, the fluid in the rear lines was bleeding out. There are a lot of curves along Old Mill Road. By the time she reached that sharp one, all the fluid in her rear lines would have been gone."

Pete swore under his breath. Zeke pushed out from under the car and went to check the front brake on that side. He found the same thing. "Jesus. I wasn't whacked, Pete. Somebody messed with her brakes."

Thirty minutes later, Zeke and Pete were standing in front of Detective Monroe's desk. The detective had leaned as far back in his chair as possible.

"Let's calm down, gentlemen," he said.

"Bullshit! I'm not about to calm down." Zeke planted his hands on the blotter and leaned forward to get nose to nose with the detective. "Someone tried to kill Natalie Patterson. Send one of your men out to inspect the brakes on her car. The bleeder valves, front and rear, were open. Every time she so much as touched that brake pedal, she lost fluid. Whoever did it meant for her to die in that accident, Monroe. The speed limit out there is fifty-five except for in the curves. You ever been going that fast on a narrow road, come to a curve, and lost your brakes?"

"No, I can't say I have." Monroe ran a hand over his balding head. "Listen, I can understand your being upset. It was a serious accident, and children were involved. But even you must admit that this story is a little far-fetched. A gander chases a midnight prowler off the property. The next morning, Mrs. Patterson's brakes fail. You're making assumptions and tying the incidents to the Patterson murder. In my line of work, you learn early on not to join the dots unless the picture makes sense, and this one makes no sense."

"Why doesn't it?"

"Your theory is that Mrs. Patterson saw something when she was inside the house that may implicate the killer." Detective Monroe raised his bushy eyebrows. "What, exactly, do you imagine she saw?"

Zeke stared into the detective's eyes. Suddenly they seemed as glassy and lifeless as a snake's. "Excuse me, but I believe I'm on the wrong side of this desk to be asked that question. The bleeder valves on that car were loosened. Someone deliberately tampered with those brakes to make Natalie have an accident when she left the farm. Going either direction, the speed limit is fifty-five, and she would have encountered sharp curves. Last week, she blithely wandered through Robert Patterson's house, looking for goblets while he was possibly being murdered out in the garage. If you can't connect those dots and see that there's a strong possibility she saw something that may get her killed, you're a poor excuse for a cop."

"That's Mrs. Patterson's story."

Anger roiled within Zeke. "But you don't buy it?"

"Whether or not I buy it is beside the point. I have to look at the facts, Mr. Coulter, and right now she's the only person who had a reason to want Robert Patterson dead."

"The only person you've found," Zeke corrected. "And the only person you will find if you don't get your head out of your ass."

Monroe pushed to his feet. "For all I know, Mrs. Patterson loosened her own damned bleeder valves. Now that the sale of her farm has come to light, she's our primary suspect, and she knows it. She may be feeling desperate. What better way to throw suspicion off herself than to stage an attempt on her own life?"

Zeke had never in all his life wanted to hit a man so badly. "Her kids were in that frigging car, Monroe. You can't honestly believe she would deliberately put their safety at risk."

The detective shrugged. "That depends entirely on what kind of person she is. If she murdered Robert Patterson, she obviously doesn't place a high value on human life, now does she?"

Pete grabbed Zeke's arm. "Come on, son. Getting yourself thrown in jail won't help the situation."

Zeke jerked his arm free and leveled a finger at the detective's nose. "Bring your superior in here *now*. I want a witness to the fact that we've reported an attempt on Mrs. Patterson's life and you're blowing us off."

"May I ask why you feel that's necessary?" Monroe asked.

Zeke straightened his shirt and endeavored to calm down. When he'd managed, he returned the detective's smile. "Connect the dots, Detective."

* * *

Naomi's face lost color when Pete told her that someone had tampered with the brakes on Natalie's car. She glanced bewilderedly at Zeke and shook her head.

"What are you saying?"

Pete finger combed his graying hair. "I know it's scary, honey. I don't want to believe it, either. But those bleeder valves didn't open by themselves. Someone tried to kill our girl."

Naomi shook her head again. "She has no enemies. Why would anyone want her dead?"

Zeke explained his theory that Natalie might have seen something she shouldn't have while searching Robert's house. "Maybe the killer's car was parked on the street. Maybe he left a monogrammed cigarette lighter lying on the coffee table. Maybe he was actually inside the house and he thinks she saw him. God knows. All I can say with any certainty is that someone set her up to have a serious accident." He looked at Pete. "You said it a hundred times yesterday if you said it once. It was a miracle they got out of that wreck alive."

"This is insane." Naomi cupped a hand over her eyes. "Like we're in a *Law and Order* rerun. Things like this don't happen to people like us."

Pete slipped an arm around her shoulders and led her to a kitchen chair. Once seated, she lowered her hand from her eyes. "How could *anyone* want her dead? You must be mistaken. If she'd seen something in that house, she'd know it, wouldn't she?"

Pete lifted his hands. "God knows what she saw, but she must have seen something. It's the only explanation Zeke and I can come up with."

For the first time since Zeke had met her, Naomi looked

her age. Her face had gone ashen. Her skin looked like wax that had melted slightly and slipped downward, making her eye sockets seem deeper and her cheeks sunken. "If you're right and someone tried to kill her, he may try again."

Zeke sat across from Naomi and took her hand. "We won't let that happen," he assured her.

Naomi straightened her shoulders, and traces of color returned to her face. "How can we keep her safe?"

Zeke sat back on his chair. "First of all, she can't be left alone. And unless she's with me or Pete, I don't think she should leave the house."

"What about the club? You've almost finished the renovations. She can't let her business go under. How will she support herself and the kids?"

Zeke almost said that from here on out, he would take care of Natalie and the kids, but the problem was more far-reaching than that. The club wasn't merely a source of income to Natalie, but a necessary component of who she was.

"When she goes in to work, Pete or I will go with her," Zeke settled for saying. "Meanwhile, we have to come up with some other people who had a motive to kill Robert. As things stand, Monroe is focused mainly on Natalie."

"Why hasn't he arrested her, then?" Naomi asked.

"They probably haven't built a strong enough case against her yet."

Naomi got up and started to pace the kitchen floor. "And in the meantime, they're not looking for the real killer."

"Chances are, no. They think they've got her. All they have to do is prove it."

Pete sat back on his chair. "How do we go about coming up with other suspects?"

Zeke repositioned the saltshaker. "We start with Grace

Patterson. Maybe she knows something. If not, we'll talk to Robert's girlfriends. Someone hated him enough to want him dead. We just have to find out who."

Natalie entered the kitchen just then. She stopped just inside the archway, her expression turning inquisitive when she saw the three of them speaking in low tones and looking so solemn. "What?" she asked.

Zeke hated to burden her with more. She stood slightly hunched, as if it were too painful to straighten her spine. Like it or not, though, this wasn't something that could safely be kept from her.

"Come sit down, honey," he said.

A wary look entered her eyes as she moved to the table. She walked as if the floor were made of eggshells, a telltale sign that it wasn't only her chest causing her discomfort. Considering the fact that her Chevy resembled a crushed aluminum can, Zeke wasn't surprised. She was fortunate to be alive.

As she sat down, she said to her mother, "I came down to get Chad some more sherbet and 7 Up. The pain medication is still upsetting his stomach."

Naomi stood up. "I'll take care of it." As she stepped to the refrigerator, she asked, "How's Rosebud feeling?"

"Bored," Natalie said with a wan smile. "Valerie's about to give up on keeping her in bed. I think she's going to be fine." She looked back at Zeke and her father. "You were powwowing about something serious when I came in. Are you going to tell me what, or keep me in suspense?"

Zeke glanced at Pete. The older man rubbed his jaw, apparently none too anxious to answer his daughter's question. Zeke sat forward, folded his arms on the table, and, as gently as possible, told Natalie what they had learned at the wrecking yard. At the news, her eyes went almost black with terror.

"You think someone tried to kill us?" she asked incredulously.

Zeke wished with all his heart that it wasn't necessary to burden her with this. "Actually, honey, I think the kids being involved was pure happenstance. Whoever messed with the brakes was trying to get you, not the kids."

Her throat convulsed, her small larynx bobbing like a marble under her cleft chin. "But that's crazy. I didn't see anything at Robert's house."

"You must have seen something," Zeke insisted gently. "When you got there, do you remember any cars parked on the street?"

She shook her head. "I didn't really notice. At the time, I didn't know I needed to pay attention to things like that."

"How about once you went inside?" Zeke felt a little foolish—a male version of Nancy Drew, sifting for clues. Only this wasn't a game. He truly believed Natalie's life was on the line. "Whether you thought it was significant at the time or not, you must have seen something to implicate the killer, honey." He threw out a few possibilities, but Natalie only shook her head. "Go back to that moment when you stepped inside," he suggested, "and tell us what you saw, room by room."

Naomi came to stand by the table, her hands laden with a drinking glass and bowl. She remained there as Natalie launched into a halting description of Robert Patterson's residence. The picture that began to form in Zeke's mind was of garish opulence—gilded statues, paintings framed in gold, furnishings straight from a Hollywood film set. Robert had clearly enjoyed luxury, but nothing Natalie recalled seemed significant otherwise.

"Back up," Zeke said as she began describing the study. "What was that you said?"

She gave him a blank look.

"You saw papers on his desk?"

She nodded. "It's strange, actually, because Detective Monroe told me there were no papers found on the desk." She shrugged. "I figured they were unimportant and one of the investigating officers moved them or something."

A cold feeling inched up Zeke's spine. "Did you look closely at them?"

"No, not really. Right after I noticed them, I saw Grandma Devereaux's goblets."

Those damned goblets again. "Think, Natalie. It may be extremely important. Did you notice anything about those papers?"

Her dark brows pinched together in a frown. "It was a contract of some kind. I remember thinking at the time that I couldn't care less about Robert's business dealings anymore, and then I saw the crystal. I got so upset then that I never looked at the papers again."

"But Monroe claims the contract wasn't there?"

Her gaze clung to his. "You think that's it, don't you? That something in that contract identified the killer."

Zeke's heart was pounding in double time. "I think it's highly possible that you saw his name on that contract and didn't register it."

When Zeke got Detective Monroe on the line a few minutes later, the policeman was less than friendly. Zeke got straight to the point.

"There were no papers lying on Patterson's desk," Monroe insisted after Zeke explained. "I was one of the first people on the scene, and I took meticulous notes. No contract, Coulter. If it had been there, I would have seen it."

"That doesn't rule out the possibility that it was there when Natalie went into the study."

"What do you surmise, that it developed feet and walked away?"

Zeke made a mental note to get this man fired before this was over. "No, I surmise that someone removed it from the desk. On her way out, Natalie heard a door latch click somewhere in the house. The killer may have still been inside."

"It's an interesting theory, Mr. Coulter, but I'm the detective handling this case. Why don't you just relax and let me do my job?"

"Because, as far as I can see, you're not doing it," Zeke replied. "That woman—Patterson's girlfriend. She says Robert got a phone call and sent her away to go shopping for a few hours. Patterson obviously meant to meet with someone. He and that someone chitchatted in the study over a few glasses of wine. They could have been discussing a business deal."

"Yes—or it may have been a meeting between exes to discuss the sale of a certain farm."

Zeke's blood ran cold. In that moment, he knew beyond a shadow of a doubt that the police were concentrating almost solely on Natalie being the killer.

Chapter Seventeen

Later that afternoon when Zeke and Natalie went to see Grace Patterson, she served high tea. The woman fascinated Zeke. Over his lifetime, he'd known a few wealthy people, most recently and inarguably the wealthiest, the Kendrick family. But he'd never met anyone so ostentatious as Robert's mother. She reminded him of a character onstage, the props around her carefully selected and arranged to convey her queenly importance.

When she greeted them at the door, she was dressed in a black tunic and pants made of soft, silky stuff that flowed around her when she moved. With her pale complexion and blond hair, the effect was stunning, which he suspected had been her aim. Women of her social standing always dressed to make a statement, he supposed, even in mourning. To finish off the outfit, she wore low black heels with feathers across the insteps. Slippers, he guessed, because no one in her right mind would wear shoes like that outside.

She led them into a beautiful room to the right of the entry hall that sported a collection of what appeared to be priceless antiques. Near the fireplace, refreshments awaited them on a tea table encircled by four wing-back chairs. He wasn't surprised when Grace sat down first. Someone of royal lineage couldn't be expected to remain standing while lesser beings were seated.

"Please, join me," she said with just enough warmth to seem sincere, but with enough coolness to convey that their visit was an inconvenience.

Natalie, still in great discomfort from the accident, sank gratefully onto a cushion. Zeke was almost afraid to settle his considerable weight onto the chair beside her. His luck, he'd bust the damned thing. As he lowered himself gingerly onto the seat, he took in the amazing assortment of small cakes, cookies, and bite-sized sandwiches arranged on flowery, gilt-edged platters. They'd come to talk, not eat a meal.

As Grace poured tea with practiced precision, she said, "It's lovely to have you come, Natalie, but I must confess to some puzzlement. On the phone, you mentioned wanting to ask me some questions?"

Natalie accepted the cup and saucer that Grace offered her. Holding the saucer in her left hand, she settled back on the chair, using her right hand to sip from the dainty little cup. She seemed to feel more relaxed in these surroundings than he did.

"The children and I were in a serious car accident yesterday, Grace."

Robert's mother almost spilled her tea. "Oh, dear God," she gasped. "Chad. Is he all right?"

Anger put a glint in Natalie's eyes. "His ribs are badly bruised, but he's fine otherwise. You do have two grandchildren. Aren't you equally concerned about Rosie?"

Grace's cheeks went pink as suddenly as they'd gone pale. "Of course. How is she?"

"She got a nasty bump on the head," Natalie replied. "Fortunately, it doesn't appear that she has a concussion."

"Thank goodness." Grace returned her cup to its saucer without clinking the china. "I'm delighted to hear that they're both okay."

Zeke couldn't fit his finger through the handle of his cup. Instead he had to grasp it between his thumb and forefinger. "Actually, Mrs. Patterson, Natalie misspoke. The wreck wasn't an accident."

Grace's blue eyes went wide. "What do you mean?"

"I mean that someone tried to kill Natalie yesterday. By chance, the kids were in the car with her when it happened."

"Dear God," Grace whispered.

Natalie looked so drained that Zeke took it from there, telling Grace the story from start to finish. "We believe that the name of your son's murderer was on that contract, Mrs. Patterson, and that he believes Natalie may have seen it. Rather than risk exposure, we think he's trying to shut Natalie up before she remembers what she saw and goes to the police."

Grace began plucking nervously at the voluminous sleeves of her tunic, and then, with such suddenness she clinked the china, she set her cup on the table, pushed to her feet, and walked over to a secretary against one wall. When she returned to her chair, she carried a fifth of scotch. She poured a generous measure into her teacup, and then slid the bottle toward Zeke.

"No, thanks," he said. "I have to drive."

Zeke sneaked a glance at Natalie. Her expression told him more clearly than words that she'd never seen her ex-mother-in-law in such a state. The woman drained her cup in four gulps and poured herself another measure of scotch.

The first infusion of alcohol seemed to calm her a bit. She relaxed against the padded backrest of her chair to consume the second dose more slowly. "No one knows more about Robert's business dealings than I," she said shakily. "If someone is trying to kill Natalie, isn't there a strong possibility that he'll come after me as well?"

Until that moment, Zeke had been trying his damnedest to like this woman. Now disgust burned at the back of his throat like acid. She wasn't worried about Natalie or her grandchildren, only about herself. He gave her a long, measuring look, decided that the more frightened she was, the more useful she might be, and said, "You're right. I hadn't thought of that. He may come after you."

She took another swig of whiskey. "I kept telling Robert to clean up his act. Do you think he would listen? Now he's dead, and I may be next." She sent Zeke a panicked look. "What am I going to do, hire round-the-clock protection? Where does one find a bodyguard?"

People like Natalie had volunteers to protect her, Zeke thought. Someone like Grace Patterson had to pay for that kind of loyalty. "A security company might be a good place to start," he said, not convinced the woman was even in danger. "If they can't help you, maybe they'll know someone who can."

Grace started up from her chair. Zeke stopped her with, "First things first. Getting protection is a stopgap measure, Mrs. Patterson. You can't live in fear for an extended period of time." When she started to get up again, Zeke quickly added, "Even the best of protectors will relax his guard sooner or later. If the killer wants you out of the way, he'll wait for his chance, and eventually, he may breach your security."

Zeke waited for her to sit back. Then he went on. "The first and most important thing we need to do is give the police more to work with. As long as your son's killer is at large, you'll be in grave danger, and so will Natalie and her children."

Her eyes huge and imploring, Grace shakily asked, "What do you need to know?"

At four o'clock that afternoon, Zeke had the dubious pleasure of visiting Detective Monroe's office again. The plump, aging cop looked no happier to see Zeke than Zeke was to be there. They settled at opposite sides of the gray metal desk, glaring at each other like opponents in a death match. Zeke tossed a paper onto the blotter.

"I visited with Robert Patterson's mother this afternoon. She gave me a list of individuals who had reason to want her son dead. Most of them are iffy—dumped girlfriends, a few businessmen he gave the shaft, that sort of thing. But the young man at the top of the list bears looking at. Robert Patterson cheated him out of more than four million dollars."

Monroe unfolded the paper, looked at the name, and said, "Keep talking."

"Stan Ragnor, thirtyish, a real estate broker with a surveying degree who works under his own shingle. He's a sharp young man with a nose for developable land. A year ago, he found Robert Patterson a large piece of prime development property just outside Crystal Falls, a hundred acres zoned for rural residential, a minimum of ten acres per parcel."

"I know what rural residential means, and he's not sounding like a killer yet." Monroe tossed down the paper. "Get to the point."

"Ragnor is an eager beaver. Went back to college in his early twenties to get the surveying degree, worked for a while in the field down in California, and then moved back to Oregon, determined to make a go of it here. He fell on the idea of selling real estate, quickly realized his expertise lay in development, finally struck out on his own, and was champing at the bit to make his first fortune when he met Patterson. Unfortunately for him, he was still wet behind the ears when it came to business negotiations and thought a man's word still counted for something."

"How does this tie him to the murder?"

"Just hear me out. Ragnor had done his research and discovered that the city of Crystal Falls and the county have a joint twenty-year development plan to accommodate urban sprawl. In certain areas within a ten-mile radius of the city limits, they will allow land presently zoned rural residential to be rezoned to RS, residential standard density. Ragnor went door-to-door, trying to convince the landowners in one of those areas to list their ten-acre parcels with him. All totaled, he secured over a hundred contiguous acres, a veritable gold mine. Then he did all the necessary legwork to be sure sewer systems, access streets, and traffic studies wouldn't throw a wrench in the fan blades for a subdivision. When he had a bulletproof package, he presented it to Robert Patterson, one of the biggest developers in town."

"Go on," Monroe said, showing a little more interest now.

Zeke sat forward on the chair. "In deals like this, a real estate broker can make a killing if he handles it right. When Ragnor presented the deal to Patterson, he asked for an exclusive, three-percent listing agreement on all the lots as well as on all the houses that would one day be built on them. It was a great offer to Patterson, roughly a fifty-percent cut in Realtor fees, and it was equally lucrative for Ragnor. Figure it out. On average, you can go with five lots per acre, and they sell from ninety to a hundred grand a crack. Ragnor stood to make over a million on the lot sales alone, plus a lowball figure of three million on the homes, which would go for at least two hundred grand each, more likely four, raising his take to six million."

Monroe whistled. "The boy stood to make a bundle."

"Exactly. In return, he agreed to walk the development project through for Patterson with the city, meeting with engineers and city planners. Ragnor found the pieces of land, negotiated to get the owners to sell, and then worked his ass off to put the deal together, trusting Patterson to keep his word and treat him right when the land was subdivided. In the end, Patterson cut him out of the deal."

Monroe raised his eyebrows. "Sounds to me as if Ragnor is one stupid son of a bitch. No one does business without a contract nowadays."

"I'm not here to discuss smart business tactics, Monroe. I'm here to tell you about a young man who trusted Robert Patterson and got the shaft in a very big way." Zeke thought of Natalie and all the years she'd remained in her marriage, believing she might save it. Robert Patterson had been a master at manipulation. "Patterson knew how to string people along. He told Ragnor that he wouldn't sign a listing agreement on lots and houses that didn't yet exist. He kept putting Ragnor off, working him like a dog in the meantime, promising that he'd happily sign on the dotted line when the time was right. Ragnor stood to make megabucks, so he continued to work long hours for over a year to make everything fly. When the city finally dropped the gavel, giving the go-ahead for a huge subdivision, Patterson let Ragnor do even more legwork. According to Grace Patterson, there are countless angles that must be handled in a project that size, and Ragnor did it all, only to have Patterson laugh at him when it was all said and done, telling him that there was no way a two-bit Realtor was going to make almost as much money on the deal as he was. He went to another Realtor, offered one percent, and the guy leaped at it. After all his hard work, all Ragnor got out of the deal was an initial three percent when Patterson bought the original parcels."

Monroe picked up the piece of paper again and studied the name. "I'll check him out."

Zeke nodded. "Do better than that, Monroe. Put him under a magnifying glass. Talk to Grace Patterson yourself. She heard Ragnor threaten her son's life. I'm telling you, Natalie didn't do this. The longer you focus on her, the longer it will be before you solve this case."

Natalie had just turned off the downstairs lights to head upstairs for bed when the phone rang. It was almost eleven, and she couldn't imagine who would be calling so late. She flipped the living room lamp back on and ran to the kitchen.

When she answered the phone on the fourth ring, a woman asked for Natalie Patterson.

"This is she," Natalie replied.

"Are you the owner of the Blue Parrot?"

After the events of yesterday, Natalie felt uncomfortable answering that question until she knew more about the caller. "With whom am I speaking?"

"This is Nancy Steingold with Iron Clad Security. I'm calling to notify you that the security alarm at your business has just gone off. The police are on their way there now."

"The alarm at my supper club has gone off?" In all the time Natalie had owned the business, this had never happened.

"You'll probably want to be there to speak with the police and reset the alarm when they're finished checking things out." Ms. Steingold paused and then said, "Most times, these are false alarms. Something goes haywire—a motion detector or a faulty door latch that jiggles in the wind and breaks the magnetic field."

Natalie had no motion detectors inside the club. Because of the cost, she'd gone with a basic perimeter system that went off only when a door or window was forced open. "Thank you for notifying me."

"No problem. I hope it turns out that everything is fine."

After breaking the connection, Natalie ran to her father's bedroom. "Pop?" She tapped on the door, then opened it and flipped on the overhead light. "The security alarm at the club just went off. I need to go to town."

Pete swung up to sit on the edge of his bed. He wore oversized white cotton pajamas with burgundy stripes. He reached for his pants. "You should call Zeke and tell him we're going in. He may want to go with us."

"He's probably at the supply store. He goes in every night to do books, I think."

"Then call him there and see if he'll meet us at the club." Pete shook out his pants. "I don't like the sound of this."

Natalie didn't like the sound of it, either.

"Is there any money there?" Pete asked.

"I always pull down the tills and make a night deposit at the bank on the way home. There's only start-up cash in each till, around three hundred total, and I always keep both tills in the safe when I'm closed."

Pete huffed. "What would a thief take, then, bottles of booze and frozen food? Unless it's kids, that doesn't make sense. Call Zeke. Tell him we'll be leaving in about five minutes."

Natalie closed the door and hurried toward the kitchen. Naomi appeared on the upstairs landing as she passed through the living room. "What's going on?"

"The alarm at the club went off." Natalie continued into the kitchen, flipped the lights back on, and grabbed the phone book to look up the number of Zeke's store.

An hour later, Zeke and Natalie stood just inside the front entrance of the Blue Parrot. Zeke glared at the doors as if they could be intimidated into providing answers. The police had just left, and they were as bewildered as Natalie and Zeke. No false alarm, this. The front doors of the club had been forced open. The puzzling part was that they'd been forced open from the inside.

Natalie stared at the marks on the interior surfaces of the wood. "This makes no sense. I've heard of people breaking into a building, but I've never heard of anyone breaking out."

Still studying the doors, Zeke curled a wonderfully strong arm around her shoulders. "There's an answer to this riddle, Watson. Just give me a minute to come up with an explanation."

Natalie smiled in spite of herself. At the most stressful of times, this man could always lighten her heart somehow. She looked up at him—at his sun-bronzed, chiseled face, brilliant blue eyes, and glistening sable hair—and she believed, truly believed for the first time in her life, that every woman on earth was destined to meet one man who had been created especially for her. She just hadn't looked long enough or hard enough to find him.

"How does a burglar end up inside a building and have to break his way out?" he mused aloud. "He would have had to be in here when the place was locked up and the alarm was set." He no sooner spoke than his gaze flew to hers. "The doors," he said softly. "My brothers and I have been leaving them open to let in fresh air while we work in here."

"And you think someone sneaked in?"

"It's the only explanation I can come up with."

"But you didn't work here today."

Zeke glanced behind him. "No, but my brothers did." He pointed to the patched flooring. "That wasn't done when I left yesterday. While Jake and Hank were here working, someone slipped inside, hid somewhere, and waited for them to leave."

Natalie rubbed her arms and shivered, glancing uneasily around the room. "But, Zeke, your brothers would have left this afternoon sometime, and the alarm didn't go off until around eleven. If the burglar was locked in here, what did he do all those hours?"

Zeke turned a slow circle to survey the room. "Good question. As far as you can tell, nothing's been stolen. That rules out theft as a motive, and the place hasn't been vandalized, the only other reason I can think of for someone to be in here."

Natalie had no answers, which only added to her bewilderment when Zeke suddenly yelled for her father, who was in the bar area, looking at the wall repairs. "Get Natalie out of here, would you, Pete?"

Natalie frowned. "Why the sudden urgency for me to leave?"

"You should be resting." Zeke grasped her elbow, led her outside, and plucked the keys from her hand. "I'll see you when I get home. Okay?"

Standing on the shadowy sidewalk, Natalie sensed that there was something she was missing. As her father exited the club and came to stand beside them, she glanced at the entrance doors of the building. Then an awful thought struck her. "Oh, my God. You think the place has been booby-trapped?"

Pete peered through the gloom at Zeke's face. "How'd you reach that conclusion?"

"It's not a conclusion, exactly, more a safety precaution. After yesterday, I'm probably a little paranoid. It just strikes me as being strange that someone would hide in the building and wait so many hours before forcing the doors open to get back out. To be on the safe side, I want to look things over again."

A chill moved over Natalie, and she looked anxiously at her father. Pete stepped closer to grasp her arm.

"He's right, honey. I need to get you out of here."

"Why can't we just call the police?" she asked. "We can all wait outside until they've checked everything out. That's their job, after all. They're trained for things like this."

"I'll call them," Zeke assured her. "But I don't want you anywhere around while they're checking things over." He turned to her father. "Take her home, Pete. As soon as I'm finished up here, I'll head home, too. If you'll wait up, I'll stop by to let you know what we find."

Natalie didn't see why she couldn't wait on the sidewalk Surely that would be safe enough. She felt her father's hanc tighten over her arm, his grip conveying urgency and fear. I hit her then, and her heart started to pound like a triphammer.

"Oh, *God,*" she whispered. "You think there could be a bomb in there. Don't you?"

Zeke stared at the building for a moment. Then he drew his cell phone from his belt. "I don't know what to think, Natalie. But I'm not going to rule out any possibility until the cops have checked the place over."

Pete tugged on Natalie's arm. "Come on, honey. Let's get you out of here."

"No!" Natalie refused to budge. "It's *my* club, not Zeke's. I can't let him go back in there while I go home where it's safe." She laughed shrilly. "I mean—well—a bomb is farfetched, but no telling what else he may have done. The ranges are hooked up to propane. What if he punctured the lines or—"

"Natalie," Zeke said softly.

If he had yelled, she might have ignored him. But the low timbre of his voice made her fall silent. He stepped closer and cupped her chin in his hand. In the streetlights, his eyes glistened like sapphires. "I understand how you feel. Honestly. If I were in your shoes, I wouldn't want to leave, either. But you have to think about Chad and Rosie."

Her pounding heart stuttered a beat.

"They've already lost their father. What will happen to them if they lose you, too?"

Natalie remembered how frightened Chad had been when she'd been taken to the police station for questioning. He'd been afraid she might never come home, that he and Rosie would be left all alone.

Zeke bent closer. "You can't take foolish risks. They need you too much."

"But you can take foolish risks?" Natalie tried to imagine losing him, and just the thought made her feel panicky. She didn't know when she'd come to love him so deeply and need him so much. She only knew she couldn't face life without him now. "I don't want anything to happen to you."

Zeke took her hand and led her around the corner of the building to Pop's truck. He seemed to relax marginally when they were farther away from the structure. "I don't want anything to happen to me, either," he assured her. "But one of us needs to stay to lock up after the police have gone through the place again. I'm elected."

"Why?" she cried. "Because you're a man, and I'm a woman?"

"Yes." He opened the passenger door of the truck. "Call me old-fashioned. Call me archaic in my thinking, if you like. I'm not wired to let the woman I love put herself in danger, plain and simple. You'll go home and stay with the kids while I take care of this. I promise not to take any stupid chances."

He caught her at the waist and bodily lifted her onto the truck scat. Natalie was still protesting as he fastened her seat belt. "I'm a grown woman, for heaven's sake!" she cried when he started to shut the door. "You can't just stuff me in the truck, pat me on the head, and send me home."

Her father climbed in on the driver's side and started the truck. "Nattie, you're going home if I've got to hogtie you. Enough said."

"I can't believe this."

Zeke leaned in and quickly kissed her. "We'll fight about it later. All right? You've got two kids to think about. I don't." He gently kissed her again. "Go home and take care of them. As soon as I'm finished here, I'll be along."

He slammed the door before she could say more, and the truck was rolling forward before she could react. Natalie twisted on the seat, relieved to see that Zeke was already talking on his cell phone, hopefully to the police. She faced forward again and sent her father a glare. She was so angry she was shaking.

"This is absolute baloney. That's *my* club. If anyone should stay, it's me."

Her dad pulled out onto Ninth and accelerated. At the stoplight, he flashed her a grin. "I like that boy. You've landed yourself a keeper this time, Nattie girl. Stop fussing and just marry the man."

Natalie didn't know what possessed her, but before she thought it through, she said, "You landed yourself a keeper once yourself. Why don't you follow your own advice, stop fussing, and just marry her again?"

Her aim had been to make her father mad. Instead he only smiled and said, "I've been thinking along those same lines myself."

Zeke got home about two hours later. After parking his truck in the drive next to his house, he headed straight for the Westfields'. He saw Natalie coming to meet him as he started across the field. In the moonlight, she looked ethereal—like an angel floating over the grass. When they'd closed the distance between them to about twenty feet, she stopped to wait for him, her arms hugging her waist, her black hair trailing across her face in the night breeze.

"What're you doing out here?" he asked.

"I was watching for your headlights."

"You're supposed to be resting."

"I've been so worried I couldn't shut my eyes, let alone sleep."

Zeke slowed his stride. When he reached her, he couldn't resist lifting the strands of hair from her pale cheek. Then, as if drawn to her by a magnetic force, he had to taste her mouth—just one slow taste. He leaned away to give her a wondering look when she didn't kiss him back.

"I'm fine," he assured her. "You shouldn't have worried."

"What did the police find?"

"I'm almost embarrassed to say. They didn't find a damned thing."

Her shoulders relaxed slightly. "Thank God. We just overreacted, then?"

"It seems that way. I guess it's a case of too much, too late. Ever since I saw the damage to your car, I've been jumping at shadows. Tonight at the club, I saw those doors and convinced myself it was another attempt on your life. I didn't want to be caught with my guard down again."

"A burglar breaking out instead of in is definitely odd. Pop and I thought your theory was plausible. Better to be safe than sorry."

"Monroe didn't see it that way. He was totally pissed."

"Monroe was there?"

Zeke looped his thumbs over his belt. "When I called them back, I must have been pretty convincing. Someone contacted him at home. He came in to check things out himself. I felt like a total idiot when they didn't find anything."

She took a deep breath and released it. Then she frowned slightly. "We need to talk, Zeke. I wasn't happy about the way you handled that situation. You were very dictatorial."

"Do we have to go there? As it turns out, there wasn't any danger after all."

"You did say we could fight about it later."

Zeke preferred to make love to her. But he could tell by the stubborn set of her chin that it wasn't in the stars. "I'm sorry. I didn't mean to be dictatorial."

"Shoving me into the truck and ordering me to leave wasn't dictatorial?"

"I didn't shove you. I very carefully lifted you in. And I didn't order you, exactly. I just asked you to go home."

"Ha. A request isn't what I heard."

Okay, so it had been more along the lines of an order. Zeke thought about it, trying his best to see her side, but no matter how he circled it, he knew he'd react the same way again if the situation repeated itself. He loved her too much to do otherwise.

"Okay," he conceded, "it was an order."

"I'm not all right with that. I don't appreciate being told what to do."

Zeke rubbed beside his nose and dug at the dirt with his boot heel. "I'll try not to do it again." Until next time. "I understand, honestly. It's just—"

"It's just what?"

Zeke suspected that he was digging himself a very deep hole. "It's just that where I hail from, no man worth his salt allows the woman he loves to be in danger if there's any way he can protect her."

"Women in the military fight in the front lines now, Zeke."

"My woman won't." There it was—a hole big enough to swallow him.

She held up a hand near her temple as if to ward off anything more until she got that processed. "Wait a minute. Back up. Your woman? Are you referring to me?"

He gazed off at nothing, trying his damnedest to think of a way to rephrase that so it sounded better. Only that wouldn't be honest. "I reckon I am. You're a woman, and I'm thinking that you're mine. If I'm mistaken about that, you'd best tell me so now."

Her chin came up again. "I care very deeply for you, Zeke."

Uh-oh. They'd reverted from loving each other to caring very deeply. Not a good sign.

"And I want to have a relationship with you," she went on. "But that doesn't mean I plan to be your possession—more precisely, a lesser being you can order around. I make my own decisions. I don't need a man, however much I may care about him, to make them for me."

"You can make your own decisions. I don't have a problem with that at all."

"Then why wouldn't you allow me to make my own decision tonight?"

"Because that was different."

"No, it wasn't. I wanted to stay, and you wouldn't let me. You made me feel like a child who couldn't be trusted to make her own choices."

Zeke rubbed beside his nose again. "Don't blow this all out of proportion, Natalie. I've got some set ideas about a man's role when it comes to protecting his loved ones. That's it, plain and simple. It has no bearing on you making your own choices the rest of the time."

"I'm afraid it does. I won't be treated like a child. I endured it for almost eleven years, and I won't again."

"Are you comparing me to Robert?"

"Does the shoe fit?"

Zeke bit down hard on his back teeth. "You tell me."

"You're not going to back down an inch on this, are you?"

Zeke felt his temper rising. "Nope. You want to go buy a car? Fine. Go on the road to sing? Fine. You can make any damned decision you want, no objection from me. But I'll be damned if I'll let you enter a building that I have reason to believe may blow up. If that makes me dictatorial, then I'm dictatorial, and I'll always be dictatorial. We can talk it to death all night, and that's not going to change."

"I see."

Zeke had a bad feeling she was about to walk away, and the worst part was, he'd have to let her go. He couldn't say what she wanted to hear and then go back on it later. That wasn't the way he was made.

Just as he feared, she did an about-face and headed for home without another word. He watched her go for what seemed a small eternity, and then his Coulter temper hit boiling point.

"Okay, fine!" he yelled. "You win. The next time a building may blow to smithereens, I'll kiss you for luck and send you in while I go stay with the kids! When I'm picking up the pieces later, I'll feel fine about it because it was your decision to make! Will that make you happy?"

She spun back around. "You're being deliberately obtuse, narrowing everything down to this one instance! I need you to tell me you won't do it again. I can understand your not wanting me to go in the building, Zeke, but you had no right to treat me like a child!"

"If I thought of you as a child, I'd turn you over my knee right now for acting like one."

That was the wrong thing to say. She doubled her fists and came storming back to him. Then again, he decided, maybe it had been exactly the right thing to say. She wasn't walking away from him now, anyway.

She stopped about five feet from him. "What was that?"

"What was what?"

"Did you just threaten to turn me over your knee?"

"I never threaten."

"Well, then, make like a frog and jump on it."

Zeke remembered that first morning when she'd flared at him in anger. He'd thought then that she was the most beautiful woman he'd ever clapped eyes on, and his sentiments hadn't changed.

"Well?" she challenged. "Put your money where your mouth is, cowboy. Don't just stand there paying it lip service."

Zeke struggled not to smile. He outweighed her by a hundred pounds. Now he knew where Rosie had gotten her gumption. "Natalie, this is silly."

"What's silly about it, that you made the threat, or that I'm not running?" She was so angry her voice throbbed.

"I didn't mean it as a threat. It was a figure of speech, nothing more. I'd never turn you over my knee."

"I should hope not. You can probably do it, but you'd better pack a lunch if you plan to try."

Zeke could see that he'd hurt her pride. He was also starting to realize that a lot more was troubling her than the incident tonight. *Robert.* Zeke had obviously resurrected some very unpleasant memories when he'd lifted her into that truck. Looking back on it, he guessed maybe he had treated her like a child. He hadn't meant it that way.

"Can we agree on one thing?" he asked.

"What, that you're bigger than I am?"

"That, too. I clearly am. But I was thinking more about

the original bone of contention. If I give you my solemn oath that I'll never interfere with your inalienable right to make your own choices and decisions, will you compromise on the protection issue and let me do my manly thing when a dangerous situation crops up?"

"Your *manly* thing?" she echoed.

"That's essentially it, isn't it, a man thing? I have a protective nature. I know it's old-fashioned, but that's the way my dad raised me, how I believe good men are supposed to react. I can't promise you I won't do it again. It's instinctive for me, not a decision, not a choice, and I don't think I can change it."

"I'm not okay with that."

"I'm sorry if it makes you uncomfortable."

"That's all you can say? It's a deal breaker for me, Zeke."

"Isn't that a little like shooting the horse to cure hoof rot? When you look at the whole picture, it's a minor thing, isn't it? If I never act that way at any other time, don't you think you can live with it every twenty years or so?"

"Every twenty years or so?"

"How many times over the next fifty years do you reckon we'll be worried about bombs or gas explosions?"

She bent her head and toed the dirt with her sneaker. When she looked up at him again, her eyes ached with uncertainty. "Will you swear to me that you'll never treat me that way again otherwise?"

That was a promise he could make. He also made a mental note to talk with her later about this independence issue. She clearly had some serious hang-ups that he needed to tiptoe around. "I swear that I'll never treat you that way otherwise, only in what I believe may be life-threatening situations. And I'll try not to be dictatorial if it ever happens again."

"It was as if you didn't hear me. I thought you considered me to be your equal, and suddenly I didn't even have a vote."

Zeke's heart caught. "I never meant to make you feel that way. You'll always have a vote, Natalie, and in most instances, it'll carry more weight with me than my own. It's just—*damn.* I'm new at this. Cut me a little slack, all right? A month ago, I was a bachelor with no one to worry about but myself. Now I love you and those kids so much it makes me crazy when I think something might happen to one of you."

"How do you think I felt?" She splayed a hand over her chest. "What if the gas lines had been tampered with, and the smell just wasn't strong enough to notice yet? What if there actually had been an explosive device in there? You acted like the big, strong man who'd take care of everything, and all I could think about was your getting blown to pieces if you went back inside."

Hearing it put like that made Zeke feel like a heel. "You're right," he said, his voice rasping like sandpaper over a cheese grater. "I wouldn't like feeling that way. I'm sorry I did it to you."

"Here's the thing that bothers me. I never saw a hint of autocracy in you, and suddenly there it was, as if you'd only been humoring me until then. Can you see why I found that upsetting? I can't be with someone who only pretends to respect me."

Zeke folded his arms to keep from reaching for her. "I'm not just pretending, honey. Where is that coming from?"

She closed her eyes and let her head fall back, as if she

were gathering her thoughts. After a moment, she said, "Maybe I'm overreacting. In my marriage, I was never Robert's equal. He refused to talk with me about his business. If someone came by the house to meet with him, he sent me shopping or told me to go watch a program. He didn't even want me in the room. The decisions were all *his* to make, and I just had to be happy with the results. For so many years, I was on a fast track, with him doing all the steering. He chose our home, and then he chose the furnishings. He even hired a fashion consultant to dress me. If he had business problems, he never shared them with me. It was as if I had no brain. When I filed for divorce, I swore I'd never live like that again."

"And tonight I acted exactly like Robert."

She dropped her chin to look at him. "Not exactly like him. In that situation, I think he might have gone home with the kids and let me handle it."

Zeke smiled. He couldn't stop himself. "I'm sorry I acted like a jerk. Next time, I'll handle it with more finesse, I promise."

"But you'll still send me home."

He nodded.

"Even if it's a deal breaker for me?"

Zeke didn't want her to walk away again, but he couldn't make promises he knew he might not keep. "Would you settle for a nose job?"

She peered through the gloom at him. "Pardon?"

"It's a big sucker. I know it for a fact because it's sitting smack dab in the middle of all my brothers' faces, too. I could get an inch whacked off the end and never miss it."

"What's your nose got to do with anything?"

"It's a flaw I can fix."

She stared up at him, looking pensive. "It isn't a flaw. I love your nose."

Zeke narrowed an eye at her. "Honey, if you love this schnozzle, there's only one explanation. You're crazy in love with me. That being the case, can you really walk away over something that may not even happen again?"

Her mouth twitched. "Foul play. You expect me to simply accept that you're occasionally going to act like an autocratic jerk?"

"Yep, that pretty much covers it, occasionally being the key word. The rest of the time, I'll be Mr. Easy."

She ran a speculative gaze over him. "How easy, exactly?"

"Crook your little finger and see."

Chapter Eighteen

The following morning Natalie received a call from Grace Patterson to inform her that the coroner's office had released Robert's remains for burial. The funeral would be at eleven a.m. on Thursday at Ehringer's Funeral Home. Viewings had been scheduled for Wednesday night between six and nine.

Natalie went up to Chad's room immediately to tell him the news. Her son was propped up against a mound of pillows, deeply engrossed in *Harry Potter and the Order of the Phoenix*. She sat on the edge of the bed, grateful yet again to Valerie for buying Chad the book. It had provided him with a much-needed escape, not only from the pain of his bruised ribs, but also from the sadness of his father's death.

"Hi," Natalie said, reaching to smooth his rumpled hair. "It's good to see that you ate a good breakfast."

Chad kept a finger in the book to save his place as he closed the cover. He glanced at his empty plate, still on the nightstand. "Grammy made blueberry pancakes."

Natalie nodded. "Your favorite, I know. She's spoiling you. What'll I do with you when she goes home?"

Chad smiled and shrugged. "No blueberry pancakes. Okay, Mom?"

Natalie laughed and turned her gaze to the open window. Just outside, a pair of robins sat on the limb of the old oak tree, warbling happily in the morning sunshine. She found herself wishing she were as carefree as those birds, that Robert were still alive, and that everything was right in Chad's world.

"Your grandma Grace just called," she finally said. "The funeral will be at eleven on Thursday. There will be viewings in the mortuary chapel tomorrow night."

Chad pushed the book off his lap, forgetting to keep his place. He sank against the pillows and closed his eyes. "What's a viewing?"

Natalie swallowed hard. "That's where friends and members of the family can go in and say last good-byes in private." She swallowed again, trying to dislodge the suffocating lump at the base of her throat. "The casket is open, and there are pretty flowers all around. It's usually in a small room that's very quiet, and one or two people go in together. With the door closed, you can feel as sad as you want, and no one will see."

"Mom?"

Natalie curled her hand over his. "What, sweetie?"

"I'm kind of scared. I've never seen a dead person. Is it going to be awful?"

"Not awful. Your dad will look just like always, but it'll be like looking at a wax carving because his spirit has left his body."

"Do you think his spirit is in heaven?"

Natalie prayed so. Since Robert's death, she had come to

understand him in ways she'd never been able to when he was alive. "I'm sure of it," she replied.

"But he did bad things," Chad whispered. "What if God wouldn't let him in?"

"If you were the one making the decision, Chad—if you held the keys to the gates and your dad was standing outside, would you turn him away?"

"No, but he was my dad, and I loved him."

"Do you think God loved him any less? More, I would think, because He could see into your father's heart."

Chad lifted his eyelashes. "Will you go with me? I don't think I can do it alone."

"Absolutely. I already asked Grammy if she'll watch Rosie. We're all set."

Zeke stopped at the edge of the Westfield yard to give Chester a Ritz cracker, a token of friendship to promote future goodwill. The gander quacked happily, ate what he could of the cracker with the first chomp, and then pecked the grass for crumbs. Zeke circled the bird and angled his steps toward the rear of the house. He was surprised to find Natalie sitting on the back steps.

She jumped with a start when he said her name. "Zeke." She smiled and patted the step beside her. "Think of the devil, and he shall appear."

"'Morning, Bright Eyes."

The dimple flashed in her cheek. "Why do you call me that?"

"Because you have fabulous eyes. Whenever I see them, I feel like the sun just came out."

As Zeke moved toward her, he wondered if he would ever tire of looking at her. This morning she wore faded old jeans and a gray Oregon Ducks T-shirt that had seen better days, but she still managed to look beautiful. Her hair fell loose to her shoulders in a cloud of jet curls. Her mouth was still slightly swollen from the heated kisses they'd shared just before dawn.

As he sat beside her, she said, "The funeral will be Thursday. It hasn't really been that long since Robert died, but it feels to me as if a month has passed."

Zeke rested his arms on his knees and joined her in gazing toward the barn. "A lot has happened since Friday night. It seems like a month to me, too." He glanced over at her. "How's Chad handling it?"

"He's sad. We talked once, but otherwise he hasn't said a whole lot." She shrugged. "I'm worried that it will all of a sudden hit him, and he'll fall apart. He loved Robert. I don't question that. But it's also about chances lost. You know? He wanted so badly to make his father proud of him someday, and now he'll never be able to."

Zeke felt as if a cold fist were squeezing his chest. Having been a boy himself once, he could understand how Chad must be feeling. It was important to a young man to earn his father's respect.

"How are you handling it?" he asked.

She went back to staring at the barn. "I feel sort of empty," she confessed. "I wish that he weren't dead, that life had given him and Chad a few more chances. He was so young. It's difficult for me to wrap my mind around the fact that he's really gone."

"The funeral will help. It'll give all of you a sense of closure. Are your folks going?"

"Pop and Valerie will be there. Mom is staying home with Rosie. I don't think she's old enough to go." She rubbed her slender hands together. "In fact, it's difficult for me to even let Chad go. A part of me would like to spare him the awful finality of it."

"He needs the finality, Natalie. He'll be okay."

"I hope so."

"Trust me. The kid's got grit." Zeke listened to the birds sing, which reminded him of why he'd come. "Are you ready for some good news?"

"Please," she said with a laugh.

"I've scheduled a grand reopening for Friday night." Zeke hurried to add, "If you're not feeling up to performing yet, no worries. The karaoke equipment is being delivered today. Frank can play a few tunes in between. And if things get dull, I'll play my fiddle."

Her eyes twinkled. "I definitely have to be there to hear you play."

Zeke grinned. "I don't just *play* the fiddle, darlin', I flat make it sing. I'm holding you to your promise of a good old-fashioned hoedown."

"I'll love it. Maybe we can do it at the club."

Zeke grew serious again. "I placed some ads in the newspaper. They'll start tomorrow night and go through Sunday. My sister-in-law, Molly, Jake's wife—she's the little redhead you met in the ER waiting room—is really good at stuff like that, so I got her to help me lay them out. Nothing fancy, but they'll get the word out."

Her eyes went sparkly with tears. "Thank you, Zeke. I've been so wrapped up in everything else that I haven't even thought about reopening the club. Madness. If I don't, I'll go under."

"You won't go under. Friday night you'll have a packed house, guaranteed. You're not just hosting a karaoke bash;

you're offering cash prizes for the best three performances of the night, decided by audience vote."

"Cash prizes?"

"I floated you a loan, remember? I tacked that on. You can pay me back when the club starts turning a profit again."

She leaned sideways and kissed the underside of his jaw. "Thank you."

"Is that the best you can do?" He chased her mouth with his and kissed her deeply. When he finally lifted his head, he whispered, "Now, that's more like it."

The following evening Natalie accompanied Chad to the funeral home. The instant they entered the building, the scent of flowers assailed her nostrils, and her skin felt as if it had been painted with sugar water. She clung to Chad's hand, not entirely sure if she did so to comfort him or herself. The assistant director, a pretty young blonde in a dark blue suit like flight attendants wear, met them in the foyer. Natalie kept glancing at her lapel, expecting to see gold wings.

"Right this way," she said kindly. As she led them down a hall, she added, "From six to seven is reserved for family members only. The deceased's mother already left, so you shouldn't be disturbed." At the door, she stopped and graced them with a gentle smile. "There's a buzzer just inside. If you need anything, don't hesitate to ring for me."

"Thank you." Natalie watched the woman walk away, then turned to look at Chad. "You ready, big guy?"

Chad nodded, but his brown eyes were huge. Natalie grasped his shoulder as she opened the door. They entered side by side, Natalie steeling herself to be strong, Chad trembling. It was a shock to see Robert lying in a coffin.

Why, Natalie wasn't sure. Of course he was in a coffin. Chad stopped in his tracks. Natalie could see a fine film of sweat on his forehead.

"It's okay, sweetie."

Chad nodded and moved forward again. When they reached the casket, Natalie slipped her arm around her son and stared stupidly at Robert's reposed features. His blond hair gleamed like burnished gold against the white satin. The mortician had done a beautiful job of making him look natural. Natalie kept thinking he might open his eyes and smile, only he didn't.

Chad said nothing. He just stood there, staring at his father as if he'd been turned into a pillar of salt. Natalie reached out and laid her fingers over Robert's folded hands. He felt like a lump of frozen chicken that had been set on the drain to thaw. She wanted to jerk her arm back, but for Chad's sake, she didn't. *Robert.* He was really and truly dead. His eyes would never open again. His chest would never rise and fall as he drew in breath. He was gone, his life snuffed out like a candle flame.

"Dad!" Chad cried. And then he started to sob. "Oh, *Dad.*"

Natalie curled her arm around the boy's waist to keep him from collapsing. The sound of his sobs made her want to weep, and pretty soon, she did, for Robert, who'd never learned to love, and for her son, who was being forced to grow up way too fast.

When Chad had cried himself out, he and Natalie sat on the wing-back chairs near the casket for a while. Then, by unspoken agreement, they got up to leave. Chad stopped at Robert's side first. Then he whirled away and almost ran from the room. Natalie hurried after him.

When she stepped out into the hall, she saw Bonnie Decker sitting on one of the straight-backed chairs along the opposite wall. Her eyes swollen from weeping, Bonnie inclined her head at Natalie and then averted her face. Natalie wanted to say something, only she couldn't think what. And there was Chad to worry about. He'd already raced up the hallway and disappeared through one of the doorways.

Natalie's maternal nature won out. She hurried after her son. But as she left the building, her thoughts were with that lonely young woman inside who'd come to say her last good-byes to a man who hadn't understood or appreciated her devotion to him.

Zeke climbed the ladder to the hayloft of the Westfield barn, guided there by the muffled sounds of Chad's heartbroken sobs. Natalie had phoned Zeke a few minutes before, upset because her son had disappeared again. She'd asked Zeke if he would mind coming over to help her find him. Zeke had heard the boy crying the moment he entered the building. He'd stepped back out to signal Natalie so she wouldn't be worried. Now he was faced with the self-appointed task of talking Chad through this and getting him calmed down.

The loft was darker than hell, the only light that of the moon, which leaked in through the open hay doors. Zeke had to follow his ears to locate Chad. As he moved in the boy's direction, his feet touched on bales one moment and loose hay the next, making him lurch. The smell of alfalfa dust burned his nose. Personally, Zeke had never understood the appeal of haylofts. Hay was itchy, scratchy, nasty stuff that only made him want to sneeze.

Almost invisible in the deep shadows, Chad was huddled

in a front corner near the hay doors. Zeke lowered himself to sit beside him. Dust billowed up again, making his eyes water. "Hey, buddy. Pretty rough night, huh?"

Chad snorted and almost choked on a stifled sob. "I w-went to see m-my d-dad," he squeaked.

Zeke looped his arms around his knees. He tried to imagine how he might feel if he lost his own father. Not a pleasant thought. It hardly seemed fair that a kid who hadn't quite turned twelve should have to live through that kind of pain. Unfortunately, it had been Zeke's observation over the years that life was seldom fair.

"I'm sorry you've lost him," Zeke whispered. "I know how you must have loved him. I sure do love my dad a lot. When he dies, I'm going to cry like a baby, no two ways around it."

The admission seemed to ease Chad's embarrassment, and he started to sob again without restraint. Zeke decided this was no time for talking. Instead he curled an arm around the boy's back. Chad didn't resist. He just leaned against Zeke's chest and cried his heart out.

Zeke settled back against the wall of the barn, straightened the leg closest to Chad, and prepared to wait it out. He lost track of time. When Chad's sobs began to abate, Zeke didn't know if he'd been sitting there for minutes or hours, and it didn't really matter. The most important thing on his agenda right then was to be exactly where he was.

When Chad was drained of tears, he whispered hollowly, "If I hit a home run, my dad won't be there to see."

Zeke rested his cheek against the boy's hair, which had the same texture as Natalie's. "No, he won't be there in the flesh. But I believe he'll be there in spirit, watching over you."

Chad's chest jerked on a soft, residual sob. "You think?"

"I know it," Zeke replied. "Be quiet for a second, Chad, and just feel who you are. Not your body, not your voice, not what you see. Just sit here with me in the darkness and feel *you.*"

Chad relaxed against him and fell quiet for a time.

"The part of you you're feeling right now will never die," Zeke whispered. "How could it? *Who* we are, all our feelings and thoughts, don't just stop. I think that part of us leaves our bodies and continues to exist. Some people say we go to heaven, where there are pearly gates and streets paved in gold. That sounds kind of hokey to me. I think heaven is right here around us, and we just can't see it, a beautiful, peaceful parallel existence in the presence of our Creator. Sort of like a two-way mirror, where the people on the other side can watch us, but we can't see them."

Chad stiffened. "So you think maybe my dad's right here?"

"I do. Even if he wasn't good at showing it, he loved you. Maybe in time, when he knows you're going to be all right, he'll drift farther away and only visit when you need him, but for right now, I imagine he's sticking pretty close. He'll be there when you hit that home run. Someday when you hold your own son in your arms, he'll be there, smiling over your shoulder."

Chad took a shaky breath and sighed. "I wanted to hit a homer and have him take my team for pizza."

Zeke smiled to himself. Pizza. It seemed like a silly wish on the surface, but when Zeke imagined all the kids in their uniforms, storming the pizza parlor to celebrate, he understood that it wasn't about the pizza at all. It was about a young boy who'd never had his father pat him on the back and brag about his accomplishments. *Chances lost.* Chad mourned all the times when he would excel and his dad wouldn't be there to share the moment with him.

"I'm not your dad," Zeke said carefully, "and I know I can never begin to take his place, but I'd be honored to take your team out for pizza when you hit that home run."

Chad stirred to look up at him through the shadows. "That's what the fathers do."

"Yeah, I know. I've been meaning to talk to you about that. A good moment hasn't presented itself. And right now isn't a good one, either."

"You're in love with my mom, aren't you?"

Zeke nodded. "Yep, Stetson over boot heels."

Chad sniffed and wiped his nose. "Are you going to marry her?"

"Not without your permission, I'm not."

"Why?"

"Because she's your mother, and you're the man of the house. I'm old-fashioned about that kind of thing. I need to ask for her hand. Normally a guy asks the woman's father. But in this case, you have more say than Pete. That's only fair. The man you choose will end up being your stepfather." Zeke let that hang there for a second. "Like I said, right now isn't the time to talk about it. In a few weeks, maybe, when you're feeling better."

"Does my mom know you're going to ask me?"

"Yes."

"What if I say no?"

Zeke thought about that. "Well, I reckon I'll wait a spell and ask again. She's like a bad habit I can't kick."

He felt Chad smile against his shirt. "Don't tell her that. She'll get pissed."

Zeke chuckled. "I hear you."

They sat in the darkness, not speaking, comfortable with the silence. Again, Zeke wasn't sure how much time passed. The shadows felt heavy with sadness, which was as it should be. For now, the future and what it might hold was only a glimmer neither of them could see very clearly.

Finally, Chad said, "I feel better now. I'm ready to go in."

"You sure? I was just getting comfortable."

"I'm sure. I don't feel as sad now about my dad. It's good to know maybe he can see me. Thanks for talking to me."

Zeke patted the boy's shoulder. "No problem. That's what friends are for."

After they reached the ladder, Zeke went down first and then stood at the bottom, watching to make sure Chad didn't fall. When the kid's feet touched ground, he kept one hand on a rung as he turned around.

"You can marry my mom if you want," he said.

Zeke shook his head. "That's not a decision that you should be making tonight. It'll keep for a few weeks."

Chad shrugged. "I won't change my mind. You were my friend before you started loving my mom. I think I'll like having you for a dad, and you'll be a good dad for Rosie, too."

That was one of the finest compliments Zeke had ever received. "Thank you. I think I'll like having you for a son, too. No throwing tomatoes, though. Deal?"

"Deal." Chad started from the barn, and then he suddenly stopped. "I guess you don't want to go tomorrow."

Zeke slowed his steps. "To the funeral, you mean?"

"Yeah. You don't have to or anything. I was just thinking—well, you know—that it might be easier for my mom if you came."

Zeke nodded. He had a hunch that Natalie wouldn't be the only one who might need a strong arm to lean on. "You're probably right. I hadn't thought about that."

"Does that mean you'll go with us?"

Zeke nodded again. "Sure. Just in case your mom needs me, I should probably be there."

The following day passed in a blur for Natalie. She felt as if she were on autopilot. She moved, talked, and did what she had to do, but nothing seemed real. At odd times throughout the afternoon, she imagined her brain was a tangled jumble of electrical wires that had frayed and shorted out, leaving most of her circuits dead. In a distant part of her mind, she worried about Chad and how he would handle the funeral, but not even her concern for him penetrated the numbness that seemed to have overtaken her body. She was grateful for Zeke. He moved through the haze of unreality, big, strong, and solid, his voice a deep rumble that soothed her in a way she couldn't understand.

The funeral was unremarkable. Grace, impeccably dressed in relentless black, wept into a tiny black hanky edged with lace. When Natalie watched her sobbing, she felt nothing, just an awful emptiness, as if her heart were a blackboard and someone had erased it. Chad was the only one who cried real tears, and even then Natalie felt nothing. It wasn't necessary because Zeke was there, a rock for Chad to lean on. Zeke seemed to know all the right things to say. Natalie couldn't string words together to make a complete sentence.

She didn't know what was wrong with her. It was like being locked in a dark closet with only her head poking out.

She could see and hear and respond to questions, but nothing could penetrate to actually touch her.

After the funeral, Zeke drove them home, Natalie on the front passenger seat, Chad, Valerie, and Pop in back. Even the drive didn't seem real. Natalie turned a section of paper towel in her hands, wondering where it had come from and why she had it. She hadn't shed a tear all day, had no desire to cry. So why was she wringing a paper towel?

What had it all been about? That was the question that kept circling through her mind. After a simple supper, Natalie went upstairs to give Rosie her bath and put her to bed. It was the strangest thing to go through the motions of normalcy—to feel the warm water on her fingers, to slick soap over her daughter's soft skin, to run a brush through tangled black curls, to hear herself reading a bedtime story aloud, injecting expression into words that didn't register on her brain.

When Rosie had drifted off, she went to Chad's room to check on him because that was what mothers were supposed to do. Her son had fallen asleep reading his Harry Potter book. Natalie leaned against the doorframe, feeling heavy all over.

Valerie came up behind her in the hall. "You okay?" she whispered.

Natalie straightened away from the doorjamb. "I'm fine." She drew the portal closed so their voices wouldn't disturb Chad. "You know what I've learned from all this?"

Valerie's suntanned face looked oddly pale. "No, what?"

"We're all just chickens that haven't gotten their necks wrung yet."

Valerie did an about-face and hurried back downstairs. Natalie moved toward her room, thinking about distan thunder and cool night breezes. All she wanted was to close her eyes and let her mind go black.

She'd stripped down to her bra and panties when Zeke entered the room. Even in the darkness, she knew it was Zeke by the sound of his boots on the old hardwood floor. She tossed her dress toward the closet, not caring if it got wrinkled or walked on.

"If Valerie sent you up, there's no reason. I'm fine. I'm not sad or anything."

He took a step toward her. "I know. That's part of the problem, isn't it, that you can't feel sad?"

She sat on the edge of the bed and stared at him. He was a tall silhouette without a face, which made it easier to talk to him. "What's it all about, Zeke?"

He came to sit beside her. She wanted him to say all the right things to make her feel alive inside again, like he did for Chad. But instead he said nothing. It made her angry. She knew he had the words she needed to hear, and he just wouldn't give them to her.

"How about a walk?" he asked.

"What?"

He pushed up from the bed and went to her bureau. After rifling through the drawers, he returned and tossed jeans and a top on her lap. "Put them on. You need to get out of here for a while."

"I don't feel like walking."

"I know. That's why you need to go."

That made no sense, but her thoughts were so disjointed she couldn't compose an argument. After she dressed, Zeke hunkered down in front of her and slipped her bare feet into her sneakers. He jerked too hard when he tightened the laces, making the blood rush to her toes, but she couldn't muster the energy to complain.

After he led her downstairs and outside into the night, she asked, "Where are we going?"

"Does it matter?"

Keeping a hold on her hand, he pulled her along behind him, angling across the yard and up the rutted gravel drive toward the road. When they reached the asphalt, he set a lazy pace, not speaking, not pressing her to share how she felt. A good thing, that, because she felt nothing.

As they walked, she concentrated on putting one foot in front of the other and breathing in and breathing out. That wasn't easy. Her feet and her lungs were at almost opposite ends of her body. She became so focused on just moving that she was surprised to hear herself say, "I should feel sad, and I don't. I loved him once. He was the father of my children. How could I look at him and feel nothing?"

Zeke swung to a stop. In the moonlight, his eyes shimmered like molten silver. "Sweetheart, you've been through one hell of a week. You're exhausted, physically and emotionally. The mind is a fabulous mechanism. When life gets to be too much, it shuts off. The sadness is there, way deep. You'll begin to feel it when you can deal with it. For now, you're just riding the wave and going through the motions."

"You don't think I'm terrible?"

He hooked an arm around her neck and drew her against him. "God, no. I think you're wonderful. Don't beat up on yourself for not feeling sad. Eventually you will, if for no other reason than because Robert was the father of your children. Just give yourself time."

Natalie made fists on his shirt and leaned her weight against him. "Oh, Zeke, I love you."

He pressed light kisses on her hair. "I know you do. And you know what else?"

"No, what?"

"I think you need a good, old-fashioned affirmation that you are very much alive."

She closed her eyes, listening to the steady rhythm of his heart. "How do I do that?"

"Let me show you," he whispered.

The next instant, he swept her up in his arms, carried her across the ditch that ran along the road, and went out into the field. When he set her on her feet, she glanced around them. "We can't make love here."

"Why not?"

"It's someone else's property."

"I repeat, why not?"

She giggled even as he slipped an arm around her waist and lowered her into the tall grass. Minutes later, as she crested with him on a wave of sheer sensation, Natalie stared dizzily at the moon, glorying in the fact that she could feel again. *Alive.* Zeke definitely made her feel gloriously alive.

She could only hope that fate allowed her to have a future with him.

Chapter Nineteen

By Friday night, Natalie felt sufficiently recovered to attend the grand reopening, and exactly as Zeke had predicted, the Blue Parrot was packed. Karaoke buffs swarmed to the club, hoping to win a cash prize for the best performance. Unlike before, when people had come only to have dinner while enjoying live entertainment, these folks stayed, following their meals with rounds of drinks, which generated large margins of profit. Halfway through the evening, Natalie took inventory of the bar stock and feared she might run short before closing time.

Seated at a table near the stage a few minutes later, she tapped her toe to the music as she gazed at the crowded dance floor. "I can't *believe* this," she told Zeke, who sat across from her. "Just *look* at all the people, and they're having so much fun."

He grinned broadly and winked at her. "Still a classy place, too," he said, giving her sequined red gown a long look. "The first time I ever saw you wearing that dress, I ran so fast the other way, I almost tripped over my own feet."

Natalie saw the smoldering heat in his gaze and knew it

held promises of indescribable pleasure for her later. "Why did you run?"

"I knew you spelled trouble."

She laughed, feeling wonderfully lighthearted. Business was up, her son had come through the storm and seemed to be dealing with his father's death, and she was wildly in love with a dreamily handsome cowboy who wanted to spend the rest of his life with her. It didn't get any better than this.

"I'm glad you didn't run far," she said, hoping he saw the promise in her eyes as well.

"Me, too. Although I have to warn you, life will never be tame for us." He jabbed a thumb toward the five tables behind them that members of his family had commandeered. "Mix all of them and the Westfields together, and we're going to have something going on constantly. Weddings, birthdays, babies being born, kids getting sick or hurt, and marital problems now and again, just to keep things interesting."

"Whose marital problems?"

A twinkle warmed his eyes. "Theirs, of course. We'll never have any."

Natalie laughed. "I hope not. You don't fight fair."

He gave her another heated appraisal. "Making up will have its benefits."

"Stop it. We're in a public place."

"Dance with me?"

A moment later, they were on the floor, swirling to a slow love song. Natalie felt as light as air in his arms, and her heart swelled with happiness as she looked into his eyes.

"I spoke to Chad," he whispered huskily. "We have his blessing. Will you marry me?"

He looked so solemn that she couldn't resist teasing him just a little. "I've already said yes, so the biggest question is when. I've always wanted a June wedding."

He narrowed an eye at her. "Forget June, lady. I'm not scaling that roof all winter. After the first snow, I'll fall and break my neck."

Natalie followed the pressure of his hard thigh, taking three gliding steps backward. "Snow will pose a problem, I suppose. A Christmas wedding, then? We could say our vows by the tree. Wouldn't that be romantic?"

He shook his head. "It snows around Thanksgiving. How about mid-October? That'll give the kids some time to settle in at school and come to terms with losing their dad. If we leave for a week or so, we can still be back for Halloween so Rosie can hang pumpkin drawings all over the house, and we can carve jack-o'-lanterns together."

"An autumn wedding?" Natalie imagined the falling leaves and the crispness of the air, and suddenly it seemed like the most perfect time of the year for them to begin a life together. "All right. Mid-October. That sounds lovely."

Zeke lifted a dark eyebrow. "Another question. Where do you want to live? I'm willing to lease my place out or sell it if you'd like to stay at the farm."

Natalie couldn't believe he would offer. "With my family?"

"I'm used to a crowded household. I can handle it again."

She smiled and shook her head. "We'll be close enough living next door. My family's crazy, in case you haven't noticed."

"I like their brand of crazy. It's your call. I honestly don't care where I live as long as I'm with you."

"Your place," she whispered. "If I want to go over, I can. When they get on my nerves, I can stay at home."

He nodded. "Do something for me?" he asked huskily. "Sing 'Forever and for Always' next."

Natalie wanted to kiss him. "You've got it, cowboy."

A few minutes later when Natalie returned to the stage, she looked directly at Zeke as she began singing the requested song. When she got to the part about staying right there forever in his arms, he pushed up from his chair and moved slowly toward her. She continued to sing as he scaled the steps and came to stand with her behind the mike. On the last line of the refrain, he harmonized with her, saying that he meant to keep her forever and for always. And then he drew a sparkling diamond ring from his shirt pocket.

Natalie was so stunned that she stopped singing in the middle of a number for the first time in her life. She stared up at him with tears of happiness welling in her eyes, scarcely able to believe that this wonderful, handsome man meant to put a ring on her finger in front of so many people. She was even more incredulous when he dropped to one knee.

"Oh, Zeke, *no!*" she cried. "Get up. This is crazy."

"Go, Zeke!" Hank yelled. Jake let go with a shrill whistle, his deep voice resounding in the suddenly quiet room when he said, "I've been trying to take him to his knees for years, Natalie. Make him stay there for a while."

Zeke flashed her one of those slow, lopsided grins that never failed to make her bones melt. Then he said, "Natalie Westfield Patterson, will you make me the happiest man alive by agreeing to become my wife?"

Natalie's throat went so tight that all she could do was nod. Zeke slipped the ring onto her left hand, then pushed to his feet and bent to kiss her soundly on the lips, no easy task with the guitar between their bodies. Everyone in the house applauded wildly. Then they began calling for the rest of the song, with both of them singing this time.

It was the most beautiful moment of Natalie's life—and without question her most memorable performance, not because her delivery was perfect, but because every word came straight from her heart, and she had only to look into Zeke's eyes to know that the words came straight from his, too. He really and truly wanted her, forever and for always.

At a tender age, Natalie had given up on dreams of true love and lasting happiness. For the last several years, she'd been grateful for a so-so life and had allowed herself to expect nothing more. Now, suddenly and inexplicably, all the wishes she'd made as a young girl were coming true. Right when she'd convinced herself that there was no such thing, she'd finally found a handsome cowboy prince and love to last a lifetime.

Earlier, Zeke had asked if she was prepared for all the upheaval their combined families would bring into their marriage. Natalie was ready for anything. She wanted a life with this man. He was surely heaven-sent. She believed with all her heart that God had looked down on her miserable, sad little life and decided to send her a hero.

When the song ended, Zeke kissed her again and left the stage to return to his seat. People in the audience began clapping their hands and stomping their feet, calling for Natalie to begin another number.

Feeling content and complete, Zeke sat back to enjoy the performance. Natalie was a brilliant flame in the red dress, so beautiful that half the men in the room couldn't take their eyes off of her. Zeke didn't mind. She loved him, and she'd just promised him forever by letting him slip that ring on her finger. Let them look and eat their hearts out. The lady was taken.

As always, she electrified the air before she ever opened her mouth to sing again. The dancers fell silent, and people at the tables went motionless. As though to build the suspense, she caressed the handle of the mike and smiled at the crowd. "This next number is one of my favorites because it can be so much fun. I hope you'll keep the beat and sing along with me."

She settled the guitar on her hip and strummed a few notes, her dimple flashing in an impish grin. Then, her voice a honeyed explosion of magic, she shouted, "Sweet Home Alabama!" The crowd cheered and whistled. The dancers began to stomp their feet and clap their hands to the music. Grinning at their enthusiasm, Zeke sang along, too, tapping his toe to keep time. *Natalie*. She was a born entertainer, blessed with an uncanny ability to captivate an audience.

Pretty soon, the vibration of stomping feet was making Zeke's table jiggle. Watching Natalie, he suddenly got an eerie, inexplicable sense of impending disaster. His heart started to pound. His body tensed. The crazy thing was, he had no idea why. Perhaps it was a sixth sense kicking in to give him a vital few seconds of forewarning so he would be able to react quickly.

Then he saw it—a slight shift of the sound-system platform suspended above the stage.

He leaped to his feet with such speed and forward momentum that he sent his chair flying backward. Natalie turned her dark head to look at him, her brown eyes filling with question. Running toward her, Zeke thought, *Oh, God—oh, God!*

It was as if everything happened in slow motion. Zeke had to cover only a few feet—six to ten, at the most—but it seemed to take an eternity. He saw the platform above Natalie break completely loose from the ceiling on one side, plaster raining so slowly downward that it seemed to float like feathers. Natalie glanced up, her face contorting with terror. Her guitar slipped from her hip and fell in a wide arc, the neck grasped in only one of her slender hands. Beyond her, Frank Stephanopolis jumped up from the piano bench, turned, and tried to run.

Zeke saw it all unfolding before him like a scene in a movie. His boots impacted so hard with the floor with each running step that jolts went clear through his body. Trying to save herself, Natalie hunched her shoulders, threw up an arm to protect her head, and fled toward the edge of the stage. *Not quickly enough.* Zeke had no idea how much the speakers, amps, and framework weighed, but he instinctively knew that it was enough to kill anyone unlucky enough to be standing below.

Natalie. In a last, desperate attempt to reach her before the platform collapsed on the stage, Zeke pushed off with one foot in a flying leap. He caught Natalie around the waist, carrying her along with him as he hit the steps and rolled. He heard screams and shouts, followed by a deafening explosion of noise.

When Zeke and Natalie came to a stop, he rolled a final time to come out on top and hunched his body over hers to shield her from the falling debris. A two-by-four struck him across the back. A speaker fell beside them, one corner colliding sharply with his hip.

Then, almost as quickly as it happened, the noise stopped, and a hush fell over the room. It lasted only an instant before chaos erupted. Running footsteps, screams and curses. Zeke lifted himself off of Natalie, frantically running his hands over her arms and legs to check her for injuries.

"Are you all right?" he cried. "Are you hurt anywhere?"

"Fine, I'm fine. What happened?" Even as she asked the question, she looked toward the stage and screamed, a long, high-pitched wail, followed by, "*Frank!* Oh, dear *God! Frank?*"

Zeke sprang to his feet and ran toward the stage where Frank Stephanopolis lay buried under the demolished platform. *Motionless.* Even as Zeke tore at the boards and sections of blue plywood to reach the unconscious piano player, he yelled, "Someone call an ambulance!"

Natalie despised speckled linoleum. Zeke's sports jacket draped over her shoulders, she sat on the edge of a chair in the ER waiting room, holding a vendor cup of cold coffee between her hands, wondering vaguely how her life had become such a nightmare. Frank Stephanopolis was in surgery. He had sustained a serious head injury, several broken bones, and a crushed pelvis. The doctor who'd come out to see them a while ago said that the piano was all that had saved Frank's life. The platform had crashed onto the Baldwin first, sparing Frank's body the full impact of all that weight.

Sharon Stephanopolis, Frank's wife, sat huddled across from Natalie on an ugly green chair, her hair mussed, her eyelids smudged with mascara. She was a thin woman with a bony, angular face and dishwater-blond hair. Every once in a while, she glanced at her watch.

"It's been so long," she said again. "Surely he's out of surgery by now."

Natalie shook her head. "It's been only forty minutes. Have faith, Sharon. He's going to be all right. He has to be."

Sharon looked at her imploringly. "Why does something like this happen to someone like my Frank? He's such a good man. He's never hurt anyone."

Natalie felt as if a party balloon were being inflated inside her chest. Every time she looked into Sharon's pain-filled eyes, the pressure increased. She wanted to say that the collapse hadn't been intended for Frank, that it should have fallen on her. But if she so much as hinted that the collapse hadn't been an accident, Sharon would ask a dozen questions.

Natalie had no answers yet. Zeke had driven her to the hospital to be with Frank, and then he'd returned to the club to see what had caused the platform to collapse. He'd called her on the cell a few minutes ago, his voice taut with worry, to tell her that the eyebolts anchoring the sound-system platform to the ceiling had been cut nearly in two. *Not an accident.* That was all Natalie could focus on. Zeke hadn't overreacted the other night after the burglary at the club. Someone had indeed sneaked inside and hidden until Jake and Hank left, and the place had been booby-trapped, just as Zeke had suspected. He'd only guessed wrong about the threat. Someone had spent all those hours compromising the eyebolts, expressly to make the platform fall during one of Natalie's performances.

After first hearing the news, Natalie had been frightened. Now she just felt furious. *Frank.* He might die because of her. He had two little boys and a wonderful wife. Sharon was right; he had never harmed anyone so far as Natalie knew. And now he was in surgery, fighting for his life because someone wanted her dead. How could this happen to a nice man whose sole endeavor in life was to create beautiful music for the pleasure of others?

Why? The question circled endlessly in Natalie's mind. She'd seen nothing significant inside Robert's home. She had an insane urge to run outside the hospital and scream, *"I don't know anything, damn you! Leave me alone! Leave the people I love alone!"* Worst of all, according to Zeke, the police were saying that the collapse had been an accident caused by too much weight on weakened supports. They believed the bolts had snapped under stress when people in the crowd had started stomping their feet. Zeke swore up and down that any idiot could see the bolts had been cut, but Monroe had just accused him of being an alarmist.

Natalie felt so tired. So awfully, horribly tired. The events of the last week were a jumble in her mind. Before ending their conversation, Zeke had made her promise not to leave the ER waiting room alone. It was madness. Someone was trying to kill her. Things like this didn't happen in Crystal Falls, yet it *was* happening. Her grand reopening had culminated in a grand disaster because someone wanted her dead.

Natalie was staring into her coffee, pondering the absurdities of that when her mom and dad arrived. Naomi sat on one side of her, Pete on the other. Each of them curled an arm around her. Natalie looked at Sharon and felt awful. Frank's wife was the one who needed family around her right now. Unfortunately, Sharon and Frank's relatives lived clear down in Modesto.

A half hour later, the surgeon came out to speak with them. Still dressed for surgery with a blue cap on his head, he sat beside Sharon.

"He's out of the woods now," he began.

"Oh!" Sharon covered her face with her hands and started to weep. "Oh, thank God."

The doctor patted her shoulder. "He was a very lucky man, Mrs. Stephanopolis. If he'd been standing under that platform, he wouldn't be with us now. As it is, he'll be a week in the hospital, recovering from the surgery, and convalescing at home for at least twelve weeks after that."

He went on to describe the injuries that Frank had sustained in the accident, which Natalie knew hadn't been an accident at all. She couldn't focus on all the medical jargon. She was just relieved that Frank hadn't lost his life.

"When can I see him?" Sharon asked.

"He's in recovery now." The doctor glanced at his watch. "An hour or two. The nurses will come get you when it's okay for you to see him."

Tears streaming, Sharon nodded and closed her eyes. "Thank you, Doctor. Thank you so much."

Before the physician left, he turned to Natalie and her parents. "Are you relatives?"

Natalie's tongue felt like a wad of cotton. She pried it loose from her teeth to say, "No, I'm Mr. Stephanopolis's employer." *And the person who almost got him killed.* "We'll stay with Sharon until she can go in to be with him."

The doctor nodded. "That's good. The waiting is always easier with company."

Three hours later when Natalie crawled into bed, her head was filled with jumbled recollections of Zeke's parents and siblings, who had arrived at the hospital right after the doctor left. She smiled, albeit sadly, as she slipped under the covers, remembering Zeke's prediction that their life together would never be calm with so many people on both sides of the family to cause upheaval. Natalie liked his mom and dad, and she had been relieved to see Jake and Hank, who had stuck to her like glue, accompanying her even when she walked up the hall to the ladies' room. It had been almost as good as having Zeke at her side. *Almost.*

Zeke had called from the club several times to give her updates as he dealt with the police and then tried to clean up some of the mess while the employees closed. Natalie imagined him shifting debris, sweeping up plaster, taping frayed wires to prevent fire, pulling down the tills, and then making a night deposit at the bank, all necessary tasks that she'd been unable to do herself. She was deeply appreciative of the fact that he had stayed to take care of things. But at the same time, she ached to feel his arms around her.

The yearning and need she felt for him made her feel small and selfish. Sharon Stephanopolis was sitting beside her husband's bed right now, praying for his life. Zeke would come to her soon, whole and healthy. He would slip under the blankets and gather her close in his arms. She'd be able to touch him—be able to feel his hands, so big and gentle, on her body. He would come, and then everything would be all right again.

On that thought, Natalie slipped into an exhausted sleep, dreaming of him beside her.

Sometime later, Natalie awakened when the mattress sank under someone's weight. *Zeke.* She smiled drowsily and lifted her arms to him, so glad to have him with her that her pulse quickened even though she was still half-asleep. She curled her hands over his shoulders, vaguely registered that they didn't feel like Zeke's, and bleated in surprise. Before she could scream, a hard, cruel hand clamped over her mouth, shoving her lips against her teeth with bruising force. Terror slowly dawning in her sleep-fogged brain, she stared at the shadowy shape of a man above her.

"Dumb bitch!"

Not Zeke. She instinctively clawed at the dark blob of a face above her. Her nails sank into soft flesh, which, yet again, definitely didn't belong to Zeke. *Panic.* Just that quickly, and Natalie was fighting for her life. Only he was all over her, a large, heavy body that anchored her to the mattress. Her legs, caught under the sheet and blanket, were useless. She could fight only with her hands. The man swore, grabbed the extra pillow, and shoved it over her face to muffle her screams as he wrestled to grasp her wrists.

Natalie bucked and strained to move, but her arms and legs were pinned. Her assailant's knees bracketed her thighs, pulling the sheet and blanket as taut as a straightjacket around her body. Horror welled within her. She tried futilely to scream, but the pillow was cutting off her airflow and muffling any sound she might have made. She attempted to twist her face free, but the man's forearm anchored the down over her nose and mouth.

She couldn't see, couldn't wriggle away. Her lungs grabbed for oxygen that wasn't there, throwing her body into a convulsive struggle for breath. Natalie had always imagined herself putting up a good fight in a situation like this—scratching, clawing, and kicking. Now, helpless to move, she could only lie there, fighting frantically to breathe. The man wasn't that much stronger than she was—she'd felt that when she touched his shoulders and clawed at his face—but he had the advantage of greater weight and the bedclothes to help hold her down.

An awful airless pounding filled her head. Her chest convulsed spasmodically. Her muscles began to twitch as her lungs caught short, her yawning mouth drawing in only pillowcase. *Oh, God.* In some distant part of her mind, she knew she was dying.

How long could she go without breathing? That question became her only focus, not who this was or how she meant to get away. Everything narrowed down to that one question—how long could she hold on? Her mind swirled with an awful, airless need for oxygen. Her fingers clutched frantically at nothing, her nails lacerating her palms and drawing blood. A heavy, black panic descended over her.

Dying. She saw Robert's still face. She thought of her children, who needed her. She shoved with everything she had, trying to jerk her wrists from the man's grip. Then, in a last, desperate bid for freedom, she arched her body and attempted to throw him off of her. Nothing she did made a difference. The next breath she tried to draw was stopped short, only the pillowcase fluffing up her nostrils and into her mouth.

Zeke stepped up onto the porch rail, a dilapidated wooden support that wobbled more precariously each night from the repeated jostling. He definitely needed to marry the lady, he thought. This was nuts. He gripped the roof, lifted his weight with his arms, and flung up a foot to gain purchase on the shingles. With a twist and a roll of his body, he was lying on the roof.

As he pushed up on his hands and toes, he heard a muffled sob. *Natalie?* He wondered if she was dreaming. No small wonder. The poor woman had been through so much over the last seven days that it was a miracle she was still sane. Zeke crept toward her window, hoping to awaken her from the nightmare with a kiss. God, he loved her. He could almost taste the sweetness of her mouth as he curled his hands over the windowsill to climb into her bedroom.

As one foot touched down on the interior floor, Zeke froze, his startled gaze riveted to Natalie's bed. He couldn't actually see what was happening, only that the shadowy shape hunched on the mattress was too large to be a woman. He swung his other foot in over the sill and sprang forward.

"Hey!" he yelled.

The man—as Zeke drew closer, he could tell for certain that it was a man—whirled around, his face a whitish blob in the moonlight that came through the window. With a bestial snarl, he leaped, his body striking Zeke's with such force that they both crashed to the floor. Zeke barely felt the impact. *Natalie.* In a rush of disjointed thought, he put two and two together and knew that this flailing, cursing assailant had been trying to harm her.

Rage ignited in Zeke's veins, turning his blood molten. He hooked a leg over the other man's thighs and rolled with him. When Zeke came out on top, he didn't bother with throwing punches. He went straight for the bastard's throat, biting in hard with his thumbs at the larynx. It wasn't a decision or even a thought; Zeke just wanted him dead.

Still gasping for breath, Natalie lay huddled on the bed, staring stupidly at the two men struggling on the floor. Zeke had her assailant by the throat. The man clawed uselessly at Zeke's wrists and thrashed his legs. *No contest.* Zeke was by far the stronger. In the moonlight, she could see the muscles on his back and shoulders bunching with the force of his grip.

It took a few seconds for Natalie to regain her wits. When

she did, she sprang off the bed and ran to Zeke. "Stop!" she cried. "Zeke!" She grabbed his arm. "Zeke, please. You're killing him! Stop it!"

At first, Zeke didn't seem to hear her. Then, slowly, he loosened his hold on the man's neck and sat back on his stomach. "Move, you son of a bitch, and I'll finish you."

The man grabbed his throat, rasping for oxygen. Natalie had an unholy urge to kick him now that he was helpless. Fortunately the door to the bedroom crashed open just then. Pete entered first, Valerie and Naomi right behind him. Valerie held a lamp in her hands and looked prepared to bean anyone who moved.

Still weak at the knees, Natalie sank onto the edge of the bed, grateful for the air that filled her lungs each time she breathed.

"The bastard was trying to smother Natalie with a pillow," Zeke told Pete. "Somebody call the police before I kill him."

Valerie set down the lamp and raced from the room. Hands at her hips, Naomi stood over Zeke and the other man. "Death is too easy. Let me have five minutes with the son of a bitch."

Two hours later, Zeke and Natalie sat beside each other at the kitchen table, all of her family, except for the kids, seated around them. Natalie had just gotten Chad and Rosie settled down and back to sleep, and Detective Monroe had finally arrived to fill them in on Natalie's attacker and explain why the man had tried to kill her. Oddly, the detective, who'd never been reticent in previous meetings, seemed to be searching for words.

Smoothing a hand over his balding head, Monroe finally

met Natalie's gaze. "It's not often in my line of work that I find myself needing to apologize, Mrs. Patterson, but I was dead wrong about you."

Natalie shifted on her chair. She was glad to have Zeke's arm around her shoulders. With his free hand, he toyed with her fingers and gently touched the gouges on her palms left by her fingernails. "I guess even cops are allowed one mistake, Detective."

"I came damned close to destroying your life." The policeman looked so shamefaced and sincerely distressed that Natalie felt badly for him. "Saying I'm sorry doesn't seem like enough."

"All's well that ends well," Natalie pushed out. "Naturally I wish that you had believed me sooner. My children could have been killed in that car accident. But I also understand that yours is not an easy job, and the circumstantial evidence did point to me."

The detective puffed air into his cheeks. Then he smiled slightly. "Thank you for that. I feel really rotten for putting you and your family through all this."

Zeke tightened his arm around Natalie. "Who is the son of a bitch?" he demanded. "Natalie says she never saw him before."

"That's true. She didn't. But unfortunately he had seen her." Monroe drew a small black notebook from his jacket. As he opened the binder, he said, "The man's name is Mike Salisbury. On the way to the station, he wouldn't talk, but once we began interrogating him, he broke down and told us everything." Monroe frowned at his notes and then glanced up at Zeke. "You were on the right track, thinking the killer was a Realtor. You were just suspicious of the wrong one.

Turns out that Mr. Salisbury is another broker who got ripped off by Patterson, like Stan Ragnor."

Zeke ran his hand over the sleeve of Natalie's robe, his touch soothing her as the detective went on.

"Salisbury and Patterson had a written agreement to split the profits fifty-fifty on a land deal out on Twenty-seventh Street," the aging policeman said. "Nothing notarized or drawn up by an attorney, just a simple preliminary agreement that one of them had typed up. On the day of the murder, Salisbury discovered that Robert Patterson had negotiated an exclusive two-party contract with the property owner behind his back, cutting him out of the deal." Monroe's plump face darkened. "When Salisbury confronted Patterson, Patterson just laughed, saying the initial agreement wasn't worth the paper it was written on. Salisbury had gone there, prepared to do murder, and Patterson's attitude so enraged him that he followed through with it."

Natalie shivered and leaned closer to Zeke. "Just like that? How can anyone take the life of another person and live with himself?"

Monroe just shook his head. "There's no understanding human nature most times, Mrs. Patterson. I've spent three quarters of my career wondering what goes wrong inside people's heads. On the outside looking in, it's hard to figure how anyone can commit murder over money. But it happens. People get desperate, and they can't see any way out. The first thing they know, they've got blood on their hands."

"Why did Salisbury want Natalie dead?" Zeke asked.

Monroe flipped to another page, then closed the notebook. "He was terrified that she knew his name and might go to the police when she finally made the connection. The man's wife is terminally ill with leukemia. Being a Realtor with a sporadic income, he couldn't afford health insurance, and when she got sick, her medical expenses almost ruined him. Lost his car several months back and had to buy a junker, and now he's on the verge of losing his house. Backed into a corner financially, he saw the land deal with Patterson as his only chance to pay off some of the bills and give his wife the care she deserved during the last days of her life."

Natalie recalled that terrifying moment when she'd stared through the windshield at the back of a slow-moving cattle truck. Her kids had almost died over a land deal. A part of her could understand Salisbury's rage at Robert, but her sympathy for him ended there. Chad and Rosie had never harmed anyone.

Monroe looked directly at Natalie as he continued. "Salisbury had been under incredible pressure, and when Patterson tried to cheat him, he snapped. Unfortunately, you happened along at the worst possible moment and almost caught Salisbury red-handed. According to him, after carrying Mr. Patterson out to the garage, he left without remembering to get the contract that he and your ex had drawn up. He'd just reentered the house to collect it when you walked in. He dove into a closet, hoping you'd leave. He'd parked on the next street over. There was nothing to tie him to the murder but that contract."

"And when Natalie went into the study, Salisbury thought she'd seen it," Naomi inserted hollowly.

Monroe nodded. "Fear of getting caught drove him straight over the edge. I've seen it happen more times than I like to count. A law-abiding citizen commits one crime, and then, to avoid prosecution, he finds himself doing things he never dreamed possible. He didn't want to be arrested and have to leave his sick wife. His answer was to try and make sure that Mrs. Patterson didn't remember the contract and go to the police."

"Thank God he botched all the attempts on her life," Valerie murmured.

"I'll say," Gramps seconded. "Was he the one who cut the eyebolts at the club?"

Monroe nodded and glanced regretfully at Zeke. "That was a brilliant move, actually, very clever for an amateur. If the platform had fallen on Mrs. Patterson, chances are good that it would have been ruled an accident."

"I told you the bolts had been cut," Zeke said, his voice a low growl.

The detective nodded again. "I apologize for not taking you seriously." He lifted his shoulders in a weary shrug. "I'm just thankful that Mrs. Patterson wasn't hurt and her kids are okay. Looking back on it, it's a miracle that Salisbury wasn't successful in at least one of the attempts." He smiled sadly at Natalie. "I've heard of people having guardian angels. Yours must have been working overtime."

Natalie shivered, remembering that horrible moment when she'd seen Frank buried under debris. Even with the piano to protect him, he'd been seriously injured. If not for Zeke's quick reaction, she would have been killed. Perhaps she did have a guardian angel, she decided.

"How did Salisbury know which bedroom was Natalie's?" Pete asked. "He could have just as easily climbed through Valerie's window."

"The night that Salisbury sabotaged Mrs. Patterson's car, she ran to her window when she heard the gander honking," Monroe explained. "Salisbury says he heard her call out and got a clear look at her in the moonlight, so he knew where she slept." The detective sighed and shrugged again. "All his attempts to kill her and make it look like an accident had failed. In frustration and panic, he finally resorted to a personal attack to get the job done."

Natalie closed her eyes and touched her throat, grateful that Zeke had arrived in time to stop the man from suffocating her.

Monroe went on talking, but his voice seemed distant, and the words no longer registered in Natalie's mind. That was fine. She'd heard enough. It was over. Now she just wanted to put all the ugliness behind her.

Moments later, her parents escorted Detective Monroe to the door and bade him good night. When they returned to the kitchen, the room fell absolutely silent. Everyone sat around the table, staring off at nothing. For once, even Gramps seemed to be at a loss for words.

Valerie finally broke the silence. "How can a perfectly normal guy who's never broken the law go off the deep end like that and murder someone? Even worse, how could he bring himself to try to kill Natalie, who'd never done a thing to him?"

"It sounds as if the man's been under an incredible amount of stress for a long period of time," Zeke said softly. "Losing someone you love isn't easy. Add in financial problems and getting cheated out of the money you need to recover, and a lot of people might lose it."

Naomi propped her elbows on the table. "My mother died of cancer. I saw what it did to my father." She looked sadly at Natalie. "Over a period of time, he lost everything he'd worked for all his life, just trying to give her proper medical care. It changed him so. He'd always been a jovial, carefree man, and suddenly he yelled about nothing and never laughed anymore. One night I got a call from the police station, telling me he'd been picked up for shoplifting. I couldn't believe it. My dad was honest to a fault. He'd never stolen anything in his life." Naomi's eyes went bright with tears. "Come to find out, he'd stolen some Maalox to settle Mama's stomach."

Pete nodded. "I remember that. When we brought him home, he sat on the sofa and cried like a baby. Everything he was, everything he'd ever prided himself on being, had been stripped away." Pete waved his hand. "He never would have killed someone, though. That's totally over the edge."

"Totally," Valerie agreed. "Monroe can say what he wants, but in my opinion, anyone who can be driven to commit murder probably always had the propensity."

Gramps agreed with that theory, and everyone spent a few minutes rehashing the events of the evening. Finally Natalie passed a hand over her eyes and said in a taut voice, "I'm sorry, but I don't want to discuss this anymore. Okay, guys? It happened, it's over, and now I just need to move forward."

"Amen," Gramps said.

Naomi went to make tea. Valerie hopped up to put some cookies on a plate. Pete unearthed his stash of bourbon and poured everyone a shot. Conversation turned to mundane matters—the weather, a hinge on a cupboard that needed to be replaced, and a farming equipment exhibition scheduled for the following week. Natalie deeply appreciated everyone's attempt to act normal when nerves were still raw and emotions ran high.

Thirty minutes later, she walked Zeke outside. Once on the back stoop, he held her gently in his arms—nothing more, just a wonderful hug that seemed to have no beginning and no end. Natalie could have leaned into his warmth and strength all night.

"You're exhausted," he finally whispered against her hair. "Maybe I should just stay home and see you tomorrow."

She curled her fingers into fists to clasp his shirt. "I need you tonight."

He ran a big hand up her back, his thumb doing fabulous things to the knots in her muscles. "If I come, will you promise to sleep? Nothing more. You're so shaky it scares me."

Natalie smoothed her hands over his shoulders, loving the power she felt beneath her palms. It was true; shock and exhaustion had her trembling. And the fact that he realized it and wanted nothing from her because of it nearly brought tears to her eyes. "Oh, Zeke, I love you so."

His lips found the sensitive hollow beneath her ear. In a whisper that seemed to penetrate to her very bone marrow, he said, "Go upstairs, Bright Eyes. I'll meet you there."

"Why not go up with me like a normal person? Everyone knows we're getting married. Pop won't mind. Really. I think he knows that you come."

"What he suspects and what he knows are two different things." He leaned back to cup her face between her hands. "If you were any other woman on earth, I'd probably say yes. But you aren't." He gave her a slow, sheepish grin. "Don't hang me for being old-fashioned. All right?"

She nodded because she sensed that he needed her to.

"You're going to be my wife," he whispered. "I've got your reputation to think about."

As exhausted as she was, Natalie giggled. "My reputation. I see."

"You're special." He kissed her eyebrows and the tip of her nose. "You're the mother of my children, those already born, and those to come. I never want them to hear stories about their father sampling the milk before he paid for the cow. I want them to believe you're above reproach."

Natalie looped her arms around his neck. "Oh, God, I'm marrying a Neanderthal."

"Actually, it's been proven that Neanderthals aren't in our chain."

"Don't split hairs. You're archaic."

He grinned and lightly kissed her. "You wanna throw me back?"

She tightened her hold on his shirt. "Never, Mr. Coulter. You're a keeper. I'll work on your impossibly old-fashioned ideals and get you straightened out."

He chuckled. "Good luck. They're ingrained. If my father knew I was sneaking into your room and sleeping with you under your father's roof, he'd kick my ass all the way to Timbuktu and back again." His dark brows snapped together. "Come to think of it, he'd kick my ass if he knew I was sleeping with you, period. He's of the opinion that a man should be so in love with a woman that he'll leap in with both feet without a trial run."

Natalie thought about that for a moment. "And you aren't that deeply in love with me?"

He bent his dark head and gently nipped her bottom lip. "The night I swore I loved tapioca, I made the leap, lady. There was no turning back then, and there's no turning back now. Not for me."

Natalie looked up at his shadowy features and loved him so much her heart hurt. The beauty of it was she believed him—absolutely, unequivocally, without any reservations.

As long as he drew breath, he'd be there for her. "There's no turning back for me, either."

He caught her wrist, drew her hand from his neck, and kissed the ring he'd slipped onto her finger earlier that night. It seemed to Natalie that a century had passed since then. "Forever and for always," he whispered.

And then he vanished into the darkness.

Natalie just smiled. She suspected that he would be waiting for her upstairs when she got there—Johnny-on-the-spot, as constant and dependable as Old Faithful.

That was such a lovely feeling to hold close to her heart as she went back inside to tell her family good night.

Epilogue

Zeke grabbed third gear, and Natalie snuggled happily against his side. Man and wife, at last. She was glad to have the ceremony behind them and the rest of their lives ahead of them, especially the next week, which was to be their honeymoon. She couldn't help but envision their romantic stay at the coast, with beachfront motel rooms equipped with fireplaces, patios that opened onto the ocean, long walks at low tide, and sex without Rosie anywhere nearby.

Not that she didn't adore her daughter. It was just—well, Rosie did have a way of entering a bedroom at inappropriate times. Zeke laughingly called her a faulty little timer that always went off at the worst possible moment. Natalie couldn't disagree with the description, even if Rosie was the sweetest interruption on earth.

"I love you," she said, snuggling closer to Zeke on the front seat and putting as much husky desire into her voice as a woman could possibly muster.

"Prove it," Zeke replied.

Natalie was thinking of ingenious ways to do that without making him drive into a ditch when her cell phone rang.

She stared at the leopard-skin-encased gadget, wishing it would tuck itself into the glove compartment and shut up. This was her honeymoon. Her *first* and *only* honeymoon. She really didn't want to answer that phone.

"How about if I ignore it?" she asked.

Zeke slanted a laser-blue glance at the ashtray, where she'd deposited the hated device—traveling contact with her crazy family. "Chad could have broken his arm. Better answer it."

Natalie sighed and grabbed the phone. "Hello?"

"Hey, Mom! It's me."

Chad. He didn't sound mortally wounded, and she'd been gone less than five minutes. Natalie forced herself to say very sweetly, "Hi, honey. What's up?" She would have gone to the bank on the fact that it was nothing earthshaking—nothing her mother couldn't handle anyway. "Are you okay?"

"I'm fine. I just wanted to tell you I've changed my mind. I don't want a Sea Lion Caves T-shirt. I want a hat from Bandon."

"Hmm. And that's all?" Natalie heard her parents yelling at each other in the background. "What are Poppy and Grammy fighting about?"

"No big deal. Gramps doesn't want to put in a dishwasher, and Grammy says she's leaving again if he won't."

Natalie settled back against the seat and smiled. She could almost see her parents squared off over the dirty dishes. Pop would either watch Naomi leave or call Sears. Natalie had her money on Sears. Pete Westfield loved his ex-wife with all his being and, quite simply, couldn't live happily without her.

"How's Rosie?" she asked.

"She's fine. Just don't forget. Okay, Mom? I want a Bandon hat."

"I'll remember," Natalie said with a twinkling grin at Zeke. "If anything else comes up, you have our number."

"Love you, Mom."

Natalie blew kisses into the phone. "I love you, too, sweetie."

As she broke the connection, she turned to kiss Zeke, only to smack her lips against a large manila envelope. She reared back to stare at it and then at him. "What's that?"

He grinned and flapped the envelope at her. "Open it and see. It's a last-minute wedding gift, something to make you remember this moment for the rest of your life."

Natalie took the envelope from him and stared at the return address on the upper left corner. "Who is Granger Enterprises?"

"Just open it," he said, smiling with satisfaction.

Natalie worked her thumb under the tape. When she peeked inside, she could decipher nothing from the blur of print and drew out what appeared to be a contract. As she read the top page, she saw the title of her song, "If Only," midway down the page.

"What is this?" she asked again.

"That," he said slowly, "is a contract of purchase, Mrs. Coulter. I sent your song off to several agents, and one of them ran with it. You just sold it to a big-time recording artist, Roger Granger."

Roger Granger was the new phenomenon in country-western music, a male vocalist who had blasted his way to the top of the charts and was holding steady. Natalie sat there, staring at the jumble of print, unable to make sense of it. "I can't believe it. You're joking. Right?"

Zeke just shrugged. "Things like this happen when someone writes a dynamite song and puts it to music that rocks. Granger loves it. The agent says he plans to do a duet with a famous female vocalist—a he-said, she-said kind of song, which will require you to do just a little more writing to insert the male viewpoint."

Natalie had heard songs done that way, and her imagination immediately clicked into gear. *Oh, yes*. The song lent itself perfectly to that. She just couldn't believe that a famous singer loved the words and the melody. It was, like, the biggest charge of her life—*almost,* anyway.

"You're on your way."

Just then the check fell out onto Natalie's lap. She stared incredulously at the amount. Then she burst out laughing. "This *has* to be a joke."

Zeke looked over at her. "No, and I'm going to laugh all the way to the bank with my share. You can pay me back for the renovations to the club with that check, darlin'."

Natalie barely heard him. She was still staring at the amount of the check and recounting the digits.

"That's after ten percent for the agent. All you have to do is sign, sweetheart, and you've not only got representation you've got your first sale. A big one. I've learned a few things over the course of this adventure, namely that good songwriters can make a killing."

"Oh, Zeke."

He grinned and dipped his head to steal a quick kiss. " asked you once. I'll ask you again. What the hell are yo doing in a Podunk town like Crystal Falls? You were bor for Nashville, darlin'. You're wasting your time here."

Looking up at his dark, sun-burnished features and thos blue eyes she loved so much, Natalie knew exactly why sh was in Crystal Falls—and why she meant to stay. Someone else could go on the road and scrabble to make it big. If she could sell her songs, she'd be happy. The most important success of her life was sitting right beside her, a wonderful, handsome, loyal man who would always love her, even when she burned the eggs, and who would believe in her even when she'd lost faith in herself.

She'd had songs in her heart all her life. This man was the best song of all—a sweet melody that had come to her when she was least expecting it, like all of her really good songs always did. Only she didn't need to rewrite any of the lines to make him perfect.

He'd come to her that way.

"Count on Catherine Anderson for intense emotion and deeply felt relationships."
—Jayne Ann Krentz

The Coulter Series by Catherine Anderson

BLUE SKIES 0-451-21075-1

Carly Adams feels as if she's been given a new lease on life. Born with a rare eye disorder, she's been blind until a recent operation restored her sight. Now she's eager to experience the world—which includes a handsome cowboy by the name of Hank Coulter.

PHANTOM WALTZ 0-451-40989-2

A long-ago accident has left Bethany Coulter confined to a wheelchair—and vulnerable to heartbreak. But there's something about Ryan Kendrick, the handsome rancher who's so sweetly courting her, that makes her believe she can overcome every obstacle—and rediscover lifelong, lasting love.

SWEET NOTHINGS 0-451-41015-7

When Molly Wells shows up at Jake Coulter's ranch, she has nothing but some extra clothes, a stolen horse, and a fear of the ex-husband that threatened to rule her life. She's heard Jake is a real-life horse whisperer, but she has no idea that his talents will work their magic on her.

Available wherever books are sold, or
to order call: 1-800-788-6262

Anderson/Coulter O38

Carnival Elation

7 Day Exotic Western Caribbean Itinerary

DAY	PORT	ARRIVE	DEPART
Sun	Galveston		4:00 P.M.
Mon	"Fun Day" at Sea		
Tue	Progreso/Merida	8:00 A.M.	4:00 P.M.
Wed	Cozumel	9:00 A.M.	5:00 P.M.
Thu	Belize	8:00 A.M.	6:00 P.M.
Fri	"Fun Day" at Sea		
Sat	"Fun Day" at Sea		
Sun	Galveston	8:00 A.M.	

TERMS AND CONDITIONS

PAYMENT SCHEDULE:
50% due upon booking
Full and final payment due by July 26, 2004

Acceptable forms of payment are Visa, MasterCard, American Express, Discover and checks. The cardholder must be one of the passengers traveling. A fee of $25 will apply for all returned checks. Check payments must be made payable to **Advantage International, LLC and sent to: Advantage International, LLC, 195 North Harbor Drive, Suite 4206, Chicago, IL 60601**

CHANGE/CANCELLATION:
Notice of change/cancellation must be made in writing to Advantage International, LLC.

Change:
Changes in cabin category may be requested and can result in increased rate and penalties. A name change is permitted 60 days or more prior to departure and will incur a penalty of $50 per name change. Deviation from the group schedule and package is a cancellation.

Cancellation:

181 days or more prior to departure	$250 per person
121 - 180 days or more prior to departure	50% of the package price
120 - 61 days prior to departure	75% of the package price
60 days or less prior to departure	100% of the package price (nonrefundable)

US and Canadian citizens are required to present a valid passport or the original birth certificate and state issued photo ID (drivers license). All other nationalities must contact the consulate of the various ports that are visited for verification of documentation.

We strongly recommend trip cancellation insurance!

For further details call 1-877-ADV-NTGE or visit www.GetCaughtReadingatSea.com

For booking form and complete information
go to www.getcaughtreadingatsea.com or call 1-877-ADV-NTGE

Complete coupon and booking form and mail both to:
Advantage International, LLC,
195 North Harbor Drive, Suite 4206, Chicago, IL 60601